JANE RILEY grew up in New Zealand, married an Englishman and lives in Sydney, Australia. She has a degree in French and English Literature and has worked in public relations and publishing. For more than twenty years she freelanced as a writer and editor and has completed the Faber Academy course in Australia. She is the author of the novels *The Likely Resolutions of Oliver Clock* and *Geraldine Verne's Red Suitcase*.

The Mudlarkers' Club

JANE RILEY

ONE PLACE. MANY STORIES

HQ
An imprint of HarperCollins*Publishers* Ltd
1 London Bridge Street
London SE1 9GF

www.harpercollins.co.uk

HarperCollins*Publishers*
Macken House, 39/40 Mayor Street Upper,
Dublin 1 D01 C9W8
This edition 2026

1
First published in Great Britain by HQ,
an imprint of HarperCollins*Publishers* Ltd 2026

Copyright © Jane Riley 2026

Jane Riley asserts the moral right to be identified as the author of this work.
A catalogue record for this book is available from the British Library.

ISBN: 9780008778491

This novel is entirely a work of fiction. The names, characters and incidents portrayed in it are the work of the author's imagination. Any resemblance to actual persons, living or dead, events or localities is entirely coincidental.

All rights reserved. No part of this publication may be reproduced, stored in a retrieval system, or transmitted, in any form or by any means, electronic, mechanical, photocopying, recording or otherwise, without the prior permission of the publishers.

Without limiting the exclusive rights of any author, contributor or the publisher of this publication, any unauthorized use of this publication to train generative artificial intelligence (AI) technologies is expressly prohibited. HarperCollins also exercise their rights under Article 4(3) of the Digital Single Market Directive 2019/790 and expressly reserve this publication from the text and data mining exception.

Printed and bound in the UK using 100% Renewable
Electricity by CPI Group (UK) Ltd

To my oldest and dearest friend, Jane

April

Chapter 1

The day Adam left, Gemma took her heightened emotions, her now ex-mother-in-law's hot-pink wellies, and a pair of yellow Marigold gloves down to the Thames foreshore. It was mid-morning and never had the timing of the river's low tide been so perfect. Whenever life caused Gemma stress – and even when it didn't – she went down to the river to search for objects from the past. Gemma mudlarked.

There was a strong wind and a smattering of rain. The sun was trying but failing to be seen. Gemma was beyond caring. Normally a fair-weather mudlarker, on this day it could have been snowing and she still would have been out here, meandering across the pebbly silt with her head down, looking out for anything that caught her eye. It could be a sherd of Victorian salt-glazed stoneware, a lead token, a farthing, a Thames garnet or a plastic Christmas cracker ring. Some days, there might be nothing at all. It wasn't necessarily about the finds. All that mattered was giving yourself over to the search. It was meditative mindfulness without having to sit cross-legged with your eyes closed or colour between the lines. One of her patients – a septuagenarian named Miriam – used to spend every hour of her chemotherapy sessions colouring in. Until she got Occupational Overuse Syndrome in her right wrist and had to find something else to do, which seemed so utterly unfair. One of her pictures was still hanging in the staff tearoom.

Gemma walked with as much speed as she could in wellies that were half a size too big. In her haste, she'd forgotten to put on extra socks for padding. A blister was forming on one heel already. Her rucksack bounced on her back as if in time with her pounding heart and throbbing head. Her eyes had filled with tears and, although the wind was trying its best to dry them out, her world felt like it was completely under water.

The day had begun like any other ordinary Saturday. Gemma in bed with a cup of tea – decompressing from her week at the hospital by scrolling social media – and Adam out for a run. He'd got into running shortly after they started dating. In those early days, she'd taken it up too, because new love made her want to do everything he liked doing. But in the end, she had to admit (to herself as much as him) that it wasn't her thing. Now, he was part of a club and was training for a marathon, and she sporadically did Pilates.

After watching Instagram reels of animated cats and skits by wannabe comedians, Gemma started playing around with the ageing filter on TikTok. In an instant, her face morphed into what it might look like in forty- or fifty-years' time. It was funny, fascinating and horrifying all at once. She saved the picture to show Adam.

When he returned, she was in the kitchen making a coffee.

'Good run?' she asked.

'It was okay,' he answered.

He leant against the counter and took a gulp of water from his bottle. His cheeks were red, his skin glistening with sweat and his chest still heaving.

'I have just the thing to put a smile on your face,' she said, reaching for her phone. 'Actually, it's truly frightening. Me as an old woman.' She laughed and showed him her wizened face. 'That's who you're going to wake up next to one day.'

Adam stared at the picture. She was expecting a chuckle at least, but all he did was frown and chew his lip. Maybe he was preoccupied with work, which he seemed to be a lot these days. She tried to distract him.

'Come on, let's do you,' she said.

'No.' He shook his head. 'I don't want to.'

'All I have to do is take a photo.'

'I'm not in the mood, okay?' His tone was curt.

'What's got into you?' she asked. Lately he seemed permanently bad-tempered and grouchy and she'd had enough.

'Look, Gem …' He pulled at his neck as if it were sore. 'I don't know how to say this—'

'Say what?' Adam was never usually one lost for words.

His sigh chewed up the air. Something was clearly bothering him. Was it his job? Or could it be his dad? They'd always had a turbulent relationship, which only worsened when his beloved mother, the perpetual peacemaker, died six months ago. Or could it be that he was sick? She had a patient once who, after getting a terminal cancer diagnosis, hadn't told their partner. Gemma held her breath.

'I … um …' he mumbled. 'I guess there's no other way to say it.' He paused. 'I'm leaving.'

'Pardon?' She froze, her mug halfway to her lips. She repeated his words in her head, just in case she'd misheard.

'I've met someone—'

'You've met someone?'

Gemma closed her eyes and pressed her temples. The words coming out of his mouth didn't make any sense. She pulled out a chair and sat down heavily.

'What do you mean, you've met someone? You've been having an affair?'

He nodded.

She felt utterly sick. 'Who with? For how long? Actually, don't answer that, I don't want to know,' she said, even though she did. Or did she? She just couldn't bear to hear the answer. She immediately switched into practical mode. The nurse in her began seeking to fix the problem. While she couldn't change the past, surely she could do something about their future together? She carried on. 'Don't you think we should talk it out? Go to marriage counselling? Do something!' She hit the table. Coffee sloshed. This was horrendous. She was in a soap opera from which she couldn't escape. She was a cliché.

He didn't say anything.

'Please, Adam, there has to be something—'

'It's not like you can shove a drip into our relationship. It can't be solved like that.'

'Don't you dare belittle my work!'

'That wasn't my intention.'

'Well, you're doing a great job of humiliating me on all fronts.'

'I'm sorry. I honestly didn't mean for it to turn out this way.' To Gemma's ears the apology sounded feeble and far from genuine.

'Really? How *did* you mean it to turn out?' she said sarcastically. 'You thought sleeping with someone else would be fine? That it wouldn't hurt me?' she snapped. 'That ageing filter may have seemed silly to you, but I was *genuinely* thinking we were going to wake up next to each other with age spots, wrinkles and jowls. Throw in a kid or two. Maybe even grandchildren.'

'Actually, I haven't been happy for a while. I feel …' He paused, then continued. 'Well, it's more what I *don't* feel …' He couldn't finish the sentence and gave her an apologetic smile. Since when had he become such a coward?

'You don't feel what?' she interrogated him. Her mind trying to make sense of what he was saying – or rather, what he wasn't.

'Look, I still care for you, Gem,' he told her, as if that was supposed to make her feel better. 'But I don't want to be with you anymore. I don't think it's – *we're* – working. Not like it used to.'

'It isn't?' Gemma said, as much to herself as to him. Very quickly, she tried to condense the past few years of their six-year marriage into a thirty-second thought bite. Sure, they'd been arguing more than usual and were spending less time together, but that's what happens when you have a stressful job, work long hours and have different interests. Gemma had thought their relationship was merely going through a short-term blip. All marriages had them. You couldn't be together for years and not have challenging times, could you? 'But I don't understand.' Her voice wavered. She didn't want to break down. She must stay strong and calm. There will be a way through this, surely?

'We used to have so much fun, be on the same wavelength, be more than just mates,' Adam said.

'I thought we still were. We're husband and wife, for heaven's sake.'

He chewed his lip.

'Okay, so if you feel that way, let's work on getting it back.' She looked at him expectantly, hoping for a flicker of agreement. 'It's not too late to try, is it? I'll give anything a go.' She didn't care how desperate she sounded.

He shrugged, a non-answer answer.

His silence made her want to cry. 'The grass isn't always greener, you know?' she said sharply. 'Anyway, what's this woman got that I haven't?' As soon as she uttered those words, she wanted to retract them, because she wasn't sure she could handle his answer, whatever it was going to be.

Thankfully, he saw the look on her face and dodged the question, explaining non-committally, 'It's not as easy as that—'

'Isn't it?'

'I'm sorry, Gem. I've fallen out ...' He paused.

'Oh,' she said, as she realised with terrible clarity what he was going to say, and how her dreams of fixing their relationship were, most likely, fanciful. 'You mean, you don't love me anymore?'

He looked at his feet.

'And you're in love with this other woman.' Now, she might actually throw up.

He nodded.

'Oh, my God, is she in your running group?' The thought just came to her. 'Is that why you're going for longer runs, then coffee afterwards? Are you even going running?'

'Gemma, please—'

'Well, is that all I get?'

'She's my physio,' he said softly.

'Your physio? Isn't she, like, in her twenties?'

His silence spoke volumes.

Her head spun. All at once, the sight of him revolted her.

'I suppose, you'd better leave then, hadn't you?'

Without saying anything more, he walked out of the kitchen. She heard him climb the stairs and go into their bedroom. She stood up and leant on the table to steady herself. How had she not seen this coming? Had she been blind to reality? Why hadn't he said he was unhappy? Or had he tried, and she hadn't wanted to listen? She couldn't remember. Her head swooned. Her body was jittery.

It felt as if she were looking down on herself from above, except she didn't recognise the person she saw. She'd become someone different, yet she didn't know who exactly. It was the same with Adam. Suddenly her husband was not the person she'd thought he was. They were no longer the couple she'd assumed they were. Everything was not what she had believed it to be.

Gemma stood up and wiped her eyes. She didn't know what to do, whether to stay in the house or go out. But where do you go after your life has fallen – no – been torn apart? She felt agitated. She wanted to get out of herself, step out of her skin and leave all this dreadfulness behind.

She heard Adam clomp down the stairs. He stopped in the kitchen doorway with a weekender bag in each hand.

'I'm going then,' he said.

She nodded but didn't look at him.

'We'll need to talk properly about the next steps.'

How could she possibly think about what came next when she was still trying to compute what was happening now?

She could tell he was still looking at her.

'Just go,' she told him.

He quietly turned and walked down the hallway, letting the front door slam behind him. She exhaled slowly.

Even though he'd left, she didn't feel relief. The matter-of-fact announcement of his affair and how he'd simply walked out swirled in her mind. It seemed surreal. She couldn't properly conceive any of it being true. It was confusing, disturbing and hurtful. Oh, God, she needed to do something. She couldn't stand in the kitchen surrounded by memories of happier times while she felt so rejected and lost. She couldn't stay a minute longer. She had to get out.

The one thing guaranteed to calm her was mudlarking. The gently lapping water of the river would soothe her. Concentrating on what was hidden in the foreshore would focus her mind, allow her to think. It would enable her to feel a little more like herself.

Yes, that's what she'd do.

She went to get her gear.

Chapter 2

It was only a ten-minute walk from the terrace house in a quiet back street in West London to the Thames. She took the quickest route down to the waterfront where she would pass by the Georgian houses and pubs that lined the northside of the river. When she reached a wrought-iron streetlamp and a sign that read 'No cycles', Gemma veered off the footpath onto a set of lichen-covered steps leading to her favourite spot on the foreshore. Wild daisies were blooming among thistles and weeds edging the riverbed. A seagull squawked, a jogger's tread slapped the path, and in the distance an overland train clattered across the bridge. There was noise, yet it was peaceful.

Gemma paused for a moment. Her heart was pounding and she was breathless, as if she'd been running. She felt stressed and tense. She closed her eyes and breathed in deeply. The air was damp and smelled of impending rain. Another breath in and another one out. The panic lessened. The nausea eased. She opened her eyes, took to her knees and focused her gaze on the hotchpotch of pebbles, rocks and mud. To the uninitiated, that is all it looks like, but when you train your eye, the exposed shore comes alive with the remnants of the river's thousands of years of history. This is what mudlarkers want to discover.

With the river at low tide, a couple of dinghies lay stranded on the shingle. Metres away, the water was flat and shimmered like an oil slick. As far as she could see, there was no one else on the beach or the river. A rock dug into her knee. She moved to a squatting position. Annoyingly, her kneepads were still at the house – she'd forgotten them in her haste to escape. Gemma zoned in on a small area directly in front of her. Noise from traffic, pedestrians and roadworks became distant and indistinct. Modern life began to fade, and the frenetic pace of the city dissipated. Time seemed irrelevant.

Although this section of the river revealed less than parts closer to the city, where life and industry had been more concentrated in the past, things could still be found. Sometimes pieces from the eighteenth and nineteenth centuries relating to the rows of Georgian houses along Strand-on-the-Green, or objects from the various pubs, some of which date back four hundred years. Eventually, she spotted a rounded piece of glass lodged in a small trough in the mud. Holding her breath in anticipation, Gemma carefully scrapped away a fine layer of sandy mud to reveal a bottle. She tugged at the neck, but it was stuck. She removed more mud, immersing herself in the task. She wanted, for a few minutes at least, to be transported to a long-ago world, parallel to this one, where she could let her imagination wander – and wonder about the stories behind the objects she unearthed. Where she could forget that her life had just been turned inside out and what it meant for her future. She knew it wouldn't be easy, but if she could, for a moment, push it all from her mind – pretend, even, that the previous couple of hours hadn't happened – then the act of mudlarking would give her comfort.

Finally, after some gentle persuasion, out popped a narrow, clear-glass bottle resembling an oversized test tube. It had a moth-coloured stain at its base – residue of whatever liquid it had once held that, without the protection of a stopper, had long since evaporated. She turned the bottle over, wiped away muddy debris and imagined what had once been inside. Victorian medicine, perhaps? And who had owned it: a doctor or a patient? She rinsed it in a pool of water, dried it on her top and slipped the bottle into a pocket of her rucksack. She could make use of it to store her collection of centuries-old pins found mudlarking.

Immediately, she spotted another piece of glass. This time a modern-day marble. It came out of the mud easily, like a gobstopper popping out of someone's mouth. She held it to the sky, the yellow and orange swirls making it look as if she'd plucked a tiny planet from the solar system. She rolled it between her palms, felt its cool smooth surface, then dropped it onto a smooth patch of silt. The marble rolled effortlessly for a moment before hitting a small rock. It fell into a small hollow in the mud and nestled there as if content with its next resting place.

Gemma straightened up and looked out across the river. What a cruel irony it was that the most important attribute for mudlarking was a sharp pair of eyes. You need to be able to spot straight lines and perfect circles among the wonky, unsymmetrical features of Mother Nature. The curve of a button, the straight line of a tile, the bend of a buckle. So, where had her sharp vision been in her marriage?

If Adam had not been happy, why hadn't she realised? When had he first strayed? What had Gemma done – or not done – to make Adam feel and act how he had? She had so many questions. Her mind was in a muddle and she was unable to come up with a definitive answer to anything. She picked up a stone and threw it with force. It skimmed the water once, then sank. She threw another, and another. As the last of the ripples faded away, she stared blankly ahead, no longer searching for anything, her thoughts now preoccupied with the disintegration of her marriage.

Despite Adam's devastating change of heart, she still loved him. Not the falling-in-love way when you're first married – she didn't think that lasted forever – rather, the comfortable love where you don't have to navigate the world alone. She loved the security and comfort she had felt in her marriage.

But what about the man she had married?

Just as no relationship is all symmetry and perfect circles, nor are people. Everyone is full of quirks and crooks and imperfections. Sometimes, it's actually the idiosyncrasies you fall in love with. When Gemma met Adam, she was okay with him having to have the last word or the way he left clothes all over the bedroom floor. What she admired was his impressive drive and ambition. With his running, he didn't just jog around their suburb a couple of mornings a week, he trained for a half-marathon. When he said he wanted to upskill in his senior pharmaceutical management position, he enrolled in an MBA and did it part-time while working full-time. The commitment he put into everything was inspiring. He was a boundless force of energy that continually astounded Gemma. He exhibited the sort of self-assurance she would have liked a small stake in. A twenty-per cent share would have been nice.

Sure, sometimes Adam could be so driven that occasionally she felt a little bit forgotten about. But isn't the secret to a successful marriage accepting that your partner is as flawed as you are?

What if she'd excused some of his flaws as being inconsequential when, in truth, they'd been detrimental to her? To their relationship? Clearly, there'd been cracks and she'd been blinkered to them. Had she been living a lie?

Gemma began to cry. Her vision blurred and she didn't see a weathered brick stuck in the mud, angled off-centre. She clipped it with her boot, lost her footing and landed with a thud, grazing her hands. She rolled onto her back and very quickly a wet patch began soaking her bottom. *Is this what it's come to,* she thought, *lying in a puddle, staring at the sky, having to accept a fate not of your making?*

She turned her head to the river. Two large swans lifted themselves out of the water. Their wings flapped loudly, agitating the river below. Skimming the waterline, they flew away, honking their departure. Gemma looked up at the sky and let the world around her carry on, as it always had and always would. Yet, here she was, her world having changed irrevocably.

What on earth was she to do? One option was to stay there until the river came to take her away. Because it would. Where there's a low tide, there's a high one, and the Thames goes in and out every day like clockwork, rising in some parts by more than seven metres. She wondered what would be said about her if the river took her as its own and she was eventually found? One female, circa mid-thirties, pale-skinned and freckled. Chipped around the edges and with a broken heart. Dressed for gardening but without a spade. Possibly lost. Foul play only attributable to the husband, who decided his significantly younger physiotherapist was worthy of, not only treating his rotator cuff, but breaking up his marriage.

Chapter 3

When Gemma got back, the house was very quiet and still, as if frozen in time. Normally, she liked the quiet, but this felt eery. Shoeless, she padded inside, barely making a sound herself. A part of her hoped Adam would jump out from behind a door and give her a fright, and say it had been one big – albeit misjudged – joke. The other part hoped she would never see him again.

In the kitchen, his stained teacup sat in the sink. Her mug was on the kitchen table, sitting in a puddle of cold coffee from when it had sloshed out. In the living room, his shoes had gone and so had his iPad. She wished, for once, to still see the untidy reminders of him. In the bedroom, the bed was unmade and his side was unusually messier than hers. From the wardrobe, most of his clothes had vanished, and on his bedside table only a glass of water remained. There was now only one toothbrush and one towel in the bathroom. Near the basin, a ring of hardened toothpaste indicated the spot where his electric toothbrush used to sit, and there was a strong smell of his favourite musky cologne, as if it had been spilt. It was like he'd taken the best bits of himself and left the worst for her to clean up.

She caught sight of herself in the mirror. She peered closer at her reflection; her face looked strained. When had that near-permanent frown line between her eyebrows and the tiny creases at the edge of each eye appeared? It was like her face had once been folded into an origami crane, then unfolded and pressed flat in an attempt to remove the creases so the paper could be folded into something new. Already, it was a portent of what was to come and it made her anxious. Her future had just been screwed up and thrown out, and she didn't know what it resembled anymore. She looked away from the mirror, took off her sludge-caked jeans and draped them over the bath to wash later.

Now, in just her pants and favourite striped mudlarking T-shirt, Gemma went downstairs to the kitchen. It was way past lunchtime and she'd eaten nothing all day. Her stomach wanted something, although she didn't know what. She opened the freezer. Sometimes Adam liked ice cream for dessert. There was none. Which was probably a good thing because she couldn't bear the thought of turning into the romcom stereotype of a jilted woman sobbing into a tub of ice cream. Still, frozen peas weren't doing it for her. She looked in the fridge. There was little to help mop up her sadness. Perhaps cheese on toast? With lots of cheese. And a glass of rosé.

Or a bottle.

No, she wouldn't get drunk. That was another romcom cliché right there.

To hell with it. She poured a large glass of wine and made cheese on toast.

When the toast was done and the cheese browned on top, she went to the living room and sat on the sofa. Adam hated eating in front of the TV and the thought of food getting lodged between the cushions or falling onto the carpet. She balanced the plate on her lap and alternated between sips of wine and bites of food. It made her happy to spite him. But when a piece of crust fell from her fingers, bounced off the plate and landed onto the upholstery it made her miss him, and she got teary all over again. Why couldn't things go back to how they once were? It was so much easier hanging on to hope than acknowledging it was over and having to accept rejection. She couldn't process losing Adam let alone the future life they may have had together: children, travel, joint friends, and, probably, their house.

How she loved their little home. It was a modest terrace and possibly a little dated but perfect for them. When they bought it, they were enamoured by its proximity to the river and nature, and yet only a half-hour train ride into Vauxhall in South London. It was close to the shops, some pubs and a good primary school. They'd wanted to do a full renovation but had only been able to afford to repaint the interior. Despite never having painted a thing before, they did it themselves, together. Adam even agreed to – albeit reluctantly – change the 'Magnolia' cream kitchen to a muted yellow that matched the daffodils in the back garden and have a soft dusky blue in their bedroom. They'd laughed at their inexperience and occasional blunders, and bonded over joyful dreams of creating a life together. How naive that now seemed. She poured a second glass of wine and pulled out her phone. Would it be torturous to look at photos from the past, of their wedding and the holidays they'd been on? She needed reassurance that the previous eleven years of their relationship hadn't been a complete waste of time. Or, worse, that her conviction she'd been Adam's soul mate, lover, lifelong partner and friend – as she thought he had been for her – was a mere figment of her imagination. Probably this had been true at the start of their relationship, and hopefully, for some of their marriage, but clearly this was no longer the case. Had she become unlovable? What a dreadful, disturbing thought. No one wants to think of themselves as undesirable, and yet, was this now her?

She had to stop this line of thinking. It was far more palatable to think about the times when she was certain they'd both been in love.

They'd met through work when Adam was a medical sales rep

for the pharmaceutical company where he still worked, and he'd been tasked with informing her oncology nursing team about his company's products. As he did his presentation, and while she was trying to concentrate, something unexpected came over her – a hot flush of desire that was impossible to ignore. She liked how he appeared confident but not cocky and had remembered everyone's names after only a single introduction. He switched between being earnest and cheeky, which Gemma found appealing. And she was – still was – attracted to his big hazel eyes and strong jawline. So when, at the end of the day, he asked if she'd like a drink sometime, she'd said yes.

Gemma found her two favourite wedding photos. In one, they're standing under the white-rose-decorated country house pavilion after being announced as husband and wife. In the other, they're walking hand in hand through the garden with the sun setting in the background. What a fabulous day it was. How in love she'd been. How enamoured with Adam and the thought of what was to come. How she'd had no doubts that they'd stay together. How she'd had no doubts about the man she'd married.

She swiped away the photos and put her phone on the table. After a large gulp of wine and a nibble of cold, hardened cheesy toast, she got up and took the dishes to the kitchen. Even though everything around her was familiar, it looked different, off-centre. Standing in her yellow kitchen used to feel like being comfortably cocooned in an egg. Now it seemed to be a suffocating reminder of her abandoned eggs and the children she would no longer have with Adam. Her world had shifted and she no longer seemed to belong anywhere. She felt helpless and hopeless. Lost.

Gemma wondered if she would ever be found again.

Chapter 4

For the rest of the weekend, tears regularly caught Gemma off-guard, dripping and pooling like tiny puddles after rain. She tried distracting herself, and to get solace, by documenting her latest finds in her diary-cum-journal, which she started the first time she ever brought home a mudlarking object. She noted where and when items were discovered, any interesting pieces of information she learnt online, as well as observations about herself and her life. Adam had never understood why she felt the need to log the 'river junk she insisted on bringing home'. She eventually gave up trying to explain.

On Sunday night, she discovered a lone sock of Adam's at the bottom of the laundry basket. It was navy with yellow bananas, part of a pair she'd given him at Christmas. She took it out and went to find its partner. But he'd taken all his underwear and every sock. Did he know it was missing? Or did he not want it because it would only remind him of the wife he also no longer wanted? Ugh. Even this single, solitary piece of wool was upsetting. It represented everything that she now was, alone and lonely. Half of a pair. She hid it in one of his empty drawers.

Then she took off her wedding ring because what use was that anymore? The marriage was over. She put it out of sight in a decorative trinket box she never used. Her skin was pale and indented from where the ring had sat for the past six years. Even though she could still see its imprint, it felt strange and unnatural to not feel it on her finger. She played with her engagement ring. It was modest but pretty. She liked it. Perhaps if she wore it on another finger it could represent something else. What that would be, she'd figure out later. She moved it to the middle finger of her left hand.

Those two seemingly small acts packed a massive emotional punch. She felt as if she'd been knocked down and winded. On Monday, she called in sick and stayed in bed for two days. It was as if her heart had been struck down by illness, a melancholic sickness. An ache nestled deep inside, which she feared would never go. It was a form of grief she hadn't experienced before. She didn't know what to do, how long it would last, nor how she'd be able to move forward. She felt heavy, as if drugged by sadness, and she couldn't seem to think clearly or rationally. She was reminded of objects she'd found in the Thames, that the river had worn down, chipped and snapped until they no longer resembled their original form.

She also couldn't bear to face the fact that she was now completely on her own in the house and in her life. It wasn't the solitude she minded as much as the loneliness. The feeling of being alone in the world, of not quite belonging. A familiar feeling that Gemma was shocked to be reminded of. She had been adopted as a one-month-old. Before her parents had told her, just after her tenth birthday, she'd always wondered why she wasn't like either her parents or her younger, non-adopted brother. Why she liked spending time in the garden finding ladybirds or collecting shells and sea glass on the beach, and no one else in the family had been keen to join her. When she was five, she'd asked her mother why she had freckles and they didn't. Had she drawn them on Gemma's face with a permanent marker for fun and hadn't been able to wash them off? Her mother had responded with 'you're unique', as if that was all Gemma needed to know.

Learning why her freckles would never come off and that her parents were fully supportive of her wanting to find her birth parents, if she ever desired to, was such a relief that any questions she may have had were annulled. Not only that, but because every friend and family member had known from the beginning, her status as 'adopted' was normalised. In fact, it became irrelevant. She understood it as merely another way for people to have children.

Yet despite all of this, there had forever been a hole that needed filling. Where did she come from? What was her heritage? Now, as she was left wondering about her future, questions about her past began to re-surface. And it all added to the confusion and overwhelm of the past few days.

In the end, Gemma realised it would be her work and her patients that would help her keep it together and distract her from self-absorbing thoughts. She'd much rather talk about her patients' lives and dreams, which she hoped did them as much good as it did her. It was getting used to no longer having anyone at home to distract her or keep her company that was the problem.

On her first day back, it was the last day of treatment for one of her patients, which was a much-needed mood boost. As usual, Barbara, the head nurse, had brought in cupcakes. It was becoming a tradition, but Gemma suspected it was mainly because Barbara and her husband were recent empty nesters, and Barbara wanted to continue baking without her husband complaining of being unable to eat it all. She'd made strawberry vanilla cupcakes with buttercream frosting, sprinkled with freeze-dried strawberries. Barbara had excelled herself.

An old patient, Joe, returned for his fourth round of chemotherapy in four years, which wasn't great news, but he was always good company. Gemma put aside a cupcake for him.

'Do you love us that much that you couldn't stay away?' she

joked when he walked into reception. He'd put on weight and it rather suited him.

'I didn't think I'd be seeing you again either,' he said. 'But history has a disturbing way of repeating itself.'

'Let's get your vitals done. I think your favourite spot by the window in the treatment room is free. I've got you a cupcake for later.'

'Thanks, Gemma. So how are you doing? Any news since I was last here?'

There's so much news, she wanted to say. But she just told him about the Georgian button she'd recently found. There was no need to upset him or herself by talking about Adam and the breakdown of her marriage. As it was, she'd not yet mentioned it to anyone. It was as if saying it out loud would render it more concrete, more real. Something impossible to reverse should Adam suddenly – improbably – change his mind. It also felt shameful to say 'he's left me' as if her character and integrity – not just his – were in question.

'Did you know that the eighteenth century was the golden age of button-making in Britain?' she asked, as they headed down the corridor.

'No, I did not.'

'It was an era of vanity and dressing to impress. The button I found is large and has a floral motif. I love to imagine who might have worn it. Ostentatious buttons were often on the coats of flamboyant men who were keen to stand out from the crowd.'

'It wasn't mine then. I'm not that old or flamboyant.' Joe laughed. 'You really love mudlarking, don't you? I'm sure you've told me once before – I can't remember – but have you been doing it long?'

'About five years. I took it up when we moved closer to the Thames.'

'And what do you do with all the things you find?'

'I store most things in Tupperware containers,' she said, taking

Joe's temperature. 'But not before I've carefully cleaned them so they don't get damaged, then dried them out or done whatever needs to be done, as best I can, to preserve them. The mud is oxygen-starved and so it has amazing preservation properties. Except that means some things start deteriorating very quickly as soon as they're removed from it.'

'You should have them on display.'

'I suppose.'

'That way others can enjoy them too. Your husband at the very least.'

Gemma smiled to hide her discomfort at the mention of Adam. It was time to change the subject. She noted the thermometer reading, put the blood pressure cuff around Joe's arm and asked him to squeeze his fist. 'Are you going to treat yourself to a new hat again, to wear while you're having treatment?' she asked, keeping her eyes on the monitor.

'I think I will. We're coming into summer, so a panama might be the go-to.'

'Very dashing. And how's the furniture restoring business?'

'Excellent. There's either been an increase in inheritances or more people have discovered the benefits of reviving something rather than throwing it away and replacing it with something cheap and mass produced. As you lot here know, there's nothing like the joy of bringing things back to life.' He slapped his leg and laughed at his joke.

Gemma always enjoyed chatting with Joe. There was never any topic too dark or off-limits for him. 'Your blood pressure and temperature are looking good,' she said. 'Are you ready for chemo round four?'

'As ready as Tyson Fury. Let's give this thing my best right hook.'

On Friday evening, not long after she'd got home, she received a call from Adam. She glared at her phone. They hadn't spoken since he'd walked out, and she suspected that if she didn't answer, he'd keep trying until she did.

'Hi,' she said, toneless.

'Hi, how ar—' He stopped. He probably realised that it was unlikely she was doing great, far from it, and that he was the sole cause. 'I ... uh ... wanted to get a couple of things. Can I come over?'

'Now?' she said. While she didn't fancy speaking to him, she definitely didn't want to see him. A long, hot bath was far more preferable to a stilted interaction with the man who no longer loved her.

'Yeah.'

She forced a smile. She'd read that if you smile while saying something the other person doesn't want to hear, it disarms them. 'Tell me what you want and I'll leave them in the porch.'

'Will you be out?' he asked, as if horrified she might have a social life.

'No. Yes.' She corrected herself because now she'd have to go out to guarantee she wouldn't see him.

He paused. 'Okay, but it's raining.'

'The porch is covered.'

'Fine,' he sighed.

She supposed he was being conciliatory. There was no point arguing now, was there? He told her what he wanted: some books from work he'd forgotten to return, his portable speaker, some clothes and his Kindle. 'We also need to talk some time,' he added. 'About moving forward. Selling the house and all that.'

Gemma swallowed. Selling the house? It would be inevitable, of course, but her mind had yet to properly entertain the idea.

'Not that I'm trying to rush you,' he said quickly.

Except he was!

'You can stay for as long as you like. Until ... well ... I suppose until we come to an agreement.'

She sighed. It was all too hard.

'I also wanted to give you my new address. In case you get mail for me. I've set up a redirection but sometimes, you know …' His voice trailed away as if he expected her to commiserate on the likelihood of an unreliable postal service. She felt nothing for his concerns about his post, rather she was affronted and hurt that already he was thinking about the practicalities of their separation.

'Text it to me,' she said.

'Okay.'

'Is that it?'

'Yep.'

She hung up and went to check the local tide chart. It was neither high nor low, yet it would be low enough for a short time at least. After leaving the items Adam requested in a box in the porch, she went to find her boots and rain jacket, and left the house.

When she returned, the items were gone.

But, so too were other things, which she realised over the course of the next twenty-four hours. His umbrella, a framed photo of his parents, and the Nutribullet she never used. She'd completely overlooked the fact that he still had a key.

The next day, after organising for a locksmith to change the locks, and not giving a toss about the more expensive rate because it was a Saturday, Gemma finally felt up to telling her mother about her marriage breakdown. It helped that Gemma didn't have to go into too much detail before her mother's strong sense of justice fired her up so much that she unleashed a fury of indignation on her behalf.

'How dare he, how dare he!' her mother repeated. 'He's despicable.'

'He said he wasn't happy.'

'There are far better ways of getting around that. Now, *you're* unhappy!'

Gemma nodded despondently.

'Shred his business shirts,' her mother said with a hint of glee in her voice.

'What?'

'You'll feel so much better. I did that once. Before your father. But that's another story.'

'You know I'm not as hot-headed as you are. Anyway, he's already taken his business shirts.'

'Oh, darling, I am so sorry.' Her mother sighed.

'I keep thinking, what did I do wrong?'

'You didn't do anything wrong. Don't think like that.'

It was nice of her mother to stick up for her so vehemently, but Gemma knew that it takes two to make a relationship work.

'Yeah, but sometimes doing nothing or having your head in the clouds isn't always the best strategy either,' she said. 'I must have been stupidly blind to his needs and wants. I didn't mean to be. I really didn't mean to be.'

'Don't beat yourself up. He shouldn't have jumped into bed with someone else, no matter what. It doesn't solve anything.'

'Maybe we never should have married ...' Gemma's voice cracked because that wasn't something she'd ever thought she'd say.

'Oh, Gemma, darling. Listen, I want to come and see you. I'd drop everything and come up to London tomorrow, but we've been having staffing issues at the charity shop, and I don't think I'll be able to find anyone to fill in at such short notice.'

'Thanks, Mum. I'll be okay.' As much as Gemma thought it would be nice having her mother stay for a bit, she preferred the idea of moping on her own for a while. Her mum would only want to tidy the house.

'But I'll come down another weekend,' her mother said. 'Wait a minute ... I'm looking at the diary. Next weekend is out because I'm doing a charity walk and then, the following weekend—'

'Don't worry,' Gemma interrupted. Her mother's busy social life was admirable but she didn't want to hear about it. 'We'll work something out.'

Next, Gemma called her brother. May as well get all the family informed at the same time. Rich lived in Spain, and Gemma's only niece, three-year-old Sofia, was on her way to speaking better Spanish than English. Gemma worried that one day she may not be able to converse with her at all. Even Rich preferred speaking Spanish. Or maybe he liked showing off. Gemma had never been sure.

'*El cabrón!*' he shouted down the phone after she'd told him. Although Gemma didn't know what it meant, he was clearly, kindly, as outraged as their mother had been.

'*El* …?' she said.

'Bastard, Gemma. He's a bastard.'

A much longer discussion ensued because Rich was a detail-oriented man and liked asking questions. At the end of the call, he promised to be in contact more often to check on her, which she greatly appreciated but doubted would actually happen.

'Call me anytime, though, yeah?' Rich said. 'If you want to vent your anger at *el cabrón*, I'm here. Anytime.'

And from then on, *el cabrón* became Adam's new nickname. If nothing else, it made Gemma laugh in a sardonic I-can't-believe-I-have-a-bastard-of-a-husband kind of a way.

Chapter 5

Three weeks later, Gemma was persuaded by two of her old nursing friends that it would be good for her to have a night out. Before this she hadn't been in any mood to socialise. She'd wanted to hide her reality from the world, so that no one got to see how much she was hurting and she didn't have to explain. Nothing had radically changed, but she now felt a little more amenable to receiving counsel from friends. She wore her red dress, because nothing says 'I've got this' like the colour red, even though it seemed like she wasn't in control of anthing and she was losing everything rather than 'getting' anything. When she arrived at the bar, a gin and tonic – her favourite – was already waiting for her.

'Here, come on, give us a hug.' Mel got up and squeezed her tightly. The familiar smell of her honey-scented body moisturiser was unexpectedly comforting. 'How are you doing?' she asked.

'Exhausted. A marriage break-up isn't good for your beauty sleep,' Gemma answered wryly.

'Are you okay to talk about it?'

'I didn't want to at first, but I think I'm okay now.'

'Do you think this is really it for your marriage? You're not going to have a trial separation?'

Gemma shook her head. 'Adam has made it very clear he

doesn't want to be with me anymore.'

'Oh, God, you poor thing.' Mel squeezed her hand.

'I can't believe it. It's awful, just bloody awful,' Simone said. 'And you had no idea?'

Gemma knew her friend didn't mean to sound accusatory, but she still couldn't help but feel ashamed. She shook her head.

'I'm sorry, Gem. He shouldn't have cheated, no matter what,' Simone said.

'It's pathetic,' Mel said with disdain.

'Look, I knew a distance had formed between us,' Gemma admitted. 'But I thought it was life and work getting in the way, you know?'

'It is hard knowing what the normal stresses and strains of life are and what's not,' Simone said. 'Dave and I have been going through a bit of a thing. Mainly because of the kids. We can barely have a conversation longer than thirty seconds without an interruption. They take over your life. I can't even go to the bathroom without one of them trotting in and asking questions. I think it's better when they can't talk.'

'It drives you nuts,' Mel agreed. 'I'm done with the baby and toddler stage. It can only get better from here, surely?'

'That's what they say,' Gemma said light-heartedly, pretending she was perfectly fine listening to her friends talk about their children when it only highlighted how their lives were diverging. She was losing touch with her best friend from school, Anushka, who had married two years ago and already had two children. Gemma understood her life was so busy with her young family and a challenging full-time job that she had less time for socialising. But it only made Gemma feel more on the outside than ever before.

'Until they become teenagers.' Simone was still talking. She rolled her eyes and gulped some wine.

Simone, who'd moved into cosmetic-aesthetic nursing because it was less emotionally taxing and paid more, had a long-term partner and twin toddlers whom she called her little rascals, even though Gemma thought they were the cutest children she'd ever seen. Mel, a cardiac nurse, had one child and said she didn't want another because of the state the world was in. Gemma thought that the world was always in a state so what did it matter?

She didn't like that she was being flippant, but envy could do that to you, couldn't it? What mattered to Gemma was that she was the only one without a partner, and had no idea when, or if ever, she would have children. She and Adam had talked about trying for the past couple of years. Or rather, Gemma had been keen while Adam had been more reticent. He had kept making excuses about it not being the right time, and she'd been waiting patiently for when that might be.

She sipped the last of her drink. The liquor bottles lining the mirrored wall behind the bar counter shone prettily under the lights. Though she wished the dark green velvet booth seats didn't remind her of a sofa she'd been eyeing up in a furniture catalogue, which Adam said he loved when she'd showed him, the week before he left. She'd imagined it in their living room, a more fashionable alternative to the one they'd picked up cheaply on eBay when they first moved in.

'Anyway, I think you're better off without Adam,' Simone continued. 'I always thought he had a supercilious air about him, as if he thought he was better than everyone else. And recently he was always giving some vague excuse for his absences at our social gatherings. Was he really always busier than the rest of us?'

'Simone!' Mel said.

'Sorry.'

'But I loved him,' Gemma said defensively, her eyes smarting. 'I kind of still do. I know I shouldn't and I don't want to but …' She rubbed the velvet seat and watched the pile darken and lighten. As much as Simone's words hurt, deep down, she was beginning to see that maybe she was right. It was true, Adam had been skipping events and Gemma hadn't thought to question his reasons. And if she was honest, he had developed a habit of mocking her 'lowly paid' job, when he should have been praising its worthiness.

'You know we're always here for a chat or a cry,' Mel said. 'Life can suck and you shouldn't have to handle it on your own.'

'Exactly,' Simone said. 'And whenever you're ready, we'll help you get back on the dating scene, won't we, Mel? Even though its ages since I dated, and I probably wouldn't know what to do!' She laughed.

From Mel's handbag came the sound of her and Tom's wedding song. They only got married last year and every time her phone rang, Mel liked to remind them that 'Perfect' by Ed Sheeran had been their first dance. 'Sorry,' she said. 'I think it's Gabriel. He likes saying goodnight to me if I'm out. I know I should nip it in the bud before he gets too dependent, but I kind of like it.' She did a single shoulder shrug, then, answered.

Gemma reached for her phone to check the time. It was going to be a long night and she wished she didn't feel that way. She loved her friends, but their lives were now busy in a way that hers wasn't. A text had come in from Georgie, her friend from work.

I'm at a party. My friend has been trying to set me up with this guy, Harry. To be honest, he's not my type. But he is yours. Why don't you come and meet him?

Gemma groaned inwardly. Why did everyone think she was ready to date again? It was ridiculous. Just because her marriage was most certainly over, it didn't mean her heart and mind had suddenly reached a place of acceptance and were ready for something new.

I'm out with friends, Gemma wrote.

Come after.

Gemma replied with an emoji of a man dancing. She wasn't going to go but she didn't want to be a killjoy.

I'm being serious. Be spontaneous.

Gemma had always admired Georgie's zest for life and going to a party with her was never dull. But Gemma feared that Georgie was going to rope her into blind dates, date nights and online dating sites in a search to find her a partner. She'd rather swing from a trapeze in a skimpy leotard than do any of that.

Sorry, Georgie, another time.

Gemma slipped her phone back in her bag as Simone returned with another round of drinks. Gemma drank half the glass in one go. Anything to help soothe the pain of feeling so alone while in company.

Chapter 6

Gemma woke up the next morning with a mild hangover to add to her heartache. Yet she was pleased there was going to be a low tide after work. She'd be able to get in a good two or three hours of mudlarking while it was still light. It wasn't always easy to get the timings of the tides to fit around her job and everyday life. Although one bonus of now being on her own was that she was able to go out more frequently and spontaneously than when Adam was around. At least once or twice a week was her ideal.

That evening, the river near Richmond looked almost as blue as the sky and the plants lining the path were tinged in gold. It was the perfect soft, angled light which made it easier to spot objects that might otherwise be invisible under harsher, more direct sunlight. The foreshore seemed glowing with promise. Gemma closed her eyes and listened to the gentle sound of the water. Its lapping was rhythmic and soothing.

She took her time walking the length of the beach where the water met the mud and the stones by the waterline were slippery from the tide. Even with experience at 'getting her eye in', as mudlarkers like to say, she was still amazed by how much could be found washed up by the tide. She spotted a hypodermic needle, dark-brown shards from a twentieth-century broken beer bottle, three chalk-white clay pipe stems and a little glass apothecary bottle. Nothing noteworthy or that she hadn't seen before. Not that she minded. It was pleasurable enough to be able to forget what was going on in her life and to soak up the atmosphere. Just to be alone with Mother Nature.

Up ahead a wave rushed in and rushed out to reveal a small china vase, sitting incongruously on top of the mud. Gemma walked over to it and picked it up. It was sweet and not very old, but she didn't want it. She returned it to the shoreline, wedging it into the mud. She stood up and breathed in the crisp spring air tinged with the smell of the riverbed.

After a few slow inhales and exhales, she turned her gaze back to the mud. That's when she spotted something gold submerged in the silt, its curved corner being repeatedly cleaned as the water washed over it. It was glinting so brightly that her heart skipped a beat. Gold was the ultimate treasure. It's what larkers and metal detectorists dream of finding, and the older, the better. Gemma pulled it out of the mud. It was a watch. Not old. Vintage at a push. Disappointingly, she suspected it was fake, because Adam had a replica Rolex once and, like this one, there was no serial number on the back.

Of all the things she could have found, it had to be something that reminded her of Adam. Even by the river she couldn't escape him. Should she leave the watch for someone else to find or take it with her to dispose of? Either way, as far as she was concerned it was rubbish and a sham. Much like her marriage.

Feeling huffy and sad and sorry for herself, she sat on a dry area of shingle. She lay back on her elbows and gazed at the vast expanse of sky, which looked like a giant piece of Wedgwood pottery, Georgian blue with white porcelain clouds. Tears sprung from a seemingly never-ending well of them.

'Are you all right?'

Gemma startled. Two legs in beige slacks, with brogues that shone like polished copper, were standing next to her. She recognised the voice.

'Hi, Timothy,' she said, wiping her eyes and trying to sound cheerful. 'I'm cloud spotting.' She pointed skywards, hoping to distract him from seeing that she'd been crying.

'You can't fool me,' he said, wagging a finger. 'The clouds are moving far too quickly to enable any true spotting.'

Timothy was seventy-six, 'or thereabouts' as he once told her, and lived on one of the houseboats that lined the Thames, not far from where Gemma lived. She was loosely acquainted with him because on the days he volunteered at the British Museum he caught the same train to Vauxhall as she did to work. He had an angular face softened by glasses and doe-like eyes which made him look kind and gentle.

'What are you doing down this end of the river?' she asked.

'Visiting a friend. I saw you lying down and thought you might have fallen.'

She sat up. 'I'm just having a moment.'

'Don't get up on my behalf,' he said. 'Although if you do, I'll hang around. Just in case. If you're anything like me, you'll get dizzy if you stand too quickly.'

'Thanks, but I'm rather mucky. I wouldn't touch these gloves if I were you. The Thames may be pretty clean nowadays but that doesn't mean it's pollution-free.'

'True. Years ago, a friend of a friend was struck down with Weil's disease. Nasty thing that. Comes from rat wee in the water. Have you found anything interesting?' Timothy peered at the gravel around his feet.

'Not today.'

'Ah, well.' He shrugged. 'I used to mudlark, too, you know, until my wife needed more care.' He looked wistful, then his face brightened. 'I was a complete amateur, mind you, but I developed a particular interest in the World Wars. Finding bullets and lead balls became my thing. Now I've got a bad back. That's why museum volunteering is so good. There's no bending over.

Especially if I only wear slip-ons.' He laughed.

Gemma became aware that she hadn't been fully focused on what Timothy was saying, which was a shame because at any other time she would have enjoyed sharing stories about mudlarking.

'Are you sure you're all right?' Timothy asked again.

'Uh-huh,' she answered vaguely.

'Well, enjoy your mudlarking and I'll no doubt see you at the station on Monday.'

Gemma watched Timothy tread carefully in his smart shoes towards the footpath. He turned to check on her. She waved. He waved, too, and disappeared down the street. Except now that Timothy was gone, Gemma wanted him to come back. The only socialising she'd done with him was on her commute, but he was a sweet man and good company. She sighed and got up.

She looked down at the gaudy gold watch next to her feet and for the first time ever, wished this was one item she had never found. She kicked it but it barely moved. Even here, it felt as if Adam was winning. Gemma wasn't a competitive person but, in this instance, she decided it was game on.

Without bothering to remove her gloves, she gathered her things and hurried home as best she could in sludgy wellies, probably resembling, as Adam once disparagingly remarked, a trauma cleaner fleeing a garden crime scene.

Once home, she went to the chest of drawers in her bedroom and pulled out the sock she'd hidden. It may have been out of sight, but it hadn't been out of mind. She'd thought it cute at the time but now the bananas, angled as they were into smiles, appeared to mock her. She took it to the kitchen and got the scissors. She held up the sock and cut off the toes. Next, she went for the middle of the foot, then across the ankle. Her mother was right. It felt good. With each snip her discontent dissipated. She sliced and diced the bananas until they resembled a jigsaw puzzle, only this one couldn't be pieced together again.

For a minute, Gemma gloated over her vengeful destruction.

But the feeling didn't last. Too quickly, she felt unsatisfied and hollow. What's more, she felt bad for the sock. It wasn't its fault Adam had done Gemma wrong. It had been in perfectly good condition, too. What a waste. She gathered up the frayed pieces and threw them into the rubbish bin.

Thank goodness, this month was nearly over and very soon she could start a new one afresh. She went to find her journal and took it to the kitchen table. Carefully laying out her recent finds, she began to document them.

April Discoveries:
One Georgian button made from a brass alloy to look like silver. Two heavy handmade iron nails, one of which has its maker's mark stamped on the shaft. A sheep's jaw, which gave me such a fright because I thought it was human! Two bottles: one a translucent green apothecary bottle, the other resembled a clear-glass test tube. How I now feel more of a connection to the Thames than to my actual friends. How sometimes the kindest people are those who are staring death in the face. How violence (even in the form of scissors to a sock) is never the answer. And how, now, my future is scarily unrecognisable.

May

Chapter 7

Gemma first started collecting things when she was a child and lived on the south coast. She didn't know it then, but the washed-out pieces of glass and sea-polished pebbles she took home from the beach meant that she was well on her way towards becoming a larker. When she moved to London to study nursing, the only times she beachcombed was when she was visiting home or if she was on holiday. It wasn't until she and Adam moved near the Thames that she realised how much she missed being near water. Regularly, she'd take herself down to the river to clear her mind and unwind from a tough week at work.

The first piece of history she discovered was entirely accidental. She and Adam had had a row. Over what, she couldn't remember. But she'd left the house intending to walk off her exasperation and took to the exposed riverbed where the tide was at its lowest. There, a shoelace came undone and bending down to tie it up, she noticed a triangular shard of blue and white pottery popping with brightness among the grey and red rubble of the foreshore. She picked it up, felt its smooth shiny surface and wondered what it had once been. She put it in her pocket to find out.

Gemma didn't know then that to ferret around the riverbed and take away what you found required a permit, or that what she'd done even had a name. Nor did she know that she should have washed the piece of pottery with warm water and a toothbrush, then dried it out slowly, keeping it away from heat so it didn't get damaged. Instead, she taped it to the pin board above the radiator next to her desk and began searching online for what object it may once have been a part of. Her fragment featured the blue edge of a wing and a puff of cloud, a teasing snippet of a larger story that, Gemma discovered, turned out to be inspired by a Japanese fairy tale and the designs of revered Chinese porcelain. 'Willow Pattern' tableware became fashionable and ubiquitous during the eighteenth and nineteenth centuries and was the most common type of pottery found by mudlarkers.

Although the piece may not have been valuable, it became so to Gemma. Who had eaten off it? Did it belong to a shipbuilder's wife or a pub owner? How had it ended up in the river? Had it broken and was considered rubbish? And where were its siblings? Were they close by, or had they dispersed randomly and arrived at different parts of the river? Would they ever be found? Gemma was amazed at how many questions had arisen from this single three-by-two-centimetre fragment.

When she'd got home, she was so excited she wanted to tell Adam. But he didn't seem to get it. He thought she was making a fuss over a dirty chunk of ceramic (his words) that was better off in the bin (his words again). In fact, looking back, Adam had always been dismissive of her hobby. So much so, that, deep down, it was as if he'd chipped off a tiny splinter of her that never got reattached. Why on earth had she put up with it?

Even so, it didn't make her stop. In fact, it made her want to do it more, and Gemma quickly learnt that you had to keep abreast of the tides in order to regularly hit the foreshore. Now, Gemma printed out the tide charts for the next three months. She fixed them to the fridge door and planned her next outing. She fancied going into the city, into the heart of old Londinium.

The next convenient low tide would be the second Sunday of May at one in the afternoon.

Bankside, on the south side of the Thames, was busy and noisy with tourists and buskers, trains and traffic. Walking across Millenium Bridge, her rucksack on her back, a fellow pedestrian called out, 'Hey, Dora, what are you exploring?' Gemma laughed and waved. She didn't care if someone called her the name of a TV cartoon character. She was in a good mood because she was about to spend several hours with ghosts of the past and had everything she could possibly need. Kneepads, wellies, rubber gloves, Ziplock bags, a dry bag, a trowel, a foldable rain jacket, sunglasses, hand sanitiser, tissues, a Thermos of tea, a filled bread roll and a bottle of water.

As she reached the steps leading down to the beach, Gemma tuned out from everything around her. The modern world receded. Even the clatter of the trains at Blackfriars Station faded. The grey rubble beneath her feet became her focus. The dirty sky hung low and the slowly receding tide sloshed and rippled, in parts creating small pools and in others, exposing freshly eroded blue mud. That was where Gemma was drawn. To see what would reveal itself from beneath the erosion.

After fifteen minutes, Gemma found a nail bent into the shape of a 'J'. She wasn't well-versed in nails so was unsure of its age. She would keep it in order to find out. All she knew was that there was every kind of nail wedged in the riverbed relating to all the different trades and industries that had ever existed by the Thames. Shipbuilding. Furniture making. Shoe cobbling.

She tucked the nail into a bag and was about to look down again when she was distracted by the sight of a man with a clipped strawberry-blond beard and tousled hair. He was metal detecting, and his detector was beeping more loudly than she'd ever heard one before. He was shouting at it as if it were a disobedient toddler, but, like a typical toddler, the detector was ignoring him. For a moment, Gemma felt sorry for him. He'd yet to be calmed by the river. When his continued disgust at the detector didn't stop, she changed her mind. He was disrupting the peace. She turned and headed in the opposite direction.

A woman, older than Gemma, was also mudlarking nearby. They exchanged greetings but nothing more. Neither wanted to encroach on the other. When Gemma noticed something round and flat with a dull shine, she bent over to pick it up. It was a button. Possibly pewter, with a rainbow-tinged patina. She washed it in the water. Had this come from someone whose clothing got caught leaving one of the wherry boats which once crossed the river? Or had it, sinisterly, come from someone who'd drowned? Gemma gently wiped it dry on her jeans and put it in a bag.

Her next finds were not so exciting. A snippet of a clay pipe handle and a chunk of blue and white pottery. Two things she already had. She left them in the silt for the tide to decide what next to do with them. She wandered a bit more, until, feeling hungry, she found a spot near the mossy wall and sat down. She got out her lunch and poured herself some tea.

The woman she'd passed earlier was edging closer. She stopped and peeled something out of the mud. Her face lit up at the sight of it. But it was so small, Gemma couldn't tell what it was from where she was sitting. The woman was now removing a glove and trying to take a photo of it. Then she dropped her phone and Gemma could hear her curse.

'Everything okay?' Gemma called out.

'I've cracked my phone screen,' the woman replied. 'But look.' She held up her discovery.

Gemma squinted. The woman was too far away.

'A thimble,' the woman said. 'It's squished flat but it's a thimble all right.' The woman strode up the beach. 'Here, see.' As she approached, the foreshore turned from sepia to technicolour with her brightly patterned head scarf and chunky bangles.

'That's lovely,' Gemma said.

'Shame it's so flattened I can't put a finger in it. Wouldn't it be fabulous to be the first person to wear it since it was lost in the river?'

For a moment, Gemma imagined her thumb inside a hundred-year-old thimble.

'You wouldn't mind taking a photo of me with it, would you? I've got a mudlarking Instagram account but it's just I'm not very good at taking selfies, and I usually don't bother. My phone camera should still work,' she said, handing Gemma her mobile.

'Sure.' Gemma got up and took a few photos with the woman's phone. 'Nice earring, by the way.' Gemma pointed to the gold filigree flower in the woman's right ear.

'Earrings,' the woman corrected. 'I'd never wear only one. How old do you think I am? Twenty?' She flung her head back and laughed.

'But you really do only have one,' Gemma said.

'What?' The woman touched her ears. 'Oh, you're right. The other one must have fallen off. I can't have lost it! They were my grandmother's.' She frantically scanned the ground immediately around her feet and continued talking. 'Nana gave them to me when I was ten, just before she died and I've treasured them ever since. Oh, no, I can't see it. Please don't let it be lost.' The woman's voice faltered. She pressed her hands together and closed her eyes.

'Okay, don't panic,' Gemma said, but the woman was now running down to the waterline.

Gemma packed up her lunch and followed her. 'It'll be here, I'm sure,' she said, catching up to her.

'But what if it's not? I could have lost it anywhere. It's the only thing I have of Nana's.' The poor woman was about to cry.

'Why don't we go back to where you started and retrace your steps?' Gemma suggested.

'Yes, okay,' she said with a sad smile. 'But you don't have to come. I didn't mean to interrupt you.'

'It's all right, I don't mind. It'll be like we're mudlarking, we might find more than just your earring.'

'You're being very kind.'

'I'm Gemma, by the way.'

'Phyllida with a Y.'

'So where are we walking back to?' Gemma asked.

Phyllida thought for a moment, then explained. 'I started at the access steps by Tate Modern. I walked down them, and headed straight to the water, looking for a find line. Then I, more or less, followed it all the way here.' She plotted her movements with a hand.

'At least it's not a tiny stud,' Gemma said, trying to stay positive. 'We should spot it easily if you lost it here.'

'I hope so.'

They lowered their gazes and very slowly made their way along the beach, scouring the mud and pebbly rocks around their feet. If something caught their attention, they stopped to get their eye in.

'I'm not even finding anything interesting, let alone my earring,' Phyllida said in resignation.

'I know,' Gemma agreed. 'But don't worry, I'm sure we'll find it,' she added, with none of the doubt she actually felt. 'Have you been mudlarking long?' Perhaps a distraction might temporarily ease Phyllida's worry.

'Off and on for two years, but when I went on long-service leave, I started doing it more regularly. It's so much better than metal detecting, don't you think?'

'I don't know. I've never done it.'

'See that guy over there?' Phyllida pointed to the man Gemma had seen earlier. 'He's doing it all wrong. He's waving the thing like he's vacuum cleaning. He'll do a shoulder in, if nothing else, and he'll not find a thing.' Phyllida shook her head disapprovingly. 'If you ask me, it's the men who like to metal detect. They're desperate to find a stash of treasure, something of monetary value. It's that caveman, hunting thing. Now look at him. He's having conniptions with his contraption. He'll never experience the Zen-like nature of the pursuit if he keeps that up. Oh, well. Some people.' She flung her hands in the air as if the metal detectorist symbolised her despair for the world in general.

A Thames Clipper boat travelled past, heading east down the river. Its wake pushed the water into a continuous ripple until it energetically sloshed the shoreline, kicking stones and turning pebbles.

'It never fails to amaze me how many secrets the river holds,' Gemma said, again to liven the conversation.

'Thousands of years of them,' Phyllida agreed. 'So, what's yours?'

'My secret?'

'Sorry, I didn't mean to be so forward. It's a failing of mine. You don't have to answer.'

Gemma thought for a minute. 'Put it this way, it's nice to find things instead of losing them.'

'You can say that again.'

Gemma paused to pick up something she spotted.

'Oooh, what's that?' Phyllida said excitedly.

'Just a button.'

'Oh.' Then, 'It looks in very good condition. Eighteenth century, perhaps?'

Gemma examined it closely. It was a cute little button. She slipped it into her pocket. 'Okay, let's keep going.'

In the forty-five minutes it took for them to get to the pedestrian walkway at the top of the access steps, nothing that even resembled a speck of gold glinted back at them.

'I guess that's it then,' Phyllida said.

'What if you retrace your steps from the very beginning of your journey to here?' Gemma suggested. 'You never know ...'

Phyllida nodded but she looked sad. 'Thanks for helping.'

'My pleasure. What's your Instagram handle? I'll follow you.'

'You don't have to.'

'No, I want to.'

'Well, okay, then,' Phyllida said. 'It's tide dash phylly. Yours?'

'You don't need to follow me. I barely post and when I do, it's not that exciting. Are you going to do any more mudlarking?'

'No, I might sit here for a minute and contemplate the point of finding other people's lost possessions if we can't even keep hold of our own.'

'I'm really sorry we didn't find it.'

'Don't worry about me, off you go.' Phyllida gestured for Gemma to return to the foreshore, her bangles making one last clunk before her hands rested in her lap as she gazed out to the river.

Chapter 8

Gemma turned and headed back down the stone steps towards a cluster of rotting wooden footings. It was always good to look in places where things could get trapped and accumulate, never making it back into the river, like in inlets or by walls and posts. She zoned in on the sludgy mud and poked around at the base of the footings. For a long moment, she completely lost herself to history.

Until the high-pitched beeping of a metal detector brought her back to the present. The detectorist was only a few metres away. She was about to return her gaze to the exposed riverbed when she noticed him taking something out of the mud that caught the light and winked.

'Hey,' Gemma called out.

The man looked up. He had mud on his face and wind-tousled hair. 'Hey,' he called back cheerfully.

'Can I ask what you found?' Gemma jogged over to him.

'Um, well ...' The man seemed as perplexed by his find as he was by her sudden arrival. He stared into his cupped hand.

'Sorry,' Gemma said. 'I'm not trying to be nosy. Only a woman I just met lost an earring. I was wondering if you'd found it?'

'I don't know,' he said. 'Have I?'

He unfurled his hand. A gold flower earring lay in his palm

like a piece of royal treasure on a velvet cushion.

'That's it!' Gemma clapped her gloved hands. 'Phyllida!' She shouted and turned in the direction of where she'd left her at the top of the steps. But Phyllida was no longer there. 'I can't believe it. She was there a second ago!'

The man curled his fingers back around the earring and brought his hand closer to his ripped T-shirt. 'Really?' he said looking at her suspiciously.

'No, honestly, I know how this must sound but it's true. This other mudlarker …' Gemma looked back at the spot where Phyllida had been in case she had returned. 'She was, literally, sitting up there only moments ago. She must have just left. We've spent the last hour trying to find her lost earring.'

'And you reckon this is it?'

His distrust was palpable but she didn't care. 'I *know* it is because I commented on the one she was wearing. This is amazing. She'll be so happy.' Gemma smiled, hoping to have convinced him, although he definitely – and probably understandably – wasn't going to part with it that easily. 'How about I call her and she can confirm it with you?' she suggested.

Gemma pulled off her gloves and got out her phone. Then she remembered. The only way she could contact Phyllida was through Instagram and now she'd forgotten the name of her handle.

'Oh, God.' She sighed. 'I can't call her because I don't have her number! We only just met, as I said. She told me she was on Instagram so I can send her a direct message, but I don't know when she'll see it.' Gemma bit a thumbnail and felt her face redden, as it always did whenever she felt panicky.

The man studied her for a moment, then his face relaxed. 'You know what?' he said. 'Don't worry about it. I believe you. Anyway, a single earring is no good to me. I'm a matching pair kind of a guy.' He laughed.

'Are you sure?'

'Yep.'

'Thank you. You're a man after my own heart. And definitely Phyllida's. About the single earring thing, I mean,' she reiterated pointing to an earlobe.

He smiled. Gemma took the earring and put it in one of her Ziplock bags. 'Thank you so much. I hope the river gifts you something else today.'

'To be honest, I get excited when this old machine makes a noise, let alone finds something.'

'Well, have yourself a very noisy day!' She was so happy for Phyllida, she had to resist the urge to give the man a hug.

On the train on the way home, Gemma found Phyllida on Instagram. She followed her and sent her a direct message with a photo of the earring.

It wasn't until later that evening that Phyllida replied. *Honey, you've made my day*, she wrote. *But don't even think about putting it in the post. What if it gets lost again? Why don't we meet for a mudlark and you can give it to me then?*

Gemma had never considered mudlarking to be a social activity. It had always been something she did by herself, for herself. Her solo escapism. Yet, perhaps it would be nice to go out with someone who's as enthusiastic about the pastime as she is.

An hour later, when Gemma was getting ready for bed, she received another message from Phyllida.

There's going to be a lunar eclipse in the early hours of Monday morning and a low tide. What are the chances? I'd love to mudlark then. Would you? We could do it at the spot we were today. The best time is going to be between exactly four-twenty-nine and five past six in the morning. Hardly sociable hours! I won't be offended if you say no.

It was an enticing invitation. The thrill of seeing a blood moon and not having to wander the foreshore alone in the dark would compensate for having to get up so early.

Why not! she replied.

Chapter 9

'When I'm finished with all this cancer business, I'm going to properly shake up my life.'

Gemma's first patient of the week, Jenny, had recently started her second round of chemotherapy. Gemma called Jenny her favourite repeat customer, which made Jenny chuckle. It was an in-joke, and Gemma suspected Jenny knew she wasn't the only one she attributed the compliment to.

'How are you going to do that?' Gemma asked, as she hung the chemo line.

'After my first round, my husband and I booked a holiday in France, which was lovely and all that but we could have picked somewhere different. At the very least, somewhere I'd never been to before.'

'Where are you thinking this time?'

'Rwanda. Trekking to see the gorillas.'

Jenny was seventy-nine. Gemma knew, from friends of her parents who'd done it, that gorilla trekking was challenging, but she wasn't about to put a dent in Jenny's enthusiasm. 'Wouldn't that be exciting?' Gemma said.

'Maybe too exciting for Derek. He has a heart condition.'

'Ah,' Gemma said, checking Jenny's vital signs: blood pressure, pulse, respiratory rate and temperature.

'My thoughts exactly. At our age, you've got to tone down the excitement, and consider the cost of it all, plus travel insurance. What about you? Have you ever shaken up your life?' Jenny's tiny body nestled into the curves of the large black armchair as though it were about to swallow her whole.

'Not really. I like things as they are. I like my job. I like my house …' Gemma let the words trail off as she realised that Adam had done such a superlative job of shaking up her life that she didn't need to. She gritted her teeth, determined not to lose it in front of a patient. 'There you are. You're all set up. Will you be all right if I go and check on another patient?'

'Of course. My son gave me a travel book for my birthday. I'm going to do some armchair holidaying. Hopefully it'll take my mind off all of this.' Jenny waved her free hand to indicate the IV line. Then she sighed and buried her head in the book.

After Jenny, Gemma had four other regulars: Doug, Sophie, Michelle and Hugh. Her day was looking reassuringly repetitive. Greet the patients, administer pre-meds, hang the chemo line, monitor patients' vitals, say goodbye. Then, she had a new patient, Andie, a fifteen-year-old skateboarder whose impending intensive treatment was not one she wished to inflict on anyone, let alone a teenager whose life had barely begun. So when Andie asked if she could skateboard down the disability ramp when they left, Gemma said, 'Of course you can,' even though it wasn't strictly allowed.

Lunch ended up being later than usual – at half-two – because Doug had an immediate reaction to the chemotherapy and suddenly found it hard to breathe. Once they'd fixed the problem, Gemma sat with him until she thought he was recovered enough to be left again.

Gemma's colleague Georgie was in the staffroom, finishing a salad. 'Is Doug okay?' she asked.

'He's shaken but stoic,' Gemma said. 'I'm going to recommend that a friend or family member sit with him next time in case he has another adverse reaction.'

'Good idea.' Georgie skewered some kale.

Gemma unwrapped her sandwich and took a bite.

'Hey, you know that party I wanted you to come to?' Georgie said. 'I got chatting to another guy, much more my type, and he asked me out.'

'A real-life dating invite!' Gemma said. 'How very noughties.'

'I know. You should try it.'

'No, thanks.'

'Oh, come on. All you seem to do is work and mudlark.'

'I like my hobby.'

'I know and that's good. But it's like you're so preoccupied with the past that you're not thinking about the future.'

'How can I think about the future when I'm still trying to get my head around the present?' Gemma didn't mean to raise her voice.

'I know, sorry.'

'At least with the past, it's comforting and reliable. Much like M&S pants,' Gemma said.

'M&S pants? If they're the only type of undies you wear, we've got to take you shopping.'

Gemma had no desire to go lingerie shopping.

'Once you wear silk and lace, you'll never go back. And, if you want to meet someone again …' Georgie raised her eyebrows.

'I don't want to meet anyone. I'm not even divorced yet.'

'That doesn't have to stop you. You're separated.'

'That may be fine for others but not for me.'

'You'll get there.'

It was time to change the subject. 'I thought you were supposed to be telling me about this guy you met,' Gemma said.

Georgie smiled and got a faraway look in her eyes. 'His name's Johnny and he's a product designer. He's taller than me, but not by much, and his eyes are like Marmite—'

'Marmite?' Gemma said. Was this the same person who

preferred reading non-fiction to avoid purple prose and metaphors?

'Yes, dark like the night. And best of all, he didn't flinch when I said I don't care about football – he's a fanatic – or that I've been known to walk in my sleep.' Georgie gazed into her salad as if her new date was sitting on a chickpea and waving at her.

'Wow, the love bug has bitten,' Gemma said.

She ate some more of her sandwich but found she'd lost her appetite. Whether Georgie's infatuation lasted or not, the fact remained that Gemma was about to lose her last single friend.

Chapter 10

On the morning of the lunar eclipse, Gemma got up at 4 a.m. and pulled on the clothes she'd left next to the bed the night before. Downstairs, she gathered the rest of her items she'd left by the front door: headtorch, bucket, gloves, kneepads, phone and, most importantly, the earring in its Ziplock bag.

When she got to the pedestrian access at Bankside, there was a chill in the breeze and a smell of algae. The Thames brooded, dark and uninviting, and the lights of the city bled into the water. At their agreed meeting place there were three people but no Phyllida. Gemma waited and looked up at the sky and the most striking moon she'd ever seen. Collecting the leftover light from all the sunrises and sunsets happening around the world at the same time, it glowed an orangey-red against the murky sky. It was like a motionless balloon which wanted to fly away but couldn't.

'Who suggested getting up so early in the cold and the dark?' Phyllida startled her from behind. She was swaddled in a green jumper and matching beanie, her curls exploding out the bottom like a bloom of black flowers.

'Well, I don't think I'd have come down here on my own, so thank you for the invite,' Gemma said. 'Just look at that moon.' She couldn't take her eyes off it.

For a moment, they both gazed up in awe.

Then, breaking the silence and reaching into her rucksack, Gemma said, 'Before we do anything else, let me give you the earring.'

Phyllida pressed the bag with the earring in it to her chest. 'You've no idea how much this means to me.' Phyllida shook her head as if she couldn't imagine it either. 'It's incredible you found it.'

'The detectorist, you mean,' Gemma said. 'It was just lucky he was near me.'

'It was meant to be! What if I hadn't met you and told you my Instagram handle? And what if you hadn't gone back to the foreshore? I'm a big believer in fate and karma.' Phyllida nodded sagely. 'Did you get the man's number? It'd be nice to thank him personally.'

'Sorry, I didn't.'

'Never mind.' Phyllida looked down at the earring, sighed, then tucked it into her bumbag. 'Shall we go further down the river so it feels like we have the moon to ourselves?'

They made their way slowly in the opposite direction of the other mudlarkers and moon-gazers. It was hard to focus solely on mudlarking, though, and they probably spent as much time staring at the moon as they did looking down at the mud. Still, they made some finds: a fragment of an eye ointment pot (possibly nineteenth century), a green-glass marble that once sat in the neck of a Codd bottle to keep fizzy drinks from going flat, a rusted key that was so small Gemma imagined it had once unlocked a diary, a Boy Scout badge, and a couple of passports.

By 6.30 a.m., the moon was becoming fainter, the sun brighter and the air a little warmer.

'I brought coffee,' Phyllida said. 'And oat bars. Do you have time for breakfast?'

'Sure, thank you,' Gemma said. 'I just have to be at work by nine.'

'What do you do?' Phyllida asked as they found a dry spot closer to the embankment.

'I'm an oncology nurse.'

'I love that. But it must be hard.' Phyllida poured two cups of coffee from a Thermos and unwrapped two large slices of homemade muesli bars.

'Sometimes,' Gemma said. 'I love my patients and the routine. It doesn't involve shift work, I'm a Monday to Friday nurse. And when it gets tough, I like coming down to the river.'

'Do you have a partner you can unload on?'

Here we go, her new reality of having to explain her personal life. 'Not anymore,' Gemma said. 'My marriage recently ended.'

'I'm sorry.'

Gemma shrugged as if it was no big deal, even though she was still hurting acutely. 'It's been an adjustment, that's for sure.'

Gemma played with the engagement ring she was still wearing. Perhaps it was wrong to keep it just because she liked it. She could always give it to the river for another to find and enjoy. What story would someone in the future make of it, she wondered?

'You poor honey.' Phyllida patted Gemma's knee. 'I was with the father of my son for three years. We never married and he did a runner when Samuel was born. Couldn't handle it or something. Anyway, I've been married to Robert for ten years, he is the most gorgeous, caring man I've ever been with. What I'm trying to say is, decent men are out there. You're young, you'll find someone else.'

'I can't think of anything I'd like to do less than start dating.'

'Give it time. You don't want to be on your own forever.'

'These oat bars are delicious,' Gemma said in a bid to change the subject.

'Thank you.' Phyllida nodded appreciatively.

For a minute, they sat in silence watching the sun light up the incoming tide and a used Coke bottle bobbing in the shallows. The peach-coloured horizon reminded Gemma of the gold-rimmed glassware her mother inherited from her grandmother. There was nothing better than being caught between the then and the tomorrow, cocooned in the now. Gemma closed her eyes and let the new day warm her face.

'You know,' Phyllida began. 'I've been thinking lately how great it would be to be part of a club. Yet the only one I've been able to find is the Society of Mudlarks and Antiquarians which is very exclusive. It only ever has fifty members, a permanent waitlist and you have to have some decent finds under your belt. No good for amateurs like us.'

'Oh,' Gemma said. She'd never thought of mudlarking as a group activity before.

'I'm talking about a bunch of enthusiastic larkers like us who meet up once a month or so to talk to about what they find. I fear I'm boring my husband to death with all my stories.' Phyllida chuckled.

Gemma laughed too, although she hoped that wasn't why Adam had left, because she'd been boring him to death. Although, perhaps that would be a more preferable reason than finding out she was unlovable.

'Anyway, it's something to think about. If you hear of one, let me know,' Phyllida said, pulling out her phone. 'Let's exchange numbers so we don't have to rely on social media messaging. I'd love to go mudlarking again.'

Gemma was a little taken aback by Phyllida's assumption that they were now regular mudlarking buddies. Still, she gave Phyllida her number. Phyllida immediately sent her a text and Gemma's phone pinged faintly in her backpack, as if someone was trying to make contact from across the other side of the world.

'I'm in Hackney, so getting to the city part of the river is easy,' Phyllida said. 'What about you?'

'I'm out west on the train line.'

'Lovely. There are plenty of good spots to mudlark right along the Thames, aren't there?'

Gemma nodded, quietly absorbing Phyllida's unbridled enthusiasm.

'Well, I really enjoyed that.' Phyllida stood up and brushed the foreshore from her trousers.

Gemma looked out at the river stones by the waterline that were slick with the tide and realised that she had enjoyed it too.

Chapter 11

At work, Joe was her first patient of the week. He looked drained and pale, and walked slowly, tentatively. Yet he was still able to give her a smile. He'd brought in a gift, the size of an A3 card wrapped in tissue paper.

'My wife and I were in a second-hand shop on the weekend and saw this. It made me think of you,' he said, handing it to her.

'Oh, Joe, I can't accept this,' Gemma said.

'Think of it as a birthday present or an early Christmas present, whichever comes first. Anyway, you may not want it.'

'It's very sweet of you to think of me.'

'Open it.'

He looked so pleased, she couldn't not.

'It's an old printer's tray,' he said, once she'd ripped off the paper. 'It's not large but it will hold thirty-five items. I've cleaned it up and given it a good dowsing of oil.'

For a moment, Gemma thought she was going to cry. How could this man, who was going through so much, have the time, energy and desire to think of anyone but himself?

'I didn't like the idea of your precious finds being stuck in Tupperware,' he said.

'They're only precious to me.' Had she over-glorified the bits and bobs she'd scavenged from the river?

'That's all that matters. Send me a photo when it's filled.'

'But I'm not allowed to accept presents. A box of chocolates at a pinch.' Gemma glanced around in case Barbara was within earshot. 'Let me pay for it.'

'It wasn't expensive,' Joe said. 'Less than a box of Lindt chocolates. Have you noticed how much chocolate costs these days? Exorbitant.' Joe pulled a face in disgust. She couldn't tell if he was joking or not.

'Okay, well …' She chewed a lip.

'That's the way. Now let's get today over and done with.'

That night, Gemma fetched her containers and sandwich bags of mudlarking finds from the chest of drawers in the spare bedroom and took them to the kitchen. She cleared the table of the salt and pepper grinders, the energy bill, the used mug and the morning's toast plate. She lay down the printer's tray and took out every object she'd brought back from the river and spread them out. It wasn't everything she'd ever found. Only the things she really wanted. Greed or hoarding aren't admired in the mudlarking world.

She wasn't sure if she had enough items to fill the slots because not everything was small enough. Objects such as the perfectly formed native oyster shell from the early nineteen hundreds and the stem of a clay pipe were too wide or too long. But the Georgian button and the wedge of Staffordshire slipware were perfect fits. She put things in and took them out, moving them around until the display took on a pleasing aesthetic. She carried it carefully into the living room and placed it on top of the coffee table. There were more spots to fill, and it could do with a glass top to protect the pieces from dust. But for now, it would do.

She took a picture to show Joe.

Then, she sent the photo to Anushka, whom she hadn't heard from in a while, as a way of keeping in touch. Her friend replied kindly with a compliment, even though Gemma knew she didn't share her love of history or collecting. In any case, it did prompt a discussion on when they might be able to catch up again. A few dates were mooted and Anushka said she'd confirm in a few days.

It was when Gemma was putting away some of the now empty sandwich bags into a kitchen drawer that she found a photo of her with her mother. It sat incongruously next to the paper clips, screwdriver and Post-it Notes. She was four and she was sitting on a sofa next to her mother, mimicking her mother's crossed legs, head angled to one side, and a cigarette in one hand. What was striking was not that she was pretending to hold a cigarette like her mother but how physically unlike they were. This was nothing new, but for some reason, she saw it more clearly than she had before. It was also a stark reminder of every other difference between herself and her parents. Where her mother had blonde hair and brown eyes, Gemma had brown hair and blue eyes. While her mother was sporty and good with languages (just like Spanish came naturally to Rich), Gemma was neither. Nor did Gemma share much with her father, who was olive-skinned, good with words and worked as an editor.

So, who was she like? Her birth mother, her birth father or a mix of them both? When she was younger, she'd been mildly curious to know, but she'd never cared to find out because she had never once felt unloved or less wanted once Rich came along. She had a lovely set of parents and, up until her death last year, an adorable mother-in-law, Adam's mum Gwendoline. Why be greedy and ask for more?

Yet now, something had changed within her. Adam's leaving had made Gemma feel alone, vulnerable and lost. It was like she didn't know who she was anymore. It was as if she'd finished one life and was forced to begin another but didn't know where to start. Not only that, but she didn't even know her origins or about the people who made her. Her heritage was as blank as her future.

Gemma traced a finger over the photo of her mother. What

she saw now was not what was staring back at her but what was missing. A tear slipped off her cheek onto her mother's perm, smudging the curls and blurring her smile. For the first time, Gemma wondered whether delving into her beginning would help right her future. Would finding out about her birth parents make her feel found? Was it now time, as a thirty-six-year-old with a future unknown, to search for someone with freckles that didn't wash off?

Chapter 12

A week later, on Sunday night, Gemma was lying on the sofa watching television, filing her nails and doing Wordle. Adam's leaving had gifted her an annoying abundance of hyperactivity, as though if she let herself relax for a minute and do just one thing at a time, she'd remember just how alone she was. A message from Phyllida about mudlarking made her sit up.

You'll never guess what I found yesterday!

Gemma replied. *Let me try. A Tudor coin?* It could be anything, of course, yet Phyllida sounded excited.

I wish, Phyllida replied.

A Roman roof tile?

No.

This could go on all night. Not that she'd have minded, not in the least. *I might need a clue.*

Maybe I misled you with my overly excited first text. It's not that rare or desirable. It's a coffee and chicory essence bottle from the 1940s. Completely intact, half-buried at the waterline. Phyllida sent a photo of an iridescent green-glass bottle.

That's beautiful, Gemma replied.

I have another question ... Phyllida let her statement hang expectantly in the air.

Gemma waited.

Then, *I can't stop thinking about the idea of being in a club. I know that one attraction of mudlarking is its introverted nature, but there's knowledge, support and sociability to be gained in doing things in numbers, isn't there? What if we started our own?*

The only clubs Gemma had ever been involved with were the Girl Guides when she was a child, but that was only for a year, plus the Nurses' Union and that didn't count.

You see, I'm on long-service leave and don't know what to do with myself! Phyllida added.

Gemma put her phone down. She needed a moment to consider Phyllida's suggestion. Did she want to be part of a club? She picked up the nail file and turned back to the TV. She was watching a reality show set on an island where only those with toned muscles and fake tans were allowed on. It fascinated her. Stupid really. Perhaps it was the trainwreck nature of the relationships, albeit manipulated and scripted by the producers, which made it entertaining. Or perhaps it was because it meant she didn't have to think about her own relationship in which she felt as abandoned and cut up as Adam's sock.

What occurred to Gemma as she watched the pretence and play of the show was that the contestants had been thrown together with people they'd never met before. They could be whoever they wanted to be. Gemma had no desire to be someone she wasn't nor to flaunt herself to get the attention of others, yet being part of something where you shared a common interest did appeal. Where other members knew nothing about you. Where she didn't have to feel lonely all of the time. Here she was having another quiet evening on her own. Mel had messaged earlier in the week to invite her to a dinner party. But she'd declined on the basis she'd have been the only single person, and that two of Adam's friends were also going to be there, and she was far from ready for that kind of social event.

The sound of her phone ringing cut through her thoughts. It was Phyllida! How keen she was on the idea, while Gemma was still mulling it over.

'Oh, great, you're still here,' Phyllida said when she answered. 'Did you see my last text? I'm sorry to interrupt your evening, but I'm suddenly excited by the idea and I don't want to let it go. Of course, I don't want to push you into doing something you don't want to do ...'

Well, she kind of was, but Gemma also found that she didn't mind.

'So, what do you think about starting a club?'

'I do like the concept,' Gemma said.

'We could meet once a month and have a show and tell. Maybe in a pub, and we could go on mudlarking excursions as well. It'd be like a book club, but instead of books as our common bond, it'd be mud and what we find beneath it. Anyone could join, even total newbies. Do you know other mudlarkers who'd like it, too?' Phyllida was breathless with enthusiasm.

'Sorry, no.'

'Me neither!' Phyllida said as if it was hilarious. 'But we could recruit, couldn't we? I've had years in sales and marketing. It'd be a cinch. Shall we do it?'

Phyllida's eagerness was a little confronting, but it was also infectious.

'I suppose what I'm saying is,' Phyllida continued, 'if I started one, I'd need at least one other person. Would that be you?'

Although Gemma wasn't prone to making spontaneous decisions, let alone ones with people she hardly knew, she said yes.

Monday morning, Gemma thought she was going to miss her usual train again. She'd got into the habit of going to bed late and sleeping through her alarm, even when she hadn't been mudlarking during the night. But this week, of all weeks, she couldn't afford to be late as they were due an unprecedented number of patients and were understaffed.

There was no time for breakfast and she had to run to the station. She only just got on the train, seconds before the doors closed. She paused to get her breath back, then searched for an empty seat. She spotted Timothy sitting on his own, looking dapper in a jacket and bow tie.

'You're cutting it fine,' he said.

'I know.' She sat down opposite him. 'I really have to do something about my tardiness. Are you off to the museum?'

'Yes, we've got a training day to brush up on our tour guide skills. I was hoping I'd see you again. I wanted to check that you were all right after I saw you by the river.'

'Thank you, I'm fine. Perfectly fine.'

Timothy studied her as he might an Old Master painting, which was a little disconcerting because she couldn't be sure what he'd discover. 'Have you been mudlarking again?' he asked.

She nodded. 'I might be getting addicted,' she whispered.

'Ah, yes, the adrenalin buzz of the find. Nothing like it.'

'I met someone the other day who wants to start a mudlarking club.'

'What a wonderful idea.'

Now, it was Gemma's turn to study Timothy. 'You wouldn't be interested in coming along, would you?'

He looked surprised. 'Me? But I don't mudlark anymore.'

'You've done it, though, and you love history. This woman, Phyllida, thinks there should be a club that's totally inclusive, for amateurs rather than experts, from newcomers to regulars. Where we can share our knowledge and finds, and chat about mudlarking. Anyway, you wouldn't necessarily have to mudlark. You could bring along things you've found in the past and, if nothing else, you might be able to give us some tips.'

Gemma realised her enthusiasm for having Timothy come along was for her own benefit as much as it was to help Phyllida boost numbers. The thought of socialising with complete strangers generally made her anxious.

'I wasn't sure initially,' Gemma said. 'But Phyllida was very persuasive. I should also warn you that there's only two of us at the moment. Hardly a proper club.'

'So, who is this Phyllida?'

'All I know about her is that she's on leave from work, has a son and is very keen.' Gemma let out a nervous giggle. It was beginning to sound random and strange.

'Except you know she loves mudlarking and that's all that matters.'

'True. Anyway,' she continued, 'if you did want to take it up again and were worried about your back, I can recommend a good pair of kneepads so you could do it on all fours.'

'I may never get up again.' Timothy laughed.

'Our first meeting is in two weeks,' Gemma said. 'Phyllida suggested the appropriately named Mudlark Pub by London Bridge. If nothing else, we'll have a drink and a chat and see how it goes. You're more than welcome to join us.'

'Why not?' Timothy said. 'It could be a hoot.'

May Discoveries:
Another nail – rusted – which I think is handmade and from a nineteenth-century ship, although I can't be certain. A late eighteenth-century pewter button with a beautiful rainbow patina. A tarnished 1996 penny (shame it wasn't a rare 1933 penny!). Two blue medical face masks that went straight into the bin. A green-glazed medieval pottery sherd, which unfortunately is too large to fit into the printer's tray Joe gave me. An indeterminate iron bar that disconcertingly I imagined using on Adam. I had to quickly walk away from it to banish the thought. Then finally – and this was beautifully unexpected – a new friend who shares my love of mudlarking.

June

Chapter 13

Timothy was waiting for Gemma outside the pub. As usual, a corner of a handkerchief poked out of the top of his breast pocket and he smelt like fancy cologne. He'd come from the museum and she, straight from work. She hadn't had time to change out of her nurse's uniform. Her face felt flushed and her skin sticky. The Tube had been stifling and at six-thirty in the evening, there was still warmth in the sun.

'Sorry, I'm late. I had emails to catch up on,' she said. 'We weren't told at nursing school how much admin there'd be.'

'Don't worry. I've been people watching and wondering if any of them were fellow mudlarkers. One thing I've learnt is that people don't always present how you think they might. Take you, for instance. When I saw you by the river that day, you'd bucked the trend for drab mudlarking clothing with your yellow gloves and pink boots.'

Gemma looked down as if she'd forgotten she wasn't still wearing said yellow gloves and pink boots. She laughed.

'I inherited the boots from my late mother-in-law, along with a silver toast rack and a floral teapot,' she explained. 'They were her best gardening boots. She only had them a few months before she died and they were in excellent condition, so I thought why throw them out? I liked Gwendoline. She was almost like a second mother and it's nice to be reminded of her.'

'I like that and the colour is eye-catching. Then, take me …' Timothy gestured to himself. 'I bet you don't know what another of my hobbies is.'

Gemma's mind was so full from work that she didn't have the capacity for a guessing game.

Thankfully, Phyllida arrived and she didn't have to. Although if she did, she'd have probably said something like pigeon racing.

'Gemma!' Phyllida said with gusto, her large gold earrings swinging as she spoke. 'And you must be Timothy.'

'Spot on,' Timothy said. 'Are we the club?'

'There's one more. I think he's already here.'

The Mudlark Pub was, ironically, full of office workers and, according to the pavement chalkboard, fried food and regional hand-pulled ales. They followed Phyllida to a corner table where a man with a mop of strawberry-blond hair was waiting. He looked familiar but Gemma was unable to place him.

'There he is,' Phyllida said. 'Everyone, this is my favourite metal detectorist, Nick.'

The man stood up and gave a bashful half-smile.

'Haven't we met before?' he said, shaking Gemma's hand.

'Surprise!' Phyllida shouted, startling Gemma, who then remembered.

'Of course. The earring man.'

'That's me.' Nick grinned. He was wearing black jeans and a dark grey T-shirt with a tiny white guitar on the top left-hand corner.

'Would you believe it?' Phyllida said dramatically. 'Fate intervened yet again and the other day by the river, we were both there at the same time. I didn't know if Nick was my jewellery rescuer but, naturally, I had to find out—'

'—and here we are,' Nick said.

'Timothy,' Phyllida said gravely, turning to him. 'This man

saved my life.'

'Hardly.'

'Nick, when you found my earring, I couldn't believe it. Neither could my husband. I broke open the bubbles and we celebrated as if it was my birthday.'

No one knew how to respond to that, so no one did. Instead, Timothy offered to get a round of drinks.

'You can buy them at the table via the App,' Gemma explained, but he'd already gone.

'Isn't he a darling?' Phyllida said, sitting down and fishing out a notebook and pen from her handbag.

'This looks serious,' Nick said.

'Don't mind me. I like being organised and menopause has given me a sieve for a brain,' Phyllida said.

Nick shot Gemma a look of bewilderment. Gemma shrugged. What did she know about menopause? Only that her mother had a collection of hand-held paper fans which she jokingly promised to bequeath to Gemma and, knowing her mother, she probably would.

'Don't worry, I don't bite. My mood swings are minimal.' Phyllida let out a high-pitched laugh which made them both jump.

'Why don't I help Timothy with the drinks?' Gemma suggested, glad to have something to do.

Eventually, they were all seated.

'This is so exciting,' Phyllida announced. 'When I mentioned a club to Gemma, I wasn't even sure if *she'd* want to come. I just love the idea of meeting people from different walks of life who share a common interest, knowing our mudlarking tales won't be tiresome. Shall we start by introducing ourselves?'

Gemma wondered if Phyllida had been a teacher in a former life.

Phyllida continued. 'Tell us who you are, why you started mudlarking and what you love about it. And if there's something you're searching for—'

'The answers to my questions,' Nick blurted out.

'My third wife,' Timothy said as if it was a competition on who could make the best joke.

Gemma giggled and Phyllida nearly choked on her wine. 'Aren't you two the comedians?' she said. 'How about I go first and we can go around the table?'

She cleared her throat. 'I'm Phyllida, as you know, and I'm fifty-five. Not that I want to highlight any birthday candle privilege,' she added, giving Timothy a smile. 'I've worked in sales and marketing at the same company for so long that I qualified for a sabbatical and I've finally taken it. But I didn't know what to do with myself! I've never not worked ever since I was thirteen when I had a job at the local newsagents. You've no idea what a knot I got myself in about being at a loose end. The guilt I felt ...' Phyllida shook her head.

'That's when my husband told me to stop being so silly. That I deserved a break and to just get on with my me-time. He was also the one who said I should get serious about my mudlarking hobby. So, I listened to him, like I always do, and now I'm loving it so much, I'm not even sure I want to go back to work.' She sighed dramatically.

'Well, *I'm* not jealous,' Nick said light-heartedly yet with obvious envy. 'What I wouldn't do to have a break from work. Anyway, you haven't said what you love about it and what you're searching for.'

'Oh, yes. I like the stories behind the objects we find and I'd love to uncover a penny lick glass.'

'Which is?' Nick asked.

'It's a small glass in which ice cream was sold from the mid-eighteen-hundreds to the nineteen-thirties. It only held a few licks of ice cream, although its shape made it appear as if it held more. When you finished your ice cream, you gave the glass back to the seller and it was used again. Unfortunately, health and safety didn't exist back then and germ transmission was rife. It became the ideal vessel for spreading diseases like cholera and tuberculosis and was the reason they stopped being made.'

'The innocence of the times,' Timothy said.

Gemma nodded.

'Ignorance more like,' Nick added.

'Would you like to go next, Nick?'

Nick scratched his head as if trying to remember who he was and what he was doing there. 'I'm Nick and I'm a newspaper reporter,' he began. 'I'm now freelancing after losing my job during COVID. I was sort of being truthful when I said I'm looking for answers to my questions. But I'm afraid I've never mudlarked. I inherited my dad's metal detector and thought I'd give it a go. Even though I sometimes used to go with Dad when I was a kid and I like history, I admit I was a bit disparaging of the hobby. I used to wonder why anyone would get excited over a poxy old mud-caked curio—'

Phyllida drew a sharp, audible intake of breath. 'Nick, how could you?'

'It's blasphemy.' Timothy nodded.

'Oh, sorry,' Nick said, looking at Gemma to ascertain whether they were being serious or not. Gemma tried not to smile.

Then Phyllida batted the air. 'We're only joking.'

'Okay, phew.'

'Still, you mustn't describe anyone's find as poxy,' Gemma said, because, really, who did he think he was?

'Very true, Gemma,' Phyllida agreed, writing who-knew-what in her notebook. 'Just like no question is too silly, no find is too terrible.'

'Of course. I'll never do it again,' Nick said. 'Shall I keep going?'

'Please do.'

'So, yeah, I've only used the metal detector a few times because it started playing up and then it stopped working. It was old and not in good nick. That was when I met Phyllida the other day and she suggested I try mudlarking because—' He mimed quotation marks in the air. '—It's arguably more enjoyable and much less noisy. I didn't think she was being serious about a club, though, and I wasn't going to come at first. I still don't really know why I'm here. I'm curious, I guess.' He tried to hide his bewilderment by taking a swig of beer.

'Curiosity is the hallmark of an excellent larker,' Phyllida said. 'Is there anything you'd like to discover?'

'I guess everyone wants to find the cliched "treasure", don't they? Or something Roman. I've just been assigned to do a feature on the two-thousand-year-old Roman house that was uncovered not far from here at that multi-million-pound office development. I'm fascinated by London's Roman history.'

'That sounds amazing,' Gemma said.

'Yes,' agreed Phyllida. 'You must keep us updated on that story. So, Timothy, you have the stage.'

'Evening all,' Timothy said. 'I'm a retired businessman and I volunteer as a guide at the British Museum. I believe I've got all my marbles for someone in their late seventies and I even have some Roman ones.'

'Really?' Nick said in awe.

'Really.'

'Wow.'

'I'd love to say I found them mudlarking but I didn't. I'm a bit of a collector and several years ago, I purchased them at an auction. My wife passed away four years ago, but I've got my daughter and the grandchildren to keep me busy. I live not far from Gemma and we struck up a friendship based on the timings of the trains. I'm here to support the endeavour but with dodgy knees and a bad back, I'm not sure how active I'm going to be.'

'We don't mind. It's the knowledge and enthusiasm you bring, and the stories you can share that's more important,' Phyllida said.

Timothy nodded and smiled. Pleased, Gemma imagined, at Phyllida's praise.

'Lastly, Gemma.'

'Hi everyone.' She stupidly did a little wave.

'Speak up, honey. It's getting loud in here.'

Gemma coughed and began again. 'I'm an oncology nurse and I've been mudlarking on and off for about five years. I started as a way to de-stress and then I got the bug. I love how it forces you to slow down, and you never know what's going to come out of the mud. It's exciting knowing there are worlds within worlds waiting to be found.' She paused because nerves were making her speak quickly.

'There are so many things I'd love to find. One is a pilgrim badge which travellers bought in the Middle Ages in the hope they'd be rid of a sin they'd committed or cured of a disease or ailment. They were like the first souvenirs.'

'Have you seen the collection at the British Museum on the third floor?' Timothy asked.

Gemma shook her head.

'Maybe we could go on an excursion there sometime?' Phyllida had definitely missed her calling as a primary school teacher.

'I'd like that,' Gemma admitted.

'I recommend the café on the ground floor. The baking is excellent and the treacle tart my favourite.'

'I had a slice of carrot cake there once and it was pretty good,' Nick said.

'I think we're getting off topic.' Phyllida waggled her pen.

'Sorry, boss.'

'Oh, Nick, I don't want you to think I'm the boss,' she said, in a way that suggested she didn't mind too much at all.

He smiled. 'Okay. But seriously, do you think we should give the group a name?'

'Yes, we must have a name,' Phyllida exclaimed. 'Is there a collective noun for mudlarkers, I wonder …?'

'A murder of mudlarkers?' Nick emphasised 'murder' as if he were acting in an Agatha Christie play.

'Too macabre,' Timothy said.

'How about a mischief then?'

'Isn't it a mischief of magpies?' Gemma said.

'You're right.' Nick nodded.

'Don't magpies like to steal shiny things and we're not meant to be stealing anything?' Gemma didn't like to dampen Nick's enthusiasm.

'Something less offensive might be nicer,' Phyllida suggested. 'Like a drift. A drift of mudlarks.' She gestured with an elegant swish of an arm as if mimicking the image.

'Adrift in the river …' Nick pondered the idea.

'You definitely don't want to be adrift in the river,' Timothy said with a tone of warning in his voice. 'You could drown. I know someone who once discovered a body.'

'Nasty.' Phyllida pulled a face.

Gemma was similarly shocked and was reminded of the jaw bone she found which was, thankfully, nothing to do with a human. But Nick's eyes lit up in crime-loving delight.

'Wow,' he said in awe.

'You see, if you're not careful, tides and currents can whisk you away and you could die a theatrical if wholly unnecessary death,' Timothy explained. 'You always need to know what the tide is doing and where your nearest escape route is.'

'Excellent advice, Timothy,' Phyllida said. 'So, back to our name …'

'We could just be The Mudlarkers' Club?' Gemma suggested. She didn't see the point of puns or euphemisms. Her line of work was full of the latter and she wasn't convinced they benefited anyone.

'Yeah, let's keep it simple,' Nick said.

'The Mudlarkers' Club it is then,' Timothy agreed.

Phyllida wrote it down before anyone could change their mind. 'Now, if everyone's still keen, I thought I'd suggest some ideas on how the club could work.'

The three of them looked at each other and nodded.

'I was thinking – and please offer other suggestions if you disagree – that we meet monthly. Perhaps in this pub? It's central and easily accessible by public transport. Where are you based, Nick?'

'Hammersmith, near the Ravenscourt Park Tube stop.'

'Excellent.' Phyllida noted it down. 'If someone can't make a meeting, they should text out of courtesy. It's obviously not imperative to come to every meeting, but attendance should be fairly often. Otherwise, I suppose, what's the point? Does everyone agree? And if you know of any other mudlarkers, or potential mudlarkers, feel free to invite them.'

'Sounds good to me,' Nick said.

'Me too,' Gemma added, particularly liking Phyllida's informal commitment to being club secretary.

Phyllida continued. 'I thought our meetings could focus on show and tells, where we bring along a find for the month and tell everyone about it – our best or our worst, or the most interesting or unusual find. Perhaps do some research before you come. The more stories the better. You wouldn't be a mudlarker if you weren't always asking questions and liked discovering the answer. Indulge yourself and indulge us in every snippet of history you uncover. What do you think?'

'We're all made of stories, after all,' Nick added.

'And you'd know that better than the rest of us,' Phyllida said. 'Now, Nick, you do you know that you need a permit, don't you? It's the same for metal detecting. If you find anything made of gold or silver that's more than three hundred years old, is a group of coins or prehistoric metalwork, you must report it to the Portable Antiquities Scheme.'

'What if you don't know whether it is or not?' Nick asked.

'Bring it to the club! And if we don't know, we can try and find out. We can be detectives together.'

'What about going on field trips?' Timothy suggested.

'We could be separate but together,' Phyllida said, as if considering the idea out loud. 'Like when my husband and I go shopping.

He watches football on his phone while I try on clothes.'

Nick raised a hand. 'Guilty as charged. Although I like to think my girlfriend values my advice.'

'That's it!' Timothy said. 'We can give each other advice or help along the way.'

Gemma may have met Phyllida once for a mudlark but she'd never entertained going on regular field trips in a group. Mudlarking was typically a solitary venture and that's why she liked it. To be at one with nature and yourself. Then, again, maybe it wouldn't be so bad doing it as a collective, where you were there for each other. Separate but together, like Phyllida said. A bunch of history nerds happy to talk for hours about what Londoners once did along the Thames. Gemma nodded, as much to herself as to them all.

'I'd love to do it as a group,' Nick said. 'I could do with a lesson.'

'We could have breakfast if we've done an early morning mudlark or a nightcap if it's at night,' Phyllida suggested.

'And try different locations,' Timothy said. 'We'll have to coordinate with the tides, of course.'

'All in agreement?' Phyllida asked.

'Say ay!' Nick shouted enthusiastically.

'Well, you don't have to say "ay" …'

Nick swung Gemma a glance as if to apologise for being eager in a way that Phyllida hadn't sanctioned. She smiled.

'I'm in agreement,' Timothy said.

'Yes,' Gemma added. 'I guess I am too.'

'Excellent.' Phyllida made another note in her book as if they might forget.

As if out of nowhere, a bowl of chips arrived.

'I was hungry,' Nick said apologetically. 'I shouldn't have skipped lunch.' He took two chips and pushed the bowl to the middle of the table. 'Help yourself.'

'Thanks, Nick. Did anyone bring in something for show and tell?' Phyllida asked.

'Yep, I did.' Nick wiped his fingers on his jeans, then placed an object covered in tissue paper on the table and unwrapped it. 'This item is one hundred and twenty years old.'

Timothy leant forward for a better look. 'Isn't that—?'

'It is,' Nick said solemnly. 'I found it at Battersea. A corner was poking out from behind a rock. It's the only interesting thing I found metal detecting.'

'But—' Gemma said. 'It looks—'

'Yes?'

'—like a potato peeler.'

'Oh, my goodness, it is!' Timothy slapped his leg.

'As I said, the only thing of interest.' Nick was trying to stay serious. 'It's stainless steel so there's no need to report it, and it's as blunt as my ninety-year-old grandfather was sharp. Apart from that it's quite a specimen. My research revealed that it was an invention of the twentieth century by a Swiss kitchen utensil seller, who hated potato peeling after his time in the army.'

Gemma got the giggles.

'Nick, you cheeky so-and-so,' Phyllida said with a smile. If she hadn't been married, you'd have thought she was flirting with him.

'Okay, seriously, I did bring something else in.' Nick produced another item from his leather satchel. 'This is what my dad found in a field about two years ago. It's seventeenth century.'

He held up a large rusty horseshoe with nail holes around its rim.

'What do you know about it?' Timothy asked.

'How happy Dad was to have found it. You'd think he'd won the lottery. He put it above the door to our kitchen, insisting that it had to be hung upside down so his luck wouldn't fall out, not that it made sense to me to do that. Except after that, Dad's luck very quickly ran out.' Nick paused for a moment and looked wanly at the horseshoe.

'I know I speak for everyone here. We're sorry about your father,' Phyllida said.

'Yeah, sorry,' Gemma said softly.

Nick shook his head as if there was nothing to be sorry about and he was getting unnecessarily sentimental. He passed the horseshoe to Gemma. Knowing its backstory made Gemma feel the weight of its significance in her hands. How it was so much more than a rough, gnarled hunk of metal.

'Anyone else?' Phyllida asked.

'I'm sorry, I didn't bring anything,' Gemma said.

'Me neither,' Timothy said.

'Not to worry. I've got something.' Phyllida took what looked like a pen box from her bag and lifted the lid. 'A nineteenth-century glass medicine vial. I like to imagine it held some sort of narcotic medicine – perhaps an opium tincture – and that it had fallen from a doctor's bag or the hand of a dandy.'

'You could be right,' Timothy said. 'In those days, opium, otherwise known as laudanum, was prescribed for all sorts of things. Sleep. Pain. Much like germs, back then they didn't understand addiction either.'

'Aren't you a wealth of information? I could stay here and talk about poxy old curios all night.' Phyllida winked at Nick. 'But I suppose we should wrap it up. Shall we end on another tip, Timothy?'

'If you like,' Timothy said, which Gemma assumed was his answer to both questions, proving he was either a very amenable man or adept at diplomacy. 'Goodness, what to say.' He thought for a minute. 'I suppose, the most important thing about mudlarking is to be relaxed but focused. That's when you find things. Pay attention and be curious, like Phyllida said.'

Phyllida burst into applause, as if he'd won a prize. Gemma and Nick joined in so as not to appear churlish. Gemma was thankful that Timothy seemed to be enjoying himself and the club hadn't been a flop.

'Thank you so much for indulging me tonight,' Phyllida said. 'I hope this can become a regular thing. How about I set up a

WhatsApp group and I'll message about the next meeting?'

'What's up?' Timothy looked confused.

'Whats*App*,' Nick said.

'I've got The Facebook, does that help?' Timothy said, giving the social media platform capitals as if it were to be revered.

'No, but I can set it up for you, if you like?' Nick suggested.

Phyllida continued. 'Let's see … Are Wednesdays good for everyone?'

Gemma thought about her future Wednesday evenings. They were achingly vacant. Sometimes she and Adam went to the movies on a Wednesday night to break up the week. But she hadn't been to the cinema for at least four months. She couldn't even remember the last film she'd seen. Maybe she could suggest going to the cinema with Anushka.

'I'm free,' Gemma said.

'Me too.' Nick nodded.

Timothy gave a thumbs up. Phyllida made another note. Gemma wondered if by tomorrow evening the minutes would be in their inboxes.

'If it's all right with everyone, let's kick off our first official meeting at the end of the month. Because this has been more of an admin catch-up, hasn't it? Wednesday, twenty-ninth of June.'

No one disagreed.

'Okay, Timothy is now good to go on WhatsApp,' Nick said, returning Timothy's phone.

Immediately, Phyllida set up a chat group, typed a message, then beamed. Her chest heaved from delight at a successful night connecting people. 'And so that concludes the first meeting.' She snapped her notebook shut.

As Gemma followed Nick and Phyllida out of the pub, she realised that not only hadn't she been ready for The Mudlarkers' Club meeting to end, she didn't want the evening to wrap up either.

Chapter 14

It was a Tuesday night in the middle of June and Gemma was sitting at the kitchen table researching old coins on her laptop. The previous weekend she'd found a coin that was worn so smooth from years of use and friction from the swirls of the riverbed, that she couldn't make out much of its detail.

She'd cleaned it with a soft toothbrush in warm water and left it to dry on a small cloth. Its patina appeared to be either bronze or copper and, although it was extremely worn, there was still a raised bump in the centre that was most likely an image of a royal figurehead – of whom she didn't yet know. It was thinner than a modern-day coin, measured 30.8 millimetres, and had a smooth edge. Gemma loved the feel of it between her fingers and wondered how many hands had handled it, what deals it had been a part of, and who had been the last to touch it. A woman for illicit services rendered? A market trader? A pickpocket? Or was it a counterfeit coin as many were during Victorian times?

As she held up the coin to the computer screen to compare it to pictures of similar ones online, her phone buzzed with a message. She glanced at the text. It was from Adam. With her new distraction of The Mudlarkers' Club, she'd been more easily able to push him from her thoughts. It was foolhardy to freeze herself in the present, she knew, but it was proving to be a helpful coping mechanism. Her phone sounded again. She sighed and read it.

Hi, Gemma, I'm really sorry to have to tell you like this, but I didn't want you finding out from anybody else …

That was all Gemma could see without clicking on it. She put down the coin and opened her messages.

We've only just found out ourselves and I would have called you, but I wasn't sure if you'd want to talk and Mia is … well, she's not much fussed on the two of us talking anyway …

For goodness' sake, Adam, get to the point. Gemma didn't have to read on much further to see what his point was.

We're pregnant.

Gemma's dinner somersaulted.

I know this isn't what you want to hear.

You're right about that.

We weren't planning it, I promise.

Really.

I'm sorry you have to find out like this.

Gemma turned the phone over so that it was face down. Her mouth had gone dry and her heart was racing so fast that she put a hand to her chest to try and stop it. Hadn't he hurt her enough? And now this, in a text? A text! Of all the ways he could have communicated it with her. Of all the things he could have announced. Now, he was expecting, and she was expecting nothing with no one. And to think that he'd been the one in their relationship who hadn't wanted to rush into having children. She'd raised it with him in the past about how conceiving wasn't always straightforward, as experienced by her parents. Yet he hadn't seemed bothered, as if arrogantly assuming he'd be fine. And then he was! *El cabrón*. This felt like another deception and an intimation at the spuriousness of their marriage.

What's more, she was reminded, yet again, of how her future was one big question mark, scarily blank and void. Would she marry again? Would she ever be a mother? How could things that had seemed certain suddenly vanish in an instant? With those two words Adam had uttered – *I'm leaving* – her whole world had upended completely and irrevocably. She didn't want to start crying – she'd done enough of that already – but it was impossible to stay composed.

Another text message came through. She wouldn't read it. But, of course, how could she not? She wiped the tears from her cheeks. Adam continued.

It'd also be good to talk sometime – properly – about getting a divorce.

She knew this was coming but she hadn't wanted to fully entertain the idea. It was so final and the act of it, so clinical. As if with each of their signatures they could erase their vows to one another and the life they'd shared, every moment of happiness reduced to mere memory and replaced by sadness and anger, on her part at least. And what of Adam? He'd had who knows how long to consider divorce and was, it seems, not only accepting of it, but relieved and in a rush for it to happen. For her, it felt like a bombshell, she was still getting used to the idea of being separated. Not only did she dislike the term divorcee, she didn't want to be labelled one. It smacked of failure and bitterness, and a sense of pride that had been in a hit-and-run. The idea of picking over their life together like a vulture scavenging a corpse was upsetting and painful, and she knew that nothing, apart from time, would make those feelings go away. Did they really have to talk about divorce already?

She considered not replying. Then again, she didn't want him thinking that she couldn't take the news, even if she was now reduced to tears. A simple, *I know and congratulations* would suffice.

She got up to check the tidal chart. The photo of her and her mother that she'd stuck to the fridge door jumped out at her and made her pause. She felt even more drawn to it than she had before. Surely, her history was the one thing she could latch on to and claim as her own, even if it meant having to research it? How ironic that, with a few online searches, she'd easily and quickly be able to find out so much more about the small coin she'd unearthed than her own past.

Somewhere, she had an album of childhood photos, but she couldn't remember where. She left the kitchen and went searching. Eventually, she found it in the chest of drawers in her bedroom, wedged under a couple of jumpers.

She pulled it out and sat on the bed. The front cover was dented and faded and the pages inside were no longer sticky. The clear plastic sheets that were meant to be protecting the photos flapped loosely. Gemma peeled off the photo on the front page. It was the first one ever taken of her parents with Gemma as a baby. She was dressed in a white baby suit covered with tiny lemons. Her eyes were closed, her bottom lip sucked in ever so slightly. She looked peaceful. Her parents were smiling in disbelief and joy.

For Gemma – and perhaps her parents, too – this picture represented her beginning. Yet she wanted to delve deeper. To find out about the circumstances that had led to it, about what happened to her birth parents, why they hadn't wanted her, and if they ever wondered about the daughter they gave away. Rich knew everything about his squashed-face pedigree cat that liked filing its claws on the furniture, yet Gemma had no idea about her own heritage.

Suddenly, and with unequivocal clarity, she yearned to know about her past.

It was time to call her mother.

Chapter 15

The following Saturday, her mother caught the mid-morning train to London because Gemma's father needed the car to get building supplies. He was laying paving stones in their back garden, which worried her mother because, although he may be a sprightly seventy-five-year-old who'd taken up yoga later in life, she didn't think he should still be doing manual labour.

'He never listens to me, so I may as well come and see you,' she'd told Gemma.

Gemma met her mother at the train station. With her straight grey hair now shoulder-length, she reminded Gemma of a sleek long-haired hound.

'You're looking thin, Gemma.' Her mother's first words.

Gemma glanced at her thighs. She couldn't tell. She only wished that her mother didn't fuss.

'Now, what's going on?' Her mother linked her arm into Gemma's. It was a habit she hoped her mother would never tire of.

'Let's get back to my place,' Gemma said, not wishing to talk at the train station.

Her mother patted her hand. 'Well, okay, but I want to take you out to lunch. I've booked that posh place. What's it called? Audrey and someone? We'll have champagne and lobster or whatever you like.' Her mother had the opinion that splashing out on an expensive meal was the antidote to any woe.

'It doesn't need to be anything fancy.'

'I know. But why not? But first we need to get you changed. Do you wear anything other than those dirty old jeans?'

Her mother insisted Gemma change and persuaded her to wear a floral sundress she'd bought on a trip to Greece, even though it annoyingly reminded her of Adam, and some low-heeled slides she hadn't worn since last summer. Gemma didn't feel like herself. Then again, she hadn't felt herself since Adam had left. But if it pleased her mother to see her in something smarter than jeans, then she was happy to oblige. She had more important things to talk to her about.

At the restaurant, lobster wasn't on the menu, but sustainably farmed prawns were. Gemma finished the first glass of champagne before the mains came out. She hadn't expected to feel so nervous about raising her adoption with her mother, considering how it had never been a taboo subject between them.

'More bubbles?' her mother asked.

'Yes, please.' She took a large drink to calm herself.

'Is it Adam?' her mother said. 'You seem very on edge.'

'It's not Adam. It's …' She fiddled with the stem of her glass. 'Look, I know you'll be honest with me, Mum. I'm just scared.'

'Go on.'

'I guess, I want you to tell me about me.'

'About *you*?'

'What I was like as a baby and what it was like getting me.'

Her mother looked thoughtful for a moment. 'Well,' she began. 'When we first took you home, we sat on the sofa, laid you on our laps and couldn't take our eyes off you. We were bewitched.' She shook her head as if still astonished at how mesmerising a baby could be.

'I remember you being equally entranced by us,' her mother

continued. 'Your eyes were big and wide, watching us intently. This might sound fanciful but it seemed as if you were so enamoured with us and the world that you dared not go to sleep. Then we found out that you actually weren't a big sleeper, yet it didn't seem to bother you. You didn't cry like other babies did when they woke up. Not like Rich! Often, I'd go into your room and you'd be wide awake in your cot, happy as anything.' Her mother smiled with contentment, then studied Gemma. 'Is that what you really wanted to know?'

Gemma shook her head. Her mother reached across the table for Gemma's hand and held it.

'Is this about your adoption?' her mother said gently.

Gemma nodded. Her mother squeezed her hand which was shaking.

'I've been waiting for this day. You know it won't change how we feel about you. We never felt any different about you than we did with Rich. We wanted to treat you exactly the same.'

'Except when I tipped paint over his head. You weren't happy with me then.'

Her mother laughed. 'No, but we'd have been just as cross with him, if the roles had been reversed.'

'Did it feel strange to fall pregnant when you never thought it would happen?'

'Oh, yes, especially as I didn't find out until I was five months. That was a shock. We thought we'd only have you. But, of course, it was joyous and you were so excited about being a big sister, that it wouldn't have mattered how Richard came into our lives.'

The mains arrived. Two of Gemma's prawns were unpeeled and stared disconcertingly back at her. Her mother had a rack of lamb. Gemma could smell the garlic from where she was sitting.

'*Bon appétit!*' Her mother took a sip of her drink, then sliced through a piece of lamb. 'Now let me see, what can I tell you about the adoption?' She waved her meat-skewered fork as if it would help conjure up the memories.

'We didn't want to do IVF because it was very expensive and back then it didn't have high success rates. We also liked the idea of adoption to help a child who'd had a poor start in life. Initially we were in line for a different baby, but the mother had a last-minute change of heart. That was upsetting, but we'd been warned it was a relatively common occurrence. Yet everything happens for a reason. We eventually got you.'

Her mother paused, a nostalgic look on her face.

'I could talk for hours about what it was like bringing you into our lives, although I suspect you really want to know about the time before that, don't you?'

'Uh-huh.' Gemma chewed her lip.

'The problem is we know very little.'

'Like how little?'

'All we were told was that your mother was young and your father unnamed. It was common for the father's name to be missing from birth records.'

'Okay,' Gemma said, trying not to feel let down. She had – perhaps wrongly – hoped her mother had known *something* more. Like a name or an explanation. Anything that Gemma could have taken hold of and claimed as her own, the smallest piece of information to make her feel a little bit more whole. 'But surely my mother's name would be in the records somewhere?'

'It should be, but we never saw your birth certificate. When a child is put up for adoption, their birth certificate becomes superseded by an adoption certificate, which is what adoptive parents get. I'm sure you'll be able to find out about it, though. Is that what you want to do, go searching?'

'Yes,' Gemma said softly, as a single tear dropped on a prawn tail. 'I think I do.'

Chapter 16

After her talk with her mother, Gemma hadn't been able to stop thinking about her birth mother. She'd thought more about her in the past twenty-four hours than she ever had before. What did she look like? What was her job? Did she have any hobbies? Did she have other children? The more Gemma thought, the more the hole widened and the scope of possibilities about who her birth mother was and what had happened to her became impossible to imagine.

If the discussion with her mother had felt anti-climactic because of the lack of information she had to share, conversely it left Gemma feeling exhilarated and free. As if for the first time since Adam left, she had regained a sense of control over a part of her life and a new sense of purpose. She may not know what was going to happen in her future, but she could find out about her past. She would become like the Thames tides, uncovering little by little, layer by layer, the fragments of her history and, hopefully, one day she'll be able to piece it all together and make herself feel whole again.

It was Sunday night and Gemma had decided to ask Google the most significant question she'd ever posed: how to find your birth mother in the UK? From the window behind Gemma's desk, the late evening sun cast a brassy light over the garden. She'd poured a glass of wine and clicked the 'return' button. Her heart raced. She felt giddy with expectation. Then, in an instant, a whole new world opened up to her.

Gemma took a deep breath and dived in. She bookmarked an adoption finder agency, a government services website, the Adoption Contact Register, a family history website that used DNA to find familial matches and a couple of informative blogs. She read them all and took notes. It seemed that the best way to begin the search was to apply for her original birth certificate.

All she needed was her date of birth, date of adoption, adopted name and her pre-adoption name. That is, if she had one.

Gemma sat back in her chair. She'd never contemplated having a pre-adoption name. A pre-Gemma name, a name given to her by someone else. But why not? Names were easy to give. Yet the idea of it was disconcerting. As if she might have two lives.

Still, having another name, another persona wasn't going to stop her applying for her birth certificate. She found the application form on the General Register Office website and filled it in. It didn't take long because there was so little that she knew of names and dates and places. She checked it over a couple of times, feeling nervous with excitement, then pressed 'submit'.

Except as soon as she'd done so, she felt panicky because who would she find? What would she learn? What if she didn't like something she uncovered and would want to throw it all back to where it came from? But there was no turning back.

Chapter 17

It was six-thirty in the evening on the last Wednesday of the month and Gemma was the first to arrive for the second meeting of The Mudlarkers' Club. She took a seat by the window at the table Phyllida had reserved and watched as people walked by.

'Hey, Gemma. It is Gemma, isn't it?'

She looked up.

'Oh, it is,' Nick said with obvious relief. 'I was just out the back having a cheeky smoke. Have you ordered?'

Gemma was about to answer when Phyllida arrived.

'Hello, everyone!' Phyllida glanced around. 'Minus Tim? He *is* coming, isn't he?'

'I think so,' Gemma said.

'I'm getting the drinks. What would you like?' Nick drumrolled the table like he was trying, but failing, to get in time with the background music.

'I was thinking we should start a kitty so that we don't have to worry about all this drinks-shouting business. It could go towards outings as well,' Phyllida said.

'But I'd like to shout this time. Tim did it last time.' Nick was insistent. 'And here he is. Our most senior mudlarking adviser.'

'Senior being the operative word,' Timothy said. 'Evening all.'

'Welcome to our second meeting,' Phyllida announced, sounding relieved and amazed they were having one. 'Has everyone had a good few weeks?'

'Well, my permit recently came through. Thankfully, Phyllida, you told me to apply at our first meeting. And I bought a trowel,' Nick said. 'The detector is officially kaput. I thought about spray painting it gold and displaying it on a stand, but Ella dissed the idea.'

He quickly looked away. Gemma thought his eyes were welling up, although it was hard to tell.

'Are you okay?' Phyllida said gently.

'It's just sad knowing I can't use it anymore. This might sound ridiculous, but it's kind of like saying goodbye to Dad all over again.'

'It doesn't sound ridiculous,' Phyllida said.

'Maybe you can remember your dad through mudlarking?' Timothy offered.

'Yeah, he'd have loved being part of a mudlarking club.'

'You could spray paint your trowel gold instead,' Gemma suggested.

They all laughed, and it was nice that Nick smiled at Gemma in appreciation and then seemed to brighten up after that.

'Just a tip, though,' Timothy said. 'You can only use the trowel to dislodge objects or for gentle surface scraping, not for digging. You're only supposed to search with your eyes and take out what you see on the surface. The top layers of the foreshore are extremely important ecologically and digging can cause permanent damage.'

'Roger that,' Nick said.

'Have you been out yet?' Timothy asked.

'The day after I got the permit, as it happens.' Nick paused. 'Sorry, is it ok for me to skip the show and tell?' he said seriously.

'Oh. Well,' Phyllida said, looking flummoxed. 'It's not really in the spirit of things. Sharing is what the club is all about. But

I suppose if you haven't found anything …'

'I'm sorry, Phyllida, I'm only joking.' Nick laughed. 'I've brought in my find.'

Phyllida's face relaxed. 'You cheeky so-and-so,' she said.

He opened his satchel and pulled out an antique padlock from a plastic bag. 'It's pretty rusty and corroded. There are some letters at the top which are hard to decipher but you can just make out "London 1801". It looks like it's been forced open, too. Maybe someone was trying to steal something.'

'Or its owner lost their key?' Phyllida said.

'It could have been used to lock up one of the warehouses or docks along the Thames. Or even a barge,' Timothy said. 'If you clean it carefully, the letters might come up clearer and then you could do some research.'

'Electrolysis is the best way to get rid of rust,' Gemma said. 'I've been looking up how to do it and it seems pretty easy to make your own kit.'

'Do let us know how that goes,' Timothy said. 'We might all want to try it.'

'What about you, Timothy? Have you brought anything along?' Phyllida asked.

Timothy opened the box he'd put on the table. 'It's a World War Two Auxiliary Fire Service coat button,' he said, passing it around. 'The AFS was a voluntary fire service formed in 1938. During the war, fire boats played an important role in fighting fires along the Thames. But many of the bombings occurred when the river was at its lowest, which meant that access to water was extremely difficult. When the Blitz happened, it was the first time many of the AFS members had ever had to fight a fire.'

'Fascinating.'

Timothy's chest expanded as he smiled. 'I could bore you for hours on the Second World War.'

'And, Gemma, what about you?' Phyllida rushed to say, as if that was as much World War Two information she could handle in one sitting. 'Have you got something to show us?'

'I do,' Gemma replied.

'Good, good.'

'These pieces of typeset. Two are spaces and one is the letter "C".'

'Wow, how did you spot them? They look like slivers of stone,' Nick said.

'Practice, I guess,' Gemma said, feeling pleased to be on the receiving end of awe, which was in sharp contrast to what she'd often got from Adam.

'It's called "tuning your eye" or "getting your eye in",' added Timothy.

'Well done on finding them,' Phyllida said. 'But if you don't mind, I think I can go one better.' She held up a large Ziplock bag inside of which, at the very bottom, was an aqua-coloured bead like the eye of a very small bird. 'It's so tiny that I thought I should put it in the largest bag I had so I wouldn't lose it.'

Just then, a tinny sound rang out from her handbag. She raised a finger as if testing which direction the wind was coming from. 'Hang on, that's my phone.'

Answering, she turned her back on them for privacy reasons but didn't modify her volume. There were a lot of 'Oh, dears' and 'Oh, no's' before she hung up.

'I'm so sorry. That was my son. He's going travelling to Australia in three days and he's just discovered that his passport is out of date. I can't believe he didn't check earlier and now he seems to think I'm going to be able to help. I thought I'd raised him to be capable and independent. He had to be, given he was an only child of a single mother.'

'You raised him on your own?' Timothy said.

'My ex-partner got commitment phobia when Samuel was born and did a runner. But my husband Robert is a great stepdad for Samuel, even though he spoils him. The boy's now twenty-four, and I suppose I shouldn't still be worrying about him so much.'

'It doesn't matter what age they are, it never ends,' Tim said.

'I've got one child, three grandchildren and one foster grandchild and I worry about them all.'

'I've got no kids and you're putting me right off,' Nick said. It was hard to tell whether he was joking or not.

'Would you like children? Sorry if that's too personal,' Phyllida quickly added.

'Ella – my partner, girlfriend, whatever we are – she said she got broody once, but she hasn't mentioned it again. Sometimes I feel like I'm the one with the biological clock ticking and not her.' He laughed, even though it didn't sound as if he found it particularly funny.

'If you really do want children, surely you need to raise it with her again?' Phyllida said, as if she were his mother. 'I don't mean to interfere but you need to be on the same bandwidth in a relationship.'

'Don't you mean page?'

'Probably.' Phyllida shrugged as if she wasn't bothered with semantics.

'Whatever it is, you're right,' Nick said despondently, as if he'd given up long ago trying to raise the subject of children with his girlfriend.

'What about you, Gemma?'

Gemma smiled, telling herself to put on a brave face. 'No children,' she said. Then out it came. 'And as of three months ago, no husband. Adam left me for another woman and now they're having a baby.' She blushed and looked away. She hadn't expected to reveal so much so soon, nor did she want to get upset in front them.

'What a stinker!' Timothy said.

'Yeah, that's shit,' Nick agreed.

'You can do it on your own, you know. Have children, I mean,' said Phyllida. 'Back when a friend of mine was in her early thirties, she gave up trying to find someone special to have a family with and used a sperm donor. She now has a twenty-seven-year-old daughter who's a human rights lawyer.'

'Impressive,' Nick said.

'It has its upsides,' Phyllida continued. 'If your child displays unwanted traits, you can always blame the sperm donor. Ha! Only kidding. But if you do want to go down that route, my friend would be more than happy to have a chat.'

'Oh, I don't know …' Gemma was still getting used to living on her own, let alone be ready to contemplate something as audacious as using a sperm donor.

'Never say never.'

'I was considering getting a dog but worried I'd dress it up in bows and tartan coats, and that's no way to treat a puppy.' Gemma laughed. It was time to lighten the mood.

'Or a baby.' Nick chuckled and smiled at Gemma as if offering sympathy for her unlucky personal circumstances. Or perhaps it was because she'd admitted to liking miniature tartan coats.

'As we're on the subject of children, do you mind if I ask you all a question?' Timothy said.

'Ask away.' Phyllida leant back in her chair as if preparing herself to give more advice.

Timothy cleared his throat. 'I was wondering what you thought about me bringing my foster grandchild to the club?'

'The more the merrier, as far as I'm concerned,' Phyllida said.

'The problem is Laila, and I mean this in the nicest possible way, could be a liability. She seems to be rebelling at everything at the moment. She's fallen out with her foster parents, my daughter Jodie and her husband, who've had her since she was eleven, and she's started to skip school. It's such a shame because she's seventeen and so close to finishing. Last year, she had a boyfriend who was two years older and not a good influence. Then last week, she ran away from home. Jodie was beside herself.' Timothy sighed. 'Laila has so much going for her. So much potential. I've been wrestling with how I can help.'

'Perhaps parents and child need a break from each other?'

Gemma suggested, remembering a time, at fifteen, when she'd hypothetically entertained running away from home. Not because she wished to rebel but because she craved independence. To be the master of her own destiny. Little did she understand then that you can never fully be in control of anything.

'They do,' Timothy replied. 'I've agreed to have her stay with me on the boat. We've always got on well and we share a love of history.'

'How wonderful that your daughter and son-in-law are foster parents,' Gemma said. 'It can't be easy if you get attached to a child and don't want them to leave.'

'It is,' Timothy agreed. 'Jodie and Simon wanted to adopt Laila but they found out that if they did, she'd lose all ties to her birth mother and they didn't want that. They hope she'll have a relationship with her one day, but the birth mother is in prison on drug charges.'

'Oh, no, poor kid,' Nick said. 'I don't mind if she joins us, although she might not want to come to our meetings.'

'Yes, and she may dismiss the club as something only for fuddy-duddy oldies …' Timothy continued as if he was thinking aloud.

'Thanks very much,' Nick said, pretending to be offended.

'You know what I mean. I suppose what I was thinking was that being by the river might help. I'm not sure precisely how but whatever teenage angst she has going on, a bit of mudlarking might do the trick.'

'So bring her along to a group mudlark,' Phyllida suggested. 'She may be surprised and enjoy it.'

'Great idea,' Gemma added. 'I can definitely vouch for its therapeutic benefits.'

'All right let's get that in the diary next,' Phyllida said.

'Thank you, everyone.' Timothy nodded. 'Now please tell us about your bead, Phyllida.'

'Oh, yes, my pretty little bead. Look at it!'

Three heads leant forward. The small donut-shaped specimen

had rolled to the right-hand corner of the bag. They could barely see it.

'I've never found one this small before. It's a bit worn but I imagine it was once part of a beautifully decorated dress,' Phyllida said. 'Beads are everywhere in the river. If you can spot them, that is. Just because they can be colourful, they also get coated in mud like everything else. The Romans made them from glass and they were often pale blue. Later on, they were made from other materials like bone, pearl, stone and coral. From the late fifteenth century, beads were made from tubes of different coloured glass, making them look like pieces of a multi-coloured candy cane. They were used for trade. I've never found one of them before. That's my goal.'

'Nice one,' Nick said.

'Right, the kitty!' Phyllida suddenly switched to club secretary mode. 'What shall we put in to start with?'

'Twenty pounds each?' Timothy suggested.

'Doesn't it depend on what we're going to be using it for?' Gemma said.

'I was thinking a bottle of wine here, coffees there …'

'Sounds good to me,' Nick said.

'Maybe a lunch or two,' Phyllida continued. Then, her eyes lit up. 'I know! We could get guest speakers.' Phyllida was getting carried away, but Gemma was becoming accustomed to her quick-fire, and changeable, thought process.

'One of my Instagram followers is an historian, Megan O'Connor. I could see if she might like to come and talk.' Phyllida looked skyward. 'Yes, I'll do that,' she said and then documented it in her notebook. 'All right, shall we put in twenty-five each to make it a hundred and see how we go?'

Nick stuck his hand in his pocket to get his wallet. But opening it up, he found it was cashless. 'Does anyone carry money anymore?'

'I do,' Timothy said.

Gemma shook her head.

'Bring it next time,' Phyllida suggested.

'Shall we definitely go mudlarking next time?' Nick said.

'I think so. Everyone in agreement raise their hand.' Phyllida shoved two arms in the air.

Four other arms lifted, too, including both of Nick's.

'Let's check the tides and make a date. I'll send out the minutes tomorrow so we don't forget.'

Gemma resisted the urge to do a military salute.

June Discoveries:
A late nineteenth-century penny (finally my coin finds are getting older). A fragment of earthenware, which I've learnt is London salt-glazed stoneware from the early twentieth century. A Georgian cufflink set with blue glass stones, which are so pretty I wouldn't mind buying a man's shirt just so that I can wear them. A fast-food straw (why can't people dispose of their rubbish?). Three modern-day pennies which I put in the Thames charity box. And how stepping out of your comfort zone isn't so bad after all.

July

Chapter 18

When Gemma got home from work one night, there it was on the floor with two other pieces of post and a glossy flyer from the Indian place down the road. She immediately knew what it was because of the little black crown symbol next to the words 'Gov.UK' at the top of the envelope.

Gemma took it, and the rest of the post, to the kitchen and flung it onto the table, as though it was too hot to hold. Or rather, as if she didn't want anything to do with it anymore. She felt breathy and light-headed. She stared at the envelope but didn't think she could open it. Instead, she walked smartly out of the kitchen and up the stairs.

Firstly, she had to get out of her nursing uniform. Comfort is imperative when opening mail that makes you nervous, she decided. That's what she told herself when she'd delayed opening the electricity bill she received earlier in the week. It meant contacting *el cabrón*, because most of the period it covered was when Adam was still living at the house. Gemma damn well wasn't going to pay for his long hot showers, so she happily messaged him about it. He was brief and curt in his response, as he was in his last exchange about starting divorce proceedings (he asked nothing about how she was!). Thankfully, he didn't protest the payment. After a prolonged shower, she remembered to reply to the message Simone sent at lunchtime inviting her to her four-year-old daughter's birthday celebrations, which sounded like more of an excuse for the adults to party. Even so, Gemma wasn't sure she wanted to be around adorable children and married couples. She said she'd pop in as she had other commitments, so that she didn't appear churlish if she didn't stay long.

Then, eventually, Gemma returned to the kitchen.

But in her absence, the envelope seemed to have taken on a personality all of its own. Lying, seemingly innocuously on the table, it mocked and teased. It dared her to ignore its presence knowing that it made her giddy wondering what information it held inside. For it, and only it, was the segue between one life and another. It was symbolic – if not indeed the reality – of who she was and how she'd come into being. She leant against the kitchen bench to steady herself. All she had to do was open it. But the more she procrastinated, the harder it became.

She couldn't do it on her own. She decided to call Anushka.

'Hi, Gemma, how are you?' Anushka answered. She sounded a little breathless and Gemma could hear muffled noises in the background.

'I'm good ...' Gemma said, even though she wanted to say so much more, but she didn't know where to start.

'Hang on, I've just got to pay for the Tube.'

Gemma waited for her friend to be focused again on their conversation.

'Sorry,' Anushka said. 'I've got work drinks and I'm running late. I should have worked at the office today but it was my turn getting the kids from school. I don't even want to go to this thing.' She groaned. 'Are we still going to organise a movie night?'

'Yes, I'm keen.'

'Great! I haven't had a look at what's on, but I will.'

'Me too.' Gemma sighed. She suspected it was never going to happen.

'Are you all right?'

'Yeah, fine,' Gemma said reluctantly. Anushka was clearly distracted, and this wasn't the time to bother her with any personal problems. 'I'll let you get back to your night. Hopefully, it's not too unenjoyable.'

'Thanks!'

Gemma didn't put her phone down. She still wanted to talk to someone. She decided to video call her mother.

'Oh, Gemma, do you really need to see me?' her mother said curtly.

She was wearing a pale-pink satin dressing gown and her skin glistened with face cream.

'Nice to see you, too, Mum.'

'I've just got out of the bath.'

'You look very shiny.'

'Don't be cheeky.'

'Sorry …' She glanced at the envelope. 'Guess what came in the post?'

'Goodness, I don't know.'

Gemma held up the envelope to the screen. 'My birth certificate. I don't want to open it on my own.'

Her mother put a hand to her chest. 'Oh, darling.'

'I can't bear it.'

'I thought you'd be excited.'

'I want to be, but I also feel terrified.'

'Just rip it open, get it over with.'

Her mother was right, but she seemed unable to do it. Her stomach flapped like a trapped bird.

'I know it's daunting,' her mum said, softening. 'But whatever you find out, you don't have to do anything with it. It will just be. What's in there are facts that exist whether you know them or not. And didn't you decide that you wanted to know them now?'

'I suppose.'

'I'd sit down if I were you.'

Gemma sat at the table and rested her phone against a plastic container of found buttons to free up her hands.

'Imagine you're taking off a plaster. You've got to do it fast, without thinking.'

Gemma picked up the envelope.

'One, two, three,' said her mother.

A quick tear and the envelope was open. Her mother clapped. Gemma pulled out the certificate. She skim-read it, as if to linger on the words would be to learn too much.

'What does it say?'

'Well …' she began. 'My birth name was Hayley Rita.'

'Hayley.' Her mother said the word as if playing with the letters with her tongue.

Gemma didn't know how she felt about once being a Hayley. She couldn't relate to the name in any way and felt so removed from it that she almost felt nothing at all. In some ways, she felt unsettled and both displaced and misplaced. Yet, it was reassuring to think that her birth mother had named her at all.

'Carry on,' her mother said.

Gemma looked back at the birth certificate. 'My birth mother's name is Claire Rita Munroe.'

Claire. Rita. Munroe. Gemma recited the words slowly in her head as if it might conjure up a picture of what her mother looked like and who she was.

'Rita's a family name then …' her mother said.

Oh, yes, her mother had passed on part of her name! Gemma's heart skipped. That had to mean something, didn't it? That she'd cared about the baby she'd just given birth to, even if she was going to give her away.

Gemma continued. 'She was born in 1969.'

'Which makes her …' Her mother did the sum in her head. 'Seventeen when she had you.'

'Uh-huh.'

'So, is that Monroe as in Marilyn?' Her mother asked as if there was any chance she could be related to a film star.

'Mum!'

'You've got to check these things.'

'Well, you're going to be disappointed. It's with a "u".'

'Ah.' Her mother sighed. 'And the father?'

'He's not named.'

'Which is what I thought. What's the place of registration?'

'East Sussex.'

'By the sea, where we liked to go for summer holidays when you were kids. How funny.'

Gemma thought back to childhood days at the beach: Rich obsessed with making sandcastles and Gemma collecting shells for decoration. Had they once shared the beach with her birth mother? Had they swum in the sea at the same time as she had? Had they stood together in the ice cream queue? Just imagine if they had. But as Gemma did, she felt adrift again. Fabricating your back story was futile if it was littered with fantasy.

'Anything else?' her mother asked.

Gemma looked at the occupation column. 'She was still at school.'

'Gosh.'

'Yeah.'

For a moment, neither spoke. The reality of what she was reading out loud was beginning to sink in. Her past was slowly coming to life and she wasn't sure what to make of it. There were still too many gaps, and a name and an age could only conjure so much. It was like being teased with half a joke and never learning the punchline. Had Claire Rita Munroe held her baby after she was born? How long was the labour? How much had baby Gemma weighed? Did she have hair or none at all? And where was her father during all of this? Did he ever know of her existence?

Her mother said gently, 'How do you feel?'

'I thought I'd be excited to find these things out, but I'm shaken.'

'It's a lot to take in. As I said, you don't have to do anything else just yet. Take your time to let the information sink in.'

'She'll be fifty-three now,' Gemma said suddenly.

'So young,' said her seventy-four-year-old mother.

'Oh, God, she'll still be alive.'

'Still alive,' her mother repeated, as if she'd never considered the possibility either.

One minute her birth mother was a word on a piece of paper, the next she was a living human being, out there in the world right now. Wow, as Nick would say. Just wow.

'Maybe you'll be able to meet her ...' her mother suggested.

'But what if she doesn't want to meet me?'

Over the weekend, Gemma found she couldn't stop looking at her birth certificate, as if to reassure herself that it was real and it was hers. It was concrete evidence that she had a life before the one in the photo on the fridge. Nor could she shake Claire Rita Munroe from her mind. Who was she and what had her life been like?

In the end, Gemma couldn't resist googling. Who could have? There was a Claire Munroe doctor, a financial services adviser, a photographer and more. On Facebook, there were pages and pages of them. So many! But it was pointless and overwhelming. Her birth mother could have been any one of them or none. She put her computer to sleep and tried to stop putting a face or a profession to her birth mother's name.

Chapter 19

The Mudlarkers' Club met for their first group mudlark a week later. There was heat in the sun and a cowlick of cloud fringed the sky. The foreshore shone with promise. They gathered at the top of the stairs at the north end of Southwark Bridge in central London in the early afternoon. What a motley bunch they must look, Gemma thought, in their old clothes suitable for getting dirty.

'Everyone, I'd like to introduce Laila,' Timothy said. 'This is her first time mudlarking.'

A chorus of hellos and do you know what you're getting yourself into went around the group. Laila's mouth reluctantly stretched into a semi-smile as if it were a taut piece of elastic. She appeared disinterested and bored already. She was dressed all in black, with red-dyed hair and a multitude of piercings.

'Timothy tells us you like history. That's a very good place to start,' Phyllida said.

Laila glanced at her grandfather. Underneath all the attitude seemed a shy girl. Gemma felt for her. When Gemma was seventeen, she was so shy she couldn't even look dogs in the eye, let alone a fellow human being. And what about Gemma's birth mother? She'd had a baby at the same age!

Timothy nodded to Laila, encouraging her to speak.

Laila shoved her hands in the pockets of oversized baggy jeans that swamped her small frame. She scuffed the footpath with her boots. 'Yeah, I kinda like watching YouTube history videos about famous women,' she said. 'Sassy women like Boudicea and Cleopatra. Although Hatshepsut was the most badass of all.'

'Laila.' Timothy gently scolded.

'Hatshe …?' Nick started but couldn't pronounce it. Probably, no one other than Laila had ever heard of her before.

'The longest reigning female pharaoh in Kemet, and one of the most successful,' Laila explained.

'Well, there you go.' Nick sounded impressed.

'Never let anyone tell you that the youth of today knows less than you do,' Timothy said.

'And being the youngest member, you'll have the best eyesight, so I'm looking forward to seeing what you find,' Phyllida added encouragingly. 'And we have two mudlarking newbies – I'm including you in this, Nick, if you don't mind.'

He traded a look with Gemma as if to say, *Here goes Phyllida, taking charge again, but we don't mind because she's doing a very good job, isn't she?* Gemma smiled back.

'Call me what you like,' he said. 'I won't be offended.'

'Okay, good. So given we have newbies, I thought Timothy, Gemma and I could offer some tips and tricks to help us get started.'

She waited for nods of agreement before continuing. 'My advice is that as the river has a way of collating objects of similar weight and size together, if you find one item, there's a good chance you'll find more. Gemma?'

Gemma hated being put on the spot, even if it was talking about something she loved. 'Um …' Her mind had gone blank. Eventually she thought of something. 'I suppose this is kind of obvious but anything that looks green or brown is slippery. You don't want to fall on the rocks.'

'Good point.' Phyllida nodded. 'Timothy?'

'I recommend focusing on a small area at a time, especially at tide lines. A sweeping glance won't get you anything.'

'Excellent.'

'Also, remember that perishable materials like wood, fabric and leather stay preserved in the mud because it's anaerobic, without oxygen. It's when you take them out that they start disintegrating, so you need to be careful and prepared.'

'Like how?' Nick asked.

'Sealing finds in plastic bags as soon you can is a good idea. Then, when you get home, you need to implement preservation methods. For example, with wood, you don't want it splitting and warping. The best way is to freeze it and put it in a plastic bag pricked with holes to let it dry out slowly,' Timothy explained.

'Wouldn't it be wonderful to find an ancient leather shoe?' Phyllida sighed.

'You never know,' Timothy said. 'People have found all sorts of things.'

'Let's get to it then!' Phyllida let out a high-pitched laugh as if it was a call of the wild. Gemma wondered if the heat was getting to her already. 'Nick, you can trail Gemma, if you like. Obviously, you've got Laila, Timothy. And I'll float around between all of you. Sun cream?' Phyllida pulled out a tube of sunscreen from her day pack and passed the tube around, squirting cream onto everyone's palms as the sun hid behind a cloud.

Gemma adjusted her kneepads, tightened her rucksack and headed to the wooden steps leading down to the beach. There was no point waiting for the others when they were still technically mudlarking solo. There would be plenty of time to chat later.

Chapter 20

'I don't know how you guys find the things you do in all this rubble.' Nick had hurried to catch up with her as if interpreting Phyllida's use of the word 'trail' as tailgate. 'I mean look at this,' he continued. 'It's like the ruins of an industrial wasteland.'

'I know,' Gemma agreed. 'To the uninitiated, it looks like a wild mess of rocks and rubble and mud, even though you're likely to find more objects from domestic life than from industry.' She carried on walking.

'It's like the archaeological dig that's near here, the one I've been covering,' Nick said, keeping pace. 'The developers of the building site uncovered a four-bedroom Roman house with pottery, coins, copper bowls … Even gaming counters.'

'Mmm, incredible,' she said, becoming distracted by the river and mildly irritated by Nick's chatter.

But he wasn't to be subdued. 'I'd have loved to have broken that story. Since I lost my full-time gig, I've been working part-time for a small paper and taking on freelance jobs whenever I can. Which usually means you get the stories no one else wants. Apart from the dig. I made sure I got that one.'

'Oh, right.' Gemma looked longingly across the beach, wondering which spot she'd claim as hers. She may have agreed to come as a group but she still wanted the chance to mudlark by herself.

'Just quietly,' he whispered, moving closer to her. 'I hammed up the size and professionalism of The Mudlarkers' Club to give me an edge, so I'd get to write the story on the two-thousand-year-old Roman house. Don't tell Phyllida.'

She turned to him. 'Did you?' She didn't know whether to admire his chutzpah or feel a little bit used on behalf of the club.

He laughed. 'A journo's gotta do what a journo's gotta do.'

'Well, I'm sure you've covered some interesting stories and met some fascinating people,' she said, starting down the access stairs.

'And some utter bores.' Nick followed. 'You meet all types in my job.'

'Okay, I'm going over here.' Gemma pointed to a patch of stones where the foreshore bulged into the river.

'Yeah, good point, we're meant to be mudlarking! Sorry if I'm talking too much.' Nick mimed the zipping up of his mouth.

Gemma smiled. She shouldn't really criticise his high spirits because, if anything, she envied them. 'It's okay. I'm happy to chat on a break. The thing with mudlarking is that it's as much about the serenity as it is about what you uncover. On a good day, I hear nothing. The silence is bliss. But when it's not going well, I hear everything. My thoughts can be the worst of all.'

'I get it.' Nick nodded. 'It's like when I'm engrossed in my writing, that's all I'm focused on. The words, the hook, the story, the drama, the climax ...' His words trailed away as did his gaze.

Gemma pulled out a new set of gloves from her rucksack, thin black latex ones to replace the Marigolds, which had developed a split in one finger. She paused for a moment and looked to the sky. A dragonfly flew into her frame and hovered, its wings a blur of motion. Immediately, the tension in her shoulders eased and a sense of calmness came over her.

'How about I go over here?' Nick said. 'Close but not too close, yeah?'

'Sure.' Gemma placed her rucksack on a dry rock, then lowered her head and zoned in on the mud and the jumble of rust, grey and white stones drying out in the sun. Despite being part of a group, once she'd started, it was easier than she'd thought to block out everything around her and disappear into a world of her own private time travel. Here, the mud was drier and more densely covered in stones and broken brick. After a period of standing, she sat on a large rock – a remnant perhaps of the river's shipping industry – and let her eyes roam.

'Hey, I think I've found something,' Nick called out after only a few minutes. 'Is this anything?' He held up a small, round object.

'I can't tell from here,' she said. 'Keep it and I'll have a look later.'

He pulled out a string of green dog poop bags from his back pocket, as if he was about to do a magic trick with a scarf. He saw her watching. 'I didn't have any other bags,' he explained louder than necessary. 'Darryl didn't mind.'

'Darryl?'

'My dog,' Nick said as if he needed to clarify, when really she'd been questioning its suitability as a dog's name. 'He's Ella's dog, but I love him as if he were mine.'

After only a few seconds, Nick started up again. 'Have you ever found anything really valuable?'

Gemma closed her eyes for a moment. Nick may be good company, but right then she wished he'd be quiet.

'Sorry, there I go again.'

Just then, next to a chunk of terracotta rock, Gemma spotted something mustard coloured. She bent over and pulled it from the mud.

'What is it?' Nick asked.

Gemma turned the shard over, felt the smooth glaze on one side and the rougher ceramic on the other. 'It's a piece of pottery. Yellow Staffordshire slipware.'

'How old?'

'Eighteenth century, I think.'

'Wow …' he said with such wonder. You'd have thought she'd found something rare – a perfectly preserved bone-handled Tudor knife, perhaps. 'What do you think it could have been? A jug or a bowl?'

'A royal chamber pot, I'd say.'

'Ew? Really?' He pulled a face.

'Could have been.'

'You mean someone pissed on this thing? Like a real king or something?'

'And then he had his bum wiped by the Groom of the Stool.' She chewed her cheeks to stop herself from smiling.

'You're having me on.'

She burst out laughing.

'I thought I was meant to be learning from you!'

'Sorry, I couldn't help it.'

'Just so you know, you're a terrible liar.'

'I only made up the bit about the chamber pot. The Groom of the Stool really existed.'

'Yikes.'

'Come on, let's get back to mudlarking.'

'Yeah, I've got to find something really good to show everyone at the end,' Nick said, as if mudlarking had turned into a competitive sport.

After an hour, Gemma found herself at the high moss-covered wall which protected the city from the river. There, Laila was sitting, sketching.

'Sick of mudlarking already?' Gemma asked, ready for a break herself.

'It's okay. But I like drawing.'

'Cool,' Gemma said and immediately regretted it. Do seventeen-year-olds still say 'cool'?

The scratching of Laila's pencil shading was nearly as loud as the birds. Gemma noticed a tattoo on the underside of her right forearm, just before the elbow crease. It was an outline of a rabbit with the word 'Nuts' inked along one of its ears.

'Do you mind if I sit here for a minute?' she asked.

Laila shook her head. Gemma sat down and took out the Thermos from her rucksack. 'Tea?'

'No, thanks.'

Gemma poured herself a cup and sipped it slowly, looking out to the river and beyond, to the modern high-rise buildings on the other side. Timothy was walking slowly away from them in a westerly direction.

'Did you know that hobbies are a gift that came about from the industrial age in the nineteenth century?' Gemma had no idea why she was trying to be educational, particularly not to a teenager who'd been playing truant. But somehow, she felt the need to engage with her, in case Laila was hating every minute of being there.

'Well,' said Laila. 'Did you know that wealthy people have always had hobbies? Cleopatra spoke nine languages.'

'Did she?'

'Really,' Laila said, as if Gemma needed convincing.

'What are you drawing?'

Laila showed Gemma a detailed sketch of the city skyline across the river.

'I love it! You're really talented,' Gemma said.

Laila shrugged. Getting information out of her was like trying to find a completely intact clay pipe: almost impossible.

'Your grandad's a lovely man, isn't he? Do you call him grandad?' Gemma wasn't going to give up yet.

'Sometimes I call him Gramps. Or Grumps to wind him up. He's not my real grandad, though.'

'It doesn't matter. I call my mum "Mum", even though she's not my birth mother.'

'Were you adopted?' Laila looked at Gemma as if she'd suddenly gone up in her estimation.

Gemma nodded. 'Names can be names for reasons other than logical ones. My grandmother on my mother's side insisted we call her "yia yia" even though we have no Greek heritage. She just liked the whole Mediterranean thing. And feta. There was always lots of feta in her fridge.'

'Is that your adoptive grandmother or your biological one?'

'Adoptive.'

'So, you could actually be Greek.'

'I suppose.' That was food for thought. 'I like feta, too.'

'Do Greeks have freckles?'

Gemma looked at Laila and started laughing. 'I guess that answers the question then,' she said.

Laila supressed a giggle. Perhaps giggling was uncool.

'Did you know that Gramps has another hobby he loves as much if not more than mudlarking?' Laila said.

Gemma recalled Timothy once mentioning another pastime of his, but she couldn't remember if he'd ever told her what it was.

'You won't believe it,' Laila said.

'Won't I?'

'Nah.' Laila shook her head. 'It's cross stitching. Something to do with learning to darn socks when he was a kid. He does these super detailed scenes, and he's *really* good.' Laila overemphasised 'really' in a way only teenagers can. 'I love that he's challenging gender stereotypes.'

'I'd never have picked that.'

'You can't make assumptions. That's what Gramps always tells me. Never judge a book by its cover. I don't, anyway, because I don't read. Don't like it,' Laila said in a slightly sullen way that implied there was more to it than that. Then, she went back to her drawing. But curiosity clearly got the better of her because she started up again. 'Do you know your birth mother?'

The question caught Gemma off-guard as she'd not mentioned her recent discoveries about her birth mother to anyone other than her parents and Google. She certainly didn't know anyone who shared a similar backstory. 'No, I'd love to,' she said. 'But I've only just started searching for her.'

'What's that been like?'

'Weird.'

'Are you going to meet her?'

Gemma turned away and bit her lip. She didn't want to start crying again.

'You okay?' Laila asked.

Gemma nodded. Maybe she wasn't as ready to talk about this as she'd thought.

'You don't have to tell me. I get it, it's hard. I'm being fostered, if you didn't know,' Laila said.

'Timothy did mention it.'

'They're okay, Jodie and Simon, even though I'm kind of pissed off with them. They're all about openness and love for everyone, blah blah blah.' Laila sighed as if her foster parents were being such bores.

'They want me to re-establish a relationship with my mother someday. But I don't know if that'll ever happen. I'm not seeing her in prison, and unless she changes when she gets out …' She scraped a heel across the stones with her foot. Gemma immediately scoured the newly exposed mud in case there was something to be found there. 'It's like history's repeating itself,' Laila continued.

'What do you mean?'

'I never knew my grandparents because they basically disowned Mum.'

'Oh, dear …'

'Yeah. Mum's parents had immigrated from Pakistan when Mum was a child. They dreamed of Mum marrying someone from their culture or who was, at least, South Asian. But Mum always wanted to fit into the "white" world and didn't want to acknowledge her background. They clashed a lot when she was a teenager and then when she was twenty-one, she met a non-Asian man and got pregnant with me.

'You can imagine the fall out. Even though they didn't want Mum to be with my father, they also didn't believe in abortion and didn't want her to be a single mother, so they insisted they marry. That was a step too far for both Mum and my father. Anyway, I don't even know how much they really loved each other, to be honest, but they tried to stay together, pretending to my grandparents that they would marry after I was born. Mum even agreed to give me a Pakistani name to try and appease them. She chose Laila because she wanted one that was familiar to and used by non-Asians.'

'Laila's a pretty name.'

'It means "of the night". I was born at two in the morning.'

Gemma smiled. It made her wonder what her two given names meant and whether it had any bearing on why they'd been chosen, or absolutely none at all. 'So, what happened?'

'It didn't work out between my Mum and father, so Mum agreed to move back with her parents. I was about two or something. But that didn't work out either. Then Mum got in with the wrong people and here we are. All I ever wanted was a normal life with a normal mother.'

If Laila kept chewing her lip like that, she was going to draw blood.

'I'm sorry.' Gemma put a hand on the girl's back. Not for long, but long enough to show that she cared.

'I didn't mean to blab my life story.'

'Don't apologise. It sounds like you've been through a lot. How long have you lived with Jodie and Simon?'

'Six years, with a gap in between when I went back with Mum, because everyone thought she was getting her life back together. She tried.' Laila looked sad for a moment. 'It's been all right with Jodie and Simon. I know they mean well but ... I dunno ... they want me to like school and I don't. They didn't like my boyfriend. Or my tattoo. Then we had a massive argument. That's why I'm staying with Gramps.'

'I thought you had to be eighteen to get a tattoo.'

'Not in Ireland. You can be sixteen if you're with a guardian who's over eighteen. My boyfriend was twenty. We secretly took a trip there so I could get one. I wasn't going to tell Jodie and Simon before we went because they wouldn't have let me go. Plus, Trey wanted to see his half-sister in Dublin.' Laila paused, as if thinking fondly of the memory.

Gemma understood that being a teenager was never easy, but Laila's rebelliousness was completely foreign to her. Gemma had never had a desire to challenge authority. The most daring thing she'd ever done was smuggle a hip flask of vodka into a nightclub, which proved laughable. Having left it in the kitchen while she was getting ready, her housemates had drunk it without telling her, so it was empty anyway!

Laila continued. 'Trey and I laughed and laughed at the idea of him being my guardian. But I wanted a tattoo so badly. I'd decided to get one of the rabbit Jodie and Simon got me when I first moved in with them, because he'd just died. It was the second saddest moment of my life. The first was when I had to leave Mum. Or when Mum had to leave me. The first time. Whichever way around it was.'

Laila stretched out her arm so Gemma could get a better look at the tattoo. 'I called the rabbit Nuts because he was brown, and I love Nutella. I wanted something to remember him by.'

'Are you still with Trey?'

'Nah,' Laila said abruptly. 'He started mucking around with someone else. My friend caught him with some girl behind the pizza shop. I wasn't having any of that.'

'Good for you.'

'Hello, you two, what's going on over here?' Phyllida approached, waving a stick at them. 'Made any finds?'

'Yep,' Laila said.

Gemma studied her. Had Laila really made some interesting

discoveries or was she humouring Phyllida? There was something charming about her directness.

'I thought we could gather in half an hour and do a show and tell. What do you think?' Phyllida said.

'I've definitely got another half an hour in me.' Gemma packed up her Thermos. 'What about you, Laila?'

Laila did a nonchalant shoulder jig yet slipped the sketchbook and pencil in her bag and got up.

'You can come with me, if you like?' Gemma suggested. 'But no chatting, deal?'

'Deal.'

It was probably Laila's best offer all day.

Chapter 21

It turned out that Laila *had* made some finds. When The Mudlarkers' Club re-grouped on the sandy part of the upper foreshore, Laila was already laying out her discoveries for everyone to see.

'I don't know if any of this is something interesting or if it's all nothing,' Laila said, her hands finding their way into her jeans' pockets again.

'It's *never* nothing,' Phyllida said, so emphatically that Laila would have been forgiven for thinking she'd offended her. 'No, no, no,' Phyllida reiterated and peered eagerly at the collection. 'I spy some lovely bits of blue and white pottery and a buckle. That could be nineteenth century.'

'Nineteenth century?' Laila said in disbelief.

'I'm guessing, but it looks similar to one I have. And those chunks of red that resemble stones? Bits of roof tile, some of which would be medieval. See how easy it is to go back in time? Great job picking up some rubbish, too.' Phyllida pointed to the white plastic fork Laila had also found.

'I added it to my finds because it made me wonder what people in the future will think when they find our plastic cutlery,' Laila said. 'Will they say, "Check out this piece of history. What had its owner been eating before it got thrown away?" Or are they going to tell us off for inventing plastic in the first place?'

For a moment, Laila looked proud and surprised at saying as much as she had. She lowered her head and chewed a lip, a turtle going back into its shell.

'Probably both, Ley-ley,' Timothy said.

'But hopefully disposable plastic will be so rare that to find an unbroken fork will be like finding gold,' Nick said. 'Only less valuable, of course.'

'Can I take a picture of the fork and put what you said on Instagram?' Phyllida had her phone out before Laila could answer.

'I guess,' Laila said. 'But don't expect it to trend.'

'I've never been trendy, so the bar's low.' Phyllida chuckled and snapped a few photos.

'What did you find, Gemma?' Laila asked.

'A cluster of pins.' Gemma showed them a bag of eleven tiny pins. 'Some of them could have held together an Elizabethan ruff.'

'That old?' Nick said.

'They could date from anywhere between the fourteenth and eighteenth centuries, because they look handmade and copper.'

'No way!'

'Doesn't it just make you wonder who was wearing them and what for?' Phyllida re-joined the conversation after finishing her Instagram post. 'Pins were used by everyone, no matter what social class. Although a woman of distinction would have had anywhere from two and a half thousand to five thousand pins on her.'

'I believe Queen Elizabeth the First had a dress that needed ten thousand pins to hold it up,' Timothy said.

'Sounds dangerous.' Nick laughed.

'Why all the pins?' Laila asked.

'There was no other way to keep your clothes in place! They were used for attaching veils, baby swathes, hats, jewellery. Literally everything worn by anyone. Then, in the early nineteenth century, pin-making was mechanised, clothes became mass produced and fasteners and buttons took over from the pin.'

'They're so ordinary, and yet now, hundreds of years later, you're all getting excited about them,' Laila said.

'It's because they represent the history of everyday Londoners.'

'Just like your plastic fork,' Nick said, managing to get Laila to smile.

'I found a Victorian glass syringe. It's amazingly unbroken. Do you want to see?' Phyllida said.

'Cool,' Nick said, confirming that he was of a similar age to Gemma.

'Who knows how many times this was used and what for. It probably gave people disease as much as it was trying to help them.'

'Yuck.' Laila turned up her nose. 'Will it still be …?'

'Contaminated? No. I doubt any communicable disease could survive that long.'

'It may have held mercury,' said Timothy. 'For centuries, mercury was given as a treatment and cure for all sorts of ailments, until someone twigged that the horrendous side effects it caused was from metal poisoning.'

'Thank you, Timothy, you've just reminded me I need to book a blood test.' Phyllida laughed. 'To check my calcium levels – not mercury! No matter how much cheese I eat, they seem to be on a downward trajectory.'

'My mother had that,' Nick said. 'Something to do with poor absorption. My dad, on the other hand, ended up with an excess of Vitamin K. He's the only person to have ever been told to cut back on his greens.'

'You're making that up.'

'True story. He got a form of anaemia. That's what happens when you have lettuce for breakfast, lunch and dinner.'

'Let that be a lesson to you, Laila.'

'No chance of that.' Timothy smiled. Laila pretended to be

offended. 'Can I show you what I found?' Timothy held up a thimble. 'The porcelain is so white that it stood out against the grey of the mud. And, can you see, there's a tiny sailing boat painted on one side?'

'I found a silver thimble the day Gemma and I met,' said Phyllida. 'They're sweet, aren't they?'

'I don't know how old it is, if it's old at all. But I suppose it could date back to the late eighteen hundreds.'

'Something to find out, perhaps?' Gemma offered.

Timothy nodded. 'Yes, I'll have fun investigating.'

'What about you, Nick?'

'I seemed to find a lot of things but nothing I recognised.'

'Such as?'

'Oh.' He held up a small terracotta-coloured stoneware container. 'I think it's an inkwell.'

'Yes!' Gemma said. 'It's a pork pie ink pot. They were mass produced in the late eighteen hundreds to early nineteen hundreds, often, unfortunately, using child labour.'

'You could use it for your writing,' Phyllida suggested. 'Imagine what it would have been like to write an article by hand using an ink pen. I've always fancied writing romance novels.' Phyllida got a dreamy look in her eye as if she'd conjured a scene between Jane Eyre and Mr Rochester. 'You'd *have* to do it with a quill pen, don't you think? With feathers. Yes, lots of feathers and a bit of lace.'

'I think I prefer the speed of touch-typing, even if I make mistakes,' Nick answered. 'I'll happily put this on my desk, though.'

'I don't know about anyone else, but I'm famished,' Phyllida said. 'Anyone fancy a pub lunch?'

Timothy glanced at Laila to gauge her opinion. She moved a shoulder. It looked like a yes kind of a shrug.

Nick looked at Gemma, as if her decision mattered to him, but she didn't see why it would. Although, if he said yes, then she'd go too, because a group lunch would round off her Saturday quite nicely. She had to concede that mudlarking with others was not only more pleasurable than she'd originally thought, but it was also gratifyingly informative and social. She gave a nod.

'Why not?' Nick said.

They gathered their finds, slung on their rucksacks and started walking to the stone steps. Phyllida strode ahead, starting up a conversation with Laila; Timothy lagged behind getting distracted by some last-minute searching; and Nick and Gemma walked in between.

'That was really great today, Gem,' Nick said. 'Can I call you Gem?'

'Sure.'

'I feel like I've learnt so much, even though there's still much more to know.'

'I've been doing it for years and I'm still learning things,' Gemma said.

'Hey!' Nick pointed a finger at Gemma as if just remembering. 'You never said what that piece of pottery you found would have been? If not a chamber pot, then what? No lying this time, yeah?' He laughed.

Gemma was about to tell him it would have formed part of an everyday pottery dish when an ear-curdling wail sounded behind them. They stopped and turned. Several metres away, Timothy lay face down on the pebbles. He wasn't moving.

Chapter 22

'Gramps!' Laila sprinted towards him, her hair flying behind her.

Nick shot Gemma a worried look and they started running, too.

'Oh, my goodness, Timothy!' Phyllida cried, fast walking.

Laila got there first and flung herself to the ground next to her grandfather.

'Don't move him,' Gemma called out.

Timothy lay face down on the stones, his head to one side and his left leg bent. A few centimetres from one hand was a rusty hook that he must have been reaching for when he fell. He was unconscious and unresponsive when Laila touched him.

Laila was sobbing. 'Don't die, Gramps, don't die.'

'It's going to be okay, Laila. Isn't it, Gemma?' Phyllida was in such a state she couldn't stand still. She paced the sand, pulling at her top as if the temperature had suddenly risen.

Gemma kneeled next to Laila. 'Timothy,' she said. 'Timothy, can you hear me?'

He didn't respond. She put two fingers on his wrist, then held a hand close to his mouth. 'It's okay, he's breathing and has a pulse. I think he fainted.'

'Should we get his legs in the air?' Nick asked.

'Ideally, but I don't think we should move him,' Gemma said.

'Okay, I'm going to call an ambulance.' Nick got up and pulled his phone from his back pocket.

'Laila, perhaps you could fan his face to get some cooler air flowing around him.' Gemma reached in her backpack to find something Laila could use. 'This will have to do,' she said, giving her a floppy straw hat that was folded up small and good for travelling.

Laila, her shoulders shaking and eyes red, obeyed, while Nick called the emergency services.

'Poor Timothy, this is just terrible,' Phyllida said agitated. 'I can't believe it's happened.'

'The ambulance is on its way,' Nick announced.

'Thanks, Nick,' Gemma said.

Nick went over to Phyllida and took her hands. 'Big deep breaths, Phyll.'

'You're a honey, Nick, did you know that? How are you staying so calm, both of you?'

'Gemma's a nurse so if she wasn't calm, I'd be kind of worried,' Nick said. 'Are you all right, Laila? Is the hat working its magic?'

'No,' Laila said in distress. Gemma stroked her back and rubbed Timothy's back as well. Hopefully, it would make a small difference to one of them, at least.

'Gramps!' Laila cried.

Timothy's eyes had flickered open, but he looked woozy and his face was drained of colour.

'You're alive!' Phyllida shouted. 'Oh, my goodness, I think I'm going to pass out.' She bent over and rested her arms on her legs.

'It's okay, Phyllida,' Nick said kindly. 'There's no need to panic.'

'I believe I am alive,' Timothy mumbled. 'What happened? It feels like I've been hit by a car.'

'You had a fall,' Gemma said.

He started to lift his head, but the effort proved too much.

'Don't try and get up. Can you tell me if it hurts anywhere?' Gemma asked.

'This leg for starters,' he said, trying to point to his bent left leg.

'My arm. Both wrists. A hip. And my face. It feels grazed.' Timothy sighed. 'All over to be honest. I'm probably just in shock. It's no good people of my age doing stunts.'

'What?' Laila said horrified.

'Don't worry, Ley-ley. I think I tripped on a rock.' He pointed vaguely behind him. 'Although if I remember correctly, I got dizzy before the rock. Mmm, hard to say the sequence of events.' He closed his eyes.

'Do you mind if I take a look at your leg and remove your shoe? I'll be gentle,' Gemma said.

Timothy tried to help pull up a trouser leg. He groaned. Gemma gently took off his shoe.

'Can you wiggle your toes? Move your foot?'

There wasn't a lot of movement and his lower leg was beginning to swell. Not only did Gemma not like the look of it, but she was worried he had other injuries that weren't immediately obvious. She pulled his trouser leg down and patted his thigh. Just then, the high-pitched whine of a siren sounded.

'Excellent, here's the ambulance,' Nick said.

Timothy grumbled.

'It's all right, mate. If you haven't been in an ambulance before, it can be quite fun. Think of it like a car chase, fast cars and sirens.'

'I'd rather be in a Lamborghini,' Timothy muttered.

'Now you're talking.'

Timothy nodded, then closed his eyes in pain.

'Okay, stay there, I'll go and flag down the Lambo.' Nick ran to the access stairs and waved his arms at the ambulance.

'It's okay, Gramps. Help is here,' Laila said, patting his hand.

'I don't want to go to hospital,' Timothy moaned. 'I really, really don't like hospitals.'

'Grandma was in hospital for a long time before she died,' Laila whispered to Gemma, as they watched Nick direct the paramedics. 'She never came home.' Her bottom lip trembled.

'I see,' Gemma said. 'We'll have to do all we can to appease him then. But hospital is the best place for him right now.'

'Okay, everyone, help is here,' Nick said, joining them as the paramedics began assessing Timothy. 'Is Phyllida all right?'

Gemma nodded and looked over at Phyllida who'd wandered away from them and was muttering to herself. 'She's shaken but I think she'll be okay. I don't know about you, but I'd like to go to the hospital and wait with Laila.'

'Absolutely. I will, too,' Nick said. 'Is that all right, Laila? We'll sit with you until we know Timothy's diagnosis. We can bore you with old-people talk.'

Laila gave a half-smile and nodded.

'All right, we're set to go,' one of the paramedics said. Timothy was now on a stretcher, wrapped in a blanket, his eyes were half-closed.

'Can I come with you?' Laila asked.

'Sure, love.'

Timothy managed a small half-smile for a few seconds before he ran out of energy to do even that.

'Go on, Laila,' Gemma said. 'We'll meet you at the hospital. Which one are you going to?' she asked the paramedic.

'St Thomas's.'

Gemma nodded.

'Phyll!' Nick called out. 'Timothy's going now.'

'Coming,' Phyllida shouted.

But the paramedics weren't waiting around. They were already carrying Timothy to the ambulance.

'What did the paramedics say? Is he going to be okay?' Phyllida asked. 'I feel terrible. Like it's my fault. If I hadn't invited you to join the club, Gemma, you wouldn't have invited him and then he wouldn't have come and—'

'Don't be silly, Phyllida, it was an accident,' Gemma said.

'Yeah, that's just nonsense talk, Phyll,' Nick added. 'We're going to meet them at the hospital. We'll take the Tube from Mansion

House. You don't have to come if you don't want to.'

'Of course I'm coming,' Phyllida said, as if horrified they would have thought otherwise. 'Might need a stiff drink, though.' She let out a nervous laugh, then noticed something a couple of metres away. She went over to it.

'Timothy, you've forgotten your fishing hook!' she shouted, waving the rusted implement. 'I think it's eighteenth century, too!'

But Timothy, Laila and the paramedics had already reached the pavement and were no longer within earshot.

Chapter 23

At the hospital, Laila was sitting at the end of the third row of chairs in the waiting room, a lost soul among other lost souls. One of her legs jiggled as she cradled her phone, but she seemed unable to concentrate on it or anything around her. A baby in the front row was crying, which only added to the tension hovering around them.

'Hey, kiddo,' Nick said.

'Hey,' Laila said quietly.

'Oh, honey,' was all Phyllida could manage to say.

'Any news?' Gemma asked. They sidled past Laila to sit in the three seats beside her.

'No.'

'He's in good hands now, so you don't need to worry.'

'It's hard not to. He's old, you know?'

'He's only in his seventies, isn't he?' Nick said.

'Seventy-six. That's nearly eighty,' Laila said, as though her grandfather had entered his second century.

'But he's pretty fit and healthy for his age,' Gemma said.

'I guess.'

For a moment, they didn't speak. The baby's wails ricocheted off the linoleum. As much as Gemma loved babies, she dearly wished this one would pipe down. Phyllida, who'd been unusually quiet on the way there, seemed happier now that she'd started on her mini bottle of white wine, which she purchased from the corner store near the Tube station.

'Anyone hungry?' Nick asked.

'Gosh, yes, we never got to have that pub lunch,' Gemma said.

'I think we need something to keep us going. I'll go and see what I can find.' Nick got up and sidled past them to find a vending machine.

'Maybe some water too?' Gemma called out.

'On it.'

'Laila,' Phyllida said in between sips. 'Are you going to call your mum to tell her what's happened?'

'*Foster* mum,' Laila said curtly.

Phyllida looked taken aback, and Gemma realised that she hadn't been privy to their conversation on the foreshore.

'I know it hasn't been easy between you recently,' Gemma said. 'But she does need to know. Timothy's her dad.'

'Yeah, but I don't want to see her. Can't we wait until we know what's up with Gramps?'

Gemma looked at Phyllida. It was a fair point. While Gemma didn't know what it was like to fall out with a parent, she did know what it was like to fall out with a husband. And right now, if she saw Adam and his pregnant girlfriend walk in, she'd scarper down the corridor in the opposite direction, pretending she'd been called to assist in an emergency. Alternatively, she'd hide behind the vending machine Nick had found. Because there he was returning with four chocolate bars and four bottles of water.

'I wasn't sure what everyone's preferences were so I got a KitKat, a Snickers, a Mars and a Twix. Take your pick. Laila, you go first.'

Laila took the Snickers but left it in her lap. Gemma said she didn't mind, even though her first choice was the Twix. Phyllida shook her head as if she wanted none of it.

'Politeness isn't part of the rules. Go on.' He waggled the bars at Gemma.

She took the Twix. 'Thanks.'

'Phyllida? You have to have one.'

'Well, okay, then.' She sighed and took the Mars.

Nick stared at his lap. He looked sad all of a sudden.

'Are you all right?' Gemma asked.

'Yeah.' He sighed. 'I just had a flashback to the last and only time I've ever called an ambulance. It was when Dad—' He suddenly choked up. 'I'm sorry,' he said.

'It's okay,' Gemma said.

He shot a glance at Laila who was looking at her phone. Then he turned his back on her and, lowering his voice, continued. 'I can't believe how much I miss him. We had a connection, a bond, you know, that I hadn't properly appreciated until he was gone. There wasn't even any warning that he was going to go. It was bam! A heart attack. You can't prepare for that.' He played with the KitKat bar absentmindedly. 'I've even started smoking again. I thought it might make me feel better.'

'Oh, no, you don't want to be doing that,' Phyllida said. 'But is it helping?' Phyllida asked as if she was tempted to accompany her wine with a fag.

'In the moment, but it's a stupid habit, I know.' He glanced back at Laila. 'Anyway, enough about me.'

'Are you all right, Laila?' Gemma asked.

'I'm okay, but hospitals are depressing,' Laila said. 'I can't believe you want to work in a place like this.'

'She wants to make people better,' Phyllida said through a mouthful of caramel chocolate, which made the consonants sound squishy and gooey. Clearly, she did want the Mars. 'The thing is, Laila, we're here for you and Timothy. Why don't we organise a roster of visits for him, assuming he's going to be staying in here for a bit?'

'Even if he doesn't, we could arrange visits and meal drops for him at home,' Gemma offered.

'Excellent idea,' Phyllida exclaimed, waving the water bottle. 'Hang on, I've got a notebook and pen somewhere in my bag. I'll take notes.'

'What do you think, Laila?' Gemma said.

Laila nodded but she still looked as if she might cry again. 'I'm just worried about Gramps in the future.'

'How do you mean?'

'It's his stupid houseboat.'

'I thought you liked it,' Gemma said.

'I do. But he's got *so* much stuff. He likes collecting and hates throwing things out. What if he has another fall and no one's around to help him? Even *I* tripped over his pile of *Antique Collecting* magazines last week and I wasn't even drunk.'

'You drink?' Phyllida asked as if shocked.

'Don't tell anyone,' Laila whispered.

'But you should have said so before!' Phyllida exclaimed. 'I'd have bought you a wine as well.'

'Phyllida!' Nick said.

She snort-laughed.

'Geez, can you drink some more water? Anyway, back to Timothy's houseboat. Is it really as bad as you say, Laila?'

'Yeah, it really is.' She nodded. 'It's hectic.'

'Do you think he's not coping living on his own?' Gemma asked.

'He's fine. He just can't be bothered cleaning and tidying. It was when Grandma died, you know …'

'I get it,' Gemma said. 'Still, it's not ideal.'

'I reckon we should add declutter Timothy's houseboat to the list,' Nick suggested.

'Another good idea!' Phyllida said.

'But he won't like us throwing out his stuff,' Laila said.

'We don't have to throw anything out. Just tidy and rearrange.'

'We certainly don't want to do anything to upset Timothy, do we, Nick?' Gemma added, giving Nick a look that said, *let's try not to rock the boat, okay?*

Nick nodded. 'We only want to help.'

'That's right, we only want to help,' Phyllida repeated gently.

'Do you think we could check absolutely everything so that nothing's a hazard? And maybe we could get him one of those bracelets with an emergency button in case he has another fall?'

'Good idea,' Gemma said. 'Let's make his home as safe as possible.'

'Okay,' Laila agreed. Finally, she opened the Snickers bar. 'I've had enough, now. How long are these people going to take?'

As it happened, it took the length of time that Laila needed to finish eating the chocolate bar before a doctor appeared and called her name.

Laila jumped up and went over to the doctor. They all followed. 'How is he?' she asked.

'He's stable but he has a broken ankle and a badly sprained wrist. He'll need to stay here for a few nights. But his age means—'

'See, I told you.' Laila shot the three of them a look.

'And you are?' The doctor looked questioningly at Nick, Gemma and Phyllida.

Gemma was about to say 'friends' when Laila spoke. 'They're family,' she said assuredly.

Gemma looked at Laila and for a split-second pictured her as Gemma's daughter. Or perhaps a younger sister. Either would have been nice. Nick and Phyllida, thankfully, didn't dispute their pretend familial status, and the doctor nodded.

'Can we see him?' Laila asked.

'I'm afraid he's sedated. I suggest you go home and get a good night's sleep. You can come back in the morning.'

The doctor gave a perfunctory smile before leaving.

'Poor Gramps,' Laila groaned. 'He's going to hate it.'

Gemma didn't like to say that that was probably why he'd been sedated. 'Come on, let's get you home,' she said instead.

Then Laila started crying. 'Is he really going to be all right?

What if something bad happens to him?'

Nick looked as if he was about to put his arm around her before deciding it wasn't appropriate.

'He's in the best place he could be right now,' Gemma said. 'He'll be home before you know it.'

'Give me a hug, right now.' Phyllida, clearly feeling none of Nick's awkwardness, opened her arms wide and pressed Laila to her bosom. 'Everything's going to be just fine. I know it, in my heart.'

A muffled thanks came from the direction of Phyllida's chest.

As they walked to the carpark, Gemma tried to recall the state of the spare bedroom. There was a bed, of course, but it was unmade and covered in random things – ironing that needed doing, the manual to the vacuum cleaner which last week started playing up, and a couple of coats she planned to list on Vinted. Nothing that couldn't be sorted at a moment's notice.

'How about you stay with me tonight?' she suddenly said to Laila. 'I don't think you should be on your own. Or maybe, you'd prefer to be on your own … Either way, the offer's there. You can stay for as long as Timothy's in hospital.'

'There you go again, Gemma, another good idea!' Phyllida said.

'Are you sure?' Laila asked.

'Of course.'

'Well, yeah, thanks.'

Nick looked at Gemma and nodded respectfully. But was it that admirable to offer a bed to a teenager whose guardian had been rushed to hospital? If Gemma was being honest, it was getting a little lonely being in the house on her own.

'Don't you need to get approval from your foster parents?' Nick said.

Laila groaned.

'True,' Gemma agreed. 'And Jodie needs to know what's happened to her father.'

'But what if she says no?' Laila asked.

'I'm sure she won't. I can talk to her.'

'Will you?'

'Yes, of course. I'll explain everything and tell her who I am and all that.' Gemma sounded more confident than she felt. Because did she really want to get involved with a family she knew little about when she was still wrestling with her own parental issues? What if Jodie took umbrage and Gemma inadvertently made Laila's situation worse?

'Thanks, Gemma.' Laila smiled at her appreciatively.

Oh, God, it was too late to back off now.

Chapter 24

'This is full-on. Do you actually live here?' Laila said in astonishment when they walked into Gemma's kitchen. It had taken both Gemma and Nick on speakerphone to convince Jodie to agree to letting Laila stay with her. The tipping point was learning of Gemma's involvement with the club which, Jodie said, Timothy hadn't stopped raving about. The joy on Laila's face made their meddling worth it. 'It's like an archaeological dig and a garden shed combined,' Laila continued. 'I thought nothing could rival Gramps' houseboat.'

Gemma could see how you might think that, what with her kitchen table clustered with stacks of Tupperware containers, the bottle of WD40 for cleaning bits of iron, box of disposable gloves, and muddle of random objects she'd collected from the Thames.

'It would be nice to have a dedicated workroom but as I don't, this table has to be it. Anyway, I only need to keep a small corner free for eating,' she said, even though these days, more often than not, she ate on the sofa.

'I didn't mean to be rude. I kinda like it.'

Laila picked up something from Gemma's small bone collection.

'That's a cow's tooth,' Gemma said. 'They turn black when

they're in the mud for a long time. It was probably from butcher's waste.'

'Eww. And this?'

'The bowl of a clay pipe. Isn't it pretty? The decorative carved theatre curtains mean it was probably sold at a theatre. You wouldn't believe how many pipes there are, especially at the city end of the river. Sometimes, if you're lucky, you can find a teensy bit of original tobacco still stuck at the bottom.'

'Could you smoke it?' Laila's eyes lit up.

'I don't think so.' Gemma laughed. She pulled out a chair and offered Laila a seat. 'Do you want a drink? Tea, coffee?'

Laila sat down. 'I only drink hot chocolate.'

'That's right,' Gemma said. She sometimes forgot how young Laila was and how she may not yet have acquired a taste for tea or coffee. Despite Gemma's love of tea, she decided to join Laila in having a hot chocolate. She pushed aside a pile of mudlarking paraphernalia to clear space at the table for the mugs and a plate of pink wafer biscuits that were probably stale but would have to do.

'Don't tell Timothy that we're overloading ourselves with sugar,' Gemma said.

At the mention of Timothy, Laila's eyes smarted.

'He's going to be just fine,' Gemma said. 'I promise you.'

'But he's going to be so lonely in hospital. He'll hate it.'

'We'll visit him, like Nick said. In fact, why don't I message everyone and organise to go tomorrow? We could bring in a mudlarking find to talk about. He might like that.' Without waiting for Laila to answer, she messaged The Mudlarkers' Club on WhatsApp.

Laila sipped the hot chocolate and looked over some of Gemma's other found objects.

'So what's happening about school?' Gemma asked. 'Can you take some days off?'

'It's still the holidays.'

'Oh, right.' Gemma had forgotten how long summer holidays

used to be. 'When do you go back?'

'The beginning of September. I'll probably go next term.'

'Probably?'

'Don't you start,' Laila grumbled.

'I only want to understand.'

'Well, school's been hard. I'm not good at reading and writing. That's why I started skipping lessons. At first it was just the ones I didn't like but then whole days. Gramps got me dispensation to stay home for a couple of weeks for mental health reasons. Not that I have a mental health problem. Apparently, my "problem" …' Laila mimed inverted commas '… is dyslexia. I mean why label those who can't spell with a name *no one* can spell. It should just be an emoji. I could draw that, easy.'

'You could! Why don't you design one?'

'Yeah, maybe … I really want to go to art school, but Jodie wants me to do hairdressing.' Laila pretended to vomit. 'Just because I like changing my hair every month.'

'Jodie only wants what's best for you. I guess she thinks hairdressing is a reliable job.'

'Yeah, yeah, I've heard it all before. But it's not a passion. Anyway, who wants to touch other people's hair every day?'

'You've just been fiddling with a three-hundred-year-old wig curler that may have styled a wig made from the hair of dead plague victims,' Gemma said, pointing at it with a wafer biscuit that really was very stale.

'You're making that up.' Laila rocked back in her chair as if to avoid catching something contagious.

'No, I'm not.' Gemma shook her head. 'Cheap wigs were made from animal hair but expensive ones from human.'

'People paid *more* for human hair?'

'It's the same today. Many of my patients get wigs. Some, a selection. Anything to make going through a terrible time a little more dignified. But now synthetic fibre wigs are cheaper, more lightweight and easier to style than those made from human hair.'

Laila made another face. Perhaps Gemma shouldn't have referred to the realities of chemotherapy. But wasn't it good for kids to have some awareness of the struggles people can face?

'You might find that having had a break from school will make going back easier,' Gemma said.

'Or harder.'

'Do you want to get your A-levels?'

'I guess.' Laila sighed.

'I'm sure you can get help for the dyslexia.'

'Whatever.' Laila waved her hands chaotically as if it was all getting too much. 'Why do we have to keep talking about me? You're trying to find out stuff about your past which is real-life personal mudlarking. That's so interesting.'

'Yeah,' Gemma said unconvincingly.

'What?'

'It's daunting, that's all. Sometimes I wonder if I shouldn't just let things lie.'

'I get it. I used to ask Mum about our Pakistani heritage but she'd never talk about it. It was like, because her parents disowned her, she disowned them and everything to do with them.'

'Maybe one day you'll be able to find out.'

'Dunno. What bothered me more than that was eventually learning about her drug habit and the consequences of it. Unfortunately, it's not all happy shit in your social services file.'

'Huh,' Gemma said, staring into the chocolate sludge at the bottom of her mug.

'Sorry, I shouldn't have said that,' Laila said quickly. 'Look on the bright side, you could find out that your birth mother is an amazing person and that you have a sister. I always wanted a sister,' she added, as if trying to make Gemma feel better.

'Me too,' Gemma agreed.

'So there, don't listen to me. Go and find her.'

'Maybe. Anyway, before I forget, I should give you a key because I'll be out at work every day. You also might want to bring a few of your things over from the houseboat.'

'Thanks, Gemma. I'm happy to sleep on the sofa.'

'Don't be silly. I've got a spare bed somewhere underneath the junk upstairs.' Gemma gestured to the ceiling.

'You haven't seen Gramps' houseboat. I'm used to sleeping surrounded by junk,' Laila said, as though she's had to accept that mess is an indisputable part of life.

Chapter 25

Whenever Gemma visited another hospital, she found it hard not to slip into nursing mode. She was overcome with an overwhelming urge to read the patient's chart at the end of the bed, check their vitals, administer pain relief. Seeing Timothy with his arm in a sling and his leg in a cast, raised on pillows, looking pale and spent, made Gemma want to swing into action, even if orthopaedics wasn't her area of expertise. It was the heavy picnic basket she was carrying that reminded her she was now off duty. That, and seeing Timothy overjoyed to have the members of The Mudlarkers' Club crowd around his bed.

'Look at this! How nice of you all to be here.' Timothy's grin was so wide it looked as though it might split his face in two.

'Don't tell the nurse,' Gemma whispered to Timothy. 'But we've got wine and cheese. Not too much wine, though, for you, given the pain medication you're probably on.'

'Go, Gemma.' Nick gave her a small, silent clap, which could have been interpreted as gently mocking, but given he was looking at her admirably again, perhaps he wasn't.

'A great initiative from Gemma,' Phyllida said, as if Gemma had thought completely out of the box. 'And I've made chocolate brownies!' she added.

'It's only the usual stuff you bring patients,' Gemma said, winking.

'Wine? I love it. Anyway, you're a nurse. You can apply for dispensation,' said Nick.

Timothy started laughing, then winced.

'Careful,' Nick said.

'It's only a couple of bruised ribs. Nothing a bit of jollity won't aggravate, or a dribble of wine won't ease.' Gemma could tell Timothy was trying to be stoic even though he was in pain.

'Come on, Laila,' Phyllida said, and off they went to find three more chairs to add to the one that was next to the bedside table.

'How are you doing?' Nick asked, gently touching Timothy's shoulder.

'Much better now that you're here. The food is horrendous and the noise incessant, but hey-ho.'

'You'll be out in no time,' Gemma said, setting up a wine and cheese station on Timothy's meal tray.

'You brought Wensleydale! My favourite.'

'A little bird told me.' Gemma cut him a slice and put it on a cracker.

'I must thank you for being so good to Laila,' Timothy said.

'It's not a bother. It's nice having her around. She can stay as long as she likes.'

Gemma poured wine into the blue plastic picnic cups she'd not used since last summer. She'd forgotten how much they reminded her of when Adam proposed on a windy beach in Cornwall, and sand had stuck to their rims like salt on a glass of margarita. Hopefully, after tonight she'll have made a new memory with them.

'Right, we're ready!' Phyllida and Laila returned with chairs which they positioned either side of Timothy's bed. 'The nurse wasn't too pleased, but I told her a patient's mental health is as important as their physical. She couldn't disagree with that. How's everyone?' Phyllida ran the sentences together as if she no longer had time for pauses or full stops.

Like Gemma, the others must have assumed her question was rhetorical because no one answered. Then Phyllida's phone announced an incoming text. She read it, frowned and looked across to the curtains as if trying very hard to see through them.

'I think mobiles are supposed to be turned off,' Timothy said. 'Or at least in aeroplane mode – whatever that means. Apart from reminding us that we're as far away from being on an aeroplane as we could be.'

'Suits me,' Phyllida said, turning off her phone.

'Everything okay, Phyll?' Nick asked.

'Just my bloody husband,' she snapped, throwing the phone into her handbag.

'Did your son get his passport sorted?' Gemma asked.

'Yes, but he had to delay his trip. It's all fine now, though and he's off on his travels.' Then, her face brightened and she pulled out a green-glass bottle from another bag at her feet.

'Well, look at that,' Timothy said.

'Isn't it marvellous? I believe it's a medicine bottle from the nineteen-forties, the type you can easily pick up from an antique shop. And before I forget, I brought this in. The fishing hook you found, Timothy.'

'Did I find that?'

'It was by your hand when you fell.'

'I'd completely forgotten. Perhaps you could look after it for me. I don't think the nurses would appreciate me harbouring all that rust in here.'

'Of course.'

'Do you want to see what I brought in?' Nick held up a single domino. 'I found this yesterday, too.'

'There could be other dominoes where that came from. You should go back and see if the mud has revealed any more.'

'Yeah, I could. Do you want to know where I found it? I can tell you the exact spot because afterwards I had a rest on a large rock nearby—'

'Ssh.' Phyllida put a finger to her lips. 'You can't tell us. A find spot is secret only to that mudlarker.'

'But you were all with me. Kind of.'

'It doesn't matter.'

'Well, sure, but it does seem a bit silly.'

'It's just a thing, Nick,' said Phyllida.

'Okay, whatever,' he said and passed the domino to his left so everyone could get a close-up look.

'Do you know anything about it?' Laila asked.

Nick shook his head. 'I'm guessing it was from a game played by sailors and it had fallen overboard.'

'If money had been involved, they would have done it secretly, because seamen weren't allowed to gamble,' Timothy said. 'It's probably handmade, too.'

'You're like the walking Internet,' said Nick.

'Happy to be anything but injured,' Timothy said, then cocked his head in the direction of the wine and waggled his empty glass.

Reluctantly, Gemma gave him a little more wine, given he hadn't had an adverse reaction, and Laila reached over to adjust his pillows, which only proved that nursing didn't always have to involve medical intervention. He closed his eyes and let his body sink deeper into the bed. Then, he opened them again and said, 'What have you got, Gemma? Anything interesting?'

'I decided to bring in something I discovered a while ago which I thought you, in particular, Timothy, would like.' Gemma held up a bullet casing and gave it to him.

'Ah, yes,' he said. 'A .303. The type of rifle round that was used in both world wars, as well as in aircraft machine guns like the Spitfire. Have I told you that over the years I've found musket balls, lead bullets and even a bomb?'

Gemma smiled. Getting Timothy engrossed in the past and distracted from his present, was exactly what she'd hoped this get together and the bullet would do.

'Tell them your story, Gramps,' Laila said. 'The one about the bomb.'

Timothy thought for a moment before beginning. 'I was on the foreshore one day, minding my own business. I won't tell you exactly where …' He winked at Phyllida. 'When I spotted something in the rubble. It looked like a large stone. Except it was too spherical and cone-like to have come from Mother Nature. I went to inspect it. What happened next, happened so quickly I had no time to stop it.

'You see, as I was going over to the stone, I tripped on a bit of wood. I know, I know, I'm rather clumsy. The next minute my top dentures – I've had them for years – flew out in the direction of the stone. Only it wasn't a stone. At that very moment, I determined it was a World War Two bomb.'

Nick's mouth dropped open. 'Really?'

'Potentially unexploded.'

'Wow.'

'I dived for cover – not that there was any around – just as the dentures hit the bomb and I thought, this is it, there's going to be an explosion.' He paused and took a sip of wine.

'And?' Nick was practically on the edge of his chair in anticipation.

'Well, naturally, it didn't, because I'm still here.' Timothy appeared chuffed at the success of his agility. 'No casualties, only grazed knees and a muddy face.'

'And a bomb that needed to see the dentist.' Laila giggled.

'Don't make me laugh!'

'Goodness, Timothy, you were very lucky,' Phyllida said.

'Did that really happen?' Nick asked suspiciously.

Timothy smiled. 'Ah, we have a journalist in our midst.'

'It's just, dentures landing on a bomb …?'

'Well, all right, I may have exaggerated how far they flew, but they did come out and there was a bomb. The point is, there's more ammunition lurking in the Thames than you'd like to imagine.'

'What happened to the bomb, then?' Nick asked.

'Once I realised that the thing hadn't gone off, I called the police. I knew they'd want to get a bomb disposal team to defuse it. Just because it hadn't exploded then, didn't mean it wouldn't at another time. A simple fall or misstep could have easily set it off.'

'But your dentures?' Phyllida pressed a hand to her chest in expectation.

'Exactly. It's not easy talking with no top teeth. I had to repeat myself several times.'

Laila chuckled again.

'My ribs!' Timothy said.

'I mean, did you get them back?'

'I took them home to be disinfected. Dentures are expensive, you know. But before I went, I got a photo with the bomb and the disposal squad. Needless to say, I didn't smile.'

'Whoever said mudlarking was boring?' Phyllida said.

Instinctively, they all turned to Laila.

'Don't look at me! I get it,' she said.

'Have you brought in anything, Laila?'

'I was going to bring in a piece of ceramic but Gramps has seen tons of them so I left it at home.'

'Is there anything you'd like to share with us instead?'

There was a whiff of self-help group about Phyllida's questioning, which Gemma wasn't sure Laila would embrace.

Except Laila surprised her and said yes, producing a sketch of the scene by the Thames that Gemma had seen her draw yesterday. 'I did this for you, Gramps.'

'Well, how about that!' Timothy exclaimed.

'If you can't come to the river, the river can come to you,' Gemma said.

'It's beautiful.' Nick nodded.

For a moment they admired Laila's drawing, until Phyllida broke the silence.

'Now that the cheese has been decimated, anyone want a

brownie?'

Finally. Gemma had been eyeing them up for ages. Everyone took a piece except for Phyllida. She was looking at her phone again, hoping no one would notice.

But Nick did. He may have had highly tuned observational skills but he also seemed to have a genuine caring side. 'All okay, Phyll? No more dramas?' he asked.

'Ha!' Phyllida scoffed ambiguously. She slipped her phone into her bag and brushed down her skirt as if it needed de-creasing.

'Kids don't always want to cause trouble, you know,' Timothy said, which meant he'd either jumped to conclusions about what was happening in Phyllida's personal life or he wanted to take the opportunity to endorse his foster granddaughter.

Heads turned to Laila, who looked down at her lap, embarrassed.

'Life's complicated and it can be a challenge,' he continued.

'It certainly can,' Phyllida said ruefully. 'I used to think that sometimes you were better off ignoring things, except they always find you eventually.'

Gemma swallowed. It was like Phyllida was talking about her.

'I'd agree with that,' Nick said.

'They *really* do.' Phyllida nodded.

Then it occurred to Gemma. Although Phyllida seemed to be skirting around her issues, unwilling to open up about them, *she* needn't do so. What good were a group of friends if you couldn't get their advice?

'So, um …' Gemma said softly.

'What is it?' Phyllida asked.

'Can I canvas something with you all? It's not strictly to do with mudlarking but it is about searching for something.'

'Go for it.' Nick said.

'It's about a find, as I said,' Gemma began, unsure how to set the scene. 'Something that I don't know whether I *will* find, or if I really *want* to find. Well, no, I *do* want to find it. At least, I think I do.'

After this confusing introduction, Gemma told them what she'd discovered about her birth mother and how she was having second thoughts about requesting her social services file. She was worried about what she might learn – where she came from and who she was – things she may end up wishing she didn't know. 'It's not as if I dislike my adoptive family,' she explained. 'Far from it. They *are* my family. I don't even think of myself as adopted.'

'What are you wanting to find out?' Nick asked.

'I want to learn my story. At the very least, to find my birth mother.'

'That's like digging up the whole of the Thames,' said Phyllida.

'Which is what scares me. What if I uncover a whole lot of stuff I don't like?'

'You don't have to like it,' Timothy said. 'When we find a manky old sole of a shoe or a dirty bit of ceramic, we don't have to love it, but merely appreciate where it came from and what it can teach us.'

'Yeah, but once you know something, you can't unknow it,' Laila said, with the sagacity of a middle-aged woman.

'That's it,' Gemma agreed.

'Laila,' Timothy chided.

'I'm only trying to protect Gemma from finding out something she doesn't want to know. Anyway, she knows I think she should do it.'

'Thank you for your honesty, Laila,' Gemma said.

'It sounds like you want to know more,' said Nick. 'So, I reckon, go for it.'

Gemma nodded.

'All in agreement, say aye.' Nick winked at Phyllida.

The response was four very definite ayes.

The meeting really was turning into a self-help group, yet Gemma found she wasn't ready to bring it to an end.

'I guess, I'd better do it then,' Gemma declared.

Chapter 26

When a nurse came around to tell the group that visiting hours were up, poor Timothy didn't want them to go. But they promised to keep to the visiting roster to help break up the monotony.

'You're too kind,' he said.

'And I'll be here every day, so long as you-know-who isn't,' Laila said, kissing him on the forehead.

'Be nice to Gemma, won't you?'

'Duh.'

'Do you need us to get anything for you?' Gemma asked.

'No, thank you. As soon as Jodie heard about me, she dropped by yesterday with some of my things.'

'Well, hang in there, Timbo,' Nick said.

'I'll try.' He smiled wanly and raised a hand in farewell.

'Timbo?' Gemma repeated as they left the ward.

'Don't knock a nickname that's meant as a term of endearment,' Nick said. 'It's good for the soul.'

'Whose soul?' Gemma laughed.

'The recipient's, of course.'

At the lift to the carpark, they said farewell to Phyllida, and Gemma, Nick and Laila took the exit at the main entrance.

'I'm going to meet a friend now,' Laila said when they were

outside.

Gemma had wondered why Laila was wearing a skirt so short it should have been shorts.

'What friend?' Gemma asked.

'A friend-friend.'

Did that mean a friend-friend who was a best friend or a maybe-boyfriend? Gemma decided not to ask. It was probably more important that she knew where she was going. Laila disagreed.

'You're not my mum,' she said.

'I know I'm not. But you're in my care.'

'Fine. I'm going to the pub.'

'You're underage.'

'My friend isn't.'

'Is that supposed to make me feel better?'

'Dunno. That's my bus. Bye!' Laila ran across the road as the bus approached.

Gemma hoped Laila had remembered to take a key. Maybe she should text her. Or maybe she shouldn't. She sighed noisily.

Nick laughed. 'Do you still want kids?'

'How do you know I ever wanted them?' Gemma turned to look at him.

'You said so once.'

'Did I?' Gemma couldn't remember.

'I'm pretty sure you did. Hey, what are you doing now? Do you want a drink?' Before Gemma could clarify what sort of drink scenario he was contemplating, he quickly elaborated. 'My editor wants me to write a companion piece on mudlarking to go with the feature story I'm doing on the archaeological dig. I was wondering if I could ask you some questions.'

'Oh, right,' Gemma said with obvious relief, because what if he'd had other ideas? She was far from ready for any of that.

'Don't worry.' He laughed. 'I wasn't trying to ask you out. I've got a girlfriend, remember.'

'That doesn't stop some people.'

'Well, *I'm* not like that. The thought just came to me and I've got nothing to go home to.'

'What about your girlfriend?'

'She's away at a uni reunion. If we did it now, then I wouldn't have to bother you during the week. Your work must be full-on and I doubt you'll want me hassling you in the evening.'

Gemma thought about how she had nothing to rush home to either, especially with Laila going out. What's more, she did love talking about mudlarking and couldn't deny that Nick was fun to hang around with. 'Sure. Why not?' she said.

'Excellent!' Nick said. 'There's a great pub about five minutes away.'

They chatted on the way there and then found a table at the front whose window was filled with orange and pink summer flowers, so vibrant and flawless they didn't look real.

'I'm getting this,' Nick said and, before Gemma could protest, he added, 'I can claim it from the paper so don't feel like you're going to be indebted to me or anything.'

Gemma nodded and realised, as Nick went to the bar, that this was the first time she'd been out on her own with a guy since Adam had left. Even though Nick had said this wasn't a date, it was for professional purposes, it still felt strange. It also brought *el cabrón* to mind. She'd decided not to contact him about anything to do with their break-up, knowing it would only be a matter of time before he got in touch with a checklist of what needed to be done. Even if she now no longer wanted to be with him, she'd make him work for what he desired. She knew that when the divorce was eventually finalised, she would still mourn the end of them as a unit and everything that came with it.

'Here we go.' Nick returned with their drinks and a packet of nuts. She quickly pushed Adam from her thoughts. 'I don't have a pen and paper with me so are you okay if I record this?'

'That makes it sound serious.'

'Don't worry, it's not a long piece. Only for a break-out box.'

'There are far more experienced people you could be talking to, you know.'

'It's not about the experts,' Nick said. 'It's about enthusiastic amateurs. Let's begin with the mud in mudlarking. There's more to it than meets the eye, isn't there?'

It turned out Gemma knew more about mud than even she realised. She told him about tidal mud, historical mud, dry shingle and sand. The more she talked – and the more she drank – the more animated and talkative she became. Soon, she noticed that Nick's eyes had turned glassy, and he was fiddling with the as yet unopened packet of nuts.

'Sorry, am I boring you?' she said apologetically.

'Not at all. It's just I've got a six-hundred-word limit. Why don't you tell me how you got started?'

Gemma opened her mouth to begin.

'Succinctly, if you can,' he interrupted. 'Like an elevator pitch.'

Gemma's explanation ended up being more like two lift rides, with stops on every floor. Nick then wanted to know about her favourite find, which was hard to narrow down, but she decided on the sixteenth-century louse comb she found last year, with mummified lice stuck to it.

'Everyone had lice back in the day,' she explained. 'It was no big deal. If you were a knight in medieval times and wanted to impress a lady, you gave her a louse comb.'

'I'll keep that in mind.' He smiled.

She blushed. How silly! 'Sorry, if I rabbited on. I'm turning into one of those lonely people who as soon as they get any opportunity, won't stop talking.'

He laughed. Then, more seriously, he said, 'I'm sure it's been tough with your marriage and all that.'

Gemma nodded. 'It was hard enough accepting it was over but then to find out that he and his thing-on-the-side are expecting a baby when we haven't been separated long … That was a punch in the gut.'

'Ouch,' he said. 'I guess the girlfriend's not on the side anymore.'

'She's now the main course.'

Nick pulled a face in sympathy.

For the first time, she properly noticed Nick's eyes. How attractive they were, like clear-cut pale-blue stones from a piece of Victorian jewellery. Fearing she'd blush again, she stood up. 'Okay, well, I'd better be off. I suppose I should be the responsible guardian.'

'Ha-ha, yes,' Nick said. Then, 'Actually, I've just had another idea. Why don't we get a photo of you in all your mudlarking gear down by the Thames?' He gestured in completely the wrong direction of the river.

'A photo?'

'I don't mean now but with a professional. I think it would liven up the piece. I mean, it's lively already, of course,' Nick added hurriedly. 'It'll just make it livelier. Especially with your pink boots and yellow gloves.'

'Really?' Gemma asked, not because she was doubting the liveliness of her accessories, but whether it was a good idea for her to be photographed. She never liked being the centre of any sort of attention.

'Absolutely. I'll suggest it to my editor.'

Chapter 27

When Gemma got home from work the next day, Laila was in the kitchen ferociously dicing red pepper as if she was unaware of the dangers of knives.

'I'm making an omelette,' she said.

'Really? How lovely,' Gemma said. To think that it had been months since someone had cooked her a meal ... 'Hey, I've got you a present.' She took out the grocery items she'd bought during her lunch break.

'What for?'

'Doing dinner.'

Laila frowned as if trying to remember whether she'd told Gemma earlier that she would cook. She hadn't.

Gemma handed her a large tub of Nutella, then she put the milk, apples and yoghurt into the fridge.

'You remembered,' Laila said. 'Thanks.'

They sat at the table and ate Laila's omelette, which was delicious, if not a little heavy on the cheese. But Gemma wasn't going to nit-pick. For the first time in several weeks, she was reminded of what being fully relaxed in your own home felt like. As though an hour before, she'd treated herself to a massage.

'I really appreciated that, thank you, Laila.'

'My turn on the dishes, too,' Laila said.

Gemma wasn't about to argue. 'Did you see Timothy?'

Laila stood up and gathered together the dirty dishes. 'Yeah.'

'Is he all right?'

'He's okay.' Laila looked down at her scuffed black boots that seemed more suited to mid-winter snowy Balkan conditions than an unusually balmy London summer. 'I passed Jodie in the corridor.'

'Oh, gosh, how was that?'

'Awkward.' Laila made a racket rinsing the cutlery and plates. 'She said you don't need to meet her. She trusts Gramps' endorsement of you.'

'That's great. Did you talk about anything else?'

'I told her I was fine and that she didn't need to worry.'

'That's all a parent ever wants, I reckon.' Then Gemma changed the subject. 'Do you like *Love Island*? I know it's mindless but sometimes that's what I need after a day's work.'

'It's okay,' Laila said as if she needed to pretend to like it for Gemma's sake when she really didn't. 'I've got another idea. I could help you.' Laila's eyes shone like the crystal in her nose piercing.

'What do you mean?'

'I could help you find out more about your birth mother.'

'You don't have to do that.' Gemma was taken aback by the girl's interest and keenness.

'I like finding stuff out.'

'Well, I mean …'

'You are going to do it, aren't you? You got four yeses from the club. You wouldn't want to let everyone down …'

Gemma laughed. 'You're really putting the heat on.'

'Yeah, you're right. Why would you want me helping you?'

'Oh, I didn't mean it like that!'

'Well, wouldn't it be better than doing it on your own? And if you discover things you don't like, I'll be here to make you a hot chocolate.'

Gemma's heart melted. 'You're so sweet.'

'No one's ever called me *that* before.' Laila pulled an expression of disdain.

Gemma smiled.

'So?' Laila asked.

'Well, only if you really want to—'

'Of course, I want to do family-larking with you. Where do we start?'

'You mean *now*?'

'Duh.'

Gemma moved a dining chair next to her desk chair and turned on her laptop.

'It's funny,' Gemma said. 'Ever since I learnt a little more about my birth mother, I've become hyperaware of what I do and how I do it. Like, does my biological mother walk around the house when she's cleaning her teeth? Does she twirl her hair when she feels excited or on edge? And what would I say if we ever met? Would I call her Mum? Or should I call her Claire? Or would I be so nervous that I wouldn't be able to speak at all?'

'The only way to know is to find her,' Laila said.

Gemma nodded. It seemed a little strange getting reassurance from a seventeen-year-old but, as Gemma was finding out, life could sometimes be a little strange.

'It's okay, you've got me here, remember?' Laila said. 'So, what do you need to do?'

'Now that I've got my original birth certificate, the next step is to apply for my social services file which will, hopefully, have all the information that was known at the time about my birth parents and my life before the adoption.'

'Okay, let's do it.'

'It's just a form.' Suddenly, Gemma felt foolish for admitting that she hadn't been able to even do that.

'I hate filling out forms,' Laila said. 'Don't do it too quickly, that's what Gramps says, otherwise you could make a mistake.'

Gemma found the form she'd previously bookmarked. She read through the information that was needed, even though she knew it already. Her mouth went dry.

'When Gramps said don't do it quickly, he meant don't fill it in too fast, not spend all evening wondering whether to complete it in the first place.' Laila spoke so matter-of-factly that it made Gemma laugh.

'I'm being serious,' Laila said.

'I know you are. I'm just nervous.'

'I get it. Now, do it.'

'Okay, okay.' Gemma took another deep breath and started typing.

'Now press "submit",' Laila said when she'd finished.

Gemma pressed submit and let out the longest breath she'd ever exhaled. Laila gave her a high-five, then got up to make hot chocolates.

For a moment, Gemma sat there taking in what she'd just done. Her mudlarking friends were right. Surely it was better to have some information than none at all, and what she did with it could always be decided later.

From the kitchen, she heard her phone ping with a text.

'It's Nick,' Laila called out.

'Are you reading my messages?' Gemma put her laptop to sleep and left the study.

'He wants to go on a mudlark. Just the two of you,' Laila cooed teasingly.

'Laila!'

'It's true.'

Gemma swiped her phone from the table and read the message.

'See,' Laila said. 'I think he likes you.' She stirred the hot chocolates and gave one to Gemma.

'No, he doesn't.'

'Yes, he does.'

'He wants to learn more about mudlarking and doesn't know when we'll next be going out in a group, now that Timothy's in hospital.'

Laila smiled as if she couldn't care less about Gemma's excuse.

Gemma went over to the tide chart on the fridge. The next low tide options suitable for her were going to be during the late afternoons of the following weekend. Nick said the sooner the better for him, which realistically meant Saturday. It wasn't like she had anything else on, plus Nick was fun to spend time with and, unlike with her girlfriends, a child-free conversation was guaranteed. Why not?

'Are you going to go?' Laila asked.

Gemma didn't answer but sent a reply to Nick.

'You *so* are.' Laila smiled.

Just as Gemma put her phone down, it went off again. This time, in unison with Laila's. Phyllida had sent them a friendly reminder (her words) about the hospital roster for Timothy. She also included suggestions for treats they could bring in for him so they didn't double up. Laila had to tell her that she'd already given him grapes which meant Nick would have to choose another fruit. Phyllida suggested strawberries because they've been 'delish this season' and Nick replied with a military salute emoji which made Gemma and Laila giggle.

Chapter 28

Gemma waited for Nick at their agreed meeting spot at the top of the foreshore steps at Bankside. A man in an oversized coat was sitting on a large foundation post on the beach feeding a group of pigeons. He seemed unaware of anyone or anything around him other than the birds. They too were focused solely and eagerly on him and his bread. After a good fifteen minutes, Gemma wondered if Nick was going to show up. He hadn't even messaged.

She was about to call him when she spotted him jogging towards her. 'Sorry, I'm late,' he said panting. 'The trains were delayed.'

'Don't worry,' she said. 'How have you been?'

He took a moment to get his breath back, then sighed. 'Pretty crap, to be honest. But I don't want to ruin the afternoon. You've no idea how much I need this mudlark. Well, actually, you probably have.'

'You're being very cryptic.'

'If you really want to know, Ella and I had an argument – a doozy of an argument – and we've broken up.'

'Oh, no, Nick, I'm so sorry.'

'It's all turned to … well, you know …' He gazed out at the

Thames.

'You could have cancelled. I wouldn't have minded.'

'No! I suggested this mudlark to try and make me feel better.'

'When Adam left, the first thing I did was go down to the river.'

'I knew you'd understand.'

'Come on, let's sit for a minute.' Gemma gestured to the concrete bench overlooking the river. 'Tell me what happened.'

He sat and rolled his shoulders as if his explanation was going to be like doing a workout.

'Okay, so we were clearing out a few things from the house to put out in the household rubbish collection that we'd booked. Ella tried *again* to get rid of Dad's metal detector, but I wasn't having a bar of it. I don't care if it no longer works, you know? Then, out of the blue, she asked me if I was going to marry her. It caught me off-guard and I hesitated for a second. When I didn't answer straight away, she threw her arms in the air and shouted, "Well, what's the point, then?" I couldn't believe it. One minute, we were having a giggle trying to wrangle the broken clothes rack, which wouldn't stay together, and the next she's talking marriage and furious with me.

'Then, before I could properly answer, she stormed out. I ran after her but she refused to talk to me. She just left the house *and* she took Darryl. That's when I knew it wasn't good. I tried calling her so we could discuss it, but she wouldn't answer. Then all she did was send a text, saying it's over.' He looked away.

'I'm so sorry, Nick.'

He leant on his knees and put his head in his hands. 'I didn't mean for it to be over. Not like this.'

'Maybe it isn't though. Maybe it's just a blip, and she said those things in the heat of the moment,' Gemma offered.

'I don't think so. Ella isn't one for histrionics. But it was like she'd suddenly decided that it was marriage or nothing. That she was no longer happy with the status quo but didn't seem to feel the need to discuss it with me.'

He unzipped his rucksack and pulled out two cans of beer. 'These were meant to be for later, once we'd earned them, but I don't think I can wait.' He handed Gemma one. She smiled sympathetically and took it.

'I keep going over why I wasn't able to say without hesitation that I'd marry her. Does it mean that I'm not on the same bandwidth as her, as Phyllida likes to say? Or does it just mean I didn't want to at that moment but I will sometime in the future?'

'Only you'll be able to answer that,' Gemma said. 'You're in shock. Give it time.'

'Maybe I was taking her for granted.'

'Or maybe she was taking you for granted?'

'Huh,' he said thoughtfully and took a slug of beer.

'If it makes you feel better, I think that was me in my marriage. I didn't want to acknowledge that things may not have been right, or that Adam wasn't the man I thought I'd married. I never for one moment thought he'd cheat or that the marriage would end. I guess no one wants to think those things are going to happen.'

'Thanks, Gem.' He tapped his beer can against hers. Then he reached deep into his rucksack and pulled out a packet of cigarettes. 'I don't normally smoke, honestly, but extenuating circumstances, right?'

'I don't mind,' Gemma lied, but now wasn't the time to remind him of its dangers.

'Aren't we a couple of sad sacks? Still, it's nice to be able to talk about it properly with someone who gets it. I told a couple of close mates but even though they were sympathetic, I don't think they quite got it. One of them has been with his partner since he was sixteen and the other has only ever done the dumping, so hasn't experienced that kind of rejection.'

'You chose the wrong friends to tell by the sound of it,' Gemma said.

Nick thought for a moment, as if he was still trying to digest it all. 'I mean, we had discussed marriage before,' he said, like he was talking more to himself. 'And even though I knew she fancied getting married, I thought she felt like I did: that it would be a nice thing to do but not essential in the bigger scheme of things. Because weddings are expensive, you know, and you can still commit to each other without making a big fuss about it, can't you?'

'Sure,' Gemma said.

'And she didn't even let me explain. I was given an ultimatum out of the blue, without any indication that it was going to be a deal-breaker. In an instant our relationship imploded. Then there's Darryl. I love that dog. Now I don't know if I'll ever see him again.' Nick stared into the small hole of his beer can.

Gemma put a hand on his knee.

'Thanks,' he muttered, then downed the rest of his beer.

'If you ask me, she's the one missing out.'

Nick gave her an appreciative smile. 'I'm not fishing for compliments but thank you.'

'Trust me, I know what you're going through. It's really confusing when your status quo is turned on its head. It makes you revisit stuff, to try and work out why things changed, what you might have missed, whether the rejection would have happened if you had acted or said something differently.' Gemma was surprised by how much wiser she'd become.

'Yeah,' Nick agreed. 'I can't stop rewinding our whole relationship. Like it's on a continuous loop in my head and no other thoughts are allowed in.'

'I suppose we're meant to learn something from it, aren't we?'

'Like turn your failure into success?'

'Something like that.'

A tour group coming from the Tate Modern paused in front of them, then moved on.

Nick stubbed out his cigarette and dropped it into his beer can. 'I feel so guilty for not rushing to propose to her, even if it wasn't what I wanted. I hated seeing the disappointment on her face. That I'd been responsible for her whole world falling apart.'

'That must have been hard. But you've also got to be true to yourself. That's what I keep telling myself about Adam. He was only trying to be true to himself, even if he did go about it the wrong way.'

'That's decent of you. You should have a side hustle as a shrink.'

Gemma laughed ruefully. 'I've just had longer to analyse my relationship break-up than you have.'

'Sorry to burden you with my personal life.'

'It's okay. It's good to talk about it. If it really is over – and once you get used to the idea – you can reframe the future. You never know, it might turn out better than you think.'

'Is that what you thought when Adam left?'

'No! I'm all talk and no action. To be honest, I still don't want to think about the future,' Gemma admitted.

'And I thought you were giving me sound advice.' Nick laughed.

'You picked the short straw with me, then.' Gemma reached into her bag for her hat. The sun was making a lengthy appearance.

'I guess you're only good for mudlarking tips.'

'And you're only good for beers. Do you have any more?'

He shook his head. 'Sorry.'

'I take back my last compliment.'

'Fair call,' he said. 'Do you think we should actually do some mudlarking?'

'Absolutely.' Gemma nodded.

Nick crushed his empty beer can and, with spontaneous recklessness, threw it over the edge behind him.

'Nick!'

'It can be our first find.'

'You could have hit someone.'

He turned and looked down. 'But I didn't.' He grinned.

Gemma stood up and reached for her rucksack but something fell out of the side pocket. She hurried to pick it up.

'What's that?' Nick asked.

'I thought it would cheer you up but now I feel bad.'

'You bought me something?'

Sheepishly, she showed him the can of gold spray. 'It was meant to be for your metal detector, to immortalise your dad.'

'That's *so* thoughtful,' he said, as if she'd given him a box of mementos from his father's past that he never knew existed.

'Except your girlfriend tried to get rid of it and you've broken up with her, and I've just made it worse.'

'No, you haven't. You were being kind.'

'You don't have to have it.' Gemma went to put the can back in her bag. 'Anyway, I reckon you should think of mudlarking like you're doing it for your dad. That because a little piece of him is in you, he's kind of still here. That way, it doesn't really matter if you don't have the metal detector, does it?'

'I like that.' He nodded. Then, 'I guess I could spray the trowel like you suggested the other day?'

'You could,' Gemma agreed. 'But seriously, you don't have to.'

'No, I want to. I think it'd be funny.' He gestured for her to hand over the spray.

'Well, okay.' She gave it to him.

'Come on, I'll race you to the beer can!' he suddenly shouted.

They disturbed a couple of pigeons as they sprinted down the steps. The bird man had wandered off and a couple of other mudlarkers were foraging further west down the river. Nick got to it first.

'If I find nothing else, I've always got this,' he said, putting the can in his rucksack. He pulled on his gloves and scanned the foreshore. 'Are you ever disappointed when you come out here?'

'Never,' Gemma replied. 'You'll always find something, even if it's just that wonderful feeling of being in nature. It's never the same. The river, the mud, the clouds, the sky, the finds … they're always different.'

He nodded and immediately started mudlarking – or what Gemma believed he thought was mudlarking – except he wasn't doing it right.

'Hang on,' she said.

'What?'

'You're moving your head too quickly. You might be missing your metal detector, but your head isn't one.'

'Okay.' Nick laughed.

'And you need to let your mind roam free. Don't force yourself to find something in particular. Put aside your desires and ego. Observe slowly and be inquisitive. It's all here and what the tide wants you to discover today, you will.'

'Hey, that sounded good.'

'It's really about believing in the importance of the past. You either love unearthing history, or you don't. Like some people enjoy extreme ironing and some don't.'

'Extreme ironing?'

'I saw it on YouTube once.'

'When I got Dad's detector, I watched a YouTube video on how it's done. You gotta go low and slow, the guy said.' Nick extended his right arm and moved it left and right, like it was a detector.

Without warning, he started beeping as if he were a cardiac machine in A&E. Or R2D2 having a meltdown. How good it felt to have a laugh.

'Okay, let's do it.' Nick immediately dropped to the ground. Anyone watching would have thought a hand grenade had been thrown. He looked up at her. 'Please join me. I feel silly down here on my own. I promise not to make any more loud noises.'

As the late afternoon sun hit the water, making the surface of the river resemble thousands of tiny pearls, Gemma lowered her head and began to mudlark. Nick, as promised, became her shadow. She could feel him watching her and sensed, despite the silence, that he still wanted to chat. But for the moment, she was enjoying not having to. The plip-plop of the water lapping the shore and the friction of her knees against the stones were the only sounds she wanted to hear. Very soon she entered a dreamlike state that was addictively hypnotic.

'Have you ever found anything gruesome?' Nick suddenly started up again.

Gemma took a moment to come back to the present. She thought for a minute. 'A bone from part of a finger.'

'Seriously?'

'Yeah, I had to hand it into the police.'

'So, you never found out anything about it?'

She shook her head. 'It could have been two hundred years old or only two months. From a sailor or an aristocrat. You can conjure up all sorts of scenarios if you let your imagination go wild.'

'I bet. That's what I love about being a journo. I get to find out all sorts of weird and wacky stuff about people, although it's even more fun making it up. I'm writing a novel, did I tell you?'

'No?'

'It's a madcap romp that crosses multiple genres with a plot that's going off in all sorts of out-of-control directions. There are numerous story threads that go nowhere and there's no ending. Can you tell it's going to fly off the bookshelves?'

'You never know.'

'I doubt it.'

'What's it about?'

'I want it to be about a bunch of people who go on a quest. I've been trying out different experiences so I can write about them. I went caving a couple of months ago in the longest cave system in the UK. I've also done a beginner's scuba diving lesson and I really want to go in a helicopter. But that's expensive. Somehow, I need to concoct a story that involves helicopters so I can wrangle a ride.' Nick rubbed his chin.

'Please don't tell me you started mudlarking so you could use it in your novel?'

'No,' he said emphatically. 'I don't plagiarise *everything*.'

'Okay, good.'

'What about you? Any pipe dreams?'

Gemma shrugged. She didn't wish to divulge how all her dreams had evaporated when Adam left. Now she couldn't think of any she was keen to pursue.

Nick continued. 'My other dream is to one day get a scoop. A *really* big scoop where every media outlet comes knocking at my door.' He shook his head at how glorious that would be. 'Anyway, you're a cancer nurse. That's far more honourable.'

'It doesn't feel honourable when treatments fail. But, unfortunately, that's part of the job.'

'That's so tough.' He nodded.

'Sorry, I didn't mean to get so serious. On a positive note, things with Laila are going well.'

'Oh, yeah, I was going to ask you how it was going. Is she being a good housemate?'

'I can't fault her. She's cooked some meals and even encouraged me to apply for my social services file.'

'Great kid. I don't think I'd have been so thoughtful at her age.'

'I know. There's more to her than meets the eye. I think she's just feeling lost, to be honest.'

'Aren't we all,' Nick said.

For another hour, they pottered at the water's edge. Nick's chatter petered out as he, too, succumbed to the contemplative nature of mudlarking.

Soon, they took a break and found two dry rocks to sit on. Nick looked across the river to the buildings on the other side. He seemed calmer now.

'Isn't it amazing how mudlarking makes it feel as if time has stopped?' she said.

'So true.' He nodded.

'I like to think that, here, you can control time – or at least, pause it for a bit – so that nothing else matters other than the little spot of riverbed you're looking at.'

'It's exactly what I needed today.'

Chapter 29

Sunday night and Gemma and Laila were in the living room. The television was on but they were both on their phones when Timothy sent a message to the club. He wasn't happy.

The doc says I have to stay here another week because my leg is taking its sweet time to heal. A week! If it wasn't for visitors, I'd be losing my mind.

'Oh, Gramps,' Laila said.

Gemma didn't blame him. Up until then, Timothy had been a fit, independent man and being confined to a hospital bed must be making him feel like a caged animal. Still, he couldn't risk another injury by going home early.

Don't worry, we won't stop visiting, she wrote.

Thank you, Gemma.

Then, Nick joined in. *Chin up, Timbo, you'll be out in no time.*

Laila giggled. 'Nick's funny,' she said.

Gemma smiled to herself because it was true, Nick never failed to lighten any gloom.

Immediately, Nick set up another group chat that didn't include Timothy.

Let's do that clean-up and safety check of Timothy's houseboat before he comes out. Wash his sheets and towels, fill the fridge, that sort of thing.

Good idea, Gemma wrote. *What do you think, Laila?* she added, even though Laila was sitting next to her on the sofa.

Yes, definitely, Laila typed *So long as we don't throw anything out.*

Only food that's gone off, Nick added.

Duh, Laila wrote.

Phyllida had yet to make an appearance in the chat, which Gemma thought was strange. Normally, she'd have been the first to respond, but, so far, she'd been very, very quiet. In the end, they made an executive decision to do it the following Saturday, as Timothy would be getting out on the Monday. They hoped Phyllida would be free to join them.

By Monday night, Gemma was beginning to worry about Phyllida, who still hadn't replied to any of the group messages. If it had been Mel, Gemma's friend – who was so late to her own wedding everyone had thought she'd changed her mind – she wouldn't have given it a second thought. But Phyllida was always extremely punctual. Plus, Gemma didn't think she'd been her usual self when they were at the hospital.

Should she be concerned or was she reading too much into it? Gemma sent Phyllida a direct message on the pretence of whether they should organise a group mudlark if Timothy wouldn't be able to go. Gemma knew something must be up when Phyllida's eventual reply contained swearing, after realising she'd missed the WhatsApp chat. Gemma decided to call her.

'Are you okay, Phyllida?'

For a moment, there was silence. Gemma waited. A wasp buzzed in from outside and landed on the fridge. It crawled along the middle of the door and stopped on a magnet. Finally, Phyllida spoke.

'Not really, no.'

'Do you want to talk about it?'

'Maybe,' Phyllida said softly.

'I could come over to your house tomorrow after work?' Gemma suggested.

'Not my house,' Phyllida said quickly.

'A restaurant?'

The wasp was now on the dish cloth. Gemma managed to shoo it out the door without getting stung, as Phyllida said yes.

Bright flowers filled window planters at the entrance to the gastro pub in Soho. The streets were bustling with pedestrians and the roads glossy from a summer rain shower. Gemma found a free table outside, at the front. Not long after, Phyllida arrived. Her face looked drawn and her eyes puffy.

'Hi,' she said solemnly.

'Hi, Phyll.' Gemma stood up and gave her a hug.

They talked for a few minutes about this and that before Gemma got them some drinks and ordered food. Then Gemma decided to see if Phyllida was ready to open up.

'How are you today? You seemed upset on the phone. I don't want to pry but would you like to talk about it?'

Phyllida fiddled with a spare coaster. Gemma knew to stop talking because the more you filled the silence, the less likely the other person was to speak. She sipped her drink and waited. Eventually Phyllida spoke.

'Something terrible has happened.'

'Oh, no, Phyllida, what?'

'I'm losing my husband to gambling.' Phyllida stated it so matter-of-factly it was as if she'd said, *I'm losing my husband to golf*. 'In fact, I may have lost him already.'

'I'm so sorry.'

'Our finances are a mess. I had no idea. I feel such a fool, and I'm so angry with him. So angry.' She jabbed her paper straw into the glass, but it didn't provide the impact she no doubt wanted.

'How long has this been going on?'

'Nearly a year. He said he started because he wanted to clear our debts and was going to stop after a winning streak but, of course, he didn't – or couldn't. Gamblers never can, can they? The addiction gets its claws in and burrows into their subconscious.'

Gemma squeezed Phyllida's hand.

'Then, surprise, surprise, he got us into more debt and our finances have been spiralling out of control. Eventually, he came to me to fess up – too late, of course – and says he can't go on anymore. *He* can't go on anymore! How does he think I feel?' Phyllida's voice rose in pitch, trembling.

Gemma gave Phyllida's hand another squeeze. 'He can get help, you know, and so can you. There'll be a solution for it all, I'm sure,' she said, as if she were an expert in gambling addiction.

'It's dire, Gemma. I think we'll have to re-mortgage the house and borrow from family. How could he have been so stupid? How could he not have talked about it with me before doing anything rash? Especially when he knew that my sabbatical meant I'd only be paid a fraction of my usual salary.' She shook her head. 'And you know the stupidest thing of all? I can't seem to un-love him. It's like I hate him and care about him at the same time.'

'That's exactly how I felt when Adam said he was leaving me,' Gemma said. 'It's unsettling. But if you do still love him, you'll get through this. Look how brave and strong you were to raise a child on your own.'

'It seems to get harder the older I get.'

Gemma didn't doubt that. She'd seen it with patients. The more setbacks you have, the more difficult it is to keep on rallying yourself.

A waiter arrived with their meals and cutlery wrapped in paper napkins.

'There's a difference between then and now, though,' Phyllida said. 'What drove me then was the need and desire to look after my child. I was in control of the situation. Now, everything feels out of my control. I don't know what to do, where to start to make things right. I can't think straight anymore. And Robert, even though he's remorseful, has fallen apart.'

Phyllida stared at her food and said nothing more.

'Why don't we put it to The Mudlarkers' Club?' Gemma suggested. 'Look at Timothy, we've proven we can band together and help each other out.'

'But I'm so ashamed.'

'You have no reason to be. No one will think badly of you. They'll only want to help. We could raise it when we're doing the clear-out on Timothy's houseboat.'

Phyllida played with her food with a fork.

'We don't have to, of course.' Suddenly Gemma felt bad for wanting to broadcast Phyllida's personal problems to the group.

'I feel like such an idiot …' Phyllida dropped the fork and let her shoulders slump. She looked all-round defeated.

'You're not an idiot,' Gemma assured her.

'Well, Robert's *definitely* an idiot.'

Gemma nodded gently. Phyllida's husband may well have been struck down by a bout of idiocy, but she wasn't about to criticise him when she didn't even know him.

'I suppose talking about it with others might help,' Phyllida conceded.

'I think it will,' Gemma said. 'In fact, I *know* it will.'

'I do feel a little bit lighter having had this chat with you. Thank you.'

Gemma smiled and squeezed her hand again. 'Any time. But now, let's eat before it gets cold.'

Chapter 30

For Gemma and Laila, it was a fifteen-minute walk to Timothy's home. Laila was on edge, fussing with her hair and looking as if she wanted to break out into a run.

'I can't stop worrying about Gramps and how his boat is one big accident waiting to happen,' she said. 'It's the thought of something even worse happening to him ... You'll see when we get there. I mean, maybe he shouldn't be living on a houseboat at all. But the last thing he'd want to do is move into an old people's home. I just don't know what we should do.'

'Laila, you don't have to shoulder all the worry on your own,' Gemma said. 'Let's focus on what we can do today.'

'Look,' Laila said rushing ahead. 'See what I mean?' She pointed to a navy and white paint-chipped houseboat, its top deck overstuffed with pot plants, and just enough space for two deck chairs and an umbrella. 'There's hardly room to sit outside because it is so crammed with stuff. And where's a safety rail? He could topple over the edge!'

Gemma caught her up. 'Don't panic, we'll look at everything. Oh, hi, Nick.'

She hadn't seen him waiting on the path that ran parallel to the river, outside the gate by the boat. She went over to him and quietly said, 'Laila's really worked up about Timothy having another accident. She's taking full responsibility for his well-being, bless her. It will comfort her if we can do as much as possible to make the houseboat safe.'

'Of course. Poor kid.' He nodded, then called out, 'Hey, Laila, do you want to show us around?'

'You go in,' Gemma said to him. 'I'll wait out here for Phyllida.'

Ten minutes later, Phyllida came hurrying along the path, apologising for being late.

'Everything all right?' Gemma asked. 'I thought you might have pulled out.'

'I wouldn't do that, even if I didn't get much sleep last night. Robert came home late and very drunk,' Phyllida grumbled. 'So drunk he was spouting off about how much he hated himself and what kind of husband he'd become … I had to shove him in the shower and hose him down to try and snap him out of it. Then I put him to bed. I barely slept with all his talk rattling around in my head. I hoped he'd have forgotten about it in the morning.'

'Had he?'

'Thankfully, yes. And he apologised. Profusely. He's very remorseful but I know that doesn't mean he won't gamble again. He's an addict.'

'You really don't have to do this with us today, if you need to be with him,' Gemma said.

'He urged me to come, said he'd try to work out a way to turn things around. To be honest, given the state he's in, I don't think he's capable of feeding the cat. Anyhow, I cooked him a large fry-up, made him eat it, then told him to watch something trashy on the TV. I won't lie, I'd rather not be at home right now and could really do with some of that support you talked about.'

Gemma put an arm around her shoulder and hugged her gently.

Phyllida attempted a smile, then Nick called out from below deck. 'Are you gasbags coming or what?'

Gemma looked questioningly at Phyllida, who nodded.
'Coming!' Gemma replied.

Gemma took Phyllida's hand, led her to the boat's entrance and down a set of wooden stairs to an open-plan living area with timber walls and floors. Either side of the steps sat lifesize majolica dogs – replicas of Timothy's two deceased pets, according to Laila. Books lined both sides of the space in a higgledy-piggledy manner. The flimsy, jam-packed shelves looked as if they'd collapse the moment a high wind rocked the boat. Gemma thought of her mother. The haphazard storage was exactly the sort of thing that would have given her heart palpitations. What's more, she'd probably have insisted on re-organising the books in a colour-coded fashion. She'd tried it once at Gemma's place, who quickly put a stop to it.

In the middle was a brown corduroy sofa and armchair ('Gramps' special chair' Laila told them) and on the floor next to it, a tall pile of *Antique Collecting* magazines, some of which had fallen and scattered like a deck of cards. A coffee table was covered with even more books, newspapers, two antique statues, a jar of pens, random pieces of paper, receipts and other things Gemma couldn't make out. There was a furnace in one corner, with an iron, a lamp and an old clock huddled on top. The doorless kitchen cupboards exposed more hoarding, a collection of utensils and equipment, as did the open shelving. On the floor, there was a slow cooker and a stack of boxes housing various antique knick-knacks and wartime memorabilia. On the small semi-circular dining table with extendable flaps was a laptop, more paper, more books and more collectibles. Not one surface was left uncovered. Even Gemma, who embraced clutter, could see that the place needed to be tidied at least and, at most, de-junked.

'Isn't this a sight,' Phyllida exclaimed, attempting to push aside her distress and focus her attentions, for the time being, on Timothy's chaotic living conditions.

'See, I wasn't exaggerating,' Laila said. 'And you haven't seen the bedrooms.'

'Yeah, this is … What did you call it, Laila?' Nick said.

'Hectic.' Laila nodded. 'It's *so* not a place for an injured elderly man who's got the clumsy gene.'

'Where do we start?' Phyllida asked, already looking dumbfounded at the scale of what needed to be done. Or perhaps it was the combination of stress and a sleepless night catching up with her.

'I don't know. It's so bad.' Laila looked like she might start crying.

'It's okay, Laila,' Nick said gently. 'It might seem overwhelming, but if we break it down into smaller tasks, it won't seem so bad. I reckon we start by clearing all the surfaces, then sorting out the kitchen cupboards, and removing anything that's on the floor which shouldn't be.

'We can put any item he has more than one of or those we think he could get rid of in a pile under the stairs. He can sort through them when he comes home. Then we wash the stuff in the sink, dust and vacuum, and return things in a more ordered fashion.'

'Excellent, Nick,' Gemma said.

They each went to different corners of the boat and got to work. At one point, Gemma disturbed so much dust that she had a sneezing fit. Laila went to find a cotton scarf she could use to cover her face. After nearly two hours, Phyllida's phone beeped loudly. It kept sounding again and again. She frantically pulled the phone from her back pocket and scrolled through her messages, worry lines creasing her face. Gemma went over to her.

'Is it Robert?' she whispered. 'Do you need to go?'

Phyllida shook her head. 'You won't believe it. He wants to know where the beer is. I hid it before I went out. Hair of the dog may be helpful after a boozy night, but right now I don't want him touching the stuff. He also messaged saying *again* how sorry he is, asked me to buy more paracetamol and checked three times whether I'm genuinely going to come home.' She sighed. 'Isn't it enough that he deceived me and lost our money? Now I'm also lumbered with all this neediness and extra worry about him.' Phyllida pushed her hair out of her face and rubbed her temples.

'What's up, you two?' Nick asked, sidling over to them and waving a blue duster he'd found somewhere. He looked at them both and realised he'd interrupted something serious. 'Would you like to break for a cuppa?' he suggested.

'I think, in fact, it's time for a mudlarking meeting,' Gemma said. 'What do you say, Phyllida?'

Before they could sit on the sofa, they first had to remove the kitchen items Nick had dumped there. In his enthusiasm to 'Marie Kondo', he'd overlooked the fact the sofa may be a handy place to sit. Laila made a pot of tea and they found their seats. 'So what's going on, Phyllida?' Nick asked.

'I'm in a bit of a pickle, to put it mildly, thanks to my husband,' she said, staring into her lap and at her fretting hands that wouldn't stay still. Her lips began to quiver and her eyes were teary. 'Gemma, can you tell them? I don't think I can.'

'Of course,' Gemma said. She gently and considerately explained Phyllida's personal crisis, while Nick and Laila listened. When she was done, Laila went to one of the bedrooms and returned with a box of tissues.

'Take the whole thing,' she said to Phyllida. 'Believe it or not, there's more. Gramps is a fan of bulk-buying.'

'Thanks,' Phyllida sniffed.

Then Laila knelt on the floor next to Phyllida and rested her arm on the sofa arm. 'It'll be all right. I'm sure your husband can get help.'

'Exactly,' Nick said. 'There are support networks for gamblers and those affected by gambling, like the National Gambling Helpline. I did an article on it once. Interviewed a couple of gamblers. I'll fish it out for you. It's always good to read about other people going through the same thing as you are.'

'Can't you get cognitive behaviour therapy to help with gambling?' Gemma wondered out loud. 'And I'm sure there'll be financial services help as well.'

Phyllida nodded. 'Robert says he only wanted to reverse the financial mess he'd gotten us into and never thought he'd get addicted.'

'I guess the key to moving forward is being on the same page and to support each other,' said Gemma. 'That's what went wrong with my marriage. We ended up being not just on different pages, but in two different books, written in different languages.'

'Second that,' Nick said.

'Yes, how are you doing, Nick?' Gemma asked, feeling bad she hadn't thought to ask him.

'Something's happened to you, too?' Phyllida said, blowing her nose.

'Ah, don't worry about me, I'm fine.' He flapped a hand as if swatting away a fly.

'You've just heard all about me …'

'Yeah, but …'

'Come on.' Phyllida waggled her finger at him. 'It's good to get it off your chest, isn't that right, Gemma?'

Nick glanced at them all as if assessing whether to air his woes. 'Okay, so, I've broken up with my girlfriend. Or rather she broke up with me. She took the dog and I haven't heard from her since.'

'The dog as well! Aren't we a right bunch?' Phyllida said, dabbing her eyes with a handful of tissues.

'New club name: the Lost Souls of the River Thames,' Laila said drily.

'That's depressing,' Nick said.

'It was meant to be funny.'

'It would be if it wasn't true.'

'Sorry.' Laila made an apologetic face. 'But look on the bright side, we're all in it together.'

'Exactly,' agreed Gemma. 'If we can't help each other, what's the point of The Mudlarkers' Club in the first place?' It still amazed Gemma how much she'd embraced the collegial nature of the group.

Phyllida stood up. 'Come on, group hug.'

'Group hug?' Nick said, looking uncertain.

'It's better than a group cry,' Phyllida said, wrangling them together with her arms open wide.

'Okay, then ...' Nick stood up and positioned himself as if he thought a group hug meant doing a rugby scrum.

They formed a circle together, awkwardly, as if no one was quite sure how close they should get to one another. Nick caught Gemma's eye. A zing of something she couldn't immediately put her finger on went through her. He smiled. Had he felt it too? She had to look away, even though, she realised disconcertingly, that she'd have rather kept looking at him.

Suddenly, he pulled away as if he'd reached his time limit for hugging. 'Okay, Phyll, how are you feeling now?'

Phyllida sighed and pressed her palms together. 'You people are marvellous. I can't tell you how ashamed I am, but already you've made me feel like I can deal with it and there is help available. When I get home, I'll sit Robert down and tell him we need to have a proper conversation about it. No more arguing and sleeping in different rooms.'

'We really don't mind if you want to go back home now,' Gemma said.

'But I want to stay and finish the job. You help me, I help you. But I will check in with Robert.'

'Yes, go and call him. We'll get started on the bedrooms.'

Phyllida pressed her husband's number as she went up to the top deck.

By the time, she returned, they'd finished one bedroom and were about to start on the other.

'Sorry, Robert didn't want me to go.' Phyllida sighed as if feeling guilty for hanging up on her husband.

'I've got an idea,' Laila said. 'Why don't you do a video call with him and show him what we're doing? I've been doing that with Gramps.'

'You have?' Nick said impressed.

'Gramps loves it. Makes him feel less lonely. And it doesn't matter what you're doing either. The other day, Gramps watched me getting ready to go out. It actually got annoying, because he started grilling me about who I was meeting and made a rude comment about the new cartilage piercings I got the other day.' She turned her head to show them an embellished ear. 'He called me a metal detectorist's dream.'

Nick snorted.

'Trust you to find that funny,' Laila said, but she was smiling so Gemma knew that she wasn't offended.

'I love that idea, Laila,' Gemma said. Then to Phyllida, 'What do you think? Do you want to do a video call with Robert? We could all say hi and wish him a speedy recovery as if you've told us that he's been unwell. There's no need for him to know that we know what's happened.'

'I guess it would cheer him up.'

'Exactly. He'll be able to see you and you can keep an eye on him.'

So, that's what they did. Phyllida's husband was flummoxed at first by an unexpected video call with a group of people he had never met. But he soon warmed to the idea and muted the television show he'd been watching to focus on them – and hand out the occasional piece of tidying-up advice.

'This is like reality TV,' he joked at one point when Nick and Laila were debating what to do with the newspapers. Nick was trying to persuade Laila that they should all go. But Laila was worried about Timothy's reaction. In the end, they settled on keeping the last two weeks' worth and chucking the rest.

When they'd finished, and Laila had gone outside to pick some wildflowers and put them in an empty jar on the now clutter-free dining table, they congratulated each other for a job well done. Phyllida assured them that Robert would have joined in as well because he was a high-five kind of a guy, except he'd fallen asleep.

Just then, phones beeped and dinged and sang and cooed. Timothy had messaged on the group chat.

'Yay!' Laila exclaimed (trust Laila to be the first one to her phone). 'The doctor says Gramps can come home tomorrow.'

'Fantastic!' Nick said.

'But we haven't organised an emergency bracelet,' Laila cried. 'I don't even know how you get one and what they cost.'

'And Timothy needs to agree to wear one first,' Gemma said.

Laila pressed her temples. 'Aargh, it's so stressful!'

'It's okay, Laila, don't worry,' Phyllida said.

'Yeah, one thing at a time,' Nick said. 'Timothy will be much safer here after today's clean-up.'

'Why don't I call Jodie and discuss it with her?' Gemma suggested. 'It'll be up to her and, of course, Timothy, whether he gets one or not. We can seed the idea to him.'

'Hang on, let's do a quick bit of research,' Nick said, going into journalist mode. His phone came out and he began googling. No one spoke. After a few minutes, Nick enlightened them. 'Right, so there are several places where you can get medical emergency bracelets. The NHS for starters. They come with GPS tracking, twenty-four-hour monitoring and will detect hard falls. Best of all, you can get next day delivery so there won't be a long wait time. That sounds perfect, don't you think? I reckon that if you have a chat with Jodie, Gemma, and then you and Laila gently introduce the idea to Timothy. What do you say?' He looked at them expectantly.

Gemma glanced at Laila who nodded.

'We could do it in the car when we go and pick him up,' Gemma suggested, until she remembered about his daughter. 'But what about Jodie? She'll want to get him, won't she?'

'I've already told her I'm going to do it,' Laila said defiantly. 'She can visit later.'

Gemma felt bad depriving Timothy's daughter of the task. 'Look, I know you probably don't want any advice, but for what it's worth, I think you should end your stand-off and make up with Jodie. Do it for your grandfather, if no one else.'

Gemma could tell Laila was thinking it over, but she didn't respond. She was picking her nails instead.

'I think that's a very good idea,' Phyllida said. 'Oooh, and I've got another one. Why don't we surprise him by being on the boat when he returns?'

'I like it. I can bring balloons and cake,' Nick got excited.

'What can I do? You lot have to-do lists and I don't,' Phyllida said, as if they'd intentionally left her out, which wasn't the case at all.

'You've got enough going on, Phyll,' Nick said. 'You don't even have to come tomorrow, if you don't want to.'

'But I do! I'll see how Robert is and make a call in the morning.'

'Great, Phyll, we'll wait for a call from you tomorrow. Okay, are we clear on our tasks?' Nick said.

They all nodded.

'And Laila? You good?'

'Uh-huh.' She chewed a nail, looking coy. 'Just … you know, thanks. For everything.'

As they said their goodbyes at the gate to the towpath, Gemma got a sense that today had been so much more than a clean-up job. It seemed to have cemented their relationships as friends and confidantes in a way she had never thought a niche group of history lovers could ever be.

She just hoped Timothy wouldn't be upset and accuse them of unnecessary meddling.

Chapter 31

When Gemma and Laila went to the hospital to collect Timothy, he was sitting in the guest chair next to the bed.

'Look at this, two of my favourite ladies,' he said.

'You're going home!' Gemma clapped.

'Yes, and we need to celebrate,' he answered.

'There'll be plenty of time for that,' Laila said.

'Do you need to check out with the nurse?' Gemma asked.

'Done, and I've seen the doc. I'm ready to go.' His bag was packed, his hair neatly combed, and a handkerchief poked out from the top of the left breast pocket of his short-sleeve shirt. But he still had a protective boot on his injured leg and when he stood up, he had to steady himself on the arm of the chair.

'Will you really be all right?' Laila was still concerned.

'I bloody well hope so. My arm's better and my foot only aches when I try and run.'

Laila sighed and looked at Gemma. She knew what Laila wanted to say and, as it was as good a time as any, she nodded at the teenager to go ahead.

'Gramps, we ... I mean, *I* ... was thinking that it might be a good idea for you to have a medical emergency bracelet. Just in case you do something silly like go for a run and have another fall.'

'I don't need one of those! I'm done with falling. And I was joking about the run, ha-ha! No need to worry, Ley-ley.' He patted her hand.

Laila smiled at him reluctantly but turned to glare at Gemma.

'It's not a bad idea, Timothy—' Gemma began.

'It is a *silly* idea. Those bracelets are for people who have Zimmer frames or a pre-existing medical condition. I have neither.'

'No, but Gramps—'

'Ah-ah.' He waggled a finger at her. 'I don't want to hear another word about it. Come on, you two, put your arms in mine. Never has anyone had such a beautiful pair of crutches!' Timothy laughed.

Gemma picked up Timothy's bag, even though she could tell he'd rather not have had any help at all. Then she and Laila each linked one arm into his, and they accompanied him out of the hospital.

'It's looking good up here,' Timothy said with pride as he took in the top deck of his houseboat. 'Has someone swept up or has something moved?'

Although the mudlarkers hadn't wanted to disturb too much on the upper level, the arrangement of pot plants had been an obvious hazard, and it didn't look as if it had been swept or spruced up for years.

'I gave it a little tidy, Gramps,' Laila said. 'And rearranged some of the pots. I hope you don't mind.' Laila exchanged a look with Gemma. She was clearly worried about his reaction given his vehement insistence on not needing an emergency aid.

'I like it, thank you.'

'Careful down these steps,' Laila warned.

'Yes, yes.'

'Why don't you go first, Laila, and I'll follow Timothy?' Gemma suggested.

'Please don't fuss,' Timothy said.

Slowly and carefully, they accompanied Timothy down the stairs to where Nick and Phyllida were sitting on the sofa. While they wanted to surprise Timothy, they had already agreed they didn't want to give him a shock so that he ended up in hospital again. They decided that a simple joint call of 'Surprise!' would be more than enough to set the scene, rather than any sudden appearances from behind doors or an explosion of party whistles and streamers.

Laila started it off, followed by Nick and Phyllida, who in their enthusiasm flung their arms in the air, and Gemma, who was ready to steady him if he wobbled in shock.

'Goodness me!' Timothy exclaimed. 'My heart's going like the clappers. I think I'm going to have to sit down.'

'Of course, of course.' Nick shot out of his seat and helped Timothy over to his special armchair.

Timothy let out a rush of air as he sank into it and shook his head again in disbelief. 'I wasn't expecting this.'

'There's nothing nicer than a welcoming party,' Phyllida said. 'And you must say hi to my husband who's joining us by phone. I hope you don't mind.' Phyllida waved to Timothy as if encouraging a child to wave, too.

'Hello, husband,' Timothy called out.

'Hi, mate. I'm Robert,' said Robert, who sounded like he was trapped in a tunnel.

'Robert's been poorly,' Phyllida added.

'Join the club, old chap.'

Robert said something else, but Phyllida quickly lowered the sound to make it harder for the others to hear him.

'Right, who wants some bubbles and cake?' Nick went to pour sparkling wine and dish up slices of carrot cake with frosting so thick, it was like a slab of recently fallen snow.

'Where did you find these?' Timothy said, studying the champagne flute Nick gave him, as if he'd never seen it before.

'In a cupboard,' Nick said.

'I haven't seen them for years.'

'They were tucked away behind ... I don't know, something else—'

'Wait a minute,' Timothy said, looking around. 'Where's the stuff that was on the coffee table? And where are my dogs?'

The mudlarkers exchanged nervous looks.

'We did some tidying,' Gemma said hesitantly.

'And cleaned,' added Laila.

'We thought, as it hadn't been lived in a for a couple of weeks, it'd be nice to come back to a freshened-up home,' Nick said.

'Hmm,' Timothy grunted, as he took in the changes to his houseboat.

Gemma sensed collective breath holding.

'It's certainly neater ...' he mumbled.

'We haven't thrown anything out, Gramps,' Laila said hurriedly. 'But now it's, well ... it's safer. Less of an obstacle course for you.'

'It wasn't that much of an obstacle course before.'

'It kinda was, Timbo,' Nick said.

Timothy looked at him questioningly. 'Hmm,' he grunted again.

'And, Gramps, look how sparkling everything is.' Laila smiled.

'It's so sparkling, I almost need to wear sunglasses. Now, *that* would be a safety hazard.'

There was a strained silence. Gemma glanced at Laila, who looked forlorn, and then at Nick, who appeared to be forming a placatory speech but didn't know where to start. Then, there came the tinny, faint voice of Robert from Phyllida's phone.

'What was that?' Timothy said, leaning closer.

Phyllida raised the volume on her phone.

'They care about you, mate,' Robert shouted.

Timothy sat back and looked at the other members of The Mudlarkers' Club. Laila was crying now, the stress of it proving too much. 'Don't cry, Ley-ley,' he said. 'I'm sorry if I came across as rather ungrateful, but I got scared in hospital. I didn't want this to be the beginning of the end of my independence.'

'That's why we wanted to do all of this, so you *could* stay independent,' Laila said, wiping her eyes.

Timothy nodded thoughtfully. 'Yes, well, I will concede the boat was teetering on the edge of being a health hazard and I'm not the tidiest of people. But how I do despise minimalism. At any rate, I guess I shouldn't have let it get so bad, and this really is an improvement.'

'Now, you don't have to worry,' Gemma said.

'I suppose it was a mammoth task and you deserve a very big thank you.'

Laila dried her eyes.

'You've all been incredibly kind to me as it is, visiting me in hospital, bringing food and conversation—'

'It was nothing, really,' Nick said, as if jokingly brushing it off.

'I can't thank you enough.' Timothy surveyed the changes again. 'You know what? Now there'll be room for my new subscription of *Beachcombing* magazine.'

'More magazines?' Laila said in disbelief.

'If it's a digital subscription, it'll be fine,' Nick said.

'Don't be absurd, I'm not reading a magazine on a computer.'

Gemma, seeing Laila groan in despair, quickly added. 'That sounds like a wonderful magazine. Perhaps you can share it with us, too, and that way, they won't pile up here.' Gemma glanced at Laila, hoping her comment had made her feel better.

'Yes, yes, of course,' Timothy said.

'You haven't drunk your bubbles!' It was Robert interjecting again.

Timothy laughed. 'Ah, yes, of course. A toast to you all.' He raised his glass.

'But you've got to promise me, you won't have another fall,' Laila said sternly.

'I sincerely hope I won't.'

'Just don't, all right?'

He nodded and smiled. 'But if I do, maybe I'll be wearing a medical emergency bracelet and it'll be all right …?' he said teasingly, letting the proposition linger reassuringly in the air as he sipped his wine.

July Discoveries:
A shard of Yellow Staffordshire slipware that resembles a bite of almond tart decorated with dark chocolate feathering. Part of a Victorian white ceramic Gosnell Bros and Co Cherry Toothpaste pot lid. Five handmade pins and how I've just learnt that the term 'pin money' was used for the money women were given to buy clothing pins for the household. How Phyllida makes a mean chocolate brownie (it was so good, it might even inspire me to have a go at baking!). And, more significantly, whenever you find out that others are going through 'stuff', as you are, how this knowledge of mutual angst is like an elixir of comradeship.

August

Chapter 32

Gemma hadn't anticipated how Laila's departure – to return to the houseboat and look after Timothy – would leave such a vacuum. The house felt hollow and lifeless. It no longer tinkled with Laila's silver jewellery or thumped with her boot-shod feet. She wasn't there for a chat when Gemma got home from work or woke up in time for lunch at the weekend. It didn't help that the jar of Nutella Gemma had given Laila was still in the cupboard, reminding her every time she saw it of the void that her short-stay housemate had left.

It also didn't help that she was still waiting for her social services file to arrive. It seemed like a hole that would never be filled and she couldn't stop feeling like something was missing. She was at once terrified and excited about what it may reveal. She was told that within forty days – finally – she would have answers, of sorts, to her questions.

Then she thought about having her photo taken for Nick's article and the wait for the story to be published. Everything was making her anxious. Nick was certain the piece was going to run, even though it kept getting bumped for more newsworthy events. Like the war in Ukraine, climate change protests and a celebrity in a bikini who doesn't look how they did two years ago. Gemma didn't like to say she was more than happy to be bumped by *anyone* who'd had a bum-lift, and that she secretly hoped the photo shoot wouldn't go ahead.

A heatwave descended on the city and as most of her friends were either already abroad or about to go on their annual summer holiday, Gemma decided she had to keep busy. There was to be no holiday for her, now that she had to survive on her own financially. She focused on work and caring for her patients; delivered some homecooked dinners after-hours to Timothy and Laila; and checked in to see how Nick was doing (being dog-less was killing him more than being Ella-less). She kept in touch with her friends by liking their holiday snaps on Instagram but found they left her feeling empty and gloomy. While not wanting to pester Phyllida but wishing to offer moral support, Gemma sent motivational quotes to inspire her and silly reels to make her laugh (at least, she hoped they made her laugh). Sometimes Phyllida replied and sometimes she didn't. By the second week of August, Gemma decided to call.

'I'm so sorry I haven't been in touch,' Phyllida said. 'I've been focusing all my attentions on Robert.'

'I didn't want to intrude,' Gemma said. 'I just hoped things were okay.'

'After our chat at Timothy's, I went home feeling inspired. I wasn't going to let Robert destroy our marriage or our finances. Nick sent me his article, which was really very good, and from that I wrote an action plan of where we were going to get help from. Bullet lists are my forte. First up, is joining Gamblers Anonymous and finding a specialist therapist.'

'Is Robert on board?'

'He's not enamoured with the idea of opening up to strangers, but he knows he has to do something. I can tell that even having me take charge and no longer having to lie has made him feel a little bit better.'

'What about you, are you getting help?'

'I've found a support group for families and loved ones affected by someone else's gambling. I have been to one meeting, which was dominated by an eighty-year-old whose wife is fixated with playing the fruit machines and wouldn't stop talking about it. But I guess it'll help.'

'Any time you want to chat …'

'Thank you, Gemma. How's Timothy? Have you seen him?'

'His recovery is slow and he's getting frustrated. But Laila's taking good care of him, and Nick and I have dropped off some meals.'

'I was going to message the group to suggest we postpone our next meeting. Do you mind? I've got too much going on at the moment and that will give Timothy more time to get better.'

'Of course.'

Gemma sensed Phyllida's relief. Even though she was happy to delay the next meeting, she felt a little glum not knowing when they'd get together again. The regularity of their catch ups, as much as the nature of them, had been something she'd started to rely on. They offered her more than just an opportunity to mudlark. She'd gained a new set of friends, a social life and a support group she'd not had before, with diverse but like-minded individuals. There was nothing for it, she'd just have to schedule some mudlarks of her own. By the end of the first two weeks of August, she'd made six trips to the river. She didn't care what she found, or if she found nothing at all. It was about soaking up the setting, allowing the push and pull of the water to tug at her emotions and, ultimately, flush away all the negative ones.

One evening, after the sun had set, she went out at ten o'clock. She loved the river at night. Sometimes, it was a little eerie, even with her headtorch, but it was always more peaceful and tranquil than during the day. On a night like this one, when the sky was cloud-free and the moon hung suspended like one of her mother's white glass Christmas baubles, Gemma could stay there for hours.

*

What didn't fill her with joy was hearing from Adam in the middle of the month – despite it being expected. His message began sickeningly breezily, as if he was now suddenly interested in her and what she was doing.

How are you? How's your work and how's the mudlarking?

His tone was chatty and happy because, naturally, he was doing great.

Did I tell you I've been promoted?

Of course he hadn't. His disingenuity grated, she knew it was because he wanted something. Butter her up to hurry her up.

We really need to get on with the divorce.

And there it was.

I haven't wanted to hurry you but it's going to take time. I've spoken to Smithy. He's going to be my solicitor, by the way, as he's my mate, after all.

God, you really are a *cabrón*, Adam, laying claim to the friends you want in the divorce. Gemma growled under her breath and continued reading.

The first step is filling out an online application form. We can either do a joint application or one of us does it. Doesn't matter either way. Your call.

Gemma would rather swim naked in the Thames than do anything jointly with Adam.

You'll need your own solicitor, of course. But as long as you don't contest anything – you won't, will you? – then we could have this done and dusted in about seven months.

Gemma sighed. Adam had chosen to ruin their marriage, so he could do all the work to extricate himself from it.

I'm very busy at the moment, she replied. *Could you do the application?*

That was all she wrote. She'd let him stew over whether she'd contest anything. Not that she would. What was there to contest? Certainly not a change of heart.

A couple of minutes later, he sent another text.

We need to sell the house, too.

Gemma felt a stab of pain in her chest. The thought of losing her home now seemed even worse than losing Adam. The house had only ever been good to her. It was her little corner of the world and so close to the river. No, she wasn't ready. Adam added:

I've got the rent to pay here as well as the mortgage. It's not sustainable.

Gemma wanted to cry. When she didn't respond, because she hadn't known what to say, he messaged again.

I'll have to stop the mortgage payments if you won't agree.

Was he threatening her? She replied, *You don't need to be nasty about it.*

Just stating facts.

Ugh, he could be so patronising!

Well?

She gave no reply. He could stew on that as well.

Gemma?

'Oh, go away, Adam!' she shouted and flung her phone across the sofa.

Chapter 33

An hour later, when Gemma retrieved her phone from down the side of a sofa cushion, she realised Nick had messaged about the photo shoot.

Don't worry about the high tides and chance of rain. We'll work around them. You might have to stand on the tow path if there's no foreshore left. And dusk and gloomy weather will give the photos an added aura of moodiness.

Gemma thought his reply was particularly descriptive, and she wondered if he'd been in the middle of writing his novel. He continued.

It won't take long. Half an hour at most. We'll come to you and if you can dress in your full mudlarking kit, rucksack and all, that'd be great. Really appreciate it.

Now, finding out it was going ahead (ideally in the next day or two, Nick had said), she didn't feel panicky. Rather, she felt buoyed. So buoyed! She'd show Adam that she could be successful, too. Who cares if the feature was only a six-hundred-word story in a breakout box, she was still going to be in the newspaper. What's more, she'd be spending time with Nick, and he knew how to treat a woman with respect, even if her ex-husband didn't.

*

On Thursday night, Gemma followed Nick's instructions to the letter. She cleaned her boots, bucket and trowel, and even contemplated putting on lipstick, which is what her mother would have told her to do. But she never wore lipstick when mudlarking, and with her fuchsia-coloured wellington boots, she decided that was more than enough pink for one outfit. Lastly, she got out her Thermos, and made a pot of tea, to keep things truly authentic.

When Nick arrived, he introduced her to Greg the photographer, and Gemma took them the quickest way to the river. When they got there, the tide was well and truly high and threatening to spill onto the footpath. The water was the colour of slate, and the sky was inky and most definitely moody.

'So where do you want me?' Gemma asked. 'What do you want me to do?' Suddenly nerves started getting the better of her. Who did she think she was, anyway, a model or something?

'Let's get some with you looking out to the river,' Nick suggested. 'But just be yourself,' he added, as if he could tell she was feeling self-conscious.

She went to stand by the edge of the towpath, where weedy river plants formed a border.

'This is going to be great,' Greg said, assessing the scene. 'The contrast of the colours with your boots and gloves against the landscape … Excellent. Let me just check the lighting. And, Nick, I might get you to hold the light reflector when we start shooting.'

'Do I look okay?' Gemma asked.

'Of course, Gem,' Nick said. 'The only thing that would top it off is a headtorch.'

'I've got one, but I wasn't sure—'

'Yes, stick it on!' Nick said enthusiastically.

Gemma got the headtorch from her rucksack and pulled it over her head.

After a minute or two, Greg said, 'Okay, great, we're ready to go. Relax your shoulders and gaze out to the water as if imagining the treasures you're going to find.'

Gemma nodded. But all she could think about was did she really look all right, and why was one leg starting to cramp? Could she move it without having to look down and ending up dangerously close to the stinging nettles? Or worse, falling into the water? Then she thought of Adam and the sort of confidence he would exude if someone was photographing him for the paper. She needed to snap out of her self-doubt. So she lifted her head, pulled her shoulders back and said, 'Okay, I'm ready!'

'Hang on.' Nick jogged over to her. 'The headtorch is wonky.'

He stood in front of her and adjusted it. He was so close Gemma could smell the minty gum he'd been chewing and the detergent he'd laundered his T-shirt in. She studied his face and gingery whiskers, the faint redness across his cheeks from having been in the sun, and the curl at the top of his forehead.

He caught her eye and held it for a second. She was sure she stopped breathing. She realised it had been so long since she'd been this close to another man that her body didn't know what to do with itself.

Nick glanced at her headtorch. 'That looks better.' He smiled and she wished he wouldn't keep smiling at her. She wasn't sure if he was sending her a cryptic message she needed to decipher or whether he was just happy with the additional accessory.

She was probably reading far too much into it and all he was doing was being friendly. She'd no reason to assume that just because he was single he was looking for a date, let alone one with her. Which was a good thing because she wasn't ready to date. She certainly didn't want to ruin a friendship by having a regrettable rebound kiss – or worse, regrettable rebound sex – and having to leave The Mudlarkers' Club because it ended up being weird and awkward between them.

'All good now, mate,' Nick said, jogging back to fetch the reflector.

'Let's shoot off a few more,' Greg said. 'Then I reckon we can call it a night.'

After taking some more shots, Greg gave her a thumbs up and said, 'Thanks, Gemma. Got it.'

Gemma took off the headtorch and rubbed her temples. It had been a little tight. The sky had now taken on a purple hue and the humidity had risen. The air felt thick with impending rain.

Greg packed up his gear, and Nick offered to carry the light reflector and Gemma's bucket in which she'd dumped the headtorch, Thermos, knee pads and trowel. They headed back to her street.

'When do you think the story's going to be published?' Gemma asked.

'My editor assures me it's coming out on Saturday, barring a presidential assassination or a royal scandal,' Nick said.

'Anything could happen between now and then.' Greg laughed.

'I'll text you either way,' Nick said.

'Will it be online, too?' she asked, thinking of how she could send it to Adam.

'Yeah, I'll send you the link.'

Although it was petty, she couldn't deny the glee she felt at the idea of showing Adam what she'd done.

When they reached Greg's scruffy red Honda parked three houses before Gemma's, Nick said, 'I'll walk you to your house.'

'You don't have to. It's just here,' Gemma said.

'I know.'

'Nice to meet you, Gemma,' Greg called out, flicking open his car boot.

'You too, Greg. I look forward to seeing the chosen shot.'

She and Nick set off towards her house, Nick swinging the bucket so vigorously Gemma thought something might fly out. Her feet felt hot and puffy in the wellies and she couldn't wait to take them off.

'You were great, tonight, thanks,' Nick said.

'I don't know about that but as long as you get one good picture where I don't look completely daft—'

'You didn't look daft. On second thoughts, maybe when you nearly fell in …' He glanced at her with a smile. 'Just kidding,' he said.

'Ha-ha. Well, this is me.' She stopped at the path leading to her house.

'And here's your bucket.' He handed it to her but didn't look about to go. Instead, he scuffed the path like a kid wanting to ask for more cake but not knowing if he'd be allowed. 'Hey, I was wondering,' he finally said. 'Have you mudlarked at the Vauxhall part of the river, near Lack's Dock Slipway?'

'Isn't it meant to be one of the more dangerous parts of the river?'

'Yeah, I heard that. The tides can come up pretty quickly and the currents are strong. Do you want to go?'

'You haven't sold it very well.'

He laughed. 'True.'

Then she had a thought. What if Nick thought that she'd been coming on to *him* and he was asking her on a date?

'Are you asking me on a date?' she said, not intending to sound quite so horrified.

'No, not all.' He batted the idea away as if it was quite outrageous. 'I'm keen to go there and I wouldn't mind the company.'

'Right, of course. Me too.' She let out a nervous laugh. 'It's just I'm not ready to date,' she said.

'Okay, sure,' he said. Gemma thought he looked a little taken aback but couldn't tell if it was because she'd disappointed him or because she was being presumptuous.

'Not that there's anything wrong with you, of course—' she added.

'Good to know …' He nodded. 'Nothing wrong with you either.'

She smiled but it suddenly felt uncomfortable between them. She kicked a stone, but her boots weren't designed for kicking, and the most it did was slowly roll over.

'You're right, though, it is nice having company when you're mudlarking.' How funny that now she found it strangely quiet when she was down by the river on her own. 'So, I guess it's a yes, then.'

Nick's eyes lit up. 'Great! I'll look up the tides and text you.' He shot a glance back at Greg. 'I'd better go,' he said.

As the car drove away, she trundled to the front door, left her boots in the porch and flopped on the sofa. She felt tired but exhilarated. There was no denying that whatever she did with Nick, it was always easy, and he made it enjoyable. Even something as disagreeable as having her photo taken.

Chapter 34

Sure enough, on Saturday, Nick's story was published. He sent Gemma a link to the digital version while she was on the bus going home from a Pilates class. Her first reaction to the photo was, *I don't look too bad, after all, even if I'm a nobody in knee pads.* Her second was how much she loved the headline, 'Free as a Mudlark'. Nick had captured the essence and attraction of mudlarking better than she'd been able to describe it to him. Of course, the main article was far more interesting and if it wasn't for Gemma's hot-pink boots popping off the page, you could have easily overlooked the breakout box altogether.

She messaged him: *Congratulations, it's a great read.*

Thanks, he replied. Then he sent her a photo of a gold-painted trowel. *What do you think?*

She had a chuckle but felt touched that he'd used the spray. *Your dad would be proud*, she wrote.

Actually, I think he'd say it was bloody gaudy and why did I ruin a good bloody trowel? (He used the word bloody a lot, FYI).

Gemma sent him a grinning emoji and typed, *Kitsch and gaudy never goes out of style. Anyway, I like it and if you like it, that's all that matters.*

I'm going to put it on a plinth with a waffly explanation about remembering the dead and deification, and call it art. People pay good money for that sort of thing.

You never would.

Probably not. There's some spray leftover if you've got anything that needs gilding. Costume jewellery you want to jazz up?

Gemma smiled.

Did I just say jazz? I'm turning into my father.

It's all yours. Keep the spray to gild whatever takes your fancy.

Okay, thanks! Have a good weekend.

You, too.

She looked out the bus window, feeling very content. All in all, it was a good start to the weekend, especially now she knew that Nick, like her, was happy to just be friends.

Then, she re-read his story. How she'd love to show it to Adam. But, no, perhaps she wouldn't. If he chose to ruin their marriage and no longer be a part of her life, there was no need to include him in anything she did. Instead, she sent the piece to her parents and a few of her friends, who gave her all the positive endorsement she needed.

Midway through the following week, when she came home from work, on a day that was being described as the hottest day of the year so far, Gemma nearly slipped on an envelope from the local authority's children's services.

Her heart skipped a beat. There it was, in her house, her social services file. She picked it up, her hands already shaking, and took it to the kitchen. But she was too nervous to open it. She left it on the bench and went to text Laila.

I need reinforcements, she wrote.

What? Laila replied five minutes later.

Gemma explained, then asked, *You wouldn't be able to come*

over, would you?

It felt silly needing a seventeen-year-old to sit with her while she opened a letter, but Laila wasn't a regular teenager. She'd already helped to get Gemma this far, for starters, and despite her limited years, Laila understood. She knew what it was like to be all-consumed by the questions of who she was and where she came from and why she was no longer with her birth parents. Of feeling incomplete, that something was missing, and which starts slowly eating away at you.

Yeah, I'm there, Laila replied. *I'll come now.*

Thank you, thank you, Gemma wrote back. She put the phone down and left the kitchen. The sight of the envelope, which contained information on her past, was proving too much. It was finally here, and all she hoped now was that her only regrets would be that she hadn't started on this journey sooner.

When Laila arrived a few minutes later, Gemma greeted her at the door, holding the envelope in front of her.

'Here it is.'

'This is *so* exciting. Where shall we do it?'

'Let's go to the living room.'

Laila pulled off her shoes and sat cross-legged next to Gemma on the sofa. Gemma looked down at the envelope lying in her lap and sipped some of her drink.

'Just so you know, I don't mind you reading it with me,' she said.

'Okay.'

For a moment, they both stared at the envelope, until Gemma felt Laila looking at her.

'You can't rush these things,' Gemma said to explain her procrastination.

'But it's not going to open itself.'

For a second, Gemma wished it would stay forever sealed. Because what if the past was better left unopened?

'I could do it?' Laila suggested.

Gemma shook her head. The desire, rather the need, to know was strong.

The envelope flap unpeeled easily, and the paperwork slipped out as if the information had been waiting to escape. Gemma's nerves rattled. She let the envelope drop to the floor and, holding the papers so Laila could see, began reading.

'So ... you've got an aunt called Louise, your grandparents were Elizabeth and Lyndon and your mum was an office administrator,' Laila commented out loud as she leant in closer. 'Oh, and you had a different name—'

'I know.'

'Huh, interesting. And look there, that's the adoption agency your mum used.'

'Mmm,' Gemma muttered, trying to take it all in.

'Are you okay?' Laila asked, gently touching her back.

'I guess,' Gemma said. 'I suppose I was hoping for something more detailed, more personal. This is like reading a bank statement, all facts and no feeling.'

There were no sentiments or description. No photos or loving words. No hints as to what these people had been like. It was as if she was reading someone else's story. It neither cheered Gemma up nor made her unhappy. She felt at once removed and unmoved by the information, which made it feel disappointingly anti-climactic.

What's more, all it did was open up a raft of new questions. Had Claire Rita Munroe left school because of the pregnancy? Had she really wanted to work in an office, or had she rued the day she got pregnant? How much did she think of baby Hayley after giving her up? Did she believe she was showing her love by giving her baby away rather than keeping her in less-than-ideal circumstances? Did her parents Lyndon and Elizabeth ever wonder about their granddaughter? What had they thought of it all?

'It still feels like I'm skimming the surface of what happened. I'm getting basic information and nothing else.'

'Yeah, I get it,' Laila said. 'But what you really want to know about is your birth mother, right?'

Gemma nodded.

'So what do you know already?'

'Not much. Her name. Her age when I was born. Her parents' names. A job she did …'

Gemma didn't know whether her mother went on to get married or have other children. Whether she lived in England, or not, and what she was doing now.

'This is a start, though, right? You know enough to begin googling.'

'True,' Gemma said.

'Okay, let's do it.' Laila stood up.

'You've done enough for me already, Laila.'

'So?'

'So, you don't have to.'

'I know I don't, but I'd like too.'

'Don't you want to find things out about your own birth family?'

'Not with the mother I've got. I don't want to learn that my genetic heritage is addiction.'

'It may not be. Your mum might have got caught up in unfortunate circumstances, where one thing led to another. Look at Phyllida's husband.'

'S'ppose.' Laila shrugged. 'But right now, I'd rather help you with yours.'

Gemma couldn't deny how reassuring it was to have Laila by her side, an ally urging her on.

'Come on,' Laila said, reaching out an arm. 'Before you get cold feet.'

Gemma gathered the social services papers, and she and Laila went to sit at her computer.

'What are you going to search for first?' Laila asked.

'I suppose I have to go back to the beginning, like I did with the birth certificate.'

'How do you do that?'

'By looking up the United Kingdom birth and marriage records.'

And that's what Gemma did, with Laila ready to take notes, because she thought Gemma might forget the detail in the heat of the search. Knowing the names of her grandparents and her birth mother's age meant it wasn't difficult to find her birth certificate. From there, they were able to confirm that Louise was Claire Rita Munroe's only sibling, two years older than her.

Next, they uncovered a marriage certificate which revealed that when Gemma was ten years old, a twenty-seven-year-old Claire married thirty-two-year-old Steven Reed in East Sussex. So far, her birth mother had not yet left the county in which Gemma was born. Then, assuming her birth mother took her husband's name, she was now Claire Rita Reed. Knowing this, Gemma searched her new name and discovered that she went on to have one more child, a son named Benjamin Reed, who would now be twenty-three.

'You've got a brother!' Laila cried, spinning around in the swivel chair.

'Gosh, yes.' Gemma pressed her hands to her chest. She thought her heart might explode with joy. She had a half-brother, a real, blood-related sibling.

'What if he's got the collecting gene, too?' Laila said in delight.

'What if—' Gemma began.

'You could get to meet him *and* her.'

'Yes, but …' Gemma got a sudden, unpleasant sinking feeling in her stomach. 'What if they don't want to meet *me*?'

'Don't say that.'

It was a possibility Gemma had to accept. Because the reality was that her mother had kept her brother and not her. Did her mother think of her baby girl with shame and embarrassment? Was it her son whom she loved the most? Did Gemma's brother even know she existed or had Claire kept Gemma's birth a secret from everyone? She got up and went to the bathroom. She splashed her face and drank some water. Her heart raced and she leant over the basin.

'Are you all right, Gemma?' Laila called out.

When the feeling had dissipated, Gemma returned. 'Sorry, Laila. It's really overwhelming. The more I learn, the more questions I have. Questions that I don't know if I'll ever find the answers to or if I even *want* to know the answers to.'

'We can stop, if you like.'

'I think there's one more search we should do,' Gemma said.

They found one more record, and then that needed double-checking, too. Gemma searched electoral rolls. She scrolled, she clicked, she read. She found her mother's name. She checked the date of birth. Again, she read everything. She got Laila to do the same.

The sinking feeling returned. White noise pulsed in her ears.

Gemma stared at her birth mother's death certificate for what seemed like an age. Claire Rita Reed, living in East London, an admin assistant for an undisclosed company, died of cancer aged fifty-two, on 16 November last year.

Last year!

'Oh, no.' Laila put a hand over her mouth.

'I never entertained the idea she could have died,' Gemma said, stunned. 'I just never did. How stupid was that?' A tear dropped on the keyboard.

'I'm sorry, Gem. Life can be so shitty sometimes.'

'And here I was, more worried about whether she'd want to meet me! Oh, God, why didn't I do this earlier?'

More tears fell and the world became a smudge, a sheet of frosted glass. Laila rubbed Gemma's back and let her cry.

Even though, for thirty-six years, it never seemed as if she'd had a birth mother, Gemma now felt her passing keenly and desperately. The information that had previously felt impersonal, suddenly became personal. The biological mother she'd finally taken the courage to find was now not even here to meet, let alone welcome into her life. All that was left were words on a piece of paper. Gemma held her head in her hands and sobbed with an acute sense of loss – the loss of a parent, the loss of an opportunity and the loss of hope.

August Discoveries:
More bits of broken clay pipes – how many there are! But it makes sense when you know that they were only smoked once or twice before thrown away. A lead token that was used as a coin substitute for the exchange of goods and services in the seventeenth and eighteenth centuries. A black leather watch strap, whose age I can't tell. An absolutely disgusting bloated dead rat. But the worst thing of all, is the tragic and untimely death of my birth mother.

September

Chapter 35

The divorce application came via email on the first Friday of the month. It was as unemotional as Gemma's social services file, which in this case was a good thing. All she had to do was read it over and sign it. The lawyer she'd found via a friend of Timothy's was a charming man in his sixties who, somewhere along the way, had abandoned the formalities of suits in favour of golfing attire. Gemma did what she had to do as quickly as possible so she could get on with her life, without Adam.

Yet even though she was trying to be stoic, she still felt sad. There was nothing pleasant about your marriage ending, even if you knew it was for the best. It was the finality of it and the loss of what could have been. She gave in to the sorrow and cried until the tears dried up.

Then she updated her friends and family, who were all champagne-emoji supportive, and then announced the news on The Mudlarkers' Club WhatsApp chat. She knew the mudlarkers would lift her mood as much as her older friends did and they didn't disappoint. Laila kept her response simple with a single fist-pump emoji, Timothy said *Thinking of you*, and Nick sent her a video clip of Taylor Swift's song, "We are never ever getting back together", which made her smile. A long text came in from

Phyllida about how this was a new chapter for Gemma and how she was going to get through it and thrive. It was like Phyllida had amalgamated all the positive messages and reels Gemma had sent her recently and packaged it into one.

On Saturday, Gemma needed a diversion and decided to try her luck mudlarking in West London at the Hammersmith part of the river.

Grey cloud slung low like a tarpaulin and the traffic was busier than usual. She headed to Hammersmith Bridge, which was jostling with cyclists and joggers, and she scrambled down the riverbank, flattening weeds and taking care of her footing when she got to the mud. Two large mallard ducks glanced her way but seemed unperturbed by her arrival.

For the first half an hour, Gemma found nothing but some colourful pebbles polished smooth by the tide. She turned them over and admired their shiny gloss before throwing them back into the water. She didn't keep stones or fossils. It wasn't that she didn't appreciate or like them; it was more because she felt that everything that was formed by nature should stay in the river and, for practical reasons, she only had a limited amount of storage space at home.

Gemma stood up to stretch her back. She cast her gaze across the river. In the distance, sun rays cut through a dark rain cloud and a faint rainbow cupped the sky. Further west, near three wooden boats, a man had set up an easel and was painting. Closer by, a small clique of seagulls settled in the water, floating like rubber ducks in a bath. Then, only about a metre away, something glinted. It was probably nothing. A silver ring-top from a can or a fifty-pence coin. Still, she couldn't ignore it.

Wedged between two mossy stones was a ring. Gemma picked it up. It was a simple gold band with a circular pale-blue gemstone edged in gold. It wasn't old or fancy, but it was striking. Was it a real gem or coloured glass, gold plate or solid gold? She tried it on. It slid easily onto the fourth finger of her right hand. It needed a gentle wash in mild detergent but otherwise it was in perfect condition.

Whose was it and why was it on the foreshore? Had its owner lost it, or had they purposely discarded it from heartbreak or anger after the end of a relationship?

Gemma extended her arm and flexed her hand to admire the ring. The delicate, semi-translucent colour of the stone reminded her of a summer evening sky, and its gold, the sun. She did the same with her left hand. The small diamond in her engagement ring may have sparkled brighter, yet it seemed blemished somehow. It had lost its meaning and its relevance. Suddenly and with surprising clarity, Gemma realised that she no longer felt anything for it at all. She walked with purpose down to the shoreline. With the water lapping over her wellies, she pulled off the engagement ring and threw it forcefully into the river. It didn't go as far as she'd have liked, but it went far enough. It plopped unceremoniously into the water and quietly disappeared. She imagined her mudlarking friends cheering her on and Nick giving her a fist-pump in person.

Goodbye, old life. Goodbye, marriage. Goodbye, Adam.

Gemma kept the newly found ring on her finger. As she returned to the boat ramp and her belongings, she thought about the cycle of life. How it wasn't just about when someone dies, another is born, it's also when a discarded object, unwanted and unloved, is discovered and then wanted and loved all over again. Gemma had given to the river in exchange for what she had taken. She was making a new story for herself and her ring. Having originally symbolised her commitment to Adam, it now represented her allegiance to the river. She was intrinsically linked to the Thames, its history and its future. Who would eventually find her jewellery and what would they wonder about its owner?

It was difficult to concentrate after that. All Gemma could

think about was how full of strength she felt after having given her engagement ring to the Thames, to let the river decide where its fate lay. She felt a sense of release. A sense of freedom. She was Gemma Hudson, single, proud, strong.

Later, when Gemma was cleaning her new ring, Phyllida messaged on the WhatsApp group chat.

Good news, mudlarkers! Although historian Megan O'Connor is unable to give us a talk at the moment, we have another contender. Last-minute.com, I know, but Professor Rosie Simpson is free next Friday. She is an archaeological scientist and an expert in glass, and one of my son's lecturers. She promises to bring the past to life and, according to Samuel, she didn't need much persuasion. Supposedly, academics are as keen for publicity and social media followers as the rest of us. She also, he says, likes the sound of her own voice. But who knows? Maybe Samuel is being churlish because she gave him a low essay mark. Who's keen?

Gemma was definitely up for it because it sounded interesting and, she didn't have anything else on. So was Nick (probably for the same reasons). Timothy wanted to come but was still getting fatigued and didn't think he was ready for an evening out, to which everyone expressed their sympathies. Laila was a maybe, but Gemma suspected that was only because she wanted to feign a typical teenage non-plussed attitude.

Phyllida seemed so excited that she'd have gone on her own if no one else had been keen. She immediately sent an invite: *Six p.m. at The Anchor pub, Bankside. We'll start off with our usual meeting, followed by the professor at seven-thirty.*

Immediately after that, Nick messaged Gemma.

Sorry for the radio silence. Things got busy and the low tides at Vauxhall haven't been user friendly. If you still want to mudlark, there's a low tide on Saturday seventeenth. Sunset starts at seven when the tide will be at its lowest. But that's all right, isn't it? You've got a headtorch and I can buy one. How about it?

Gemma didn't hesitate. *Wonderful. Looking forward to it*, she replied. She suspected that Nick was now feeling how she did when Adam left, alone and empty. A shared mudlark was just what he needed.

Let's meet at five at MI6. I like saying that! Feel like James Bond. But it's true, the best beach access is right next to the building.

Chapter 36

Phyllida had booked a private room at The Anchor for their next meeting and their first talk by a guest speaker. She'd wanted a venue that was rich in history and The Anchor was famed for being the sole remaining river tavern from Shakespeare's time. The room had the air of a tired old stately home, with its wood panelling, long table and high-backed red damask chairs. Despite its faded grandeur, having the room to themselves made Gemma feel a little bit special – and even more so when Phyllida asked if she could make a toast to her post-divorce future. It was a little embarrassing but Gemma appreciated her friend's support. After that, they had an hour to talk about all things mudlarking (like the popularity of Nick's gold-painted trowel by other foreshore searchers), and other things that weren't (like how Phyllida's husband had started counselling). Then it was time to greet the guest speaker.

'Professor Simpson!' Phyllida said with glee. 'We're so pleased you can join us in this quaint pub, with ghosts of the past. I believe we're in good company: Samuel Pepys, Dr Samuel Johnson, Shakespeare, and most likely a bunch of pirates. Ha!' Phyllida's nerves and excitement were getting the better of her.

'Thank you, Phyllida. But please call me Rosie.' The professor was a forty-something woman in an elegant navy suit. For the first time, Gemma wished that she was sometimes required to attend suit-wearing occasions.

'Of course. Rosie it is. Now let me introduce you to everyone …'

After Phyllida had done the introductions, she sat back down next to Nick and let Rosie take over. Nick slid Phyllida's wine towards her. She smiled appreciatively.

For forty minutes, Rosie talked to them about the history of glass in Britain and London in particular, sprinkling her lecture with humorous and quirky stories to keep them interested. Or, in Laila's case, to prevent her from falling asleep. Gemma wondered if she'd had a late night. Nick, by contrast, appeared enamoured. He was leaning on the table, with his head resting in a hand, not taking his eyes off the professor. Perhaps he'd acquired a new interest in glass.

'… And that, I hope, will give you a little more insight into the wonderful world of glass in this country,' Rosie concluded. 'Now, when you're out in the field, you'll be able to recognise different shards of glass and better understand their origins. If you like, you can follow me at "profrosie" on Instagram and Bluesky. And I'm soon to launch a YouTube channel.'

Phyllida burst into a round of clapping. Nick came in a close second, with Gemma and Laila following.

'Do you have any questions?' Rosie asked.

Naturally, Phyllida did. She produced a small black iridescent bottle that had lost its bottom. 'I'd love to know what this may have contained.'

Rosie turned the object over in her hands. 'Nice. Shame it's broken. It looks like an apothecary bottle from the seventeenth century. It's likely to have contained "plague water", herbs steeped in wine. It did nothing, of course, to stop you getting the plague or to cure you of it.'

'What I'd like to know is, why was glass, as opposed to other materials, always used for bottles of medicine?' Nick asked.

'Good question. It's Nick, isn't it?'

He nodded enthusiastically.

'Basically, glass was found to be less reactive than ceramic, and coloured glass helped protect medicine from light.'

'Can you find bottles that still have stuff in them?' Laila had woken up.

'It's very rare. It's not common to find a whole bottle either, most are broken, and it would have to have its stopper, of course.'

Phyllida was then reminded of someone she'd read about who'd found an old perfume bottle with a dribble of fragrance still inside. Except it smelt so rank, they wished they hadn't been able to take the top off. This segued the conversation on to the bad smells sometimes encountered when mudlarking. Even though it wasn't Rosie's expertise, she generously gave them twenty minutes more of her time, and Gemma found herself daydreaming about a new career as an archaeological scientist.

Nick, on the other hand, looked as if he was imagining something else entirely. Gemma swallowed, as if her throat had suddenly become dry. Right then, Gemma doubted that his admiration of the professor was solely based on his appreciation of history. She wasn't jealous of the professor, was she? It was ridiculous. Nick was free to admire whomever he wanted, just as she was. Gemma excused herself to go to the bathroom. She splashed her face with water, dried it with a paper towel, then took a moment to compose herself.

When she left the bathroom and spotted the professor and Nick talking near the pub entrance, the feeling came back again. Rosie was standing close to Nick, talking, and he was typing into his phone. Rosie laughed and touched his arm. Gemma was sure professional speakers didn't usually do that to members of their audience – or was she reading too much into it? She turned and hurried back to the private room.

Phyllida was studying Laila's found luggage tag and giving her tips on how to research it. Gemma poured herself the last of the water from the carafe and drank. She told herself to pull it together. Next, she went to find her wine glass. There was still a puddle of alcohol left. She threw her head back and drank it down, wishing that the bitter taste in her mouth wasn't caused by envy. Where had that suddenly come from? Did she really like Nick? The thought made her pause for a moment, unsure what to make of it. Or, perhaps she did.

But no! What was she thinking? Having already told herself that she wasn't ready to get back on the dating scene, the last thing she should do is go to battle for Nick's attention. As she poured herself another glass of wine, prudence came to the fore. Nick would stay a mudlarking friend and that was all. She was definitely *not* going to get involved with him. Or with anybody. Absolutely not.

Chapter 37

A week later, Gemma met Nick in front of the imposing, cream and green British Secret Service building. Her heart skipped and hopped for a couple of seconds, which made her flustered. Oh, why were these new feelings trying to get in the way of their friendship? Thankfully, Nick unwittingly diverted her emotions. When he saw her, he started talking into his collar from one side of his mouth, making her laugh. 'Roger that,' he said. 'Gotta go. Suspect is approaching.'

'You're such a big kid,' she said.

'I watch too many crime shows.'

'And I bet you always want to work out who did it.'

'Of course! Isn't that the point? I love trying to be one step ahead of the show.'

'Doesn't that take away from its enjoyment?'

'That *is* the enjoyment!' he said, as if he couldn't believe he had to spell it out.

They walked down Lack's Dock Slipway, disturbing a bunch of seagulls. Nick started chatting about the TV series he was currently watching and how he'd like to try writing one some time. 'I might even do a screenwriting course,' he said.

'I'm in awe of fiction writers,' Gemma said. 'I wouldn't know where to start.'

'Trust me, real life gives you everything you need. You just need to be on alert. Everything you do and everyone you meet can form a potential story.'

'Oh, God, does that mean you could plagiarise something I do or say?' Gemma pulled a face. 'I'd better be careful then.'

'I wouldn't call it plagiarism as such. Inspiration, perhaps. Anyway, you're making out that I know what I'm doing. Don't worry, I don't. Most of what I write, I end up deleting.' He laughed as if he couldn't believe how bad a fiction writer he was. 'But enough about me. The mud beckons.'

'Yes, shall we head east first, away from the bridge, then turn back and go west?'

Nick nodded and went a few metres up the beach where there were larger rocks and chunks of pebbles. Gemma decided to hug the waterline where the stones were small. For a moment, she paused, closed her eyes and listened. All she wanted to hear was the *sotto voce* of the water. Her heartbeat slowed; her breathing deepened. And so, she was ready to begin.

For ten minutes, they larked together but alone. A stretch of cloud darkened overhead. Although the sun hadn't yet set, she almost needed her headtorch.

Then Nick started up again. He seemed to have reached his time limit for keeping silent. 'Found anything?' he asked.

'Not yet.'

Gemma squatted at the tideline, thinking she'd seen a cloth seal, a lead disc that, between the fourteenth and eighteenth centuries, was attached to woollen cloth to prove its quality and that its tax had been paid. But when it started moving and scuttled away, she realised it was a crab. It took another fifteen minutes of searching to find something much more interesting: half a French franc. She placed it into the bucket. Then Nick lifted a large key from the mud, crusty with corrosion.

'Hey, look,' he called out. 'I wonder what this unlocked?'

'Who knows,' she said, not taking her eyes off the half-metre square in front of her.

'Another good item for your electrolysis kit,' Nick said.

'I'll get you one for your birthday.'

'10 January, in case you were wondering.'

'Ha-ha,' she said. Yet she couldn't help but want to try and remember the date.

'When's yours?'

'You don't really want to know when my birthday is, do you?'

'Just making small talk.'

'We're meant to be mudlarking, you know.'

'I can mudli-task, or should it be muddy-task?' He frowned. 'Sorry, I've got a soft spot for puns.'

She laughed. Then, she spotted an iron nail. She scooped it out and found two more, heavy and bent out of shape, half submerged in the mud. She let another slop of water wash them clean.

'What have you got there?' Nick said.

'Nails. Probably from a ship.'

'Nice.'

They went into the bucket too.

'Shall we turn around?' Nick suggested.

Gemma didn't see why not. 'How long until the tide turns?'

'I reckon we've got a good couple of hours.' Nick looked up to the dusky sky as if it might give him the answer.

Gemma nodded and slung her bucket over an arm.

'You know, someone found an axe head along here,' Nick said.

'There'll be lots of pieces of flint, too, I imagine. Although I'm not very good at spotting those.'

'Flint?'

'From the Stone Age.'

'Wow.' Nick sighed. 'Any use for a goose feather?' He held up a large, perfectly formed feather.

'Beautiful! You could stick it in that pork pie pot you found,' Gemma suggested.

'Nah. I can keep it for you, if you like?'

'Sure. It's pretty.'

They mudlarked in silence as they headed towards the arches of Vauxhall Bridge. The London Eye rotated slowly in the background, on the other side of the river. The sky gradually rusted over and cast an eery glow over the water and the buildings.

Even though Nick was with her, Gemma found she was still able to lose herself in the moment, and be completely and utterly absorbed in the past. Adam was no longer dominating her thoughts, and she wasn't mulling over the death of her birth mother. There were no feelings of being alone in the world, no inner chatter about whether she remembered to take the washing out of the dryer or how she mustn't forget her brother's birthday on Sunday. She was in a lovely place of peace – even if her attraction to her mudlarking companion was something that was proving difficult to ignore.

'You know,' Nick started, his voice quieter, his tone contemplative. 'I'm really starting to get it now. I mean, I thought I did but now I really, really do. Here, with you, I feel so relaxed. I guess Dad must have felt like this when he was metal detecting.'

'Was he a journalist too?' Gemma said.

'He was a frustrated poet by night and a bored bookkeeper by day. I don't think he ever achieved what he'd hoped for. But he always made the best of things and we never wanted for much. Do you come from a long line of medics?'

'Not at all. Mum was an editor and dad was a teacher.' Gemma looked into the murky water sloshing at her feet. 'Then again, I could do, I suppose, because they're not my biological parents.'

'What's the latest with the search for your birth mother?'

Gemma gave him an abridged version of what she and Laila had found out, trying to brush over how much it had upset her.

'But even if your birth mother isn't around anymore, relatives will be. I'd be tracking them down if I were you,' Nick suggested.

'That's what Laila said. I've got a half-brother somewhere but what if he doesn't know about me? And what if he doesn't want to see me? I don't want to be rejected all over again.'

'Mmm …' Nick said, having a hard time coming up with a positive response.

They were at the eastern side of Vauxhall Bridge where the lost River Effra once entered the Thames. They had to jump over a storm relief drain that had been cut into the gravel to get to the other side. Here, there was more mud, black and sludgy like concrete before it sets. The sun now resembled a dollop of marmalade hovering between the skyline and the river.

'I could help you do more sleuthing, if you like?' Nick said.

'That's kind of you to offer—'

'—I've got links to all sorts of people,' he said enticingly.

'Sounds dodgy.'

He laughed, then he yawned. It was a long one. 'Gosh, sorry,' he said.

'Late night?' she asked.

He nodded.

'With the prof?' she added. It was cheeky, she knew, but it just came out. Except she wasn't supposed to be concerned about the professor!

'Eh? No,' Nick said, as if being kept up by Rosie was a possibility, which only annoyed Gemma more because she realised the thought of it *actually* being the professor rankled. 'I had a deadline. Anyway, why did you think I was with Rosie?'

'I saw you two at the pub after the talk.' She tried to say it nonchalantly but it seemed to come out accusatorily.

'Right,' Nick said, looking, for a second, quizzical. 'I was getting her number because I had an idea for another story,' he explained.

Oh, God, of course he was.

Nick continued. 'You know she talked about how the Romans were great at recycling? I thought it was a good environmental angle. Very topical. We caught up during the week, and now I've got more than enough info for a story.' He smiled and got a faraway look in his eye, which made Gemma feel momentarily redundant.

'Well, that's nice,' she said.

'Yeah. The prof is nice,' Nick said, mishearing her.

'I bet she is,' Gemma muttered.

'Hey, don't be like that. I hadn't been angling for anything more, but she happened to ask if I wanted to go for a drink afterwards and I had no reason not to …' He smiled sheepishly.

'Yeah, of course, that's great,' Gemma said, wanting to be pleased for him.

'We were getting on well, you know, and she's a pretty cool woman,' Nick added, as if she needed an explanation.

'She is,' Gemma conceded, even though she now wished she'd never mentioned the professor. She didn't want to turn into a sourpuss again, so she bent over to refocus on the foreshore.

'She's so intelligent—' Nick went on.

'Uh-huh.'

'— and dynamic.'

Now, the attention on Professor Rosie was really beginning to rile. Was he purposely trying to wind her up because she told him she didn't want to date?

'But she can be quite intense,' Nick added. 'And I've never been out with an older woman before.'

Gemma looked up. 'How much older?'

'Seven years.'

'Oh, well, good for you.'

She smiled, and tried to bring her focus back to mudlarking. She felt the ground beneath her front foot become quaggy and less stable and reached out for something to hold on to, but there was nothing and Nick wasn't close enough. She took a step backwards with her right leg to anchor herself, but that foot began sinking. She turned and watched as her leg and one of her ex-mother-in-law's pink wellington boots slowly disappeared into the mud, as if they had nothing whatsoever to do with her anymore.

Chapter 38

'Nick, help! My boot!' Gemma heard the alarm in her voice as if that, too, belonged to another person. Her bucket swung frantically as she waved her arms at him.

'Don't move,' he said.

'I'm not. I *can't*!'

'Okay, I'm coming.'

Even though he was now about three metres away, Nick didn't rush, which she'd have liked him to. Instead, he carefully tip-toed so he didn't get caught himself. 'You must have hit a sink hole,' he said. 'They can suck you in.'

'I know, Nick. It's happening right now.' Gemma didn't want to panic but his laissez-faire manner was making her agitated.

Gemma tried to put less pressure on her right leg so it didn't succumb to the mud. But it was impossible to maintain and only made her left foot sink deeper. Her legs were fast becoming foundation posts in the sludge.

'Don't worry, we'll get you out. I think you're supposed to keep moving so you don't get stuck.'

'I know that but I already am.'

After what seemed like minutes not seconds, Nick was close enough to reach out and grab her. He got an arm and pulled.

The only thing that moved was her shoulder.

'Ow, that hurts,' she cried.

'Sorry, but better a dislocation than drowning by mud.'

'I'm hoping those aren't my only two options.'

'Ready, go.' He yanked again but she didn't budge. 'You're going to have to take your foot out of the boot,' he said.

'I'm not doing that.'

'It's just a boot.'

'It's my ex-mother-in-law's.'

'Who cares?'

'I do.'

'Oh, no,' Nick said looking past her. 'Don't panic, but the water's coming in pretty damn quickly.'

'What? I thought you said the tides ...?' Gemma turned to glance behind her. The river water looked furious and fast-approaching. She felt her hand crush Nick's, as her body switched into flight mode, worsened by the fact that she was physically unable to flee.

'I did. I mean, I thought ... Look, it doesn't matter now. We've got to get out of here.'

'Can you try and pull me out again?'

'Okay, but this is the last time, otherwise—'

'Please?'

Her right leg exited its boot completely, but her left leg sunk further into the mud. She could hear the water behind her. It was in her ears, and in her heart, as though it was inside her as well and she couldn't escape.

'That's it. We've gotta get outta here.' Nick's voice had a sense of urgency to it that she hadn't heard before.

'Let's call a police boat,' she suggested.

'No, by the time we find the number, call them, then wait for them ...'

'I really don't want to lose the boots,' Gemma said again, even though she knew she was being petulant and irrational.

'And I don't want to lose you. Look, it's getting dark and dangerous. Come on.' Nick wrenched her arm. The bucket flew off and her left foot came free of the boot. Her socks squelched into the riverbed but the momentum he'd gained helped pull her with him. She tried to get the bucket, except it was out of her reach.

'Leave it,' he said.

The mud was cold, dense and stubborn. It resisted her every move and clung to her socks and jeans, weighing her down, not wanting to let her go. She glanced behind her.

With every tug from Nick came a rush of river water that covered her feet completely. On the next surge, they were knee-deep in water.

'It's going to sweep us away.' Gemma's voice wavered. They were floundering, out of their depth. She thought she was going to cry.

'There are some exit stairs over there.' He pointed.

'The vertical ones?' She didn't like the look of them, especially as she was now only in socks. 'They're not always stable.'

'We have to take what we can get. The river's rising at such a rate. It could carry us away before we've even realised we're not standing on anything anymore.'

Nick was right. Gemma didn't wish to dwell on how much time they had before the water level rose to such a height that the force of the current would prove too strong.

'I can't believe this is happening,' Gemma said. 'How could you have got the tides so wrong?'

He ignored her. 'Just keep moving forward.'

'I mean, I've never had this happen before.'

'Yeah, well, sometimes things don't always go to plan.'

'Mudlarking is all about planning.'

'Can you stop being contrary?'

'I'm not being con—' she started before realising her hypocrisy had been caught out. She lowered her head and attempted to run. It was impossible. Even fast wading was a struggle. Sharp-edged stones dug into her soles. She tripped on a submerged rock. Her arms flailed and the river slapped her face as if telling her off. She managed to right herself before falling in completely.

'Oh, God, are you all right? There better not be a grenade around here like Timothy talked about.'

'Don't say that!'

'Yeah, sorry. Look, we're nearly there.' Nick pointed ahead, then turned to check on the water behind them.

Gemma didn't dare look. She could tell by the pull of the tide that this was one arm-wrestle it was determined to win. Even though Nick was faster than her, he didn't let her go. His hand gripped hers tightly. The water tugged at her jeans and her thighs ached. But she wasn't going to let the river get the better of her. She kept her sight on the stairs and focused on moving towards them. It was a slow, painful process. Then, finally they were there. Nick took hold of the metal railing as the river sluiced into his legs.

'You go,' she said.

'No, you first.'

'For God's sake, you're right there. Just go,' she insisted.

He wouldn't. He was as stubborn as the damn mud.

'Quick,' he said. 'I'll give you a lift up. But be careful.'

Gemma held on to the metal posts either side of the rungs and, with Nick's help, hoisted herself up. Her legs weighed heavy with sodden denim and mud-caked socks, and the rucksack pulled at her shoulders. The narrow metal rungs were painful on the balls of her feet. The only thing keeping her going was the fear of being swept away. Halfway up, she glanced down at Nick. What was he still doing at the bottom?

'I don't know if the steps can handle both of us,' he called up to her.

'But the water …?'

'Just hurry.'

She went as quickly as she could. When she got to the top of the wall, she scrambled onto the concrete. She lay on the wall on her stomach and reached over to take hold of the metal sides.

Who knew if it would make any difference, but as Nick had done it for her at the bottom, she'd do it for him at the top. Adrenalin and fear were still pumping through her.

'Come on, Nick,' she urged.

Nick proved to be nimbler than he looked because he charged up the stairs. When he reached her, Gemma helped him onto the wall.

'Jesus,' he panted.

She nodded. A lump in her throat was preventing her from speaking. For a moment, they sat together silently, their backs to the darkening river.

Until, suddenly, he reached over and gave her a brief, tight hug. 'We're okay,' he said. 'We did it.'

Then, as if the pressure from his squeeze travelled up her neck and into her eyes, tears began to well. She pulled away.

'We did it,' she agreed. Except it was going to take more than that to help her get over how close a call they'd just had with Mother Nature.

She turned to look at where they'd been. Where she'd abandoned her boots. The tide was still coming in at pace, the water level rising by the minute. The sun had disappeared completely and the sky resembled thick dark-blue ink. Her bucket was a floating speck of black. Her boots were nowhere to be seen. She shivered. She had to get away from the edge. She stood up, adjusted her rucksack and looked down at her feet. Yet even here, she couldn't escape the water. She was now standing in two puddles of it, her jeans dripping.

'Are you all right?' Nick asked.

'Fine. You?'

'Yeah. What a rush, though, huh?' He took off his rucksack, unzipped it, pulled out two cans of beer and handed her one. She took it.

'See, I knew you'd want one.'

She looked at the beer in her hand, which she didn't particularly fancy. 'Actually, I think I just want to go home, now.'

'Let's have this first. Get our heart rates back to normal. There's no rush, is there?'

'I don't really want to be here anymore.' She put the can of beer on the wall. 'The Tube's that way, isn't it?' Gemma pointed in the vague direction of the station.

'Hang on, look at the state of you. You can't get on public transport like that.'

'I don't care.'

'I'll order an Uber,' he said, pulling out his phone.

Gemma began walking up the slipway, trying not to cry from the shock of being in danger, the relief at dodging it and the sadness at losing the boots. Nick caught up with her. His shoes made sucking noises and his trousers gave off a wet-dog type of a smell.

'I've just had an idea,' he said brightly, drinking some of his beer. 'I could use this in my book. I need more dramatic tension and to up the action.'

'You're kidding!' Gemma said rhetorically, not because she was interested.

'Don't you think that's a good idea?'

'No, I don't.'

'The characters are on a quest but at the moment, it's all a bit samey.'

Gemma stopped and turned to him. 'You're unbelievable.'

'What? What do you mean?'

'We could have *died*, and you want to turn our real-life emergency into entertainment?' she shouted.

'Hang on, I'm trying to lighten things up and anyway, they say write about what you know,' he said.

'So, write about something *else* you know,' she snapped and marched ahead.

'Hey, Gemma, wait.' Nick caught up with her. 'I'm really sorry, okay?'

'No, please, I'm done with tonight.' Gemma shook her head. She felt so rattled that no apology was going to cut it with her right now. 'You put us into a dangerous situation by getting the tide times wrong and that shouldn't happen. Mudlarking isn't meant to be scary. Ever.'

'I know it isn't—'

'I'll make my own way home.'

'Don't be like that.'

'Here's your ride.' She pointed to the headlights of a car driving slowly towards them.

'Don't be silly, come with me and I'll get out first. We don't live *that* far away from each other.'

'Guilt-payment for an Uber ride home is not going to suddenly make things right,' she said.

'I was just trying to be nice. Anyway, you could have checked the tide times, too, you know,' he spat back at her.

'I didn't think I had to. You were the one organising it.' She noticed the Uber driver staring at her. 'What are you looking at?' she blurted.

'Hey, don't bring him into this,' Nick said. 'Come on, please, let's stop arguing. Just get in the car.'

'Why aren't you getting the message, Nick? I don't want to be around you right now.'

Nick looked taken aback.

Too bad. She wished he'd hurry up and leave.

'Right. Well. That's that then,' he said soberly and got into the car.

Gemma turned her back on him without saying goodbye. She didn't want to wave or watch him drive away. She just wanted to be on her own.

Chapter 39

Gemma had always considered the Thames to be a gentle, caring friend. The sort that gives you chocolate when you're feeling down or lets you borrow a dress, even if the last time you did so, a stranger knocked red wine over you. Now, she'd experienced first-hand its other wild side, where its charming exterior hid a quick temper and wasn't to be messed with.

The following day, Gemma was still on high alert. She startled at the sound of a flyer being pushed through the front door letterbox, panicked when she nearly overfilled the bath and jumped when the phone rang. The call turned out to be Nick, who left an apologetic voice message, which she chose to ignore. She didn't want to talk to him. She felt angry, disgruntled, and annoyed at herself as much as with him. He'd nearly got them drowned, for goodness' sake!

The only problem was that on Thursday, Nick confirmed his attendance for Saturday's Mudlarkers' Club meeting. As much as Gemma loved their get-togethers, this was one she would have to miss. She did not want to see him. She gave an excuse about having to go to a family brunch with her parents who were in town. Instead, she would go mudlarking on her own on Sunday – it was imperative she got back onto the foreshore before a fear of the river set in. And she accepted Timothy's invitation for Sunday afternoon tea on his houseboat.

Thankfully, when she went out to mudlark, there was no rapidly incoming tide or terrifying quicksand sludge. By contrast, the river resembled a playful brown puddle, far from the aggressive torrent she'd experienced a week ago. Two hours slipped away as if they'd been ten minutes. She found a modern mother-of-pearl button, a tortoiseshell comb gluggy with silt, a worn-smooth bag seal, and reassurance that the Thames was still her friend.

At Timothy's, Laila had made chocolate chip cookies from scratch. 'Not from a packet,' she assured Gemma when she arrived. Not that Gemma would have been able to tell the difference. She never baked. Laila proudly shook the tin of biscuits at her, insisting she take one.

'They taste wonderful,' Gemma said.

'Laila's turning into a proper little housewife,' Timothy said.

'You can't say that, Gramps. It's sexist,' Laila said.

'You know what I mean. I was trying to pay you a compliment.'

Laila rolled her eyes at Gemma as if to say *thank goodness you're here as I've been having to deal with this ever since he came out of hospital.*

'Did you have a lovely time with your family?' Timothy asked.

'Yes, thank you,' Gemma said, and went on to tell them about her parents' move to the country so that she didn't have to keep on lying.

'Anyway, how are you doing, Timothy?' she asked.

'It's such a bore not having a body that complies with one's mind.' He smiled but it didn't cover up how tired he looked, as if after all these years, life was finally beginning to catch up with him. 'But hey, ho.'

'Another biscuit, Gramps?'

'No, thank you, Laila. Don't you have to go?'

'Yep. Sorry, Gemma. I'll see you another time.'

Timothy waited until the front door had closed and they'd seen her walk past the houseboat window, so he could be certain Laila had left before speaking. 'I hope you don't mind, Gemma, but I encouraged Laila to go out as there's something I want to talk to you about. More tea before I begin?'

Gemma didn't want any more tea, but she made one for Timothy.

'I'm keen for your advice, particularly as you've got to know Laila these past few weeks. You see, Laila's birth mother has been in contact.'

Gemma's chest constricted on hearing 'birth mother'. Is this what was now going to happen whenever she came across those two words strung together?

'Nadira will be coming out of prison soon. She says she's now clean and wants to reconnect with Laila.'

'That's wonderful news,' Gemma said.

'Laila doesn't think so. She wants nothing to do with her. And she doesn't want to go back to living with Jodie either. I don't think I'm the best person to be looking after her since the fall. Let's face it, Laila's been looking after *me*. As much as I love having her around, that's not right for a seventeen-year-old, especially now that she's back at school.'

Gemma nodded. It was a conundrum she suspected wasn't going to be solved over a cup of tea. 'Sometimes these things take time,' she said. 'Laila needs to get used to the idea of her mother being out in the world *and* interested in her.'

'I agree and I'd rather sort this out between ourselves than get social services involved. If they hear about my accident, they'll start poking their noses in and making decisions for her. Until Laila's eighteen, she's still considered a child.' Timothy rested his head on the back of the chair.

'Perhaps the first step is for Laila to get back on speaking terms with Jodie, who's clearly trying to do the best by her.'

'Jodie and Simon have such goodness in their hearts but, in

my opinion, their ordered, routine-driven and disciplined lifestyle hasn't benefited Laila as they'd hoped. She's a free spirit and needs to feel as if she has some independence. It's a case of letting the rope out slowly.'

'Has Laila interacted with Jodie at all since she left?' Gemma asked.

'Briefly, at school, I believe. I was tempted to orchestrate a proper meeting. But I didn't think it would go down well.'

'You could see if Laila would consider hearing Jodie out in a neutral place like a café and with you there to mediate if necessary,' Gemma suggested. 'Laila may project a tough exterior but she's a good kid. I suspect that deep down she doesn't want to fall out with her foster parents and would secretly like to have a connection with her birth mother.'

'I hope so.'

'How about I try and talk to her?' Gemma offered.

'Would you?' Timothy's eyes lit up.

'I can't promise anything.' She didn't like to tell Timothy that the only experience she'd had with teenagers was when she was one. But she was enjoying the connection she'd made with Laila and wanted to help. She knew how wonderful it was to have people in your life who deeply cared about you regardless of whether you were biologically related to them or not, and she didn't want Laila to lose what she had.

'No, of course not. But she listens to you. It's been nothing but Gemma this, Gemma that.' He laughed as if recalling a fond memory.

'I'll see what I can do.'

Chapter 40

The next week, Gemma was so busy with work that she didn't have the time or energy to do anything but eat and sleep. They had a rush of new patients as if cancer cells had bandied together to have a community party. With every patient who left, having completed their treatment, there were even more to take their place. It was tough but all she and her team could do was stay strong and positive. Yet it wasn't always easy, and sometimes it felt all-consuming and exhausting.

Come Friday night, she was pleased to have some time to think about her promise to Timothy. She wondered how she could instigate a catch-up with Laila that wasn't an obvious ruse for a serious conversation. She still had Laila's jar of Nutella which she could give her, but that wasn't enough. Then, she had an idea. Maybe Laila might be interested in an art exhibition – nothing she might view as fusty or boring, but something modern and edgy. There was an exhibition by an up-and-coming installation artist at the Tate and a photographic one at Hamiltons Gallery. Then, she found the one: the art of the infamous and elusive graffiti artist Banksy in Soho. She would be keen to go even if Laila wasn't. Thankfully, Laila said yes, and they agreed to meet on Sunday afternoon at the train station.

*

Gemma wasn't entirely sure how to broach the rift between Laila and her foster mother but knew that it would be better to ease it into the conversation later in their catch-up rather than hit Laila with it cold. On the train, they chatted about Timothy and Gemma's work and what Laila had discovered about the old luggage tag she'd found mudlarking. Then at the exhibition, they got so caught up in the artwork that Gemma decided to leave it until the end, as they were leaving.

'So tell me, what else is going on apart from a new haircut?' Gemma said pointing to Laila's hair, where one side had been shaved, the other kept long.

'Do you like it?' Laila said.

'Well, it kind of looks like you changed your mind halfway through.'

'Ha-ha. I like it anyway.'

Laila paused at the window of a clothing shop.

'How's school?' Gemma asked.

'It's okay.' They started walking again. 'An expert on learning difficulties is going to give me strategies for reading and writing.' Laila sounded unimpressed.

'I'm sure it will be helpful.'

'I've decided dyslexia should be called "unilexia". "Dys" means bad or abnormal and is pretty insulting if you ask me. "Uni" is like unique, one of a kind.'

'I like that,' Gemma said.

'Gramps has been helping me with my homework, too. Well, supervising really. It doesn't make it nicer, just a bit easier.'

'I could help, too, depending on the subject matter.'

'Would you?' Laila said.

Gemma's heart expanded at hearing the eagerness in Laila's voice.

'You could come over on a weekend or a Friday night. We could hang out, watch a movie and do algebra. Maybe not all at the same time, though.' Gemma laughed.

'Really?'

'Sure. I won't be offended if you don't want to. I'm not too bad at maths.'

'Jodie was rubbish. Not that she's dumb or anything. She's just not cut out to be a teacher.'

Finally, an opening. 'How is Jodie?' Gemma asked.

'I saw her the other day, if that's what you mean. She's the one who organised the teacher's aide for my "unilexia". She's angry that I was somehow allowed to slip through the cracks. Plus, she wants me to go back and live with them.'

'How do you feel about that?'

'I came up with a better idea and made her a deal. My birth mother is coming out of prison soon and she's reached out to me.'

'Really? That's great, Laila.'

Laila looked non-plussed. 'I said to Jodie that I'd consider making contact with my birth mother if she lets me continue staying with Gramps.'

'You're a tough negotiator,' Gemma said.

'Nothing in this world is free,' Laila said wearily.

'You're too young to be saying things like that. Oooh, I like that dress.' Gemma pointed to a window mannequin.

'Do you want to go inside?'

'No, it's okay. I can tell it'll be wildly out of my price range.'

'We can gaze at it longingly, then.'

For a moment, they stopped and stared at the designer dress on display.

Gemma continued, 'The thing is, you've nothing to lose by connecting with your birth mother, especially if you've got the support of your foster parents. It doesn't mean you have to go and live with her or anything.'

'It's not going to be some fairy-tale reunion, you know,' Laila said with disdain.

'I'm not saying it will be, but you won't know unless you try.'

'Even it was, there's no guarantee she'll stick around.'

'Is that what you're worried about?'

'Yeah, I could lose her again, like I've lost her before. I can't. I just can't.' Laila shook her head.

Gemma locked her arm in Laila's as they headed down the street. 'Or,' Gemma said. 'You could gain an extra mum and your life might be all the richer for it. There are risks to everything we do and often the bigger the risk, the bigger the gain.'

Laila was silent for a moment. Then she asked with an edge of defensiveness in her voice, 'So what risks have you taken in your life that have worked out?'

Gemma stared ahead at nothing in particular, trying hard to think of risks she'd taken that had worked out. None came to mind. Unless she counted giving herself over to Adam. But even that ended up failing.

Chapter 41

Gemma was about to microwave her dinner when there was a knock at the door. It was seven-thirty on a Tuesday night in September. She wondered if it was Brian Anderson from two doors down who'd letter-dropped about a car burglary and how he wanted to set up a 'neighbourhood vigilante group'.

But it wasn't Brian. It was Nick. He had a feather behind his ear and was clutching multi-coloured floral wellington boots to his chest. They were pretty but they weren't Gwendoline's.

'The plain pink ones had sold out,' he said. 'And I never gave this to you. The goose feather I found mudlarking.' He pulled the feather from his ear and handed it to her.

She crossed her arms. She was still aggrieved and fuming.

'Okay, well, anyway, I've come to apologise,' he said retracting the feather. 'You're right, I should have been more careful when I checked the tides and I shouldn't have talked about my book. I didn't mean to be insensitive about your wellies or belittle how scary it was. Trust me, I was spooked, too.'

Gemma nodded. She couldn't find it in herself to look him in the eye, even though, deep down, she appreciated his apology.

'I hope you can forgive me.'

Gemma chewed her bottom lip. 'You know, it's not like I want to be mad at you,' she admitted.

'I don't want you to be, either.'

There was a moment's pause where neither of them spoke. Gemma considered how much longer she could stay cross with him, because it was proving difficult the longer he stood there.

'All right, show me this feather, then,' she said.

He gave it to her. She spun it between her fingers and watched how the porch light made the fawn-coloured feathers shimmer. 'Actually, I think it's from a mallard duck,' she said.

'If you say so. I'm no bird expert.'

'Me neither, to be fair.' She slid it behind her ear.

'These are a peace offering.' He placed the boots at her feet. 'Although I see you've brought some new ones already.' He nodded to the black boots sitting in the hallway.

'They were cheap and now having worn them, I know why,' Gemma said.

'Well, these weren't cheap, and I hope you'll get a chance to find out why.' Nick grinned.

He made her smile as he always did. 'Thank you,' she said. 'You didn't have to.'

'I know.'

She chewed a fingernail and kept looking at the boots. Even though she hadn't quite stopped being peeved with him, she was touched by his kindness. Those gentle eyes of his didn't stop looking at her, all of which was beginning to melt her steeliness and she wasn't sure what to do about it.

'I'll be off, then,' he said, as though he'd waited long enough for her to respond.

'No!' She blurted. 'I mean, wait …'

He paused, halfway between staying and going, wondering, she supposed, exactly what she was going to say.

'I'm sorry, too,' she said quietly. 'It was unfair to make you shoulder the responsibility and the blame. I was the more experienced larker and I should have double-checked the tides and conditions.'

'It's okay, I like that you trusted me. I should also apologise for shouting,' he said. 'I'm not normally a shouty person.'

'Me neither.'

'That now makes two things we've got in common.'

Gemma had to think for a moment what the first thing was. She smiled.

'Are we good now?' he asked.

'We're good,' she agreed.

'Does that mean I can get to try out your electrolysis kit?' Nick asked.

'Is that what this is all about?'

He made a maybe-maybe-not gesture.

'You're pushing your luck,' she said deadpan.

Then he laughed and said, 'Of course not.'

And Gemma laughed and said, 'Of course you can.'

'Great!' he said.

'I suppose we could do it now, if you like?' she suggested. The relief of shedding her anger made her suddenly act spontaneously.

'But I haven't got the padlock.'

'At the weekend then?'

'That'd be great.'

'I suppose, now that you're here, would you like to come in for a drink?' The spontaneity was refusing to budge.

'Thanks, but I won't. I walked here as I'm trying to fit more exercise into my life and if I had a drink then I'd probably end up catching the bus home.'

'That's very disciplined of you.'

'It's a rare occurrence so I'd better make the most of it.' He laughed.

They said their goodbyes and 'See you on the weekend' as if nothing had happened, which was a far better note on which to end than their last contentious exchange.

September Discoveries:
Even though, sadly, September had been littered with losses – the half French franc, the iron nails, Gwendoline's wellington boots – I did make some significant finds. Such as, a gorgeous aquamarine ring which I now wear all the time; a newfound deep respect for the Thames; and how empowering it was throwing my engagement ring into the river. What's more, how I hated the thought of nearly losing Nick as a friend.

October

Chapter 42

The beginning of October could have started off better. On Wednesday, Gemma's washing machine went on the blink and on Friday, she had to tell her youngest patient, skateboarder Andie, that her chemotherapy treatment was going to be paused for six weeks because she'd developed severe anaemia and needed a blood transfusion. At least she'd made up with Nick. Deep down, she never really wanted to fall out with him and now, she had to admit that she was looking forward to him coming over on Sunday to try out her electrolysis kit – an activity she'd never in a million years do with any of her other friends or, heaven forbid, have ever imagined doing with Adam.

'So, where did you learn how to make one of these?' Nick asked when he arrived with his rust-encrusted padlock.

'YouTube. Where I learn everything.'

Gemma had set up her electrolysis kit on the outdoor table in the back garden, so that the house didn't fill with noxious fumes. She'd made a pot of coffee and bought apricot pastries because he'd mentioned once that they were his favourite. She wanted the morning to go well, as she still felt bad at how she'd treated him.

'All you need is a mobile phone charger with two alligator

clips attached to the end, a stainless-steel spoon and a bowl of bicarbonate soda dissolved in water,' she explained. 'You fix one of the alligator clips to the spoon and the other to the tarnished, rusted or mud-hardened metal item you want to clean. Hopefully, the rust will come away to reveal any previously hidden distinguishing marks or imprints. Shall we give it go?'

Nick nodded.

'You do it and I'll guide you.'

Nick followed Gemma's instructions and when the kit was ready, dunked the padlock into the bowl. Very quickly the water became cloudy and brown as the rust lifted off.

'Now, get the tongs and take it out of the water,' Gemma instructed. 'Dip it in and out so it isn't just sitting in it. I've had coins fall apart doing that.'

'That'd be annoying.'

'I know, but I don't think you should make old things too shiny and new again because then it feels like you're negating their past.'

'True,' he agreed.

'That's enough now. Put it on the towel and let's see what's engraved on it.'

Nick peered at the lock. 'C Brown & Son, London 1801,' he said.

'Excellent. Now you have a name so you can start searching.'

Nick leant back in the seat. 'Wow, how amazing is that? Do you want to electrocute anything?'

'I have a lead token and an eighteenth-century button, whose iron shank is rusted,' she said. 'But they can wait. More coffee?'

'Thanks. So, how was your week?'

'Frantic. I wouldn't mind a holiday,' Gemma said, refilling his coffee cup. 'Yesterday I started googling "best places for a long weekend". I'm thinking Amsterdam because I've never been.'

'Yeah, nice. I've been there on a stag do but didn't see as much of it as I could have.'

For a moment, neither of them spoke. Gemma looked up at the sky where to the east the blueness was striped with aeroplane contrails, and the west punctured with dark clouds. The silence felt comfortable and easy.

Then, eventually, Nick said, 'Actually, I've been thinking about you and your family stuff.'

'You have?'

'I don't want to intrude and stop me if I'm being presumptuous but the sleuth in me can't help himself,' he said. 'I want to help.' He picked up a pastry and bit into it.

'Okay …' she said hesitantly because she was cautious as to what Nick was proposing.

'Have you looked up your half-brother?'

Gemma shook her head. Nick put down the pastry and pulled out his phone. 'What's his name again?'

'Benjamin Reed, but he may go by Ben, of course.'

'Oh, God, there's a ton of them on Facebook.'

She leant over to get a look. 'You know that Facebook's passé now. He mightn't even be on it, given he's in his early twenties.'

'True. What about Instagram?' He did another search. 'No good. The Ben Reeds who've used their name for their Instagram accounts have made them private.'

'It was the same when I was looking up my birth mother's name. It's too hard,' Gemma said, taking a pastry.

Nick put his phone away. 'Okay, that's for another day, perhaps. But among the info you received, did you get an address of where your birth mother died or where she lived?'

'I think so,' Gemma said.

'Let's go there.'

'What?'

'I'll come with you. I can knock on the door and pretend I'm doing research. Which will be kind of true.'

'Are you being serious?' Gemma felt a rush of adrenalin at the thought of going to a house related to her birth mother.

'Of course. If there's a residential address on the death certificate that means she died at home rather than in a hospital. And if you know where she's buried, we could go to the cemetery.'

Gemma pulled a face. 'I don't like cemeteries.'

'Me neither, if I'm honest. My sister persuaded me to go with her to Dad's grave last weekend. I hadn't been there since the funeral. It's … Well, I won't lie, it *is* upsetting. But we tended to the flowers and reminisced at how Dad wasn't really a floral kind of a guy and how we should have planted that bright green, fuzzy type of ground cover that reminds me of the trees in Doctor Seuss books. Then, Sam, my sister, reminded me that it's Mum who loves flowers and that they're more for her than for him, which makes sense when you think about it. Everything we do for the dead we're really doing for ourselves.'

'True,' she said. 'But do you think going there helped with your grief?'

'That's the weird thing. You'd think it would do the opposite, wouldn't you? When I saw his mound, I didn't imagine him as bones in the ground but rather, as a spirit in the sky. As if the real Dad was wafting around us like smoke.' Nick waved his hands in the air expressively.

'Was that comforting?'

'Well, yeah, which was surprising because I don't believe in any of that. Yet, it helped, it really did.' Nick nodded.

'I'm so pleased.'

'Me too. Except when I thought of the smoke analogy, I wanted a cigarette. *Again*. Can you believe it?'

Gemma thought she probably could. She watched the neighbour's cat scuttle along the top of the back fence, turn to look at her, then jump into the next property.

Nick continued. 'Sam and I shared one. But afterwards, I left the packet on his grave as a votive offering of sorts and a symbol of me stopping. Because that's it. No more,' he said, slicing the air with a hand to reiterate his point.

'Good for you,' she said.

'Yeah, Rosie's been going on at me to quit, even though it

felt like I'd never really started. Like it was always going to be temporary, you know?'

Gemma gritted her teeth at hearing the professor's name. 'Well,' she said, trying to cover up her reaction. 'It was what you needed while you were grieving. I wouldn't beat yourself up about it.'

'You mean, I might get to the pearly gates after all?' He laughed. 'Are you spiritual? What with your job and all that?'

Gemma thought for a moment. 'I want to be but ... I dunno.' Then, unable to come up with anything enlightening, she asked him how it was going with the professor, because now that he'd mentioned her, she was on her mind.

'Yeah, pretty good, thanks,' Nick said. 'It's early days, of course. There's lots to like about her but there's ... Ah well, never mind.' He paused but didn't elaborate, which felt like a bit of a tease. Still, did Gemma really want to know how it was going? Or did she wish it had ended before it had properly started? Annoyed, she flicked pastry crumbs off her lap and told herself to stop prying.

'Anyway,' Nick continued. 'Back to your relatives. I know that whoever answers the door may not be a relative, but they could be! At the very least, you'll get to see the house. Maybe even inside. What if I said I was there to read the meter ...?' His face lit up with excitement.

'I think that's going too far,' she said.

'But the rest isn't?' he said.

'A part of me wants to jump in the car and do it now, the other to not do it at all,' Gemma said.

'Let's run with the first sentiment.'

Although Gemma had been curious to find out who lived at the address she had and whether they were a relative or not, she hadn't yet found the courage to go there on her own. Nick's offer to accompany her was the nudge she needed to do it.

'Okay,' she agreed. 'But can we formulate a strategy first?'
'Sure.'
She picked up the bowl of dirty water. 'I'd better change this.

If you like, you could help me zap my pieces, and we could work something out?'

'Okay, I've nothing else on.'

While Nick stayed on to help with her electrolysis, they came up with a plan: Nick would pick her up in his car – which was actually his father's 'old banger' that he'd inherited. They'd drive to the house and Gemma would stay – hide? – in the car while he knocked on the door. Then ... well, who knew what would happen next.

Chapter 43

The large dent in the passenger door made Nick's car look like an empty Coke can that someone had started to crush then changed their mind. But inside it was devoid of junk and completely spotless. It was here Gemma found herself the following Saturday while Nick drove her to the residential address that was on her birth mother's death certificate.

'Okay, let's run through what's going to happen,' Nick said, as he took a wide berth around a cyclist. 'I'm going to knock on the door and say I'm a journalist doing research on the area and that I want to ask them some questions, yeah?'

'Yes,' Gemma said. 'And if it isn't her actual address …?'

'Then I'll find out whose it is. If it turns out to be her son's – your half-brother – I'll ask a few more questions for my "research" then leave. I won't mention you at all.'

'Okay, good. I really don't want to give someone a heart attack because they suddenly find out their mum had another child they didn't know anything about.'

'Trust me, neither do I.'

'It does feel a little deceptive, though. You're supposed to do this sort of thing gently, considerately, or do it through an independent party.'

'*I'm* the independent party. Anyway, I promise I won't tell them the truth. We're being inoffensively nosy.'

'You might be used to poking into other people's business, but I'm not.' Gemma felt tense. It was exciting and terrifying at the same time.

'Hey, I get it,' Nick said. 'But don't worry, I'll be with you. Anyway, we don't really know what we'll find. The house may have been knocked down and there'll be no one to talk to.'

'It hasn't been. I looked it up last night on Street View.'

'Okay, great. Just remember to keep an open mind so you won't be disappointed. But if you do change your mind, it doesn't matter. We can simply stay in the car, look at the house, then drive off.'

Gemma nodded but doubted she'd want to do that.

The street, across the other side of town in Walthamstow, in which Claire Rita Reed died consisted of a curved double-sided row of Victorian houses. Number sixty-two was in the middle. Like most of the other houses, it had a bay window downstairs and two rectangular windows upstairs. Its white paint was peeling like old nail polish, revealing snippets of red brick underneath. The front door was a dull pink colour and either side of the tiled path leading to it was a slab of concrete with weeds. Nick found a parking space two doors up on the same side of the road.

'Faded glory springs to mind, don't you think?' Nick said.

'I was thinking more of neglect. But I like how you're trying to be positive.'

'There's no need to be negative until you've exhausted all the positives. How do you feel now that we're here?' Nick asked.

'More nervous than I already was,' Gemma said.

'Do you want to leave?'

'No. Curiosity is killing me. But if they're a relative, you do promise not to tell them what you're really doing?'

'Of course.'

'And if no one is in, you won't sneak around the back and take photos of the inside?'

'I can't promise *that*,' Nick said, as if that was the obvious second course of action.

Gemma blew out a breath of air to release some of the tension.

He touched her shoulder. 'Don't worry, I'm not going to do that.'

She nodded. He got out of the car, left the keys in the ignition and the radio very faintly playing a remake of Kate Bush's 'Running Up That Hill'. Gemma watched him put his satchel across one shoulder, pull out a notepad and pen, and walk to the house.

When he got to the front door and started knocking, she had to look away. She wrung her hands and stared at her lap. But she couldn't keep her gaze there for long. Anyone in their right mind would be burning with interest if someone else was visiting the house where their birth mother died and was trying to find out information on their behalf. Nick knocked again. When no one came, Nick stepped back from the door and sized up the house, as if he was going to scale the downpipe, prise open one of the upstairs windows and climb in.

Before he had a chance to do anything foolish, the door opened, and a woman appeared. Was it Claire Rita Reed's daughter-in-law? Gemma leant forward to get a closer look. The woman looked pleasant in a plain, mousey kind of a way. She was wearing dirty overalls and a toddler was wrapped around one of her legs as if she were a fashion accessory. Nick began talking animatedly, gesturing like he did. Maybe he was even telling her a lame joke to break the ice. The thought of it made Gemma smile. Even though she suspected Nick loved this kind of investigative work, he was also going out of his way to help her when he didn't have to. Whatever he was saying, it was working. The woman nodded and smiled, then she beckoned him inside.

Gemma rested her head on the back of the seat and closed her eyes. She imagined Nick continuing the pretence of being interested in the history of the local area while being fed tea and biscuits by a stranger.

Her eyes had only been closed for a few seconds when she was startled by a frantic banging on the car door.

'Gemma, Gemma!' Nick was calling her name excitedly.

She opened the window.

'We can go inside.'

'I thought you'd gone in?'

'I wanted to get you.'

'Who is she?'

'She's the new owner. I ended up telling her about you and she's really happy for us to go in and have a look around. They've started renovating. She's in the middle of taking off wallpaper.'

'She's not a relative then?' Gemma found herself feeling disappointed, which was awfully confusing.

'No, sorry.'

Gemma ran a finger around her lips.

'I thought maybe you'd be happy that you weren't related. The idea seemed to terrify you—'

'It did, but ...' Gemma felt so anxious she couldn't think straight.

'Come on,' Nick said gently, opening the car door. 'I think you'll regret it if you don't do it.'

Gemma closed the window, reached over the gearstick to get the keys and got out of the car. Nick took her hand and together they walked to the house in which her birth mother had passed away.

'We moved in a month ago,' the woman called Sarah explained as they followed her into the hallway. 'It's good that you've come now because the house is exactly as we bought it, apart from the principal bedroom upstairs where I've started stripping the wallpaper.'

'We really don't want to intrude,' Gemma said, already feeling incredibly like she was intruding.

'Your husband's very charming. I couldn't possibly refuse.'

'He is, isn't he?' Gemma agreed, thinking he'd taken their game of pretence far enough.

Nick gave her the sort of loving smile a husband would give when their wife pays them a compliment. It was all Gemma could do to stop herself from rolling her eyes.

'It's very much appreciated, Sarah,' Nick said. 'My wife has been wrestling with her adoption and then the search for her birth mother …' He sighed heavily as if he had been finding the whole process terribly difficult as well.

Gemma wanted to shrink into the carpet.

'So, yes, I've just had a quick look at the house sale documents when you were getting your wife. What did you say your mother's name was?'

'Claire Reed,' Gemma said.

'Yes, that's it, she was the previous owner.'

Gemma inhaled sharply. Her birth mother had owned this house! She'd lived here, had stood where Gemma was standing, had stared at the staircase Gemma was facing, had filled the place with her presence.

'I didn't mean to give you a shock,' Sarah said. 'Do you want to sit down?'

'I'm all right, thank you, though.'

Nick took Gemma's hand and squeezed it. 'We'll have a quick look around and then we'll leave you in peace.'

'To be honest, it's a good excuse for me to have a break,' Sarah said. 'You can start down here if you like and, please, ignore the mess.'

Sarah gestured for them to go into the living room, the first room to their left, where there was a fireplace, a sofa and a rug covered in small toys.

'It's so lovely and light in here but I don't know why you'd paint the walls so dark, do you?' Sarah studied the room as though she wanted to attack it with white paint immediately. 'Oh, I'm sorry.' She turned to Gemma. 'I didn't mean to criticise your mother.'

'It's okay,' Gemma said, despite suddenly feeling defensive on behalf of her birth mother, because she would have had other attributes, even if interior decoration wasn't her thing, wouldn't she?

'Are you sure you're okay?' Nick whispered.

Gemma nodded.

Next, they went into the kitchen, saw the tiny utility and the bathroom. Nick started making small talk about the joys – or not – of moving house. Gemma chimed in every so often to try and appear chatty and interested, instead of self-absorbed and overwhelmed.

'Shall we go upstairs?' Sarah suggested.

And so, the tour continued.

'This is my bedroom,' announced the toddler who had finally detached herself from her mother and decided to speak. 'I like blue.' The girl grinned proudly and surveyed her sky-blue curtains and sky-blue bedding as if she couldn't possibly have chosen any other colour.

The second bedroom was filled with boxes, either unopened or half-emptied, and a double bed, unmade.

'The junk room,' Sarah said.

'We all have one,' Nick replied, nodding to Gemma as if they really should set aside some time soon to tackle their own junk room.

'And this is the main bedroom.' Sarah took them to the last room.

A built-in wardrobe ran along one wall and there was a decorative corner chair, two bedside tables and a bed in the middle of the room. The wall behind the bed was half-stripped of wallpaper, revealing three layers of differently patterned aged paper. Gemma walked over to it.

'Isn't it fascinating seeing what was hung before?' Sarah said. 'Snippets of the eighties, nineties and noughties, I'm imagining.'

Gemma ran a hand over the wall, where the paper was torn

like a photograph that had been ripped in two. The base layer was an olive and cream pinstripe, in the middle was a beige damask, and the last a Laura Ashley floral that reminded Gemma of her grandmother's nightdresses. She closed her eyes and focused on the mix of shiny and rough textures of the different wallpapers. Had her mother chosen one of these, or maybe all of them? Gemma wanted to leave her hand there forever. Then she pressed the tips of her fingers into the wall, as if somehow something of her mother could be transferred on to her. After a moment, she opened her eyes and looked around the room again.

Perhaps this was the place where she'd died. In a bed in the middle of the room overlooking the street. A funny sensation came over Gemma. She didn't believe in an afterlife but there was no denying she felt something 'other' in the room with her. Was it her mother's ghost or, simply, Gemma's imagination? Either way, she felt strangely comforted by it. She'd made a connection and wasn't that, in the end, all she could have hoped for?

Sarah was still talking. 'I thought I might uncover Victorian or Edwardian wallpaper like I've seen happen on TV renovation programmes. I'd have kept some of that. Maybe made it a feature on the wall, you know what I mean?'

'Yes. Yes, I do,' Gemma said, an idea slowly forming. 'Look, this might sound strange, but would it be possible for me to have some of it?' she asked.

'The wallpaper?'

'Yes,' she said tentatively. 'All three.'

'My wife loves keepsakes from the past,' Nick said.

'You mean, I've got to start stripping again?' Sarah laughed.

'I can do it or, at least, help?' Gemma offered.

'It's not a bother, I'll do it. And you can have what you want. It's only going to go in the bin.'

Chapter 44

When they got back to the car, Gemma couldn't speak for a minute. A mix of emotions were rumbling through her. Even if she hadn't got to meet her birth mother, she'd been in her house and the place in which she'd taken her last breath. Some might find that morbid and distressing, but Gemma felt reassured by it. It brought her a little closer to her. She'd even come away with a memento, if that was what you could call the strips of wallpaper that now sat in an envelope in her lap.

Nick put the keys in the ignition but didn't start the car.

'Are you all right?' he asked.

Gemma nodded. 'I couldn't have asked for a better outcome, apart from getting to meet my half-brother, I suppose. Sarah was very generous letting us go inside.'

'It's pretty cool. You got to see inside your birth mother's house *and* take home a little piece of it.'

'I know. And thank you for suggesting this,' she said. 'I couldn't have done it without you. Sarah must have thought I was bonkers wanting scraps of old wallpaper.'

'It's exactly what I would have expected the Gem I know to do.'

'So, I *am* bonkers?'

'No, I mean you love history and collecting stuff. It seems

right.' Nick started the car and pulled out into the street. 'I'm glad I was able to help. Actually, I enjoyed it. I've always fancied being an undercover detective.'

'I bet you have. But … wife?' she said teasingly. She hadn't really minded how he'd pretended they were married.

'It just came out,' he said. 'I wanted to sound authentic.'

'You could have said half-sister.'

'True. Next time. Only if you want me to interfere again, of course.' He laughed. 'Seriously though, do you think you'd like to track down your half-brother?'

'I don't know,' she said. 'Perhaps if I knew he wouldn't mind being found.'

'Hang on, his name and details could be on the sale documents of the house. Why didn't we think of that before? We could go back and ask Sarah?'

Gemma shook her head. She felt so overwhelmed that she didn't feel able to do any more sleuthing. 'I think I've had enough for one day.'

'I'm sure she wouldn't mind you dropping by another time.'

'Yeah, I suppose.' Gemma agreed. 'Anyway, I could always put my details on the Adoption Contact Register, which means I wouldn't have to search. If a relative goes hunting, my name would pop up and they'd find me.'

'Why not? You've got nothing to lose,' he said, putting his foot on the accelerator. 'Back to your place?'

The houses blurred into one long multi-coloured brick wall. A vertical sheet of light rain began to fall.

'Did I tell you that Ella asked if I'd look after Darryl when she goes away?' Nick started. 'Of course, she knew I'd say yes because it's Darryl, you know?'

'That's wonderful, you'll get to spend time with your dog. Just be careful she doesn't start taking advantage of you by tugging on your heart strings.'

'Yeah, I know.' He sighed and began talking about how he

couldn't wait to finally see Darryl again and how he'll have to get him a new toy and some treats …

But Gemma wasn't really listening. Her thoughts had returned to her adoptive parents and her brother. She couldn't wait to tell them about the day she'd just had. She felt her eyes well up. Not because she was sad at what she'd missed out on but, she realised, from joy at what she already had.

They spent a large portion of the journey home not speaking. Gemma appreciated the effort it took Nick not to keep chatting. She needed to process what had just happened without the distraction of conversation. Yet tears were never very far away. All the emotions, happy and sad, pooled close to the surface.

Soon they were in her street. Nick found a free parking spot and pulled over.

'Thanks so much again for driving,' Gemma said undoing her seatbelt. 'And, well, for everything.' She told herself to not start crying now but it didn't help.

'Hey, it's okay,' Nick said, stroking her arm to comfort her. 'I'm not surprised you're feeling emotional.'

She nodded. 'Sorry.'

'Don't apologise. Here, you need a hug.' He leant towards her, and she leant towards him as far as the gear stick would allow. He put an arm around her and squeezed. The handbrake dug into her side. She moved slightly. As she did, his head turned towards her. His lips were just centimetres from hers and seemed to be getting closer. Her heart started beating so fast she thought it might burst out of her chest.

A car alarm sounded. It was so loud and sudden, it startled them both and she head-butted his chin. The lights of the car in front of them were flashing in sync with the noise of its alarm.

'Wow, that's loud.' Nick rubbed his chin and looked around to see if he could spot the car's owner approaching.

Gemma turned away, wiped her eyes and stared out the

window. She felt flustered and flummoxed. What on earth were they doing? Wasn't Nick still seeing Rosie? Hadn't Gemma decided she wanted to be single for the moment? She couldn't deny there was a spark between them, but she didn't know if she wanted there to be one. For her, it seemed too soon, despite her friends telling her on numerous occasions that she had every right to start dating again, given Adam hadn't waited for them to separate before moving on. She could hear her friend Georgie, 'You're being completely irrational. Just run with your feelings and stop analysing them.' But sometimes, that was easier said than done.

'Well, anyway, what was I was saying?' Nick asked, as if he hadn't just taken a peek into Gemma's soul and lit it up for a few seconds.

'You were saying it's okay to cry,' Gemma said, reaching to pick up the envelope that had slipped off her lap.

'Oh, yeah.' The alarm suddenly stopped. 'Thank God for that,' Nick said, giving a wave to the car owner who'd appeared on the pavement.

'Well, I'd better head off,' Gemma said, reaching for the door handle.

'Of course. See you at the next mudlarkers' meeting, I guess?'

'Uh-huh. Thanks again.'

Chapter 45

The next day was a rainy Sunday afternoon and Gemma was looking at the wallpaper strips for the umpteenth time. It seemed both strange and unbelievable to think that at some point in the past, her birth mother had touched one of these papers, if not all of them. *Her* birth mother, Claire Rita Reed. They may have looked as inconsequential as any bits of torn patterned paper, but the historical and personal value to Gemma was immeasurable.

But what was she going to do with them? She certainly didn't want them to get lost in a drawer never to be looked at again.

Then, she had an idea. It had been sitting in front of her all along: the printer's display tray. The wallpaper pieces could form the backdrop to her mudlarking finds. The Georgian button would go with the Laura Ashley wallpaper and the mustard and brown sherd of Staffordshire slipware would stand out against the beige damask.

Laila called while Gemma had been playing around with different combinations. Gemma answered at the same time as deciding that the seventeenth-century elaborately decorated clay pipe bowl would be perfect next to the olive and cream stripe. Laila asked if she could come over to Gemma's. She said it was something to do with her birth mother but didn't explain.

Sensing it was going to be a hot chocolate kind of a catch-up, Gemma got out the cocoa and filled up the kettle. Laila arrived soon after and, although she did a good job at showing interest in hearing Gemma's news and seeing the pieces of wallpaper, she was also distracted.

'Something's up, isn't it?' Gemma said. 'Do you want to tell me about it?'

Laila pulled out an envelope and placed it on the table. For a minute, she stared at it. Gemma waited.

'My birth mother has written to me,' Laila said matter-of-factly.

Gemma couldn't tell whether this was good news or bad news from Laila's perspective. She decided to channel positivity because anyone's birth mother reaching out should be considered very good news indeed. 'That's great, Laila.'

'I dunno. I haven't opened it yet.'

'Has she written to you before?'

'No. That's why I'm nervous. It feels serious, you know.'

'Drink some hot chocolate.' Gemma pushed the mug closer to Laila.

'Maybe you could read it and tell me what it says?'

'I don't think she intended a stranger to read it.'

Laila's fingers worried a tassel of hair, then she eventually opened the letter and let Gemma read it with her.

Dear Laila,
I know I haven't been a model mother and I've done things I'm not proud of. But I want you to know that the one thing I'm most proud of is you. When you came into my life, I didn't think I could love anything as much as I loved you. That's the truth. No word of a lie. I know I've made bad choices in the past but having you was not one of them.

I hear you've found a loving home with wonderful foster parents. I don't want to take that away from you, but I'd like to be in your life again. To hang out with you every so often. To do whatever you like doing.

Before you go ripping up this letter because you want nothing to do with me, please hear me out. I'm not the person I used to be. I've changed. You may not believe me and sometimes I can't believe it myself. But I feel it deep down. I'm clean now and I've been studying psychology. I reckon I could become a counsellor if I keep at it. How about that? Me, a shrink!

I've also been reading up about Pakistani history, traditions and food. I rejected so much of it when I was younger but now I want to reconnect with my cultural heritage. I even thought that maybe you could come on this journey with me, too?

The point is, I'd like you to consider seeing me again. I'm going to be out of here soon and I want to make a new life. I'm not asking you to come and live with me. I'd just like you to give me a second chance.

Love Mum x

Laila pressed a knuckle into the corner of her eye, which had filled with tears.

'I think that answers your question,' Gemma said.

'Yep.'

'You know that just as she can have had a change of heart, so can you.'

'S'ppose,' Laila mumbled so quietly Gemma barely heard it. Gemma stayed silent, letting her mull over the letter. 'It just seems scary.'

'And you know what? She's probably scared too. She's put herself on the line here by reaching out to you, not knowing if you're going to reject her or not. Neither of you will know how it'll go if you meet up but there's only one way to find out.'

'We could just meet for a drink and see what happens, I guess …'

'Exactly. Take it one step at a time.'

Laila nodded. She wrung her hands. 'Yeah, okay,' she said. 'Okay, I'll do it.'

Chapter 46

On the last Saturday of the month, The Mudlarkers' Club arranged to meet in front of the Old Naval College at Greenwich. Phyllida had suggested they head east down the river, further than they'd been before. This time, Timothy said he was able to make it, but Laila couldn't. She had to study for a school test, Timothy explained with obvious delight, which gave Gemma a similar burst of pride.

It was mid-morning, and Gemma was the first to arrive. The Thames had started to inch slowly and rhythmically away from the high-tide line. In an hour and a half the river would be at its lowest. She sat at the top of the steps leading to Greenwich beach and looked out at the grey foreshore and the last remaining timber piles of a medieval jetty.

A few minutes later, Nick sat down next to her. 'Fancy meeting you here.'

'Fancy,' she said.

'Nice boots,' he said, nodding at her footwear.

'I'll be the envy of the club.' She stretched out a leg to admire the floral wellingtons Nick had gifted her. 'How's Darryl? Have you had him to stay yet?'

'Next weekend. I can't wait.'

'I bet he'll love going mudlarking, too,' Gemma said.

'Yeah, all these river smells,' Nick agreed.

'What else has been happening?'

'This and that.' Nick paused as if not sure whether to elaborate. 'I'm not seeing the prof anymore.'

'Oh, I'm sorry to hear that,' she said, hoping to disguise her delight.

'We had some good times and she's really interesting—' He paused.

Gemma waited for the 'but'.

'I don't want to be critical, but she was quite intense.'

'She was passionate about her specialist subject matter,' Gemma said to be conciliatory. 'That isn't always a bad thing.'

'I agree, but sometimes I like things light, you know, and she didn't even laugh at my jokes. Not like you.'

Gemma felt a warm glow radiate inside her. 'Well, that's rude.'

'Very,' he replied. 'Also, she wasn't very spontaneous, which you don't have to be all the time but some of the time would be nice.'

'I dated someone like that once,' Gemma said. 'He'd virtually hyperventilate if plans had to change. He was a sweet guy, too. I always wondered what happened to him.'

Suddenly, there was a raucous 'Yoo-hoo' from down the street. Phyllida was walking with Timothy, holding his folding stool.

'Sorry to keep you waiting,' Timothy said. 'I can't walk as fast these days.'

'Don't worry about it,' Nick said. 'We were just enjoying a moment taking in the sights and sounds.'

'I was telling Timothy how I thought we should make our way east first,' Phyllida said. 'We could have a tea break in front of the Trafalgar pub, then continue to the pier before turning back. But Timothy, you must take all the breaks you need and go at your own pace.'

'Thank you, Phyllida. To be honest, I don't mind what we do, I'm just so pleased to be back out in the fresh air surrounded by history with you young people.'

'Let me carry the stool.' Nick gestured for Phyllida to give it to him, and he led the way down the steps onto the damp beach rubble. The rains of the previous few days had finally moved on and the sky was unusually clear for late October.

Nick set up the stool a few metres away from where they were going to start mudlarking, and Phyllida offered around Werther's Originals as though they were at the cinema.

'I haven't had these for years,' Timothy said.

'They're Robert's favourites.'

'How's it going with you two now?' Nick asked Phyllida.

'Much, much better, thank you. We've still a way to go but the boat has righted itself and the seas are calmer.'

'I'm so pleased,' Gemma said.

'Now, shall we start?'

Mindful of each other's personal space, they spread out across the beach. Nick, now more confident in his mudlarking skills, strode off towards a spot that appeared to be strewn with animal bones. Phyllida went down to the gently lapping shoreline, cloudy with mud. While Timothy hung back, aware, Gemma assumed, of his slower, more tentative walking. Gemma chose a spot in the middle of the foreshore where firm mud met pebbles and flinty bits of stone and concentrated her gaze on what lay before her. She let her thoughts mimic the water, coming in and going out in their own uninterrupted rhythm.

Gemma's first find was an orange brick which was blotchy with mud and had two initials carved into it. She didn't fancy lugging home a brick but did wonder who its maker was and what she might find out about it. Could it have come from the original Tudor Palace of Palentia? A few years ago, archaeologists found remains beneath the Old Royal Naval College. Gemma's imagination did a little skip and a hop back to the past. She didn't care whether she was wildly off the mark and in reality was holding an uninteresting mass-produced twentieth-century brick. She took a photo so she could find out more later and carefully returned it to the silt.

She ignored an upturned supermarket trolley and picked up a ring of wire from a champagne bottle and an abandoned vape to dispose of later. Apart from finding a Victorian button with an anchor on it and some pins, she didn't discover anything else of interest.

Following Phyllida's instruction, The Mudlarkers' Club reassembled in front of the riverside façade of the Trafalgar pub.

'Right, you lot,' Phyllida said. 'What have you got?'

Timothy held up a curved tusk with tortoiseshell markings the length of a long finger. 'I think it's from a boar. Their meat was popular with the medieval crowd.'

'All I've got is this bit of pottery whose size is the only thing going for it,' Nick said.

'It looks like a piece of red earthenware mould that was once used to make loaves of sugar,' Timothy added.

'Interesting. I'm going to look that up when I get home,' Nick said. 'What about you, Gem?'

Gemma held up her button.

'Sweet,' Phyllida said. 'My finds aren't very inspiring, I'm afraid. A bent spoon, an empty lentil can and a car wing mirror.'

'The day's not over yet,' Nick said.

'True.' Phyllida got up and stretched. 'The tide's still on the way out so I'm going to get back to it.'

'Good luck.' Nick pulled out two cans of energy drink from his bag. 'Anyone want one?'

'Why not?' Timothy said.

'No thanks, I've got tea,' Gemma said.

'Hey, are you back at the museum yet, Timothy?' Nick asked.

'Yes, last weekend. I was put on the "hands-on desk" which was a godsend as I didn't have to be on my feet the whole time. You should come along to a Friday night Spotlight tour. They're only twenty minutes and focus on a key object in the museum.'

Nick looked at Gemma as if to say, 'We'd like to go, wouldn't we?' As though he was still in his pretend role of husband. Even so, she wouldn't mind going if he asked.

'Sure, it sounds great.' She got up and brushed grit off her jeans. 'That's me done. I'm going to join Phyllida.'

Leaving Nick and Timothy to finish their drinks, Gemma found a spot on her own down by the shoreline, where the movement of the river created clumps of tiny bubbles in the water that popped excitedly, then dispersed. Every so often Nick's laughter bounced down to her like skipping stones stopping at her feet. It made her smile. Phyllida, in her all-in-one khaki overalls and hat, was so far away that she'd taken on the appearance of a plastic toy soldier. Gemma couldn't tell if she was talking to herself or singing. Either way, she seemed happier and less on edge than Gemma had seen her for a while. And this pleased Gemma no end.

Making her way in the other direction, where the river began to curve like a fishbowl, Gemma found a spot where the tideline had left a clear undulating pattern in the pebbles. She got down on her hands and knees and scanned the ground in front of her as she crawled along. The mud smelt earthy and pungent, and the water felt cold even with gloves on. Everything was grey, the river, the rocks, the sky. It was a monochrome autumn day where not even the smatterings of red-tile chips on the foreshore could liven it up. She lifted the occasional rock and poked at objects that could have been something but weren't. Waves came in and waves went out.

Then, a new wave washed in and when it retreated, there it was: a heart-shaped, hollow brooch rimmed with pearly stones, whose gold shone brightly, luridly even, against the drabness of the ground. Gemma pulled it from the mud and let another wave clean it. She held the brooch to the sky. Even though it was no longer in the water and the sun wasn't out, it dazzled like a piece of costume jewellery. The horizontal pin had lost its catch, yet it looked as if it could still be worn. It was hard to tell its age. It may have been a modern piece made to appear old, or it could have been Victorian.

There was something special about finding other people's jewellery. It was personal and emotive; sometimes sentimental, sometimes sad. Maybe this could be her thing, Gemma wondered. Like Phyllida's penchant for glass, she could specialise in collecting jewellery, gemstones and beads, old or new it didn't matter. She bagged up the brooch and put it in a side pocket of her rucksack.

Two hours went by as if they'd only been fifteen minutes. On a flatter, sandier part of the beach, close to the tall mossy wall, they gathered for another show and tell. They placed their finds carefully and with thought on the sand, as if they were making art. Nick helped Timothy lay his out, as kneeling wasn't so much the problem as was getting up again. When everyone had finished, they stepped back to admire their work and studied each other's collections like they were in a gallery and their works were for sale.

However, it was obvious which object they were all drawn to. Gemma's golden brooch illuminated the mud like a shiny foil wrapper among a pile of drab rubbish.

Phyllida noticed it first. 'Well, look at this!' she exclaimed. 'I nearly bought something similar by a jeweller who specialises in making historical-style jewellery. Beautiful pieces but eye-wateringly expensive.'

'There are letters engraved on the back,' Gemma said. 'H-A-M-A-T-A.'

'May I see?' Timothy said.

Gemma passed the brooch to Timothy who was sitting on his fold-up stool.

'The gold is very yellow, isn't it?' he said.

'Garish, if you ask me,' Nick added.

'I think it's fake, don't you?' Phyllida said. 'Not that it matters.

Personally, I think it's gorgeous. You should wear it, Gemma.'

'Well, I *am* wearing the ring I found,' Gemma said sheepishly as if it was wrong to appropriate a find for your own use. She went to show them, but her glove was covering it. 'It's got an aquamarine stone.'

But no one was listening. The brooch was still holding their attention.

'There's something about it …' Timothy said.

'Something Roman, you mean?' Nick asked eagerly.

'You and your Roman fixation,' Phyllida said fondly.

'One day, Phyll, one day.'

Timothy's eyes were closed now and he was feeling the weight of it in the palm of his hand. 'It's heavy,' he said. 'And real gold is weighty. Then again, it could be a metal that's had a chemical reaction with Mother Nature and is deceiving us into believing it's gold. The problem with this hobby is that it's tempting to start making things up, isn't it?'

'You know, somewhere along my mudlarking journey, I discovered that heart-shaped brooches were popular in Scotland in the sixteenth century as betrothal gifts. Although they were usually silver,' Phyllida said.

'Still, we don't know, do we?' Nick said. 'In my job, you can't believe anything until it's been verified. You've got to fact-check everything and do it all again just in case. If we're only making assumptions about the brooch and if Timothy's got a funny feeling about it, then it needs to be investigated.'

'But guessing is half the fun!' Phyllida exclaimed. 'When you get home, google Scottish betrothal gifts.'

'It's come a long way if it's Scottish,' Gemma said.

'Who knows how any of this stuff gets in the Thames,' Timothy said. 'I do agree with Phyllida, though. You should try and find out its backstory.'

'One time I thought I'd found a real prosthetic eye—' Phyllida began.

'As opposed to a fake one?' Nick laughed.

Phyllida sighed. 'My point is, I was convinced it had come from a human. A small human, but still. It was macabre. Until I found out it was a doll's eye from one of those creepy life-like dolls.'

'There you go,' Nick said, as if Phyllida's story perfectly summed up the importance of research.

'I could post a photo of it on my Instagram account, if you like?' Phyllida offered. 'There might be someone out there who knows something.'

'Good idea,' Nick said.

'Okay.' Gemma nodded. 'And I'll see what I can find out.'

Once at home, Gemma googled the history of heart-shaped brooches in Britain – a topic she'd never entertained having an interest in. It turned out that Phyllida was correct, the Scottish have had a penchant for them going back as far as the sixteenth century. Back then, they were simple designs made from silver which everyday people gave as engagement gifts. It wasn't until the late nineteenth century that the wealthy took a fancy to them and they become more elaborate, bejewelled and enamelled. After an hour spent down the rabbit hole of heart-shaped brooches, Gemma eventually re-emerged into the twenty-first century none the wiser.

Even so, she posted an update on The Mudlarkers' Club group chat to keep them informed. Then, she did as Phyllida suggested and put the brooch on. Despite not having a catch its pin was thick and sturdy so Gemma felt confident it wouldn't fall off. It looked out of place against her coffee-stained faded blue sweatshirt. Yet, along with her new ring, it felt as though she was on her way to becoming a walking mudlarkering display case.

October Discoveries:
A barnacle-encrusted early wine bottle. The hand-painted ceramic base of some vessel, which I think might be a teapot,

possibly eighteenth century. A hypodermic needle – yuk. A mystery brooch which is quite fancy but I'm going to wear regardless of the occasion. Amazingly, my birth mother's house. I not only got to see inside but came away with a memento of wallpaper scraps which my birth mother may well have chosen and hung. How much I enjoyed playing sleuth with Nick and how, I have to say, it's a relief not to feel jealous of Professor Rosie anymore.

November

Chapter 47

Two days later, Phyllida made The Mudlarkers' Club's second WhatsApp video call.

'I'm so glad you could all make it,' Phyllida said. 'Oh, and here's Laila, too. We haven't seen you for a while.'

Laila waved.

'Geez, Phyll, it looks like you've just killed someone,' Nick said.

Phyllida's face and apron were splattered with blood-red spots.

'I've been wrangling a pomegranate,' she said. 'Getting seeds out is, I imagine, just as messy as murder.'

'So, what's going on? You seem more flustered than de-seeding a pomegranate should ever make you.'

'Oh, no, Nick,' she said gravely. 'This is me excited.'

'Excited?'

'Someone has commented on my Instagram post.' Phyllida turned her phone to the laptop camera to show them the comment. 'Can you see it?'

Four heads leant closer. Timothy put his glasses on.

'It's a bit blurry,' Timothy said. 'Can you hold the phone still?'

'Sorry, it's my hand. I can't stop shaking.'

'Why don't you read it out to us?' Gemma suggested.

'I had to show you because I didn't want you to think I

was making this up or playing an April Fool's joke on you in November.'

'Can you tell us already?' Laila said.

'The impatience of youth.' Timothy laughed.

'Okay, here goes.' Phyllida paused, took a deep breath and began. 'Do you remember how I told you that one of my followers is historian Megan O'Connor? She's been following me for a while now and has been so wonderful at providing commentary and offering support. I try and do the same for her as she also likes mudlarking. But of course, I know nothing compared to her. Anyway, she's very knowledgeable and I trust her completely. She does want to come and give us a talk but has been too busy of late. She goes by the Instagram handle of "history rocks" if you want to look her up …'

Gemma moved to the sofa. She was getting used to Phyllida's storytelling. It reminded her of her father's made-up bedtime tales when they were children. Although he took forever to get to the action, it was the detail and his florid descriptions that made her love them.

'Did she comment on the brooch Gemma found?' Nick asked, as keen as Gemma was for Phyllida to get to the point.

'This is what Megan wrote: "I may be completely wrong, Phyllida, and I don't want to steer you in the wrong direction, but I think the brooch could be something special."'

'Something special?' Nick said.

'Megan says it's likely to be a hundred per cent gold because no other metal comes out of the river with a lustre like that.'

Gemma touched the brooch. She was wearing the sweatshirt she had on the day before with the brooch still attached.

'She also says it could be old,' Phyllida continued. 'Medieval even. And she recommended that we get someone to look at it.'

'Okay, let's do that,' Nick said.

'Gemma? You've gone awfully quiet. Please don't tell me you've thrown the brooch back into the river?' Phyllida said.

Gemma shook her head. 'I'm wearing it.' She showed them the brooch which was looking flamboyant and incongruous against her drab sweatshirt.

'Oh, my God, you can't let it out of your sight,' Nick said, suddenly panicked.

'I thought you didn't believe it was anything,' Phyllida said.

'I don't. But what if it is? How cool would that be?'

'There seems to be a lot of conjecture with not a lot of evidence,' Gemma said. 'It could just be one of those Scottish brooches from the Victorian period.'

'Or maybe it's just a cheap replica,' said Nick, reluctantly reining in his excitement.

'Or a cheap replica,' Gemma agreed.

'I'm with Phyllida. The only way we'll find out is by sending it off to the experts,' Timothy said.

'If it *is* real gold and more than three hundred years old then we'll need to give it to the Finds Liaison Officer at the Museum of London,' Gemma added.

'I tell you what, why don't I get in touch with one of the curators at the British Museum?' Timothy said. 'There's one I've met a few times. Delightful woman. She wouldn't mind having a look at it and she'll be able to tell, I'm sure, if it's old and gold. Then we'll know what we need to do with it. Or should I say, what *Gemma* needs to do with it. She was its finder after all.'

Chapter 48

It seemed to Gemma that it was always the worst and the best things in life that required the most waiting for. The interminable wait for medical results. The tedious length of time it took for a divorce to go through. The yearning for your one holiday abroad of the year.

The problem with waiting for Timothy to show the brooch to the museum curator and then waiting for the curator to offer an opinion on it, was that Gemma didn't know if the wait was going to be worth it or not. The brooch could turn out to be an inconsequential piece of contemporary jewellery. Then again …

Gemma couldn't bear it. She had to stop thinking about it. She turned off her WhatsApp notifications because the other club members seemed to be equally preoccupied and kept messaging for updates or with speculation that became more and more farfetched. Nick fabricated a story about it belonging to a Roman woman who, scorned by her lover, had thrown the brooch into the river in order to forget about him, which was a little too close to home as far as Gemma was concerned. She tried to be the voice of reason because the chances of the brooch being anything of value to anyone other than herself were so remote it was laughable.

Thankfully, she had a week of work ahead to keep her occupied.

One patient – the delightful Sister Francis, with her wicked sense of humour – was finally coming to the end of her treatment, and nursing colleague, Michael, whose baking was improving, had promised to bring in a red velvet cake.

It was a few minutes after one-thirty on Friday afternoon. Gemma was walking back to the hospital, after having gone out to get some fresh air and run some errands, when her phone rang. Light drizzle had turned to cutting rain. She had to angle her umbrella in order to minimise getting too wet.

It was Timothy. 'Have you got a minute?'

'Sure.'

'Are you sitting down?'

'I'm walking.'

'Okay, I'll sit down for you,' he said.

Gemma pressed the phone to her ear as the rain became louder and heavier. Water from a passing car splashed her legs. She quickened her pace and kept going. The hospital was just up ahead.

'Are you ready?' Timothy asked.

'Sorry, you'll have to speak loudly,' she shouted.

'It's about the brooch,' Timothy bellowed. 'My curator friend wants to schedule a call.'

'What did she say about it?'

'She won't tell me.'

'What does that mean?'

'I'd say it means something, don't you? She insisted that she talk to you because you were its finder.'

Gemma's breath caught in her throat. 'Gosh. Okay. But I think everyone should hear what she has to say. Shall we meet on your houseboat for a conference call?'

'Good idea. Let's not muck around. What about tomorrow?'

Chapter 49

Early the following evening, The Mudlarkers' Club met at Timothy's houseboat, which disappointingly, and maybe predictably, had become a little more cluttered since their clean-up, for an emergency meeting. Phyllida had convinced her husband to move their home-movie make-up date to the next night, Nick cut short a catch-up with mates at the pub, and Laila was more than happy to reduce her homework time. No one wanted to miss it.

'I'd have brought a bottle of wine if I knew we were going to have cheese,' Nick said when he saw the glass-domed cheese board on the coffee table as they gathered around Timothy's kitchen.

'That's not cheese,' Timothy said.

'Eh?' Nick went over to it.

'It's the brooch.'

Nick peered into the glass as if he were expecting to see an exotic animal from a far-away land. Gemma and the others quickly followed. In the middle of the round timber board sat the brooch like a glossy wedge of gourmet cheddar. Gemma knew they were all thinking the same thing: what was the curator going to tell them that she couldn't have told Timothy in an email?

'I didn't know where else to put it,' Timothy explained. 'And, quite frankly, my friend has made me wonder whether we need to look after it very carefully.'

'Can everyone come and sit at the table?' Laila called out. 'The Zoom call is starting in five.'

'Oh, my goodness,' Phyllida said. 'I feel queasy.'

'Me, too,' admitted Gemma.

They huddled next to each other on one side of the dining table so everyone could see the screen and, for the most part, would all be seen by the curator. Phyllida produced her notebook and a pen.

Within minutes, the Renaissance Europe expert at the British Museum, Nicola Taylor, appeared on screen. She wore angular black-rimmed glasses and red lipstick.

'Hello, dear Nicola,' Timothy said. 'Thank you for joining us. Let me introduce you.'

Introductions and small talk went on for a few minutes, which only added to the suspense and tension in the room.

'Before I tell you my thoughts on the brooch,' Nicola said. 'May I ask you, Gemma, where exactly did you find it? Don't worry, I won't tell a soul.'

Gemma glanced at Phyllida whom, she knew, had strong views on disclosing find locations. But Phyllida nodded because, Gemma suspected, her desire to learn Nicola's assumptions far outweighed anything else. Gemma told her with as much detail as she could.

'Did you discover anything else close by?' Nicola asked.

'Nothing of note,' Gemma said. 'I moved on to a different spot. I thought the brooch was modern and didn't think to spend any more time there.'

'Anyone else?'

Timothy looked into the distance as if he was trying to visualise the exact scene on the foreshore last Saturday. Neither he, nor the others, had found anything notable in the vicinity.

'Well, I won't lie,' said Nicola. 'I've seen a lot of incredible things in my time, but this brooch is something else.'

Gemma sensed that everyone, like her, was holding their

breaths.

'Before I get you too excited, I must caveat that what I'm about to say will need to be properly verified, of course.'

'Of course.' Timothy nodded.

'This is *so* exciting.' Phyllida put a hand to her chest.

Nicola cleared her throat. 'As you suspected, Timothy, the brooch is gold. Real, solid gold.'

'Excellent,' Timothy said.

'And I'd say it's Tudor.'

'Tudor?' Laila exclaimed.

Gemma's jaw dropped.

'In Tudor times, brooches didn't have catches to secure the pins when closed. They came much later. Centuries later. So, if the brooch is Tudor, it isn't that the catch has broken off, it would never have had one. Interesting side note: brooches were mainly worn for practical reasons – to fasten cloaks or adorn hats – and not purely for decoration.' Nicola paused to let them take in what she'd said.

Phyllida started taking notes.

'What do you think the stones are?' Timothy asked.

'Pearls.'

'*Real* pearls?'

'Although, in Tudor times fake and imitation gems were popular. They were often made from clear glass with coloured foil stuck on the back.'

'Interesting,' said Phyllida chewing on her pen.

'And I think it may have belonged to Anne Boleyn,' Nicola added so casually that she could have been talking about one of her museum friends from another department.

'*The* Anne Boleyn?' Nick said, incredulous.

Gemma exchanged a glance with Phyllida whose eyebrows had shot up in astonishment.

'Yes,' Nicola said.

'Anne Boleyn?' Nick repeated. 'Are you kidding?'

'I know it seems extraordinary, but I'll give you my reasons.'

'This *is* extraordinary, Nicola. Absolutely extraordinary,' Timothy said, shaking his head.

Gemma was speechless. It seemed amazing and literally unbelievable at the same time.

Nicola continued. 'Firstly, the spot where you were mudlarking – in front of the Greenwich Naval College – was where Henry the Eighth's primary palace, the Palace of Palentia, once stood. He was famous for throwing extravagant banquets and jousting matches there, including the first masquerade ball ever held in England. But, more pertinently, he lived there with his second wife who gave birth in one of the private apartments to the future Queen Elizabeth the First. And who do you think that was?'

'Anne Boleyn,' Laila whispered.

'Correct.'

'I'm sorry, Nicola, I don't mean to doubt you, but isn't this all supposition?' Nick said. 'I could say that the clay pipe stem I found there was once smoked by Henry the Eighth and who'd know?'

'Of course, but bear with me. There are two more reasons why I'm thinking this, and the latter, I believe, is the most compelling.'

'I think I'm going to pass out.' Phyllida was flapping her notebook near her face even though the houseboat wasn't as heated as it could have been, given the change of seasons.

'This is *so* much better than school.' Laila shook her head as if she couldn't believe real life could be in any way educational or thrilling.

'The brooch has three gold loops at the bottom of it, correct?'

They all glanced towards the brooch in the cheese-board-cum-jewellery-case to remind themselves of its design.

Nicola carried on. 'Those loops most likely held gemstones. And, more pertinently, this was a design feature on many of Anne Boleyn's jewellery. Like her famous 'B' necklace with the three drop-pearls.'

She held up a book to the screen to show them a painting of

Anne Boleyn wearing the said necklace.

'Awesome,' Laila said.

Gemma smiled at Laila. In a funny way, she wished for her sake that it *would* turn out to be true because of how much joy Laila was getting from this real-time history-lesson-cum-mystery quest.

'And the final reason,' Nicola said. 'Do you remember the engraving on the back of the brooch, H-A-M-A-T-A?'

They all nodded.

'When Henry was courting Anne, he showered her with gifts. Especially jewellery. Symbolic pieces that formed an important part of the rituals of love in the Court. When they married, their personal signature, which Henry had engraved everywhere – on walls, ceilings, personal items – was "H Amat A". Latin for "Henry Loves Anne".'

'If I faint, hold my legs in the air, will you?' Phyllida said weakly.

'As you can imagine, Henry regretted all of this when Anne didn't produce him an heir. He went right off her, the poor thing, and he had her beheaded. There's been no surviving jewellery of hers because he broke everything up and made into different pieces of jewellery for other royals.'

'So, if this *is* Anne Boleyn's brooch, this is the only piece that exists of hers? Ever?' Laila asked.

'That's right.'

Gemma squeezed her temples. She dearly wished that what the curator was saying was true and she had found a royal brooch that was nearly five hundred years old. Yet it seemed too outrageous, too inconceivable. Perhaps there was another explanation.

'But couldn't the inscription mean anything?' Gemma said. 'Like, I don't know, "Harry And Mary Are Together Always" or something like that?'

'Or Harry and Meghan.' Nick laughed.

'Exactly,' Gemma said. 'Maybe it was commissioned by some modern-day guy who just so happened to have the same initials as Henry, whose specialist subject matter, if he had to go on

Mastermind, was Henry the Eighth, and he thought it would be fun to emulate the king.'

'I like where your imagination is taking you,' Nick said.

Gemma smiled, pleased at having come up with an alternative, more realistic scenario because it was too overwhelming to entertain the idea of the brooch being of such historical importance. Or that little old her had found something so momentous.

'If you had to have a Mastermind specialty, what would it be?' Nick said.

'Maybe the history of the British crisp,' Gemma said. 'Or the evolution of the wellington boot.'

Nick burst out laughing. Even the curator smiled.

'Can we stay on topic, please?' Phyllida said.

'Look, it's true,' Nicola conceded. 'Gemma could be right and I could be wrong. But I've got a hunch and I know from past experience that hunches should never be ignored. My recommendation is to send photos and a detailed description to the Finds Liaison Officer at the Museum of London. If this is going to be officially classed as treasure, the authorities need to know about it.'

'Yes, yes, we'll do it right away, won't we?' Timothy said to the group.

'And one more thing,' Nicola said. 'Don't let it out of your sight.'

For the first time in the history of a Mudlarkers' Club meeting, no one spoke for, what seemed to Gemma, a very long time. After a moment, she got up and went over to the cheese board on the coffee table. The brooch now seemed to have taken on a life of its own. The stones shimmered like mother-of-pearl and the gold dazzled from the lights above shining through the glass. It gleamed regally as if maybe, just maybe, it was real bona fide treasure.

Chapter 50

The soonest Gemma could get to the Museum of London was in her lunchbreak on Monday. Even though she'd emailed the Finds Liaison Officer over the weekend and she'd yet to hear back, she didn't want to waste any time waiting for a response. She wrapped the brooch in multiple layers of bubble wrap, put it in a Ziplock bag and into a zippered pocket in her tote bag. Then, at work, she secured it in her locker and checked on it regularly in between patients. She called the museum to see if she could make a last-minute appointment, which, to her relief, she could.

'Thank you for fitting me in,' she told the officer. 'I've got something I really want you to look at.'

'Okay,' he said with minimal interest. Perhaps he was used to larkers and detectorists believing – wishing – they'd found an item of treasure.

'We – my mudlarking friends and I – think it's something important. Well, Nicola Taylor believes it could be something of historical and royal significance.'

'Oh, you're Nicola Taylor's friend?' He was interested now. 'She emailed me about this piece. Have you got it?'

Gemma carefully handed the package to the officer and watched him unwrap it. When the brooch revealed itself, he paused, stared at, then turned it over. Gemma held her breath.

'Huh,' he said, nodding.

'Huh?' she repeated. Was that all he was going to give her?

'Thank you for bringing this to us,' he said matter-of-factly. 'It's beautiful. Intriguing. We'll conduct a thorough analysis and let you know our hypothesis.'

'I mean, do you think we could be rushing to conclusions and barking up the wrong tree?' Gemma said. 'One of my mother's dogs actually did that once, it was so dumb. The cat he was barking at was in the neighbouring tree.' She let out a nervous laugh.

The officer smiled, then became serious again. 'You could be,' he said. 'But we'll find out soon enough. You'll need to fill out a form with your contact details and information on where you found it.'

'Oh, I've already done that. I emailed it on Saturday.'

'Excellent. What's your name?'

'Gemma Hudson,' she said with unexpected conviction, for it was the first time she'd said her maiden name out loud since splitting up with Adam.

'Thank you, Gemma. We'll be in touch in due course.'

For the rest of that day, Gemma could barely concentrate on a thing. The waiting and wondering were unbearable. She couldn't stop imagining if what Nicola Taylor had said was true and it was something. Something that no one had ever seen before. Something so rare and valuable …

But no, Gemma had to stop thinking like this. Because Nicola Taylor could also be wrong.

Thankfully, the Museum of London didn't keep her hanging. She heard back from them late the following day. The Finds Liaison Officer was beside himself with excitement because Nicola Taylor's hypothesis was correct. The brooch Gemma had unearthed was one hundred per cent twenty-four-carat gold with real pearls. What's more, because the inscription and its font matched the personal signature of Henry the Eighth and Anne Boleyn, they were very confident it was linked to the royals and their marriage. But why it had survived when Anne's other jewellery hadn't and how it ended up in the Thames, they'd yet to understand. If they ever would.

After receiving the Museum of London's report confirming what they believed to be the provenance of the brooch, Gemma had to sit for a minute to take it all in. Learning of a hypothesis was entirely different to finding out that the supposition was true. Gemma could hardly believe it. The brooch *she* had found was a never-before-seen five-hundred-year-old-artefact made of real gold and real pearls. She had done something few people get to do. She had touched treasure. She'd even worn treasure! It was like she'd been given the opportunity to time travel, albeit briefly, to the past. Now, she wanted to find out all she could about Anne Boleyn and her marriage to Henry the Eighth, to immerse herself in their world.

But first, she must message the club. They'll be delirious with joy.

Within minutes, their WhatsApp chat went into overdrive. After that, it took Nick only twenty-four hours to compose a press release and send it to those he knew in the media. He checked that Gemma and Phyllida were happy with the quotes he'd attributed to them and, in the spirit of The Mudlarkers' Club, got every member to approve it. The speed at which all this happened made Gemma dizzy with disbelief and euphoria.

Her symptoms were only to get worse.

On Friday evening, Nick was loitering outside the hospital when she left work.

'Oh, hello,' she said, shocked to see him. 'What are you doing here?'

'I was in the area,' he said. Then his mouth stretched into a wide grin. 'More importantly, I need to know if you're doing anything on the twenty-third?'

'Next week?' she asked, wondering why he hadn't just texted.

'Yep.'

'Um …' She had to think for a minute.

He jumped in. 'You're needed on TV.'

'What?'

'BBC Breakfast wants to interview you. In person. At their Manchester studios.'

'Are you joking?'

'For once, I'm being deadly serious.'

Gemma's stomach started doing backflips faster than an Olympic gymnast.

'How great is that?' he said.

'I don't think I can do it.' She shook her head.

'Cancel whatever you've got on.'

'It's not that. It's … well … *me* on TV? The thought of it is terrifying.' Apart from when she was the hindlegs of a donkey in a school play, Gemma had never been centre stage before. And this time, it would be her whole self, not just two limbs. 'Don't you think Phyllida would be so much better? She'd love the limelight.'

'But she didn't find it. Anyway, you're underestimating yourself. It'll be just like the interview you did with me. They'll ask the same sort of questions so you can prepare your answers. The only difference is that you'll get to sit on a comfy couch and it'll be filmed.'

'Yes, broadcast *live* to the whole country!' Gemma said. 'I'll get tongue-tied and turn mute, I know I will.'

'You won't, Gem, you really won't. You have every right to be on national television and you should own it.'

'Own it?'

'Yeah, it's the opposite of faking it till you make it. Because you haven't just found history, you've *made* history.'

'I suppose ...' Gemma felt a sense of Nick-boosted pride swell inside.

'And don't worry, I'll come with you. The whole club will come, I'm sure. The others won't want to miss out. We can get a train up to Manchester with you the night before.'

'You'd do that?'

'Of course! So, can I tell the BBC you'll do it?'

Gemma looked out at the dark street lit up by the lights of the hospital. 'I don't want to let you all down,' she said.

'You couldn't, and won't, I promise.' Nick squeezed her shoulder.

'Well, okay,' she said meekly.

'Excellent!' Nick slapped his hands together. 'Now, listen, the producer wants you to come in looking the part but to leave the mud at home – he seemed to think that was funny. Also, don't wear the nautical top you like because the stripes will create a distracting optical effect. And avoid green. It'll muck up the green screen,' Nick talked quickly. It was hard for Gemma to take it all in. 'It'll be great, Gem. You'll be great. But hey, I'd better go. I'm meeting friends. Just had to tell you in person. And don't forget. You've. Made. History.' He emphasised the last three words with a finger. 'It's so amazing.' He smiled at her proudly. 'Okay, I'm off. Speak later.'

Gemma watched him skip off down the street and took a moment to think about what he'd said. About the grandeur of the statement and the significance of what it meant. About the enormity of what she'd done.

When she got home, she immediately messaged her friends and parents: *I'm going to be on BBC Breakfast on Wednesday!* Like her, no one could believe it. Then she floated around the house as if the magnitude of her history-making was causing her to levitate. She rose to such heights that it gave her an idea. But it was one she wouldn't go through with until after the breakfast show had aired.

*

The studio set was smaller than Gemma had thought it would be, and the two presenters were shorter and the cameras larger. She felt like an upturned flower vase because Nick had convinced her to wear the bright floral wellington boots with her dressier jeans and pale-pink shirt. Despite looking smarter than she usually did mudlarking, no one on set was any the wiser. The presenters greeted her with such enthusiasm you'd have thought she was Anne Boleyn herself having come back from the dead, and then one of the camera crew wanted to know where she'd got her boots. All of which had the pleasant effect of helping to calm her down.

The presenters asked her exactly what Nick said they would. How did you find the brooch? What did you think it was? How long have you been mudlarking? What made you start? Although Gemma had answers prepared, sometimes they came out speeded up, or abridged, or not as eloquent as she'd have liked and accompanied by a nervous giggle. But in the end, did it matter? She felt that she was holding her own in front of a captive audience and four cameras and found, unexpectedly, that it wasn't so bad after all.

'Now, Gemma, the big question on everyone's lips is, will you be rewarded for the treasure you've found?' The presenter, Gregory Holterman, was a good-looking guy but he had terrible taste in ties.

'Just to be clear, I never started mudlarking for financial gain,' Gemma said. 'I don't think any mudlarker does.'

'Of course.' He raised an eyebrow which gave Gemma the impression that he didn't entirely believe her.

'You're doing it to get in touch with the past,' she explained, despite having made this point earlier. 'It doesn't matter if what you find isn't unusual or rare, it's the first time that anyone has seen it or touched it since the river claimed it. That's intoxicating. It's addictive.'

'But now that you *have* found something rare, what happens next?'

'Museums are given the opportunity to purchase the object. If none of them want it, it'll be returned to the finder. If they do – because they don't already have one like it in their collection or because it's very old and rare – there's an official inquiry to deem the piece Treasure, with a capital T. It's then valued by the British Museum and the amount is shared fifty-fifty between the landowner and the finder. In this case, the landowner is the Port of London Authority and the Crown Estate.'

'Can we safely assume that the brooch you found will be bought?'

'I believe the British Museum is interested in it,' Gemma acknowledged, but she didn't wish to dwell on the idea. Just imagine, an object she had found being on display at the British Museum …

'Incredible!' the presenter exclaimed. 'What would you do with the proceeds?'

'I don't know,' she said. 'I mean, there mightn't be any, of course.'

'Of course, but if there was?'

While Gregory Holterman couldn't seem to stop visualising the amount of the valuation, the other presenter, Heather Milligan, stepped in.

'There seems to have been a recent surge in popularity for mudlarking as a hobby. Why do you think this is?'

'I can't say for sure,' Gemma said. 'Mudlarking has been around since the eighteenth century, but as a need for money, not as a hobby. I think now more and more people are learning how much history the Thames holds and how accessible it is – providing you have a permit, of course.'

The presenter nodded with interest. 'And finally, Gemma, how does it feel to know you've discovered something invaluable to the history of the country?'

Gemma thought for a moment, trying to remember what she'd practised with Nick. She didn't want to say the wrong thing.

'Naturally, I'm over the moon to have uncovered what is

believed to be a never-before-seen piece of Royal Tudor jewellery and to have contributed, in a small way, to the archaeological finds of the city.'

She paused and looked out at the production crew and cameras. It felt like a hundred headtorches were shining on her. She imagined her fellow mudlarkers huddled together on the bed in Nick's hotel room where they were watching the show.

'Except, I wasn't the only one who found it,' she continued. 'I couldn't have done it without my friends in The Mudlarkers' Club. Nick, Phyllida, Timothy and Laila. Who knows, if we hadn't been at that particular location on that particular day, and if I hadn't been looking in that particular spot, the brooch may have remained in the Thames for another five hundred years.'

Afterwards, The Mudlarkers' Club went out for a champagne breakfast at a restaurant along Salford Quays. On their way there, Gemma took a moment to ask Laila if she'd done anything about her mother's letter.

'Yeah,' Laila replied. 'It took me a while but eventually I replied. I said I'd consider seeing her when she gets out. I didn't want to commit in case I change my mind.'

'That's great. I think you need to give her a chance, but you can take it at your own pace,' Gemma said.

Laila nodded. 'Do you think I'd be allowed some champagne?' she asked sheepishly.

Gemma laughed. 'Fine by me, but you should really be checking with Timothy.'

Gemma was pleased that Timothy enthusiastically agreed, given, as he said, "the enormity of the celebration". She imagined that the bubbles went straight to Laila's head as they did hers. Gemma had already consumed half the glass when Phyllida stood up to give a toast. Phyllida tapped her champagne flute with one of her chunky silver rings, and called on everyone's attention.

'Gemma, you've done us proud today,' Phyllida said. 'I know

how much you dislike being in the spotlight. But you rose to the occasion and showed the world – or at least the BBC's morning viewers, however many there are – how wonderful mudlarking can be.'

'Six point five million,' Nick said.

'Pardon?' Phyllida looked at him.

'Average number of viewers of BBC Breakfast.'

'Oh, my God,' Gemma said. 'You didn't tell me that before I went on.'

'I couldn't have you freaking out any more than you already were.'

'Oi,' she said, giving his arm a gentle slap. 'I couldn't help it. I felt a fraud even asking for time off work.'

'I think you were marvellous,' Timothy said. 'Just marvellous.' He started clapping.

'I'm not finished yet,' Phyllida said.

'That was a warm-up.' Timothy quickly sat on his hands.

'What I wanted to say,' Phyllida went on. 'Is that I'll never forget when Gemma and I first met that day on the foreshore when I broke my phone and we started talking. Do you remember, Gemma? You said, it's nice to find things instead of losing them. I loved that. And now, look at what you've found—'

'*We* found it, remember?' Gemma scolded light-heartedly.

'Either way. Here's to you.' Phyllida raised her glass.

'And here's to the club,' Gemma said.

As Gemma raised her glass with the others, she felt a gentle squeeze of her left hand under the table. It was so gentle she could easily have imagined it. Very quickly, she got another one. She glanced to her left. Nick smiled.

A feeling came over her that she realised she'd felt before in Nick's presence but had always tried to suppress and pretend was due to other factors. Like too much coffee or too little food in a twenty-four-hour period. Or the possibility she was going through perimenopause a decade early. Now, though, she didn't want to quash or ignore any feelings; she wanted to embrace them.

For a few seconds, it felt as if it was only the two of them at the table. If only it could have been! Why couldn't everyone else, just for a moment, miraculously disappear? All she wanted to do was kiss Nick. Oh, how she wanted to kiss him. Then she wanted to hug him and thank him for being him – caring, considerate, enthusiastic and fun. He was like the coin in the Christmas pudding you think you'll never find and, when you do, you can't believe that you have.

Yet all she could do was return the squeeze and smile back.

It wasn't until she was back home that she knew the time was right to reply to Adam. Appearing on live national television had given her the courage to make the call.

'Gemma?' Adam answered.

'Adam,' Gemma said with authority.

'Hi,' he replied with less authority wondering, she imagined, why she was calling him instead of texting or emailing.

She wasn't going to muck around. 'I want to talk about the house.'

'Finally,' he said.

She put on her sweetest voice and with a smile said, 'I know it needs to be sold and I understand your situation, but my situation is this. As you chose to cheat and to leave me, the house sale will be on my terms.'

'But …?'

'I'm extremely busy right now,' she said, hoping her emphasis on 'extremely' sounded sincere and not overly dramatic. 'I've just been on national television, did I say?'

'No. What for?' he said with disbelief.

'Mudlarking.'

'Mudlarking?' The disdain was palpable.

'Supportive as always,' she muttered. 'Anyway, my publicist tells me I have more interview requests.'

'Publicist?'

'So, I'm going to be tied up for a while. The house stuff will have to wait. Oh, and you can watch my appearance on this morning's BBC Breakfast show on iPlayer—'

'Wha—?'

'Goodbye, Adam.'

She hung up and fist-pumped the air as Nick liked to do. That'll show Adam to mock her hobby. That'll show him how well she was doing without him.

In the days that followed, the story got picked up by news media around the world and more interview requests did indeed follow. Nick automatically became her public relations manager because his contact details were on the media release and all queries went to him. But thankfully, as Nick had predicted, the flurry of interest didn't last long. Other news gazumped hers and her momentary spark of celebrity was soon over.

After that, Gemma didn't know what to do with herself. She'd found an artefact so valuable it was invaluable *and* been on national television. She still felt astounded by the whole thing – incredulous, even – but also, just quietly, a teensy bit pleased with herself.

She'd also come to the realisation that only seeing Nick sporadically, as they had been, seemed agonisingly too little. She'd developed an ache in her heart, and it was being tugged in a way it hadn't for a very long time. And this, she found, was something else she didn't know what to do with. Did he really feel the same about her or was she imagining it?

November Discoveries:
What a month! I'm still gobsmacked at my discovery because not a lot can trump the finding of a sixteenth-century brooch linked to Anne Boleyn and Henry the Eighth, can it? Well, not unless you count being reminded of how wonderful it is when a man you like squeezes your hand.

December

Chapter 51

For a few days, The Mudlarkers' Club WhatsApp chat went quiet. Gemma suspected the others were, like her, coming down from their high. Life resumed as if nothing out of the ordinary had ever happened, or that they'd completely imagined it.

Then, on the first of December when a cold snap hit and the Thames shivered with the rest of London, Nick called. Seeing his name appear on her phone made her heart dance. She twirled a strand of hair and put her feet up on the sofa.

'Not *more* media interest?' she said light-heartedly.

'No, sorry.' He laughed. 'You've had your fifteen minutes of fame.'

'Thank goodness for that.'

There was a pause. Gemma waited for Nick to say why he was calling but he didn't. They said nothing for what seemed like a few very long seconds.

Then, Nick suddenly became animated. 'Hey, I don't think I told you my news, what with all the excitement over the brooch.'

'News?'

'There's been some drama at the Roman site. One of the archaeologists has been arrested for selling stolen sixteenth-century pots in an online auction – pots he took from a different site five years ago – and I got the reporting gig.'

'That's great, Nick. For you, of course, not for the pots or the archaeologist! What an idiot he was.'

'Yeah, some people. But it turns out that's the tip of the iceberg. There's a whole black-market trade for looted antiquities out there, involving an underworld of crime syndicates, money launderers and tomb raiders. Wealthy collectors buy ancient relics without checking their sources. Night hawkers raid archaeological sites with their metal detectors and sell what they find. It's not a new thing but it's getting worse. Online illicit markets are one of the major vehicles for the international trafficking of cultural objects.'

'Gosh, who knew?'

'I know! The *Guardian* has already expressed interest in the story.' She could hear the satisfaction in Nick's voice. 'It's the scoop I've been waiting for. Even better, it's given me an idea for a new novel because I'm ditching the other one. I've got it all plotted in my head. A madcap comedic heist set in the dark world of illegal artefact trading. And when it gets turned into a movie, I imagine Daniel Craig as the lead. Or maybe it'll be a woman. That'd be better, wouldn't it? Someone like, I dunno, Michelle Yeoh …'

'They'll be desperate for the part.'

'You've got to dream big.' Gemma nodded, even though she'd always felt more comfortable dreaming mid-size.

'Anyway, how are you now that all the excitement has died down?'

'Life seems rather boring now.' She sighed a bit more dramatically than she'd intended.

'I can imagine. It's definitely been the most thrilling thing that's happened to me in a long time.'

'Me too.'

'For all of us mudlarkers, I reckon.'

'Uh-huh.'

There was another silence.

'So, are you doing anything tomorrow?' Nick asked.

Gemma went to the fridge to check the tide chart. 'I'm afraid the low tide is going to be at three in the afternoon. I'll be at work.'

'I wasn't thinking of mudlarking …'

'Oh,' she said trying not to sound disappointed.

'I fancy going back to The Anchor pub for a drink.'

'Oh,' she repeated, feeling a breath-holding moment of anticipation.

'I was wondering if you'd like to join me?'

She said yes without even thinking about it.

At night, the Thames undulated as if it were black silk and the lights of the illuminated city buildings on both sides made the river spangle like tinsel. A northerly wind had blown in that afternoon and the air was icy. Gemma walked quickly from the Tube station, along the river at Bankside towards The Anchor.

Nick was downstairs in the dimly lit Clink Bar, perched on a stool. He looked smart in a collared shirt, patterned, Gemma realised as she got closer, with tiny flowers. He'd had a haircut and had shaved off his beard. He looked good. Then again, he suited both having a beard and not having one, and she couldn't decide which one she preferred.

He grinned and waved, then stood up formally.

'Hi,' he said, semi-extending an arm and leaning towards her as if he wasn't sure whether to shake her hand or give her a hug.

She didn't know what to do either, so she did both, first taking his hand and then leaning in for a brief side hug.

'Right, I'm getting the drinks,' he said. 'I'd have already ordered but—'

'—you didn't know what I'd want?'

'No, I wanted to be sure you'd come.'

'You're in luck, I didn't get a better offer,' she teased.

'Phew.' He pretend-mopped his brow. 'Okay, what do you want?'

As Nick went to order at the bar, Gemma pulled out a stool

and sat down. She stared at the old prints on the wall in front of her and tried ever so hard to be fully in the present and to not, for one second, think about what the night may or may not hold.

'Here we go,' Nick said, returning with two drinks and a bag of salt and vinegar crisps.

'My favourite, you remembered,' she said.

'A journalist never forgets.'

'I thought it was an elephant.'

'Them, too.'

For a moment neither of them spoke.

'So ...' she started.

'Yeah,' Nick agreed. 'Here we are. Any update on the brooch?'

'No. Everyone keeps asking!'

'Sorry. I guess the museum didn't give you a date?'

'I really wish they had.'

'Oh, well, I guess we'll know soon enough.'

'Hopefully.' She smiled quickly then said, 'Have you been on one of Timothy's Spotlight tours yet?'

'No.' Nick shook his head.

'Me neither.'

'We should.'

'Uh-huh.' Gemma sucked Aperol through the straw, wishing their exchanges weren't so painfully awkward. 'Have you been mudlarking again?' she asked.

'Me? Nah. You?'

'Just the once.'

Nick nodded.

The pub was beginning to fill up and take on the smell of battered fish and chips. Suddenly Nick burst into life as if he'd finally thought of something to say. 'Hey, I know ...!'

'Yes?' Gemma said, trying to avert her gaze from the attractive wisps of chest hair visible at the top of his shirt.

'Why don't you come to Amsterdam with me?'

'What?' That was not what she was expecting.

'I'm going to Amsterdam because … well, actually, I can't go into too much detail, except to say that I've got interviews lined up for that story I was telling you about. A Dutch art detective for one.'

'You'll be working?' Gemma said.

'Yeah, it's a business trip. Didn't you say you wanted to go to Amsterdam? You could be my sidekick and carry my stuff. When I say, "pen", you can pass me my pen like we're in an operating theatre, and I'm a surgeon and you're a nurse. Oh, hang on, you are a nurse, ha-ha!'

Gemma frowned. She couldn't work out whether to take him seriously or not, nor where the conversation was going.

'You did say you wanted to go to Amsterdam, didn't you?' he said.

'I did but—'

'You'd rather go with someone else?'

'No. I mean—'

'Gem,' he said touching her knee as if in apology. 'I was only joking about the pen. Of course, I don't expect you to be my sidekick. You can go off and see the city while I do my work, and then we can, you know, do some sightseeing together. Or something.' He looked into his beer glass as if that 'something' was to be found there.

Gemma thought about how when she wasn't with Nick, she missed his infectious laughter, his enthusiasm for life, his obvious respect for and support of her. How he didn't diminish her, like Adam had, but lifted her higher than she'd ever lifted herself and kept her there, buoyant with self-belief and optimism.

'Okay,' Gemma said. 'I will.'

'Really?' Nick sounded taken aback.

'I think it sounds lovely.'

'It's just, I wasn't sure—' he began.

'Wasn't sure …?' She left the question hanging.

'About us.'

Gemma nodded thoughtfully.

'Well,' she said, feeling suddenly emboldened. 'We could go to Amsterdam as friends. Or we could go as something more.'

Nick studied her as if calculating her intentions.

She gave an enticing shoulder shrug and smiled. Then she held his gaze and didn't let it go. The noise of the pub muffled and faded so she could barely hear it at all. Someone may have accidentally knocked her on their way to the bar, she couldn't be sure. Nick leant towards her. He smelt musky with a hint of Guinness. She closed her eyes and felt his lips touch hers.

Three Months Later

Chapter 52

It was spring. Although you wouldn't have known it. Snow had fallen overnight and given Gemma's daffodils the fright of their lives. In the New Year, the house she and Adam had bought was sold. Gemma had finally felt ready to let it go and when she did, it proved less upsetting than she thought it would be. For, as much as she'd loved it, it had become an ever-present reminder of her failed marriage, and she knew that at some point she had to move on. Because she didn't wish to rush into buying anything until she felt certain about the future, she found a two-bedroom rental flat in the same area. Even though it didn't have a garden, it had a balcony, so she could pot the daffodil bulbs she'd dug up from their old garden. The best part was the view over the Thames. She didn't need to check the tide chart to know whether the river was filling up or draining away. She could pull open the living-room curtains and there it was, rippling and swelling as it always did in one way or another every single day.

After their kiss in the bar, Gemma and Nick began dating. After four weeks, Gemma started calling him her boyfriend, which stunned her as much as it did her friends. Most weeks, they spent half the week together. Sometimes it was two halves back to back. Either Gemma stayed over at Nick's or he, at hers. It felt good. It felt right. Gemma liked having a living arrangement she could dip into and out of when it suited, and having a place of her own where she could live on her terms and no one else's.

Thankfully, Nick understood her need for a sense of independence post-marriage and didn't press her to move in with him. But she knew that's what he wanted. Ironically, it was his graciousness at *not* pushing for it that was making her change her mind. After all, wouldn't it be wonderful to wake up next to Nick every day? At times, she found herself imagining them getting a dog together and going on long walks along the river and letting it explore the foreshore while they mudlarked. She even dreamed of becoming a foster parent, whether she ended up having a child of her own or not. She'd so enjoyed befriending Laila and feeling as if she was, in a small way, contributing positively to her welfare and well-being that she seriously began to entertain the idea.

It was a couple of weeks before Easter when the Coroner of the Portable Antiquities Scheme called Gemma at work. She'd been in the middle of hanging a new patient's chemo line and admiring the woman's silk turban, so it wasn't until her break that she got his message.

'It's about the brooch,' he said. 'Call me back.'

Gemma drew a sharp intake of breath. This was it. Finally, they'd find out exactly how special the brooch was. She went outside to the carpark and returned the coroner's call, feeling as though phantom moths were lodged in her chest.

'It will come as no surprise to you, I'm sure,' he said without expression, 'that the British Museum would like to acquire the piece. The brooch is an artefact of significant historical importance.'

He droned on as if reading from a pre-prepared speech. 'With every find like this, we can learn a little more about the past. To be able to share this with the world is an immense privilege.'

'Yes, I agree,' Gemma said. 'I'd love the brooch to be on display at the museum.'

'The museum would like to purchase it. They've had it valued. Fifty per cent will go to the Crown and fifty per cent to you.'

'To me?'

'You found it.'

'I know but can it go to anyone else?'

'What you do with the money is up to you. But I don't recommend spending it all at once.' The man, who had up until then sounded bored with the conversation, abruptly burst into laughter.

After the call ended, Gemma immediately messaged The Mudlarkers' Club to arrange a meeting. She didn't tell them why, although they might have guessed. They gathered at her flat the following evening where she put on a spread of gourmet cheeses, a charcuterie board and even a magnum of champagne. She'd never had one of them before. It felt ridiculously decadent, and it was. It cost more than the two nights in the Amsterdam hotel where she and Nick had stayed before Christmas. Nick thought she'd gone bonkers buying such a large bottle. But then, she hadn't told him either about her conversation with the Coroner of the Portable Antiquities Scheme. It was the hardest secret she'd ever had to keep.

Her clandestine behaviour was clearly burning a hole in everyone's patience because they bombarded Gemma with questions as soon as they walked in the door. She resisted the urge to give anything away but encouraged them to sit down and have some of the artery-clogging double-cream Brie to settle their stomachs and drink the breathtakingly expensive champagne to calm their nerves. It temporarily helped to stall the cross-examination.

When Gemma felt she'd strung them along long enough, she tapped her mudlarked ring on her glass to get their attention. 'I'm sure you can guess why you're here,' she said.

'We'd like to think so, don't we?' Timothy said.

'I had a call from the coroner.'

Phyllida gasped. Gemma hadn't even got to the gasp-inducing

part.

'You never told me that!' Nick said.

'The British Museum wants to purchase the brooch,' she said.

'Please put us out of our misery,' Phyllida said.

'There's nothing to be miserable about, I can assure you.' Gemma took a sip of champagne. She was rather enjoying being the keeper of information and in control of when it was released. 'They're going to pay for it, of course,' she added.

Nick fist-pumped the air. 'Yes!' he said.

Phyllida groaned. You'd think she was about to give birth.

'Fifty per cent goes to the finder and fifty per—'

'We know!' Timothy exclaimed. Even he was getting exasperated.

Perhaps it was time.

'I suppose you'd like to know what they're going to pay.'

'Yes!' They said in unison.

Gemma nodded, then found herself whispering the astonishingly large valuation, as if to say the six-figure amount at a normal level would render it untrue.

Nick swore loudly, Laila and Timothy had a jaw-dropping competition and Phyllida threatened to faint – again. It was becoming such a common occurrence that Gemma worried one day she *would* faint and they wouldn't notice.

'But the reason I want to celebrate is not because of how much money it is,' she said.

'That's a good enough reason, if you ask me,' Laila said.

'Sure, but we all know mudlarking isn't about finding something of monetary value. For me, the real treasure has been the people I've met and being part of this club.'

'Aw, that's nice,' Nick said.

'Shush, Nick,' Gemma said with a smile.

'You two found each other, so that's treasure, right there,' Phyllida added.

'I'm trying to be serious here!'

'Let the girl speak,' Timothy said.

Gemma sighed. Perhaps she'd been premature in refilling their glasses.

'What I'm trying to say is, I'm really glad to have met you all. When we mudlark together, we might be doing so as individuals but we're together, like a team. And, contrary to the usual code of mudlarking ethics, I believe that whatever we find is, ultimately, a group effort. So that means everyone should get a share of the spoils. I'm going to split the money from the brooch equally between all of us.'

For a moment no one spoke. Even Nick was lost for words.

After what Gemma thought was a suitable pause, she raised her glass. 'To The Mudlarkers' Club.'

Epilogue

The Mudlarkers' Club continued to meet each month and recruited four new members. Phyllida's Instagram follower, the historian Megan O'Connor, who'd first suggested that the brooch may not be fake; an American man called Mark, who worked as a marketing executive for a craft beer Nick always raved about; a radiologist who'd heard about Gemma via another nurse who was also researching her family history; and the woman who was the great-grandniece of Charlie Griffiths, the original owner of the luggage tag Laila had found.

Publicity from the brooch boosted Phyllida's Instagram following. She hit four figures which was more than Phyllida could have ever imagined but far less than Gemma knew was possible. Phyllida put her share of the money from the brooch into a bank account in her name. Even though she wanted to share it with Robert, she didn't want him to be tempted back into gambling as he was making such great strides with his therapy sessions and was committed to attending the Gamblers Anonymous meetings. Phyllida used it to start clearing their debts and gave some to her son to use for future travel or to add to his savings. Then, she put some of it aside for a holiday for her and Robert before her long-service leave was up. She was determined that Robert's addiction wasn't going to ruin their marriage. They both fancied visiting Cuba and she'd always wanted to learn the salsa. All they had to do was pick a date.

When the brooch was first put on display at the British Museum, Timothy was assigned to be its sole specialist guide because of his connection to it. Tours ran every day for six weeks. Timothy was exhausted by the end of it. Yet he loved it so much, he enrolled in a distance-learning course on Henry the Eighth with the University of Oxford. Gemma suspected he would get the continuing education bug. To appease his family and to stop them giving him flyers on retirement villages, Timothy used the money he received from the brooch to engage a housekeeper to clean and tidy the houseboat every week and to ensure all hazardous objects were kept out of falling-over reach. He was also secretly – to everyone else in his life except the members of The Mudlarkers' Club – planning a trip to Egypt, which he was only going to tell his daughter about when he was at the airport. Laila felt bad about having to keep his travel plans from Jodie, but Gemma told her that sometimes keeping a short-term secret was a necessary part of the cogs of life.

Nick eventually completed the first draft of a novel. It was still to be edited and Gemma was still to read it. If she ever would. Nick fluctuated between feeling giddily confident in his fictional storytelling abilities to depressingly negative. Just as well Daniel Craig and Michelle Yeoh were nowhere to be seen. With the windfall, he was able to continue freelancing and pitching investigative feature ideas, some of which got off the ground and some of which didn't.

Laila presented Gemma with an ink drawing of the brooch as a memento of the find and told her she was going to put some of her share of the money towards art school. She also got another tattoo, which didn't impress either Timothy or her foster parents but as she'd just turned eighteen, what choice did they have? At least she'd gone to a reputable and talented tattoo artist who replicated in intricate detail Laila's drawing of the brooch. The tattoo perched elegantly on her right shoulder blade. Gemma didn't like to ask why she hadn't thought to put it somewhere she could more easily see it, rather than in a spot that required viewing with the help of a mirror. Laila split her time between staying with Timothy and her foster parents, which made everyone happy. Eventually, she got the courage to meet her birth mother, and Gemma, dying to know how it went, organised to catch up with her the following day.

Laila was waiting for Gemma at a café in Kew. Her expression gave nothing away. Gemma held off from starting the conversation in case it hadn't gone well. After greeting each other and ordering hot chocolates, Laila eventually gave her a shy smile.

'So?' Gemma said with trepidation. 'Are you going to tell me?'

'She seemed genuinely happy to see me,' Laila said with disbelief, unable to let go of her wariness.

'You're her daughter, of course she would be.'

'I think she wanted to hug me but I wasn't ready for that …'

'Of course …'

'I could tell she was nervous like I was. Her fingernails were chewed as low as mine.' Laila looked at her black-painted nails, as if to check that they still resembled those of her birth mother's.

'I can't imagine how you were both feeling.'

'I tried to keep an open mind like you said. She was chatty and asked a lot of questions. She told me, again, how she wants to embrace her roots and learn how to make traditional Pakistani – Urdu – food.'

'That sounds great, Laila.'

'She said she'd like to teach me.'

'How do you feel about that?'

'Yeah, I wouldn't mind learning stuff but …' Laila looked out of the café window and didn't finish the sentence.

'You can take it slowly,' Gemma said. 'Trust needs to be rebuilt.

Although it sounds as if she means what she says, don't you think?'

'I guess.'

'I think having an understanding of your heritage could really enrich your life.' Gemma wanted Laila to appreciate how much more she could gain by reigniting a relationship with her mother.

'Do you feel like you've missed out on that by being adopted?' Laila asked.

Gemma nodded because she'd hit a nerve. But she wasn't about to elaborate because this was meant to be about Laila, not her. She let Laila continue.

'It's made me realise that even knowing the meaning of my name has given me something to hold on to, which I know sounds kind of woo-woo.'

Gemma laughed. 'It's not woo-woo.'

'Do you know what your name means?' Laila asked.

'My two names, you mean? I was going to find out but ...'

'Let's do it.' Before Gemma had a chance to reply, Laila was already on her phone. Then she pulled a face.

'What?' Gemma said.

'Hayley means hay meadow.'

'There goes that idea, then ...'

'Hang on.' Laila raised a hand. 'Gemma means ...' She grinned. 'Gem or jewel. How appropriate is that?'

Gemma shook her head at the absurdity of the connection. 'It's a silly coincidence,' she said.

'Maybe in relation to the brooch but, maybe, not as far as your parents are concerned ...'

Laila left the words hanging, gently and seductively, pulling Gemma into the warmth of possibility that the name her adoptive parents chose for her truly meant something.

'On that note,' Gemma said quickly to stop herself from getting emotional again. 'You'll be pleased to know that I've put myself on the Adoption Contact Register. Nick wouldn't stop badgering me about it.'

'Finally.' Laila rolled her eyes. 'You have to tell me straight away if you get any bites.'

'I promise. Now tell me, how did you end things with your mum?'

'She asked if I wanted to meet up again. I said yes.'

'Fantastic! And what about Jodie? How's it going with her?'

'We're fine. She was excited about me meeting Mum, which was nice. I thought she'd feel threatened, but I guess she does only want the best for me.'

'Of course, she does.'

Laila nodded, as if, finally, she'd accepted that no one was out to get her. That, while life could chuck things at you like a tennis ball-spitting machine, it was empowering knowing that you could tackle every ball head on.

And what of Gemma? With part of the windfall, she bought new shelving and another display case for her mudlarking finds and equipment. Nick thought her unashamed restraint amusing and nonsensical.

'I can't believe you don't want to splash out on something frivolous,' he said.

'But there's nothing else I need right now,' she replied.

'That's what frivolous means, that you don't *need* it. What about some exorbitantly expensive designer wellies?'

'Not even those.'

What she didn't tell him was that while she was happy to bank the rest of the money, she also dared to dream about the future, where the two of them bought a house together. A place they could both call home which had a whole room dedicated to their mudlarking finds and maybe, even, one for a child. But for now, she was content to continue her life as it was, especially given all that had happened in the past few months which continued to astound her whenever she stopped to think about it.

Anushka finally got in touch to apologise for taking so long to get back to Gemma and then offered the biggest surprise of all: the suggestion of a weekend away together. They treated themselves to three nights in Bath and they slipped seamlessly back into their friendship as if they'd never had a break.

It was three months later when Gemma received an email and a photo from her half-brother Ben, who had just turned twenty-four. It turns out being found was just as thrilling as discovering Thames Treasure. He seemed as overjoyed as she was at finding her. His message was littered with words like 'gas' and 'amped' as if they were about to go off on an adrenalin-inducing quad bike adventure. When she studied his picture, it was like looking at a taller, slimmer version of herself. He angled his head as she did in photos, and he had a half-smile as if, like her, he didn't feel comfortable revealing all his teeth all in one go. Gemma got a rush of exhilaration. Here was a blood relative – *her* blood – on the page and in the flesh, who wanted to connect with her and, as it turned out, only minutes away in London. Here was someone who'd be able to tell her first-hand what her birth mother was like. It would be the closest she'd ever get to feeling whole. Within forty-eight hours of his message, they'd arranged to meet in person and, on a cool spring evening after work, she nervously but eagerly met her half-sibling.

After they'd said their goodbyes and she was making her way back to the Tube, she called Laila.

'I did it!' she said. 'Now I know how you must have felt meeting your mother again. The nerves.'

Laila screamed. 'Come on, spill the tea! What was he like? Was he nice? Is he like you?'

Gemma took a breath. Where to begin? 'He was nice, yes,' Gemma said thoughtfully. 'Earnest. Bright. He got a scholarship to go to university. He's now finished his science degree and will soon start a summer placement at a biomedical company.'

'Fancy,' Laila said.

'Not so much fancy as difficult to get into. But we gelled,

despite the age difference.'

'Yay. Did you find out anything more about your mum?'

'Yes.' Gemma swallowed. She now had answers, not all but some, and they made her want to cry and laugh at the same time.

'Do you want me to come over?' Laila quickly said.

'Don't be silly, it's late.'

'Okay, okay, but what did he tell you?'

Gemma perched on a brick wall. It felt as if she couldn't process it all without sitting down. 'He said that he only learnt about me when she – Claire – was in palliative care, with only days to live. Then, the following day she lost consciousness and died a couple of days later.'

'So sad.'

'He was stunned, understandably. Not even his father knew. She told him that she'd always wanted to tell him about me, except it was the fear of losing him and what she might discover about me that stopped her. Apparently, she thought about me all the time and she urged him to try and find me, which was so lovely to hear, you can't imagine—'

'Oh, I can.'

'He said that he did want to find me but he was also scared, so he didn't do it. In the end, it was his dad who made him realise that as he's an only child, he has nothing to lose if he goes searching for his half-sister. Putting myself on the register and including both my names made his job so much easier.'

'It was meant to be! Did you find out anything about your father?'

'Unfortunately, that's something I'll never know. Ben asked her who he was but all she said was that he was a boy she knew from school and he was never told about the pregnancy. Her parents wouldn't allow it. They were very conservative and not at all accepting of her predicament. They wanted to brush it away as if it never happened, but she was four months pregnant when she found out and when the pregnancy could no longer be hidden, they sent her away to her aunt's. They organised for the baby – me – to go out for adoption as a newborn. Even though "the system" was more encouraging than it had ever been in the past of women – girls – keeping their babies, Claire's parents were not, and she wasn't allowed to have a say.'

Laila groaned in disapproval.

'I know,' Gemma agreed.

'I'm sorry you'll never find out about your dad.'

'It's okay. I've gained so much already, I guess I shouldn't be greedy.'

Laila laughed. 'Grandad is always plugging that Greek philosopher, Epicurus. "He who is satisfied with a little, is satisfied with nothing",' she said mimicking Timothy. '"Do not spoil what you have by desiring what you have not". Blah blah blah.'

Gemma laughed. 'It's kind of true.'

'I s'ppose. But just think about how much you can now learn about your birth mother. I mean, you are going to see Ben again?'

'We agreed to. We both want it to work out, so here's hoping.'

Gemma got up off the wall and resumed her walk to the Tube. She now couldn't wait to get home and tell Nick. What's more, she couldn't wait to introduce Nick to her half-brother, Ben Reed.

When spring was turning into summer and Gemma was by the Thames mudlarking alone, she uncovered something she'd never found before. It was a very worn but unmistakeable silver shilling that had been bent out of shape. She lifted it from the river. It was wet and cold and gritty. She washed it in the water. There was nothing engraved on it. But then, there usually wasn't. Old-fashioned love tokens were simply coins that had been misshapen by a lover to be given to the one they loved. If the affection was reciprocated, the token was kept. If not, it was discarded.

Gemma wiped the coin dry on her jeans and slipped it into a pocket.

She knew just who she was going to give it to.

Author Letter

Dear Reader,

Thank you so much for choosing to read *The Mudlarkers' Club*. I hope you enjoyed it! If you did I would be so grateful if you would leave a review. I always love to hear what readers thought, and it helps new readers discover my books too.
Thanks,
Jane Riley

You can also follow me on . . .
Instagram: janeriley_author
TikTok: janeriley_author

Acknowledgements

I do hope you enjoyed reading this book as much as I loved writing it. When I first discovered what mudlarking was and then got a taste for it via a Thames Discovery Programme session, I was hooked. Finding out how thousands of years of history has been, and still is, in the riverbed of the Thames is astonishing. It's only because the river is tidal that we're able to discover it – but only if you have a permit, of course! Needless to say, I could ramble on forever about the joys and wonders of mudlarking, but there are wonderful people to thank.

I am endlessly grateful to my agent Ariella Feiner for continuing to believe in me and offering wise counsel in all things writerly. A huge thanks to my editor Georgina Green for championing me and this book. It's been a delight to work with you, George, as well as the rest of the wonderful team at HQ Digital, including Priyal Agrawal, Seema Mitra, Laoise Culloo and Lou Nyuar.

Once I knew that I wanted to set a story around mudlarking, I signed up for a mudlarking tour with the entertaining and knowledgeable registered mudlarker Steve Brooker, aka 'The Mud God', where I learnt how to read tide lines, how to 'get your eye in' and spot the tiniest of tiny Tudor pins among the rubble.

The foreshore has never looked the same again. Thanks, too, to mudlarker Malcolm Russell, who kindly answered more questions I had about the ins and outs of the pastime and the dangers of the Thames. Plus, a big shout-out to everyone at the Thames Discovery Programme and their hundreds of volunteers who record and monitor the archaeology on the foreshore and help educate locals and visitors about the amazing history of London lapping at their feet.

Closer to home, I would like to thank my oldest and dearest friend, Jane Liggins for enlightening me on all things medical and nursing, as well as general bookish talk, which we've enjoyed ever since we learnt to read. To my daughters, Hannah and Amy, who read snippets of early drafts and happily indulge my brainstorming. And to my Mum, Joceline Wilson, who loves reading as much as I do and has become an adorable promoter of my books at her retirement village.

But I could do none of this without my first reader and all-round rock, Will Riley. He's believed in me from day one, provided refreshingly honest but constructive criticism, and given me space and solitude to immerse myself in the wonderful world of making things up.

Dear Reader,

We hope you enjoyed reading this book. If you did, we'd be so appreciative if you left a review. It really helps us and the author to bring more books like this to you.

Here at HQ Digital we are dedicated to publishing fiction that will keep you turning the pages into the early hours. Don't want to miss a thing? To find out more about our books, promotions, discover exclusive content and enter competitions you can keep in touch in the following ways:

JOIN OUR COMMUNITY:

Sign up to our new email newsletter: http://smarturl.it/SignUpHQ

Read our new blog www.hqstories.co.uk

𝕏: https://twitter.com/HQStories

f: www.facebook.com/HQStories

BUDDING WRITER?

We're also looking for authors to join the HQ Digital family! Find out more here:

https://www.hqstories.co.uk/want-to-write-for-us/

Thanks for reading, from the HQ Digital team